THE MOUNTAINS WE CARRY

ZAID BRIFKANI

For Duhok

First American edition published in 2021
by Zaid Brifkani

Brifkani, Zaid
The Mountains We Carry

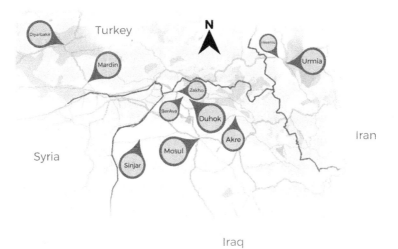

PROLOGUE

Azad

Duhok, November 1981

The last time I saw my father was two weeks ago. He came home in a hurry and frantically asked Mother to pack him some clothes. I was busy doing homework, and he gently took the book out of my hands. I stood up, full of concern, looking at his face. He took me aside and dropped responsibilities on my shoulder that were too heavy for my seventeen-year-old mind.

"Take good care of your mother and siblings, Azad!" he said solemnly. Before I asked him where he was going, he said, "The military has drafted me, and I am going to have to disappear into the mountains. Your father was not born to fight for Saddam's army."

He hugged us and kissed my mother's head, refusing to look her in the eyes so he would not see her tears. And just like that, my dad was gone. An army deserter. His name would be entered into the black government books.

A few days later, I saw his name posted on the door of the main downtown mosque along with the names of three other men wanted for desertion, a crime that brought on the death penalty. We assumed my dad was safe, already up north in the mountains with his old comrades with whom he had spent years of armed struggle against the Iraqi army.

He moved from house to house for a few days and was finally caught while trying to escape. My mother still believes someone tipped off the authorities. Two others were also found, while the fourth remained on the loose.

My uncle came earlier in the morning and picked up my mother, who was dressed in all black, including her scarf. She was already observing the darkness to come. My brother and two sisters were crying. A cloud of sorrow filled the house. We were past the stage of uncertainty and forcefully embracing the devastation.

My uncle instructed me to stay in the house with my three siblings and not dare step outside or let anyone else out. His wife was going to stay with us and watch over my sisters. I waited for my mother and uncle to leave, and when the car disappeared down the road, I grabbed my books and told my uncle's wife that I was headed to school. I was out the door before she could answer.

Walking the streets of downtown Duhok, all I can see is my father's image. Every man that passes, every poster on a wall, and every photo inside a store looks like my father, with his thick mustache, heavyset body, sharp eyes, and thick eyebrows. His silent stare follows me through the alleys. Every voice on the street and in the shops sounds like my father's, telling me to take care of my younger siblings. I left them behind, and it took some effort to distract my brother so he wouldn't follow. I want to see my dad one final time, and I don't want any of my siblings to carry that dark memory for the rest of their lives.

I turn at the intersection near the central police station and walk past the only cinema in town toward the main bus station where we are told it will go down. Today, a different show is taking place across the street. My breathing becomes labored as I hurry behind a group of men heading in the same direction. Emptied of buses, the station appears large and spacious. It's a little after ten, and dark clouds hover over the city as if they have been summoned from far away for the occasion.

I reach the corner of the station, and a police officer notices the books in my hands and stops me. "You better get back to school, boy. Right now." He pushes me hard, and I back up a few feet and leave the crowd of men being inspected as they cross the walkway into the station.

I drop my books in a corner near a tea shop and walk back toward the station. The officer is still there, instructing everyone in the full station to sit down. They are curious spectators and nosy passers-by. Perhaps some were brought there by force. I retreat to a corner of the wall that surrounds the station and lean against the cold concrete, realizing I had forgotten to put my jacket on when I left the house. I am freezing and have a hard time keeping my lips together. A dozen or so official red government Land Cruisers are positioned at every block of the main road, and every few steps there is a man in uniform spreading intimidating looks in all directions. There is no pedestrian traffic now, and no cars can move in or out of the area.

On the far end of the field overlooking the empty main road, six security officers in formal dark-navy military suits and red scarves set up three long wooden poles that connect to heavy metal bases for support. Two old men are smoking behind me, and from time to time they whisper their feelings about what is about to take place. If they are trying to be secretive, they are not doing a good job of it.

One of the men lights another cigarette, takes a deep puff, and says, "It's a shame that a known Peshmerga like Wahid Barwari would go down like this."

The other says, "I don't blame anyone for deserting the army. The war zone is a death sentence. Few come back alive now."

His companion hums in agreement. "And most of the survivors are being captured by the Iranians."

"I heard they didn't even allow Wahid's family to say their final goodbyes because of his past as a Peshmerga."

The other man sighs. "Heartbreaking. May Allah help his family. His poor wife and children."

I don't know how or when they got there, but I see my uncle and my mother standing at the near end of the open field in front of the first line of spectators. Little do the men behind me know that the 'poor wife' is standing less than fifty meters from us and that one of the 'poor children' is inches away from them.

A LITTLE BEFORE NOON, a brown Land Cruiser arrives followed by three other military vehicles of various sizes. A short, overweight man in full uniform with a black cap and a gun strapped to his waist emerges from the front passenger seat. His long mustache covers most of his mouth, and from the way the guards around him react, he seems to be the one in charge. He walks to the middle of the field, then turns in the direction of the Land Cruiser and nods a few times. Three armed men huddle by the SUV, and one of them moves to open the rear door. Joined by a third armed man at the door of the station, the three men each hold the shoulder of one of the captives as they carefully step out of the SUV.

There he is, my father, blindfolded and being led away from the vehicle and onto the field. He's wearing his favorite brown pants, but now they fit loosely on his legs, and I wonder how much weight he has lost under torture during the past two weeks. He turns his head from side to side as if looking for someone or something. I wish the blindfold would somehow fall so I could steal one more look at his eyes.

They tie my father's hands to one of the three poles. My knees shake, threatening to give in at any moment.

The two men behind me just won't shut up. Two security men walk with an elderly couple, probably in their seventies. The old man seems confused and keeps looking sideways before an agent taps on his shoulder and directs him to the front. Next to the couple stands a tall, beautiful, young woman holding a baby, barely a year old. A black scarf covers half her blonde hair, and she appears lost in her own world.

After the second prisoner is attached to the pole to the right of my dad, another uniformed officer brings the third blindfolded prisoner, a young man with torn pants and long, messy hair. The young woman with the baby starts to sob. An officer walks up to her and whispers something, after which she wipes her eyes and goes quiet.

Whispered chatter breaks out among the mass of spectators but soon quiets down after a military guard demands total silence through a megaphone. When the young man is finally tied to the third pole, the guard steps behind the three prisoners and instructs the crowd to maintain silence and order.

My mother stands a few feet to the right of the young woman with the baby, and as much as I try not to, I can imagine the emotions running through my mother's heart. I am numb; my heart is at my feet. My eyes are fixed on the baby, who is now playing with his mother's scarf and trying to free himself from her exhausted grip. He will never remember his father. His mother wipes her eyes with her scarf and turns to the old man to her left, who is struggling to maintain his balance while leaning against his cane, his eyes fixed straight toward the firing squad.

A parent should never witness their child's death, but this is Iraq, where what should be a law of nature is broken every day.

The two men behind me continue to talk and at times even giggle. I want to slap their faces. The army could tie me up next to my father if they want.

A fat officer screams through a megaphone: "In the name of Allah, the merciful. In the name of the nation, the land, and the blessed Ba'ath Party under the leadership of the long-living President Saddam Hussein." The man has terror and heartlessness written all over him. I wonder how many firing squads he has been part of. He is speaking in formal Arabic, so I can't tell which part of Iraq he is from based on his dialect. Bullets, however, only have one language.

The officer produces a piece of paper from his pocket, unfolds it, and reads the official statement aloud. With a heavy tone, he extols the blessings of the Ba'ath Party and the luxurious life it has bestowed upon the proud citizens of Iraq. We should take pride, he says, in the way Iraqis have stood against the plots of the evil foreign powers, especially the dirty *Farsi Majoos* regime. "Those who fall defending their country shall be forever remembered and respected."

My father shifts his legs as he tires of standing. He has a bad knee from an injury he sustained years ago fighting against this same Iraqi army up in the mountains.

The officer clears his throat. "And those cowardly traitors who desert the army deserve to die for their betrayal." He speaks for a few more minutes, and instead of listening, I focus on my father, tied to a wooden pole, his whole life and legacy about to be taken away by a few ruthless animals.

Then I hear my father's name over the speaker, concluding the list of the condemned. Just like that, they decide who lives and who dies, who is a patriot and who is a traitor. With the fat announcer's hand signal, three uniformed officers step behind the three prisoners, each holding a Kalashnikov. Officers from every corner scan the crowd for any suspicious movement.

I have tried to avoid looking toward my mother. I can't bear to see the look on her face. The helplessness! The hopelessness! The fear! The reality that she chose to stand and watch her life companion being prepped for death without moving a muscle because any act of interference could result in a more merciless death for her husband and possibly for the rest of her family.

As the three officers raise their weapons, I see my mother walk closer to the young woman, whose baby has finally settled down as if aware of the magnitude of the moment. My mother places her hand on the young lady's head to console her. Strangers brought together in tragedy. Even with her husband about to be executed, my mother still has room in her heart for others. This mountain of a woman who raised us while my father spent his early years fighting in the mountains will carry yet another burden.

The fat officer yells one monotonic order through the megaphone, and loud successive shots cut through the silence before piercing their targets. My father's body jerks a few times, then slides down the pole and settles on the ground. Mother covers her eyes with her scarf, and the young woman lets out a scream that fills the place. The old man with the cane lowers his head and is about to collapse, but an officer emerges from within the crowd and helps him back to his feet. My eyes roll up, and the world briefly turns dark before I am startled by the sound of another gunshot in the air as a guard warns everyone in the audience to be quiet. Their guns are now turned toward the families of the victims in case one of them decides to charge. I struggle to find tears. My heart is shattered into a million parts.

A few heavy moments pass, then a man in the first row shouts in Kurdish, "Long live President Saddam," and then claps. The military men look in his direction and smile. Many in the crowd look at each other in disbelief as they start clapping. I realize I am on my knees now, numb and in shock, with tears finally filling my eyes. I get up, turn around, and carry myself through the crowd.

I shove my way to the back and see dozens of men wiping tears from their eyes. My mother is still there, at the site of her husband's bloodied body stuck to a pole. She is stronger than I am. My heart is forever broken. My eyes have seen hell. I am nobody now.

THE ARMY WOULDN'T LET us retrieve my father's corpse for three days. The government security forces visit the house to inquire about our whereabouts and to give us stiff warnings against any activities that may disturb the peace.

After my father's burial and funeral in the village, my mother decides she is finished with the city. My sisters Dilveen and Shireen go through the motions of packing without asking questions or offering much resistance. My brother Jamil, on the other hand, pleads for an explanation for the sudden decision to leave the city for the village.

Mother has made up her mind, and nothing will make her reverse her decision. We are moving back to our village for good. The city is a place of bad omens, terrible luck, and sad memories. This means no more school for me. The excitement of my first year of high school has been buried with my father and poisoned by my mother's disdain for the city. I will not even entertain asking my mother to stay behind and let me finish my studies. At least not now while we are still numb.

I find myself unable to muster any emotions. What good are emotions? Will they bring my father back?

With my mother and siblings waiting in our uncle's truck outside, I run into the house one last time and grab my English textbook, the one thing I will carry from the city, something that will take me away from this land.

The neighbors watch us leave in defeat, some avoiding eye contact, as we head through the narrow streets to the main road leading out of Duhok.

1

Azad

Duhok, seventy kilometers from the Iraq-Turkey border,
March 1988

The March weather in the city, unlike in the village up north, is unpredictable. Though it was sunny earlier in the day, it rained in the afternoon, and now a chilly breeze has made the darkness of the night colder.

I leave my uncle's store after a long day of work flipping between the cash register and the back warehouse and head to school. Shops are starting to close for the day as customers rush to catch buses before they stop running. Life quickly dies in the downtown market as the light disappears.

Gara Preparatory Evening School is about two kilometers from downtown, where Mam (Uncle) Khorsheed's store
is located. As usual, I go there on foot, my books in one
hand and the small black Panasonic cassette player in the
other. Since my father's execution seven years ago, I have
not been able to make myself walk past the bus station. I
step into an alley and turn up the volume of the English
lesson I'm listening to on tape.

Foot traffic becomes scarcer the farther I walk away
from the city center. A boy chases me, begging me to buy
his last pack of peppermint gum. He is obviously lying; the
box is at least half full. I ignore him as I pick up the pace,
and he crosses the street to target another passerby.

Since Mr. Qais arrived at our school, I have been able to
advance my English skills beyond the school's require-
ments. I am heads and shoulders above the rest of my class,
he says, but who says that is my standard? I am determined
to speak fluent English. I want my name as a translator on
the covers of books. One day, I may even write my own
Kurdish-English dictionary.

It is dark now, and the alley leads to a wide street that
finally meets the main road heading up toward the Gere
Basi neighborhood. A broken street light buzzes, and I walk
carefully under its faint light, using whatever visibility I can
get to avoid stepping in a puddle. In this country, now a
police state, life quickly wraps up after dark and retreats to
the comfort and privacy of homes, away from the eyes and
ears of the government. Dinners are being served with
rounds of hot tea. Parents and children gather around TV
sets while more rounds of tea are served. A father may be
yelling at a child for misbehaving or not doing homework.
A mother might be scolding the kids for getting bad grades.

Yet there is laughter and joy. There are sibling arguments and displays of rivalry. There is sadness and the sorrow and missed loved ones.

An elderly man carrying a plastic grocery bag hurries past me, turns around and looks at me momentarily, then continues into the darkness.

A hand suddenly grabs my back collar, bringing me to a halt. I struggle to hold on to my cassette player and drop my books into muddy water. A violent slap lands on my left cheek, making my ears ring. Another hand shoves me against the wall of a house. Two men in military uniforms emerge from the darkness and scream at me in Arabic.

"Where are you going, you donkey?" This one is tall, with a red scarf on his head, his eyes full of anger.

The second officer, thick and short with a heavy mustache, pushes his face into mine. "Are you deaf?" he says, his voice calm but fearsome.

I don't know what is happening, but it doesn't matter. I must apologize for my crime.

"I am very sorry, sir."

Seconds of silence pass like eternity as the two officers study my shaken face and my cassette player, which is still running. "Would you care for some tea and chocolate?" the lady instructor says in English on the tape. I anxiously press a button to stop the cassette.

"Where are you headed?" the tall officer asks.

"School, sir."

All I can see is his horrifying red scarf. Growing up, we were taught that the scarf worn by the security and intelligence forces is the red line you don't cross. You don't walk in the same direction. If you see them from far away, you turn around or cross the street. If they are in your neighborhood, you disappear into the darkest and farthest corner. The red scarf is the murderous bloody sky over every city and town from the north to the south.

A car approaches from behind. I hear it slowing, but as it gets closer, it speeds away. Whoever was driving saw the government forces on the sidewalk. Surely they don't want anything to do with the unfortunate soul stopped by the officers.

The short officer lights a cigarette and paces around while his comrade frisks me and orders me to pick up my books. I clean the covers with my sleeves, and he grabs my books and flips through the pages.

Then he looks up at me. "Which school do you go to?"

"Gara Evening School."

"Oh, you are one of the idiots!"

I want to shout at him, but the anger inside will only burn me. I want to speak in English to show him who the idiot is. He thinks I go to evening school because I failed at day school. But *you* are the reason I failed three times and ended up in night school. *You*, your army, your military!

Then reason tells me to shut up and save myself another beating.

The short officer shoves his cigarette into his mouth and demands my ID. I hand it over. Looking at it, he shouts, "What's your name?"

I give him my name.

They examine my cassette player and make me play the English lesson. When they are convinced I am harmless, they instruct me to get going.

I curse myself for walking tonight, and I peek behind me. They're watching me. Soaking in sweat and anger, I cross the empty street and turn up the road, determined not to look back again.

Donkeys! Dogs! Lowlifes! I am too scared to even whisper those thoughts. In Saddam's Iraq, even your own shadow can spy on you. I resume the English lesson on my cassette player, determined to let the soft voice of the foreign lady drown out the toxic words of the officers.

THE SCHOOL IS SITUATED on a hill overlooking the city center. It brings together two worlds. It's the Mediya Preparatory School for girls during the day and then the building undergoes a total transformation at night when Gara Preparatory Evening School starts. My classmates and I are just an afterthought. A bunch of outliers. Different worlds exist within the walls of this building: gentle, romantic, and dedicated girls during the day and rough, careless, indifferent boys at night. Mostly failures and those too old for day school, Gara's students are some of the most difficult to handle. Teachers often go through the motions with little interest and drive. Students don't mind when classes are cancelled if there aren't enough teachers.

At the entrance of the school, I find three students laughing while smoking cigarettes in discreet ways that no principal can detect. Past the double metal doors in the main hallway, the custodian sits on a bench holding a broom under his left arm and pretending he has been working hard. Directly above him hangs a large portrait of Saddam Hussein in a navy-blue military uniform, smiling under a thick, black mustache. His right arm up, waving, he welcomes me. He stares down directly at me. *Welcome to evening school. Welcome to prison. Welcome to hell.*

The hallways are crowded and loud. The principal cuts through the lazy crowd and declares the end of intermission and the beginning of the second class.

I hate this place. I don't belong here. Never have, never will. I'm too old now to study with students who actually care about academics.

The principals of Kawa and Brayati day schools couldn't do much for me. I had missed four academic years in a span of nine years thanks to the war and government persecution. Those students who fall behind academically can only continue through evening school.

After my father's execution, our family had no place in the city, my mother declared. I was in no position to resist her will then, but as time passed by, my yearning for education and city life and education won.

My younger brother Jamil stayed behind and took my place as the family's male figure. It eased some of my worries, knowing that someone would watch over the family deep in the mountains in the uppermost part of Duhok.

Transitioning back to the city wasn't smooth. Not that I ever expected it to be. During the first month, I was picked up by a government squad and held at the office of intelligence for two nights. They gave me a black eye and a broken arm only to later tell me it was a simple case of mistaken identity. Even so, they told me to regularly follow up with them in the office after they found out I was the son of a Peshmerga. Despite my mother's pleas to return for my safety, I settled into a lonely life at our old house, still owned by my uncle. He refused to rent it to anyone after we left the village.

So many teachers ask me why I ended up here. Long story, I tell them. Only one so far has understood me: Mr. Qais, my English teacher. Aside from the principal, he is the only face I've consistently seen the last few years. Mr. Qais is tall and skinny with a dark complexion and heavy hair. Though he is young, his mustache is yellow at the tips, and his lips are purple from smoking. He seems to think he can ease the troubles of the world if only he'd smoke more. Though soft-spoken and shy, he's the one who has instilled a passion for the English language in me with a heart full of determination.

As I make a turn at the end of the corridor, I spot him in a brown jacket with a book in his left hand and a red pencil, as usual, over his right ear. I'm sure that half the class will be AWOL, but I'm not about to miss it.

Between classes, the principal gives me a pass. I ask for three days off to attend my brother's wedding in the village, but he only agrees to two and says he will be watching me. Friday is an official holiday, so I still get a total of three days.

The permission slip is my passport through the checkpoints outside the city.

2

Dilveen

Village of BerAva, March 18, 1988

The sound of the Quran recitation comes through the minaret of the mosque, the only concrete structure in the village. Soon, men will gather for the Friday *Jumua* prayer. Dadi, my mother, has been up since morning prayer. She made Shireen and me clean the entire house. Of course, Shireen, as usual, found every reason to slack off. In the time it took her to wash the dishes, I cleaned both rooms, set up the blankets, rearranged the living room, and still had time to help the useless creature dry the dishes.

Mother is sitting outside by the small garden. A ray of

sunlight is shining through two cracks in the old aluminum plates overhead. Sparkles of dust float above the ground, swimming in the fresh air. She is reading the Quran, her thick glasses perched on the bridge of her nose. Mother never attended school, yet she is able to read the entire Quran in its complex Arabic form.

I yell at Shireen to help me move a wet blanket outside to dry. Where did she go? I yell again, and Mother, with her white scarf draped over her gray hair and wrinkled forehead and onto the pages of the Quran, gives me a side look of annoyance as she continues whispering her recitation.

The front door opens, and Shireen has returned with our neighbor, Juwan.

"When did the two of you manage to get together?" I shout.

They both giggle. Shireen points at the plastic bag in Juwan's hand and says, "It's *khana* time."

Khana, or henna, will be the highlight of today's pre-wedding festivities. We will use it to draw on the bride's hand first and then do the same for the groom. Shireen lays a plastic sheet on the living room floor, and I grab the plastic bag from Juwan. Then the three of us circle the metal bowl we will use to make khana. To avoid getting too much dye on my hands, I wrap two clean plastic bags around them and pour the greenish powder in the bowl. Shireen adds sugar to the mix, and I motion for Juwan to pour warm water over the powder. I start mixing it in repeated circles. I can still hear the imam's voice over the mosque speakers as his sermon nears its conclusion.

Mother walks back to the kitchen and reminds us to make sure the khana is mixed well. She insists it's her special technique, but every Kurdish woman claims her technique is original even though the end product is always the same.

The greenish-brown khana is ready, and its strong scent has overtaken the house, adding to the sense of excitement for the special occasion. Weddings don't happen every day in a small village, and when they do, they belong to the entire village.

Shireen and Juwan start playing with the khana. I slap Shireen's hand as she runs her right index finger through the khana in a mischievous way. "Get away, you idiot," I yell, and Juwan laughs with satisfaction. Juwan gets a pass in this house. She is not only our neighbor but also our best friend and more importantly the beloved fiancée of our beloved older brother, Azad.

Mother summons Shireen and Juwan to the kitchen to help with the food. Soon the other women in the village will drop by to help with wedding preparations. With the two of them gone, I transfer the khana from the bowl to the metal plate to be used tonight for the formal khana ceremony. I grab a small chunk of the mushy and wet khana with my right index finger and slowly run it over the defined indentation on my left arm. The damn scar! I rub the palm of my hand over it and wish it would melt away. I feel a wave of pain under the khana from my left elbow down to my hand. I set the plate on the table, drop two red flowers on top, and head to the bathroom.

I look above the ancient metal sink at the mirror, cracked in half with a line separating each side and reflecting the broken face standing in front of it. I pull my scarf off and run my khana-dipped finger over my left cheek and to my ear. Another wave of pain. I stare at the pink scar on my cheek extending behind the earlobe, and the memories from when I was nine years old hit me again:

The green military car appears far away as bullets fly around me and my favorite baby goat. With three loud roars, the earth shakes and throws me face-down between the bushes. All I hear, smell, and see is fear. Before I can open my eyes, nauseating smoke fills my nostrils. Another roaring sound, and the ground pounds against my face. I lie motionless, shaken by unbearable pain in my left arm. I bring it to my face and suddenly feel as if it is stuck to my left cheek. I scream. I hear my father's panicky voice. More crying as the sound of bullets brings my ears back to life. I hear a distant sound from a megaphone getting louder and closer and shouting a warning in Arabic. "This is the army. Surrender. You have nowhere to go!"

I look in the mirror again. The soldiers are long gone, but their ghosts linger. The fires are out, but the burning sensation persists.

I hear two boys outside fighting over a soccer ball. And I spit at the images on both sides of the mirror.

OUR VILLAGE, BerAva, is situated near a valley in the Barwari region, seventy or so kilometers north of Duhok. For hundreds of years, BerAva has enjoyed proximity to several streams of fresh water from the Khabeer River in addition to small streams of snowmelt from Metin Mountain. Hence the name BerAva, which means "next to the waters."

Another thing that has never stopped flowing in our

village is the will to live. The elders and their predecessors have passed down accounts of the village being destroyed nearly a dozen times by the Ottoman armies, the English colonizers, and in recent years by modern Iraqi regimens. There are still remnants of destroyed buildings in the village.

In its current form, the village consists of nearly two dozen homes. Along the fresh streams of water lie dozens of farms that yield seasonal crops, including the famous Barwari apples. The apples Saddam famously fell in love with. The same Saddam whose government destroyed BerAva at least twice in the last fifteen years.

The first time was in 1969. Clashes broke out between the Peshmerga and a military unit on the main road as it was headed east toward Kani Masi. At the time, my father, Commander Wahid Barwari, led the Peshmerga unit that successfully and proudly disarmed the caravan of over fifty soldiers and sent them away on foot after burning their vehicles.

Many people think it was a mistake to let them go because the next morning a bigger military unit came, long after the Peshmerga had returned to the mountains, and it bombarded the area with heavy artillery. Half our village was destroyed, and according to my mother, people hid in the mountains for weeks before they were able to return. Many civilians were killed, including both of Jamil's parents.

Jamil and Azad were playing in the dirt next to the mosque when shells hit the farms on the other side of the village, shattering the bodies of villagers and the hearts of the families they left behind. The bodies of the victims were so badly mutilated that it was impossible to separate them, let alone identify them. The villagers resorted to burying flesh where they found it. At the time, my brother Azad was five and Jamil was four. Mom and Dad took Jamil in, and as we grew up, we thought of him as our brother. I don't remember the first time we learned Jamil is not our biological brother, maybe because it didn't matter. We are his family, and now he is a hardworking man who managed to get married before Azad.

Today, the site of the attack remains a gravesite of its own that the villagers pay tribute to every year on the anniversary of the attack. The thing that most hurts Jamil is that his parents don't have marked graves that he can visit.

Damn Saddam and his army! Damn Iran! Damn the war! Why can't we live in peace? Why is the Iraqi military always after us when we are citizens of this country? I have struggled with these questions since childhood, and every time I asked them as a child, Mother said, "You are too young to understand." Even though I've grown up, the questions remain unanswered to my satisfaction.

I often asked Mother if the Arabs hate us, and she said, "Not all of them." But her answer only fueled my curiosity. "Who hates us then?"

"People with evil minds who don't want us to live freely in our own land."

Why do they have the power to dictate that to us? How did they end up ruling us? How come we Kurds don't have our own state like everyone else on the map? Those are just some of hundreds of questions my generation has asked. Mother usually responds with a maze of historical storylines that converge with the Kurds divided by the Western colonial powers across multiple neighboring states.

I am roused from my thoughts by a knock on the door. It opens, and it's him, my brother Azad.

I drop the khana plate on the cabinet and rush to the door. "Bira, my brother, come here. We have missed you." Azad kisses me on the head and drops two heavy bags at the door. My beloved brother has lost weight since the last time I saw him two months ago. He is wearing blue jeans with a light blue jacket over a sports sweatshirt. His dark black hair is nicely combed to the left and still has the same gray spot. The family always makes fun of him for it and pushes him to get married before he's too old. His brown shoes leave mud marks on the floor as he rushes to the kitchen to hug Mother and kiss her hand.

"I was going to kill him if he didn't make it to my khana night," Jamil says jokingly as he walks in behind Azad. Shireen hugs Azad, too, and rushes to inspect his bags of goodies.

Mother excitedly paces in the kitchen. "Where is your uncle? Didn't he come with his wife?"

Azad hugs Mother again and says, "You know the villagers. They hold visitors hostage to pleasantries. They will be in shortly."

All the while, I am looking at Juwan as she steals shy looks at Azad. I can sense that, aside from my mother, this tall brunette girl with the dark black eyes is the happiest of all to see Azad.

Shireen grabs Juwan by the shoulders and yells, "Azad, aren't you going to say hello to your fiancée?"

Juwan blushes and lowers her head, then tries to free herself from Shireen's wicked grab. My mother slaps Shireen and tells her to leave the girl alone.

Azad looks at Juwan and in a soft tone says, "Hello, Juwan."

She smiles and greets him back, her cheeks as red as the tomatoes she was cutting earlier in the kitchen.

We enjoy the moment with smiles, but mother refocuses us and announces, "We will put khana on the bride in less than an hour, and the walk to Babir is not short. Let's get ready."

3

Azad

BerAva, March 19, 1988

My uncle and Jamil are already gone when I wake up a little after sunrise. I catch them outside around eight herding three goats to be slaughtered for the feast tonight. I pretend to be busy and engaged in the preparations, but Jamil catches me with his sarcasm.

"Good morning, city boy. I am glad you decided to grace us with your presence."

I walk behind him and my uncle as they take the goats to an open space behind the house, where Mam Khorsheed sharpens the large knife and instructs me and Jamil to get the first animal on the ground. A few children gather curiously to watch the action. Two hours later, we proudly finish slaughtering the animals and cutting the meat.

With our house filled with ladies preparing for the wedding, the three of us head to Mam Yasin's house for breakfast. Although Juwan is at our house with the rest of the women, she gives me a glimpse of her beauty when she and Shireen bring breakfast over.

I remember my cassette player. I must find a way to get it to Juwan, and I make a mental note for myself to ask Dilveen to deliver it to her. Just sitting inside the house fills me with pleasure. We devour hot, fresh bread, homemade yogurt, honey, and fried potatoes.

Over the third round of tea, Mam Yasin whispers to Mam Khorsheed. "Did you hear anything in the city about a chemical attack in Sulaymaniyah?"

The question takes me by surprise, and I can't tell from my uncle's facial expression if he shares my surprise.

"I was listening to the radio," Mam Yasin says. "They reported a chemical attack by the Iraqi army on the town of Halabja. It is bad. Real bad."

Mam Khorsheed takes the last sip of his tea. "I heard some rambling about it but nothing detailed or confirmed."

"Thousands of Kurdish villagers have been killed," Mam Yasin says. He leans against the wall, grunting as he moves his left leg. I notice a wound on his foot and point at it. He sighs. "It's old age, son. I noticed a wound on my heel one day after returning from the farm, but I never felt any pain. Matter of fact, I don't even know when and how that happened. I saw the local medic in Begova, and he said it was from the sugar disease. What can I do?" I can actually smell the wound when he moves. I wouldn't even need to see it to know it is bad.

"I can get you some antibiotics when I get back to the city," I say, "and will send it to Begova with one of the drivers."

He looks at me with a smile of appreciation. Jamil motions for me to end the conversation. We both excuse ourselves and head out to attend to the wedding preparations and leave politics to the elders.

Once outside, I notice the recent addition Jamil made to the house to accommodate the anticipated family expansion. He usually has a project he needs help with when I visit the village, but this time he asked local people.

"I am happy for you, brother," I say.

He puts a hand on my left shoulder and says, "It would have made more sense if you got married before me since you're older."

"Don't think like that, brother. You are the man of the house now, taking care of Mother and the girls while I'm away and busy with my studies."

He and I head into the village to get haircuts at a friend's house. A few chickens are wandering around in search of worms and insects in the mud. Most of the homes are built with stone and clay. To avoid leaks from rain, at the end of each fall season, villagers run stone roof rollers, bagordaans, along the roof to close the small pores and keep the ceiling intact and clean. A few homes are made completely of clay, mostly those that belong to old couples who defy change.

Dino, the village's mentally challenged man, emerges from between two homes, chased by a few children. As soon as he spots me, he runs towards me with snot dripping from his nose. I doubt he has showered in months. He jumps at me, yelling something incomprehensible, and nearly knocks me to the ground. I yell at the kids to leave him alone, and he passes the time with me while Jamil gets his hair cut for his wedding.

4

Juwan

BerAva, March 19, 1988

I t's late afternoon, and there is a mild breeze in the air. The tip of Metin Mountain is white with snow. Wind made the morning a bit chilly, but the sky is clear, and the wind settled down just in time for the wedding celebration.

Women and children are lined up on both sides of the road. The much-anticipated entourage of elderly men and women finally arrives with the bride. A lady in the crowd ululates with a high-pitched sound, and the rest of us ladies join her.

Later, we hear celebratory voices of the men as Jamil appears in his neat blue Kurdish *shalwal* and vest. He looks as happy as a man can be on his wedding day. His thick hair is covered with a woven cap wrapped with a black-and-white scarf. He is the center of attention.

But in that gathering, only one face registers in my heart: Azad's. The light of my eyes. In his gray *jilket kurdi* suit, he looks like a legendary Kurdish emir. With Shireen, Dilveen, and other girls next to me, I try to look as innocent as possible, but I can't help but imagine Azad being the one on their shoulders and I, the bride, in the house behind us.

He recorded a message for me on a cassette. Dilveen brought it to me earlier. He recorded it after two Arabic songs—smart, in case guards stopped him at a checkpoint and made him play the tape. They might think even an obviously personal message was coded.

"My love, Juwan: I know it has been some time since we have seen each other, but I am excited to see you soon. I am recording this in my room here in Duhok right before I leave the house to take the bus. Your picture is taped to the wall above my head, but God willing I will see you in person in a few hours if there are no delays.

I miss you dearly. I won't be able to say any of these things to you when we meet in person, but please bear with me as I go through the last few months of my studies before the exam in June. I know my mother and sisters are having a hard time understanding why I insist on studying far away. I am sure you are also anxious to see us move our relationship forward and get married.

I promise you that once I pass my exam, we will celebrate our love with the best wedding our village has ever seen. I am just so happy and lucky that you understand me. I want to become an English teacher. I must do this. I will do this for me, for you, and for our whole village, even if they don't appreciate it.

Juwan ... please take care of yourself, and if you can make a recording of your voice and give it back to Dilveen before I leave, that would be great. If you can't, I understand. But make sure you find some opportunities to say hi. I hope you like the gift. Much love."

5

Azad

BerAva, March 21, 1988

After two days and two nights of celebration with dancing, food, and good company, it's time to leave and head back to the city. My uncle and his wife have decided to stay a few more days. After breakfast, I grab my bag and mentally prepare for the all-too-familiar lecture my mother always gives me. "Why don't you stay? What is this school business you have put in your head? Why can't you be like everyone else in the village and focus on your land and your family? This school will eventually get you killed or jailed. It's not safe for you in Duhok. It is not safe for us to be apart. Anything can happen any day, any time."

By now, I am used to this rant, and I don't think she is sold on her own words. She just doesn't want me to be away. Luckily, this time my uncle is my biggest ally. He does more than defend my choices. He also asks Mother why she refuses to consider moving back to the city. With the government restrictions on movement and the constant harassment, there is little livelihood left in the village. Mother fires back by asking him why he won't live where he grew up.

"Mistekhan," he argues, "you know I live and breathe this land, but my doctor says if I have another heart attack, I may not be as lucky if I live too far from a hospital."

I hate to add more worry to her life, and I wish it didn't have to be this way. She and my siblings don't want to move with me to the city, and I won't move back to the village. That's just how it is for now.

Mother gives me a long, worried look in the living room, and I try to reassure her with a smile. I kiss her hand and promise that things will get better.

She kisses me on the eyes and sighs. "My heart will always be with you, and my prayers will always follow you."

Mother sends me off with a load of food, including dried almonds, dried figs, and my favorite: salted and roasted sunflower seeds. I drop by to say goodbye to Mam Yasin, who is delighted at my gesture.

"Azad," he says. "Please keep your ears open for any news. I hear things are getting ugly in the Soran region. The army is building up there."

I ask him to take care of his foot and promise to send him antibiotics and cream with a driver.

I see Juwan's face through the blinds of the front window. She's watching me as I walk away next to Jamil. I turn around one last time with a heart full of love and pride.

THE BUS from Duhok operates twice a week, on Mondays and Fridays. It usually runs through Zakho, stops in Begova, then heads east toward Kani Masi before turning back. Mam Khorsheed offered to drop me off at the station in his truck, but I declined. As usual, Jamil will accompany me to the bus stop, and we will enjoy talking while we walk.

It's that special time of the year when the region wears a beautiful green blanket over the mountains and valleys, spilling its love through the breathtaking scent of white daffodils. Passing through the fields of green crops, Jamil and I mull over what Mam Yasin told us earlier about chemical attacks in the Soran region. This is what our lives have become. Uncertainty about safety, security, and food. We pass through a narrow pathway surrounded by heavy bushes, then turn left and enter the cemetery where Wahid Barwari rests.

There are hundreds of graves here, and my father's is the most visible. A week doesn't pass without Dilveen and Shireen watering the seasonal flowers lining his grave. My father, like many other men buried here, left a silent legacy of bravery in the heart of Metin Mountain. I sit next to my dad's headstone and read prayers for his soul. Every time I visit, I find myself torn between proud memories and the images of his tragic death. I gently run my palm against the soil covering his body. He tells me to never let the enemy determine who I will be.

General Wahid, as many senior Peshmerga still refer to

him, joined the revolution at the age of seventeen, partici-
pating in most of the battles against the Iraqi army in the
1960s and early 1970s. In the late 1960s, peace talks took a
serious turn, and Baghdad granted the Kurds autonomy
over their region in the north. I was too young to remember,
but my parents always referred to that time as one of the
happiest for our people. Kurds were promised ministries in
the cabinet plus various administrative positions in the
municipal governments. The Kurdish region experienced a
sense of victory while all of Iraq breathed a sigh of relief.
Coexistence was visible in all of Iraq as Kurds freely traveled to the south and Arabs traveled up north with few
safety concerns.

But Iraq's leadership reneged on its promises. The self-
rule offered to the Kurds was but a show. Kurdish officials
had little say within their own ministries. The Iraqi government relocated thousands of Arab families to Kirkuk to
change the demographics of the oil-rich city. The promise
of autonomy became a pipe dream, and the Kurds finally
had enough.

The peace process official died in 1974. Young and
seasoned Peshmerga men decamped to the mountains, and
conflict with government forces broke out all over again. I
remember seeing my dad disappear for up to a month at a
time with his fellow Peshmerga, only returning for short
breaks before starting the cycle all over again. He often
came back and said they were so close to defeating the Iraqi
military and kicking it out of Kurdistan. We felt so proud
that we forgot how much we had missed him. But the
fighting continued, and we felt disappointed when Father
returned to duty with his fighting gear.

The Shoresh liberation movement benefited from the

political conflict between Iraq and Iran, with the latter providing logistical support to the Peshmerga plus easy access to its own borderlands. Iran did not love the Kurds— it was simply antagonizing the Iraqi government—but we were desperate and appreciated the help.

In 1975, the revolution collapsed when Iraq signed the Algiers Accord with Iran, offering the Shah Reza Pahlavi valuable land and access to strategic waters in return for an end to support for the Kurds. It was a bullet to the heart, and my father came home crying like a child.

I had never seen him cry before.

"The dream is gone," he said. "The dream is over. The Persians and Arabs have finally united against us."

I thought the world had stopped. Later, between the darkness of midnight and the dread of defeat, planes over-head bombed the village.

Jamil and I leave the cemetery and head to Begova. I remain mostly quiet while Jamil tries to reassure me that everything will be fine with Mother and the girls while I am away.

When we reach the bus stop on the main road, Jamil says, "Are you going to light the fire of Nawruz tonight?"

It takes a few seconds for his question to register. I had forgotten that today is Nawruz, the Kurdish and Persian New Year. How fitting that I spend the first day of our calendar year leaving my family behind and visiting the intelligence office to report my return. I place my bag between my feet and grab a handful of the dry almonds Mother had put in my pocket for the road. I throw one in my mouth and say to Jamil, "I will barely have time to catch up with school tonight. Plus, I don't want any trouble."

Thousands of households light fires on their roofs and

front walls during Nawruz, and the government usually allows it, despite its nationalistic roots, but for someone like me who is on the radar, any slip and I could find myself tortured in a dark room a dozen feet underground. I will stick to the books.

An elderly couple walks slowly toward us while struggling with their bags. Jamil and I walk forward to help them.

"We are headed to Zakho to visit our daughter," the man says. "Is the bus supposed to stop here?"

I nod. "Yes, it will stop in Zakho on its way to Duhok." As we head toward the station, I see it approach from afar. "As a matter of fact, the bus is here."

I hug Jamil and congratulate him again on his wedding.

6

Azad

Duhok, May 1988

Summer is knocking on the door, its heat and dryness arriving weeks ahead of schedule. The school year is over, but that still doesn't mean freedom for those of us in the final year of high school. We have the entire month of May to study for the comprehensive exam, which will determine our college destination. So many ifs, and so many disaster scenarios. We must get a high score to get into competitive fields such as medicine, engineering, and law, but I just want to pass and get into a university. For average students like me, there is a wide range of expectations. I have a good idea what I must do to study English

Literature at Mosul University, and I am confident in my ability to do it.

The days are long and hot, and I spend the majority of my time studying until late afternoon. For a break, I usually head to my uncle's shop for a few hours to help. He pays me, after all, and while he pushes me to go home and study, I can't sit around and get paid for nothing. But—and to be honest—I also like listening to gossip in the store.

Today, a large load of rice and flour has arrived from Zakho, and my uncle has summoned all his workers to unload and prepare it for distribution. I have never seen Mam Khorsheed sloppily dressed. Today he is wearing a full set of brown Kurdish clothes with a cap and double scarves. The pipe rarely leaves his lips, and he sucks smoke from some of the most expensive tobacco in the land. He sits at his desk, flipping through pages of the record book and giving out firm instructions about where everything goes. The server from the teashop next door brings him a cup of tea, which he declines as soon as he sees it, claiming it is not hot enough. He tells him to take it back and to tell his boss that the next one had better have a cloud of steam coming off it.

The radio is on as usual. The news reporter on the Iraqi national channel is praising the victorious Iraqi army and announcing new advances deep into enemy territory. My uncle flips the channel to the Monte Carlo French radio station, and there is a report on a possible truce being worked out between Iraq and Iran.

"After what?" my uncle says. "After both countries are burned to the ground?"

I have always been impressed by his bald tone. He can address military and secret service officials in the most confrontational tone and get away with it. They often drop by the warehouse, and on many occasions he has sent a truckload of supplies to the local officers as gifts. He always manages to present it in such a way that it doesn't look like a bribe. I wonder if these foolish officers know that for years my uncle has also been sending food to the Peshmerga in the mountains through a Christian guy in Zakho named Farhan. I found out about it last year when his right-hand man, Shafeeq, needed surgery, and I had to fill in for him.

Shafeeq is a tall, heavy man in his early sixties with nine kids from the same wife. There is nothing in the warehouse that Shafeeq's wide shoulders can't pull, push, or carry. His oldest son, Simo, recently joined the Chatta forces in a battalion belonging to their Doski tribe leader. When Shafeeq told my uncle about it, I thought Uncle would be angry that his son had joined a pro-government force, but I heard my uncle say, "That is better for him. At least he won't be deployed to the front lines with the regular army and get killed fighting Iran." Every time I question my uncle, his wisdom and access to the past humble me and put me back in my place.

Before sundown, my uncle asks Shafeeq and me to deliver a load of rice to a restaurant on the other side of town. Skillfully maneuvering my uncle's truck through traffic downtown, Shafeeq says, "My son said they will be deploying up north in the next few weeks, and judging from the heavy military presence these days, I suspect something big is going to happen." I listen quietly. "There is talk of the military extending its campaign from the Soran region northeast into our area and where your folks live farther north and northwest."

I roll down the passenger window and stick my hand

out, feeling the warm air between my fingers. "It has been like this for as long as I remember," I say.

Shafeeq says nothing.

"The military comes, and the military goes," I say. "People die, and people suffer."

Shafeeq shifts gears, and the truck jerks forward and back. Without looking at me, he says, "This time it's different, Azad. They are raiding towns and villages out there to the east of us. They are not kidding this time. Aren't you worried about your family?"

I turn to Shafeeq. He's focused on the road. "Look, Shafeeq, I appreciate your concern, but I didn't come this far in school to quit a couple of weeks before the final exams. No way."

We're quiet on the drive back to the warehouse. I know Shafeeq means well, but I've had it with all the negativity.

He senses my frustration. "I admire your commitment to education, and I knew your dad well. He would be proud of your dedication. I'm just worried about the way things are escalating, and what I heard from my son makes me worry for you and your family."

We reach the warehouse, and before I step out of the truck, I turn to him. "I appreciate your concern. Your close friendship with my dad in those days makes you like an uncle to me. But I'd be a failure in my eyes if I walk away from school."

He nods, a concerned look still on his face. But I must have a look of concern on my own face as I remember how much studying I have to do.

～

WITH THREE DAYS left before the first comprehensive exam, I am buried in my books when a little after five in the evening, I hear a knock on the door. I am not expecting any company and don't remember the last time someone showed up at my door.

I get to the door and find Jamil assisting Mam Yasin as a taxi drives away. Mam Yasin's left foot is heavily wrapped with a piece of cloth that looks stained, and he appears tired and pale. We help him inside and let him rest on the couch. Judging from the way his foot looks, the antibiotics and ointments I sent him last month have done no good. But then I doubt he has taken care of himself.

Jamil and I sit in the kitchen and catch up with the news of the village while Mam Yasin sleeps after taking a pain and fever pill. We both agree that his condition is concerning and decide to take him to the general hospital in Mosul the next day to see a specialist.

Jamil lights a cigarette, takes a puff, and asks me about my studies.

"You guys came at the worst time, man" I whisper to him.

He laughs and gently punches me on the chest and says, "There is never a bad time for seeing loved ones."

I laugh and say, "Where are the loved ones, you didn't bring them with you?"

Jamil grabs one of the plastic bags and sets it on the table. It's full of fresh green almonds, my favorite product from the village this time of the year. I quickly wash a full plate of them and set it on the table. I dip a large almond in the salt plate and chew on it, enjoying every sour particle.

After Jamil reassures me about the well-being of Mother

and our sisters and delivers their warmest greetings, I look at him and smile. "So, how is married life?"

Jamil smiles back, his face now red.

I look at him, puzzled, while he continues to smile. I give him a shove and ask, "What is that smile for, man?"

With eyes wide from excitement, Jamil says, "I am going to be a father." With that, he takes another deep puff on the cigarette, then smiles again as I get up and congratulate him on the great news.

Mam Yasin is awake now, calling on us to help him get up and get ready for prayer. We help him walk to the restroom to wash up, and when he is done praying, I look at my guests and say, "There is a nice restaurant in our neighborhood that makes the best sandwiches."

Jamil looks at me and sarcastically says, "And your point is?"

I laugh and say, "Who is hungry?"

Mam Yasin stretches his leg over the prayer rug in obvious pain. "You two go ahead. I don't have any strength to get up and walk."

"Then we will make them *seferi*," I say, "to go."

MOSUL IS about seventy kilometers from Duhok, and to get to the hospital at a reasonable time, we need to leave early in the morning. Mam Yasin has developed a fever again, so we have to take him.

Shafeeq shows up with the pickup truck before seven. Traffic is unusually high today between Zakho and Mosul, and the line of vehicles at the checkpoint moves slowly. When it's finally our turn, an officer carrying a shiny

Kalashnikov approaches our vehicle, demanding our IDs. We hand them over, and he inspects the back of the truck where Jamil and I are sitting.

I avoid eye contact, worried that something as simple as an eye twitch might trigger his thirst for interrogation and violence. Unimpressed with us, he moves back to the driver's seat and questions Shafeeq, who answers him while pointing at Mam Yasin's foot. With the guard's back to me, I study his gun. I wonder how many lives he has ended with that shiny, black barrel. He motions for Shafeeq to move on.

We stop at a shack to get some water for Mam Yasin and see a caravan of tanks and army trucks hauling heavy artillery heading toward Duhok. I stop counting at eighty vehicles. Jamil wants me to ask the old man at the store if he knows anything about this deployment, but the man avoids eye contact when he hears us speaking Kurdish, so we leave. Jamil spits out a few pleasant words at him in Kurdish under his breath.

We drive for another ten or fifteen minutes before the army caravan finally ends. Jamil and I exchange looks of concern.

Mosul is the second-largest city in Iraq after the capital, Baghdad. The city offers unlimited opportunities for business, employment, and education. Its identity has been forged by multiple civilizations over thousands of years. The Tigris River passes through the heart of the city, pumping life through its already vibrant and pulsatile nature.

The wait at the main security checkpoint outside Mosul at nine thirty is even longer than it was in Duhok. The place reeks of diesel fuel, and the sun is intensifying. A passenger Toyota Coaster minibus with a Duhok license plate passes us in the line, and the driver honks at us. Shafeeq returns the greeting with a honk of his own. I am not sure if they know each other.

The officers are friendlier at this checkpoint, and as soon as they see Mam Yasin's wrapped foot on the dashboard, they motion for us to proceed. We reach the general hospital a little after ten.

We spend the next four hours moving between various wings of the hospital. A cute female doctor examines Mam Yasin's foot thoroughly while Jamil admires her beauty. After a few X-ray examinations and consulting with her superior, she recommends amputating two of Mam Yasin's toes. The infection and poor circulation caused irreversible tissue damage, she says.

Mam Yasin is not having any of it. He adamantly refuses and angrily gets up from the examination bed, but I try to calm him down. Seeing his determination, the doctor offers to surgically remove damaged tissue from his foot instead, which Mam Yasin reluctantly agrees to. He understands Arabic, although he can't speak it. His body language alone relays his message to the nice doctor, who removes some of the dead tissue and injects him with antibiotics. She then hands us a box of wound care supplies and ointments to take with us along with a prescription for two more weeks of oral antibiotics, urging us to follow up if the foot is not better.

We leave the hospital, and in the parking lot, Jamil whispers to me, "Cute doctor, wasn't she?"

I give him a push. "Get real, man. You just got married."

He laughs and whispers back, "What's wrong with appreciating the beauty God has put on this earth?"

I am glad the conversation is forced to end when we

reach the truck and need to discuss our plan for the rest of the day.

I ask Shafeeq to make a quick stop at a bookstore. Inside, I ask the owner if he has a foreign languages section, and he points me to a shelf at the very back. I grab an English magazine as well as a level three advanced English conversation book. I pay for them and quickly head out, my empty stomach growling.

Jamil is on the sidewalk smoking a cigarette and blaming my five-minute delay for his starvation.

We head to *Al-Kahif* restaurant next to a record store and an ice cream shop. I ate here once with Mam Khorsheed. The owner, a kind older gentleman, is Kurdish but has been in Mosul since childhood. They make the best kabobs. We sit at a table by the large glass window in front, and I observe the foot traffic outside. The server arrives, and we place our orders.

Shafeeq points to a long line forming across the street. "What is happening over there?"

A large crowd, mostly young men, is gathering at the entrance to Gharnata Cinema. I stretch my legs under the table and say, "They are waiting to watch the latest Arnold movie."

Shafeeq frowns in disapproval and says, "These movies are corrupting our society. All actors are friends of the devil."

We argue back and forth, with Shafeeq fully convinced that the movie theatre in Duhok is the reason his youngest son went astray and quit school. Our food arrives, and Mam Yasin announces, "I am going to eat, and if you two keep going, maybe I'll get to eat your plates too."

7

Juwan

BerAva, May 1988

Four days of constant worry have taken their toll on me. When Jamil took my dad to the city, they were supposed to be back the next day or at most two days later. There are so many things that could have gone wrong. A few months ago, a bus full of forty laborers working on Saddam's mansion went off a cliff while descending Gara Mountain. There were no survivors. Perhaps they were held up at one of the checkpoints. Jamil has always been reckless. But not even this rattles me as much as my father's foot wound. It makes me want to vomit.

Shireen and I are heading back from a trip to the water

source when I see Jamil walking into the village by himself. I drop the jug and fall to my knees.

Shireen yells at Jamil. "Where is Mam Yasin?"

He yells something back, but I can't make out what he says. Shireen gently pulls me to my feet.

"Wallah, you scared us to death, Jamil," she says. "This girl almost died here."

Jamil picks up the half-empty water jug and apologizes. "Your dad is fine. He is exhausted from walking, so I left him at the entrance of the village to rest until I get a mule to carry him back."

Jamil borrows a mule from one of the villagers and guides it toward the farms. I follow and pester him with questions. What happened? Why are you late? Why is my father tired?

He briefs me on their visit and reassures me that my father is fine.

"So why did you take four days to come back?"

The lazy white mule is drifting sideways toward the greens, and Jamil gives it a kick to bring it back to the trail. "We were turned back at the main security checkpoint outside Zakho twice." He notices the puzzled look on my face and continues. "There is a heavy military presence on the main roads, and they are only allowing a limited number of cars to pass through."

"What's this about?"

He picks up the pace to catch up with the now-sprinting mule. "I don't know, Juwan," he says between breaths. "It's not looking good. They turned us around twice and wouldn't even allow Mam Khorsheed to drop us off with guarantees that he would return. The third time, your father got out of the car and started limping away. He told them he was going home dead or alive."

I can see my father now, resting under a large tree with his foot wrapped in a bandage. How Jamil managed to bring him all the way here from Begova is beyond me.

8

Azad

Batifa, seventy kilometers north of Duhok, July 25, 1988

I can finally sigh with relief. The comprehensive exam results arrived, and my average score is 74 percent. I would have gotten a higher average had it not been for the first exam, which I barely had time to study for when Jamil and Mam Yasin visited. But I have a decent chance of getting into the foreign languages department at Mosul University. I just have to wait two more months to find out.

That wait I can stand. What I can't stand is the current wait outside the security checkpoint in Batifa. This is the seventh time in a month I have made this trip to visit the village. Every time there is an excuse for the roads being blocked. Though we no longer see much military presence on the main roads, the checkpoints are stricter than ever. Most people turn back to the city when they are stopped, but a small number take side roads through the mountains and risk getting shot at.

It is past four o'clock in the afternoon. No one dares to ask why it's taking so long. If they don't motion for you to proceed, then you don't proceed. If you defy them, you'd better say your last prayers. Most of the cars are turning back now, but I refuse to move.

Shafeeq is getting frustrated at me. "How much longer are we going to wait, young man?"

Sweat drips down my body as I stand in the sun while Shafeeq enjoys the shade and air conditioning inside the truck. We reach a breaking point when a guard slaps a pregnant woman begging to cross while her husband watches, helpless and broken.

Shafeeq asks me to get back in the truck, and he turns us around, angry and frustrated. "We have had enough humiliation from these animals."

Ten minutes later, he makes a sudden turn onto a dirt road, angrily speeding along and leaving a cloud of dust behind.

"Where are we going, Shafeeq?"

"There is an abandoned side road not too far from here," he says, his eyes fixed on the road. "If we're lucky, we may be able to maneuver our way through and get back on the main road past the checkpoint."

Another pickup truck approaches us, but Shafeeq is not able to slow down in time to stop them and inquire.

"I guess it's a good sign that a car is coming from that direction," I say and turn my head to see if the other truck shows any signs of stopping.

Shafeeq cusses, and I turn toward the front again. A short distance ahead is a checkpoint, and as we get closer I can see a tall armed man in Kurdish clothes waving at us. Shafeeq slows down, and I see two more men on the side of the road, both armed and dressed in Kurdish uniforms.

"They must be Chatta forces," Shafeeq says as we come to a complete stop. Before he rolls the window down, he turns to me and says, "Leave the talking to me."

There are no vehicles or formal posts at the checkpoint. All three men approach our truck together. One stands on each side, and the third inspects the back. The man on my side taps on the window and demands I pull it down, which I do.

He appears to be middle-aged and has a serious look on his face. He quickly scans the inside of the truck and speaks in a firm and matter-of-fact tone. "Don't you know this road is prohibited?"

Shafeeq shifts his head to the right, hoping the closer distance to the man might garner some sympathy. "Son, we are not here for any trouble. I just need to get this young man to his mother and two sisters in their village up north, and the main road was—"

The man waves the palm of his hand at him and declares his authority: "No one crosses north past this area. We've been turning people back all week. You are no different."

Shafeeq asks his name and which battalion he belongs to, but the man only shakes his head; pleasantries will not change his mind.

"My son is also with the Chatta forces," Shafeeq says. "You may know him."

The man who was inspecting the back of the truck joins

his colleague at my window. "Look," he says in an even firmer tone. "I don't know why it's hard for you two to understand what's happening here. Haven't you seen all the military movement lately? Turn around and drive back to wherever you came from, and on the way back, think about why the military is here."

I make one last plea. "Please let us through. I must get to my family. I can just walk from here."

They step back and motion for Shafeeq to turn around. "You will be shot by our unit headquartered less than a kilometer from here if you walk. We are only following orders. The government is above us and you. So save us and yourself the headache and get out of here."

BACK ON THE MAIN ROAD, heading south where we came from, the frustration on my face and in my voice is obvious.

Shafeeq is a unique man. He can strike up a conversation with a person of any age. And with me, he always finds a way to help me see the upside. "I know you're frustrated," he says. "You want to see your fiancée. I get it, but don't worry. We'll try again."

We pass a fenced metal structure on the side of the road, and he points at it. "Do you know what that is?"

I've passed it dozens of times and never thought much of it. Three old ladies are sitting next to it, and one is busy tying fabric to a tree extending over the roof.

"That's the *mazaar*, the tomb, of Zambil Firoosh, the seller of baskets."

I am familiar with the song about him but not the history behind it.

"It's the tomb where people drop their desperate wishes, hoping they will come true."

I laugh. It's ridiculous. But I'm thinking of the lady tying fabric to the tree. "Why didn't we stop this morning when we passed it? I would have tied my own fabric so we could cross the checkpoint."

He laughs. "Now you need it even more so you can see your lover." He tells me the story in an attempt to lighten my mood: "Zambil Firoosh was a handsome man from a powerful Kurdish family. He was married and had two children, but due to some family conflicts that threatened his life, he was forced to run away, leaving his family behind. To make ends meet, he started making and selling wooden baskets that were popular at that time for storing fruits and vegetables." Now he has my attention.

Zakho's historic Pira Delal bridge, made of carved limestone, is now in our sight, and a number of kids are playing on its stone walkway. I am thirsty, so we stop by a street vendor to grab fresh pomegranate juice, and I drink it in one gulp. Shafeeq offers to pay, so I order another drink and laugh at him. We evade the street vendors pushing gum, cookies, and sunflower seeds and head back to the truck. The Khabeer River is down to its minimum due to the dry, hot weather. I watch its anemic flow, and since it's coming from all the way up north, I wish I could ask it about my family and their well-being.

We make our way down the narrow, zig-zagging road through the valley. The asphalt road is soaked with diesel and oil marks from the hundreds of Turkish trucks that pass through every day. Parts of the road are indented from the heat of summer melting the top layers. There are multiple casualties on this road every year, mostly during the winter, when vehicles slide and crash at the bottom of the hill.

Three military vehicles are parked on the side of the road, and Shafeeq slows down in case they force us to stop, but the soldiers are working under the hood of one of the trucks.

"Continue your story," I say.

"So Zambil Firoosh takes his baskets and enters a fort owned by a Kurdish ruler. While he's walking through the streets and hawking his products, the ruler's daughter, the beautiful Khatoon, sees him and immediately falls in love with him."

I turn to him and giggle. "Are you serious, Shafeeq? This is the time for love stories?"

He frowns. "Ohoooo, Azad. Let me finish the story, and then you can judge. Where were we? Yes, so beautiful Khatoon wanted him for herself and tried every possible way to get him. She pretended to be interested in his baskets just to talk to him, and she offered him gold for one. She offered a bed covered with silk. She offered him every-thing she had, but the young man was a man of God, so he declined her continuous offers. He was a *darweesh*. How could he do it?"

"So what happened to your darweesh?"

He laughs. "When Khatoon was certain she couldn't have him, she made up an accusation and sent guards running after him. He reached the edge of a cliff, hundreds if not thousands of feet above the ground, and had to choose between being caught and taken to Khatoon or jumping from the cliff. He jumped. He jumped because he was a man of God and was not about to commit a sin, not after he had repented and given God his word."

I think back to the three ladies who had come to visit the tomb.

Shafeeq seems to read my mind. "Before he died, he asked to be buried on the main road so people who pass by will remember him and pray for him. And now you see people coming to visit, and they bring their wishes there to be granted by Allah."

I question the intelligence of anyone choosing to leave the comfort of home where they can pray to Allah any time they want and travel to that site in the heat of the summer. But who am I to judge? And I'm not about to start an argument with Shafeeq.

He asks me if I enjoyed the story, and I nod. He then removes a cassette from the glove compartment and inserts it into the car stereo. After a few attempts of fast-forwarding, he finds the song he's looking for. It's by Muhammad Arif. Shafeeq turns up the volume. We approach the Duhok city limits as the sun begins to set, a half ball of orange light glowing on the horizon.

Zambil Firoosh I am, bringing baskets
    Street to street parading
    O Khatoon I am a repentant

Zambil Firoosh, you darweesh boy
    Come forward and tell
    Say the price of your baskets
    Come handsome, I am a lover

Lele Lele Lele beautiful Khatoon
    Your eyes are like the olives

I am afraid of the wrath of God
O Khatoon I am a repentant

Zambil Firoosh, you poor boy
    Come and sleep on the royal bed
    I will lay for you the silk
    Come handsome, I am a lover

Lele Lele Lele beautiful Khatoon
    You are full of beauty
    As you settle on bed and in hearts
    But you will not be my wife
    O Khatoon I am a repentant

9

Dilveen

BerAva, August 25, 1988

The last few months have brought as much uncertainty as heat. Crops are not as good as in past years, partly because of the heat and the dryness but also because the villagers' energy has been sapped. They see tanks on the main road morning and night and know that they could be uprooted at any time.

Our home has been a scene of immense stress and panic. We haven't seen Azad for months, and so far all his attempts to visit have failed. He sent word a few weeks ago through a man who was granted special permission to come into the area to retrieve his large herd of cattle. He said Azad was turned back at the checkpoints multiple times. Some villagers believed the man was a spy, so we decided not to say anything to him. The uncertainty has put Mother on the verge of an emotional breakdown.

Mam Yasin is sitting in our living room next to Jamil, his small radio in his hand, and playing with the channel locator and holding it to his ear. Lately, he and Juwan have spent most of their evenings at our house either eating dinner or coming afterward for tea. Berivan, our beautiful bride, is now almost five months pregnant, and Mother says she must be having twins because she looks too big for this stage of pregnancy. Juwan and Shireen are busy talking in the other room. I pour more tea for Mam Yasin and Jamil and set it in front of them.

"More sugar," Mam Yasin demands. "More!"

Juwan shouts from the other room. "No father, your blood sugar will go up, and we will have another problem."

I hesitate to pour more, but Jamil insists. "Put one more spoon for Mam Yasin and let him enjoy himself. Life is too short."

He and Jamil laugh and resume their chain-smoking. The battle with Mam Yasin is a lost one, so I give him one more spoonful of sugar, and he stirs the glass cup, creating waves of sugar within the dark tea.

Mother has withdrawn to the other side of the room, mumbling some prayers. The Iraqi radio channels have been flooded with victory songs for the past two days since the announcement of the end of the Iraq-Iran War. Iraq calls it a victory, but Mam Yasin insists that both sides lost.

He props up his left leg. The cloth wrap around his foot appears less soaked today, but I don't trust him when he says he is getting better. I've seen him soaked in sweat, and he rarely does enough work to sweat this much, so it can't be anything but the fever.

I sit next to Berivan and ask how she is doing, but I'm mostly paying attention to the discussion Jamil and Mam Yasin are having. As much as they try to lower their tone, and in the middle of Berivan's rant about her miserable pregnancy, I am still able to absorb a chunk of the serious man-talk in the room.

Things are not looking good. Everyone has heard about the attacks in the Soran region that started back in February and the chemical bombardment of Halabja in March. We've been seeing military movements for months, but when nothing happened, people started doubting Saddam would consider attacking this region. Mother argues that the recent heavy movement can only mean something bad is being planned.

Mam Yasin takes a quick sip of his tea and speaks in a soft tone. "We have no choice but to stay put. If at any time we realize something serious is about to happen, we will get moving and hit the mountains. After all, we are only a few hours from the border."

Mother is more engaged now but also more concerned. She cries out with a cracked voice. "Will you all get my son back here before that bastard Saddam does something to him or to us? I want to see him one more time before I die."

The room turns silent except for Mother's crying. I sit next to her and console her.

Jamil sits up straight on the other side of the room. "Mother, listen to me, I will never leave Azad behind."

Mam Yasin finally gets the Kurdish opposition radio channel to work and brings the radio to his right ear. We all listen attentively. The voice on the radio says that multiple new military units have been spotted in the direction of the Bamarni region with heavy Chatta enforcements. More than two hundred Kurdish villages have been destroyed in the Soran region since February. The news segment is followed by a patriotic song about the Kurdish revolution. Later, the announcer returns and asks everyone to be vigilant but not to panic. The Peshmerga are covering the area and will deflect any attacks.

This does not comfort us. Mother is crying harder now. We all know that a few hundred Peshmerga men armed with simple weapons can't stand against an organized army. I remember something Mam Yasin whispered to Jamil earlier: "Now that the war with Iran is over, Saddam is going to crush us Kurds." He suddenly gets up and tells Jamil to follow him. He wants to discuss what's happening with the village men.

When they reach the door, Mother asks them in a begging voice, "Please find a way to get word to Azad. Let him come. School can go to hell."

Jamil kisses her hand. "I promise you, Mother," he says firmly, "once we sense something is about to change, I will get Azad even if I have to crawl under the earth."

10

Juwan

BerAva, August 26, 1988

Father is limping again, and I know he's trying to hide it. He forces himself to perform the morning prayer while standing even though he has been performing it while sitting on a chair for months now. The soaked wrap and foul smell from his foot do not lie. He was up most of the night, and despite his misery, he still thinks smoking can cure any illnesses.

He gingerly walks outside to light a cigarette, his usual routine before dawn. I start preparing breakfast. Our food supplies are down. We have little oil left, and we are completely out of sugar. Father is also out of diabetes pills.

Last night we heard bombs in the distance. Father tried

to reassure me it was across the Turkish border, but I am not dumb. I hear a commotion outside and hurry toward the door. There is just enough light to differentiate people. Father is limping away from our house with three men, looking into the sky. Moments later, I hear a helicopter in the distance. Jamil is outside now as well, running toward my father and the rest of the men.

When daylight breaks, we discover that the military has advanced into the area in the middle of the night. Jamil and a few other men return from the hills and report dozens of parked military vehicles on the main road. We sit in Mistekhan's house, crying at the prospect of never seeing Azad again, while Jamil vows to stand by his promise to bring her boy back.

11

Azad

Duhok, August 26, 11:00 P.M.

Summer nights in Kurdistan have a special flavor to them. Duhok, especially, enjoys being surrounded by mountains that produce a soothing breeze. Sleeping on roofs has long been common from May to September. Most of the older homes, called the eastern homes, have stairs that go to the roof from an open foyer. In the newer homes, built in the last few decades and referred to as western homes, usually have access through interior stairs. The roofs themselves are usually flat with a raised concrete barrier at least four feet high for safety. Most families go up to their beds on the roof after nine or so, and many drink tea or eat fruit there. Some even take their TV set and watch whatever movie or series is playing on the main Iraqi channel.

My uncle built this house in Duhok back in the early seventies as his primary residence but later on moved to a bigger house in a nicer neighborhood. When Dilveen had serious burn injuries, my father was forced to move us to the city so she could get treatment, but in the process he had to surrender to the authorities as a potential Peshmerga troublemaker. Father took this great risk while most of his comrades hit the mountains to avoid being imprisoned. My uncle left the house for us when we moved to Duhok, while my dad was forced into exile in the deep south for several years.

It's after 11:00 P.M., and I am lying in my rusted metal bed on the roof staring at the clear sky. It is an unusually hot evening even for the end of August, but thankfully there is no humidity. A newborn has been crying for a while now, and I can hear a man yelling at his kids to shut up and sleep or he will throw them from the roof. He has to wake up early for work, he says. My next-door neighbors have guests, and they have moved their entire party to the roof. They have had multiple rounds of tea, and there is no indication of the night quieting down anytime soon. My eyes are fixed on the full moon, and I wish it could reflect an image of BerAva for me so I could find out how my family is doing. But there are only closed checkpoints, military trucks, and uniformed officers instilling fear in the poor and the helpless.

The neighbor's kids are running back and forth on the roof, carelessly stomping and playing as if it is the middle of the day. I hear two of them whispering and leaning over my side of the wall, a social crime on summer nights. I want to get up and yell at them, but their parents are good folks.

"I think he's asleep," one tells the other. "He can't hear us."

"Should we throw a rock at him or maybe make our ball bounce near his bed to wake him up?"

Wicked kids. I finally get up and hurry barefoot in the direction of their voices. To my surprise, they remain in their positions, their bodies halfway over my side of the wall.

"Mister, there is someone knocking on your door," the first says.

"Yes," the second says. "For at least half an hour now. Don't you hear?"

They both disappear before I answer.

I walk to the front side of the house and lean over the wall, looking down toward the main door downstairs. The street is dark, and I can't see anything, but as I focus with more attention, I hear the repeated knock on the door.

"Azad, come down, can't you hear me?"

It's Jamil. He collapses on the stairs, exhausted and dehydrated. I rush to get him water, then help him inside to the living room. He gulps down four full glasses. When he catches his breath, he grabs my hand. "We have to go now."

Jamil tells me that he left the village before noon and walked for hours, then was forced to hide from spotty military patrols. He then crossed over the mountain and onto the main road, where he was approached by a Chatta patrol. They questioned him for some time and then let him go. To avoid getting caught again, he had to zigzag his way through the mountains and valleys until he passed Zakho and crossed into the open, flat fields. Once there, he managed to hitchhike his way between villages and small towns until he reached the mountains near Duhok. He waited until dark, then crossed it and started his descent toward our neighborhood in Baroshki, which lies on the edge of the mountain.

"The army is within eyesight distance of the village and has begun assaulting nearby villages," Jamil says. "So far, dozens have been burned down, bulldozed, or bombed."

I absorb Jamil's heavy words with reflection. I feel guilty and selfish, but what would I gain from remaining in a village that could be bulldozed at any moment and sent back to the stone age for the hundredth time? And what are we doing anyway? Where is this struggle taking us? Most people in the city are oblivious to what's happening beyond the mountains surrounding us.

Dear Mother, you should have just accepted living in the city so we could enjoy some peace of mind and I could pursue my education, a dream I am now so close to achieving but may soon be gone forever.

It is almost 2:00 A.M., and we need a plan. Jamil takes a quick shower while I prepare sandwiches and grab two water bottles for the road. I turn on the radio, and some of the channels are playing early morning Quran while others are running music. No news!

We sip hot tea and mull our options. I hope to leave immediately and cross the mountains, but Jamil is convinced that he won't repeat his good luck. "We need a safer and more efficient way to get as far away from the city as possible," he argues.

With little appetite for food, I take a sip of my tea. "We wait until daylight." In the Ba'ath Party's Iraq, one better have a good explanation for walking the streets after midnight. "Then we head to Mam Khorsheed's house. He can drive us outside the city."

I can think of at least three security checkpoints on the main streets from here to the city center, and God knows how many more there are after that.

12

Dilveen

BerAva, August 27, 1988, 10:00 A.M.

What we feared for weeks finally happened. The military is upon us.

Mother has been sitting in the same corner and refusing to eat since Jamil left yesterday morning. She is fixated on the Quran and saying prayers. Her eyes have dried up from crying, and no amount of reassurance can cheer her up. Mam Yasin dropped by earlier to check if Jamil and Azad had made it back, sending Mother into another crying jag.

All last night, we heard the sounds of bombs in the distance, and the village men met at Mam Yasin's house to discuss strategy. Two families left last night before the meeting even convened. They packed some belongings and headed to the Turkish border. As of now, from my count, there are eleven households left. No one has seen Dino for two days. We are used to him disappearing for a few days at a time, but with the military scattered around the area, he could get shot or seriously hurt if they don't recognize his mental disability.

The consensus after the meeting last night was that we should leave the village in the morning once all families have a chance to pack. A few men pushed for moving south, toward the army, instead of heading towards the border, but they were laughed at.

Nobody slept last night. Everyone was busy making preparations, cooking food, packing clothes and blankets, and getting their children ready as the sounds of explosions grew louder.

Juwan, Shireen, and I are almost done with our preparations. Berivan has been in bed since last evening with contractions and pelvic pain. She, too, has been crying since Jamil left. Juwan has gone home to finish packing while Shireen and I attend to last minute preparations.

We hear a knock on the door and two male voices followed by the voice of a female who barges in without waiting for permission. Seti, Berivan's mother, frantically heads to the living room and calls her daughter's name. "Where is my daughter? What happened to her? My death before I see you dying and bedridden, my daughter."

I stand there speechless. Who told this lady her daughter is dying?

Shireen, standing next to me and watching the drama

unfold, can't control herself. "Welcome, Hajiya. Your daughter is alive and kicking. Can you please calm down and not scare her more?"

I pinch Shireen's arm to shut her up. By now, Mother is already in the room, attempting to reassure Seti that her daughter is fine, that she's just under a lot of stress. Berivan's father and older brother are now at the door, and I welcome them in and invite them to have a seat.

Her father looks around anxiously. "We don't have time to waste. The world is turning upside down, and we are here to check on our daughter and see what your plans are."

Upon her mother's arrival, Berivan's pain has doubled in intensity. She is crying while her father sits there and shakes his head. Her family is behaving as if we have done her wrong. Before Shireen runs her mouth further, I grab her shoulder and pull her behind me to the kitchen.

While preparing tea, she says, "I am tired of these people. Let me go back and tell them to get the hell out."

"You open your mouth one more time and I will pull that tongue out."

In the living room, I hear Berivan's father discussing plans with my mother and asking if we intend to leave. He says they are ready to go but got worried when they didn't hear from our men. One of the families that fled last night told them Berivan was sick. Of course, Seti had to come and grace us with her attitude.

"I never liked this old witch," Shireen whispers.

Berivan's parents are determined to leave, and after a few exchanges with Mam Yasin, we agree they should take Berivan with them and leave. My mother refuses to leave until Azad and Jamil return. If something happens to

Berivan after we force her to stay, her family would blame us.

At three o'clock in the afternoon, Berivan's family places her on a horse. They agree to wait for us on the other side of the mountain if she feels better. If not, they have some relatives on the Turkish side who will help take her to a hospital. In all fairness, she looks sick now, and I am genuinely worried about her. Except for us and one other family, the village is deserted. The main road is completely blocked by military vehicles. One man claimed earlier in the morning that two soldiers chased him when he went to get some vegetables from his farm for the journey. I think he was lying and trying to get the villagers to hurry up and leave.

Juwan enters our house a little before sundown carrying some packed food to be added to our stack. She looks worn out, physically and emotionally. I take her outside and try to talk to her. She immediately breaks down crying. I can read pages of worry in her eyes, and can I blame her?

I'm the village therapist now. Well, except for Shireen. I don't think she cares much about anything. If she does, she sure doesn't show it. I don't know if that's good or bad, but in the middle of this emotional hurricane, I'm happy to have one fewer person to babysit.

Juwan and I look around the empty village. Just twenty-four hours ago, it was buzzing with activity and chatter. In their rush, the last family to leave before us doesn't even stop say goodbye.

When the sun finally sets after a long and emotionally draining day, Juwan asks me to go with her to check on her father's foot. Mam Yasin is sitting outside in a chair by the door, his mind somewhere else. The foul smell is evident from feet away. The dressing we put on his foot yesterday is totally soaked now. I remove it, and half of his left foot is engulfed in puss and inflammation. Yet he's smoking a cigarette, seemingly oblivious.

"I don't feel any pain this time," he says.

I look up at him. "Mam Yasin, your foot looks worse than it did a few months ago."

I feel a pinch on my left arm scar, as if it's reminding me that a living wound is supposed to hurt. "A painful wound is a sign of healing," my doctors told me each time I cried while they changed the dressings.

It is totally dark as we move inside Mam Yasin's house. I instruct Juwan to bring a bowl of hot water, and while she holds her father's foot, I scrape off some of the puss and dead tissue. Pressing all the way to the heel, I am unable to elicit a pain response, which is not good, but I keep my concern to myself.

While helping me wrap her father's foot with a clean piece of cloth, Juwan gives him her usual speech. "Babo, you must take care of yourself. Please, for my sake, watch what you eat and stop putting this poison in your lungs." She removes the half-smoked cigarette from his fingers and throws it away. I tie the last knot in the cloth, and Mam Yasin asks me to make it tight.

Suddenly a wailing sound erupts from the sky, and a second later the ground shakes under us, throwing Mam Yasin from his chair and me and Juwan against the wall.

I slowly pull myself up, struggling to maintain my balance, then give a hand to Juwan. We find Mam Yasin on his back, groaning in pain. We help him sit up, then he pushes himself to his feet and walks with a wobbly gait. I notice a streak of blood on Juwan's forehead as she helps her father back to the chair, but it's only a minor scrape.

There is another explosion, and the entire house shakes, causing pieces of debris to fall from the ceiling. I run outside and head back home. Shireen is howling somewhere inside, and I find Mother slowly moving around, confused and dazed. Three more shells fall on our village in the next ten minutes. We're under attack in a haunted village. At around nine in the evening, we hear a helicopter hovering in the distance, and then it disappears. Mam Yasin is at the door, his cane in one hand and a small bag in the other. Juwan is behind him, holding an oil lamp and sobbing.

"Let's go!" Mam Yasin says. The serious look on his face says it all.

Realizing that leaving without her sons is inevitable, my mother leans her head against the wall and weeps. Shireen and I hold her arms and gently pull her out of the house.

We avoid the dirt road and walk through the apple farms. These trees have been with us through decades of struggle, providing life and color despite the brutality in this otherwise enchanted land. Now we are leaving them to the iron of the army.

Juwan holds the lantern as she walks next to her father, periodically looking down at his feet. Mam Yasin leads the way, and when the village is behind us, Mother asks, "Have any of you seen Dino? That kid could be anywhere and without anyone to care for him."

Shireen grabs her arm. "As if this is the time to think about that retard."

We turn a corner and march toward the mountain. We have heard no more explosions since leaving the house.

"Maybe the attacks are over," Mother says, "and we overre-acted. Should we turn back?"

Mam Yasin doesn't answer. But a few minutes later, two successive explosions light up the mountainside from behind us.

13

Azad

Barwari region of Duhok, August 27, 1988

Jamil and I leave the house at around six in the morning. The last two items I pack are my English-Arabic dictionary and a compass my father gave me as a child for doing well in school. It's old, but it gets the job done. We head to my uncle's house and find him sitting on his front porch and putting fine tobacco in his pipe. He sucks his pipe as we break the news to him.

Within half an hour, we are on the road, heading toward Zakho with Mam Khorsheed. He insists on taking us himself since he knows the way and has connections in the area. The initial plan is to drive past Zakho and go as deep into the rural areas as possible, but the heavy military presence forces us to improvise.

My uncle pulls over next to a narrow trail leading away from the road. It is the first time I've seen him cry. He hugs us and hands me two hundred dinars in case. He walks with us for a few minutes, then stops. With tearful eyes, we bid a sad farewell and set off in opposite directions.

Even after half an hour, my uncle is still watching us from the side of the road. Later, I turn and he is gone.

They say men don't cry. Well, my uncle cried, and so did Jamil and I. When the land cries, and when the skies cry, how dare the eyes not follow suit.

It is noon before we know it, and we are soaked in sweat. Our initial plan is to go east, then follow the stream north toward the Khabeer River, but it proves harder than anticipated. The side roads are all blocked by checkpoints, and we're forced to hide in a small valley near a creek surrounded by abandoned farms.

At some point, we realize it would be impossible to continue walking without being spotted, so we find a hiding place outside one of the villages. We lie low for hours and take turns napping, knowing our main struggle would come at night. At dusk, we resume our course, with Jamil taking the lead since he knows the area well. So far there is no active bombardment in the area, but we see dozens of military helicopters in the sky near the Metin mountain range.

Near midnight, things settle down except for some sporadic shells hitting the surrounding mountains from time to time. From far away, some of the villages look alive with scattered lights, but most of them lie farther south and below the red line established by the government for restricted zones.

Exhaustion takes its toll on us. After nearly six hours of walking trails, climbing hills, jumping over creeks, and swimming through rivers, we surrender to biology. I look at my wristwatch, and the time is a little after four forty in the morning. We ate the last of our food earlier, so we rest for about an hour on empty stomachs. With the dark sky still our ally, we get up and resume our course.

A little after sunrise, we reach an abandoned military post on top of a rocky hill with a good view of the surrounding area, so we climb up to get a better view. Scattered bomb craters and numerous spent bullet casings speak of prior armed clashes here. On one of the large rocks near the post, someone has written BIZHI KURDISTAN, long live Kurdistan, in red paint. Whatever happened here, Peshmerga were the last to occupy this post. Far in the distance, we can see the main road leading up to Begova, and I look at Jamil and smile.

"All right," he says. "Your compass and my expertise carry the magic."

I sit down to catch my breath and collect some energy. Jamil suddenly grabs my arm and pulls me to my feet. "Look over there." He points to a steep area about a kilometer or so northeast of us. A massive herd of goats and sheep is marching in an organized pattern.

"Where there are organized animals," Jamil says, "there is a shepherd."

Before I get a chance to respond, he descends the hill. I follow him in hurried steps. Half an hour later, we are close to the herd, and we spot two dogs frantically chasing the animals that are determined to go astray.

An old man wearing a brown shalwal and a black vest appears. "Where are you two headed? My dogs will eat you alive if you hurt my animals." The dogs are now barking at us from a distance with the man continuously signaling for them to hold off. They snarl their sharp teeth at us.

Jamil reassures the man that we are harmless and that he does not need the dogs. After some pleasantries and introductions, the man feels comfortable enough to approach. His name is Haji Rajab. He's from the village of Kesta, but he has been moving back and forth in the area for years. No family, never married, and he has over a thousand animals, including two hundred head of cattle. He needs to get them across the border. He doesn't care if he can sell them or not—it's personal. "They are my children, and I must get them to safety, even if it costs me my life."

He knows my father from decades ago, and that is comforting. And he knows the area even better than Jamil and my compass. He is headed to the border, and we decide to tag along until we get to our destination.

He offers us some meat that he cooked for himself earlier.

"Aren't you afraid of the army?" Jamil asks.

Haji Rajab answers confidently: "I am scared of no one but Allah."

14

Juwan

*Metin Mountain, Barwari region, August 28, 1988, early
morning.*

T he mountain! Our ultimate sanctuary. Where we
turn for hiding, resting, celebrations, protection,
even fighting. We have been walking for hours
along the tortuous trails. It's long past midnight, and we
have struggled against the steep, rocky trail. Finally, Father
falls and is unable to continue. In trying to catch him, I drop
the lantern, and it lands on a rock at least ten feet below and
shatters into pieces. Now we are in complete darkness.

Earlier, we could see some lights on the mountain that
Father thought were made by people from nearby villages.
Now we can't see any lights, probably because all those

people managed to descend and cross the main road, evading army units in darkness.

Dilveen and I help my father to the side of the trail so he can rest. His warm body is shaking, and he leans against a tree, too weak to move or talk as we surround him, concerned, barely able to see each other. He takes a few sips of water as I help him eat a few tablespoons of yogurt. I wet a piece of cloth and put it on his forehead. Dilveen attempts to examine his leg, but he won't let her. He is more awake now but also more agitated. He slowly gets up, disregarding our pleas for him to rest, and walks gingerly while leaning on his cane. Dilveen and I give our belongings to Shireen, and we both hold my father by his shoulders and continue our journey.

Later, Mistekhan asks for another rest break. With her and my father resting, I take Dilveen to the side. "It will be daylight soon, and we will be exposed. We need to find shelter."

She looks around. We are still on a steep edge with poor visibility. "Let's continue walking slowly," she says in a comforting and confident tone, "and when the light comes out, we'll be able to find a good place to hide." She squeezes my hand. "Hang in there. We will survive this."

I turn the other way, wipe my tears, and then walk back toward my father, who is now demanding to get going again. His pride will not allow him to admit pain or accept that he needs more help from us, the women, than he could give us.

At dawn, we set up camp in a small open area surrounded by large trees. Behind us is Metin Mountain, which extends farther east as far as we can see. The main road is less crowded with military vehicles in that direction but only because they're wreaking destruction in the villages. I see a column of smoke rising from the village of Babir, east of BerAva. Two Soviet-made Sukhoi jetfighters fly over us. Shireen screams and drops the bags from her hands. Moments later, the planes reappear, and I swear this time that they intentionally dropped lower to frighten us, though Father reassures us we are out of their sight and safe under the trees.

Dilveen points toward the mountain on the other side of the main road. "Look, there are people crossing to the other side of the mountain toward Turkey. That's good, right?" She looks at my father for validation and continues. "Hopefully, we can cross the main road without getting caught."

Gathered under a large tree surrounded by bushes, we sit in silence, desperately trying to keep worry at bay. "I wonder," I say to no one in particular, "if Berivan and her family made it to Hiror safely and are waiting for us or if they've already crossed to the other side."

As expected, Shireen has something nasty to say. "I don't want those idiots in our company anyway, so good riddance."

My father shifts his body with a grunt. "Don't blame them. They were worried about their daughter, and in times of distress, humans get tested to the limits and beyond."

I hear distant, periodic explosions, but so far it's been quiet nearby since the jetfighter scare. Dilveen and I carefully search the area for water. I hear the distant sound of a creek, and we head toward it. With Dilveen watching my back, I quickly fill our containers. Then we wash our faces and head back toward our site.

I hear something at the edge of the tree-covered area. Dilveen grabs my arm, and we duck. We carefully crawl on our knees, dragging our water containers behind us as noiselessly as we can until we reach a large tree and sit behind it. A group of men are having a casual conversation, their voices growing closer. Breathing heavily against the tree, both Dilveen and I sit and listen carefully. I want to scream, but my throat feels numb and paralyzed as the sounds grow louder and closer. I'm too rattled to recognize the language those men are speaking, but Dilveen does.

"They're speaking Kurdish," she says. "They're Kurds."

I peak around the tree and spot three young men, all wearing Kurdish clothes in full fighting gear. We stay put and observe carefully. They suddenly stop, and one of them walks to a tree not too far from us. The other two smoke cigarettes and resume their discussion mixed with laughing and giggling.

"They must be with the Chatta forces," I whisper. "They're fully armed."

She studies them and nods. "We have to go back."

One of the men throws his cigarette on the ground and yells at the guy behind the tree. "Hurry, Rashoo. What did you drink? You've been pissing for an hour now."

We take advantage of their distraction and run, leaving behind our water jugs. Before we get far, one of the men shouts, "Hey! Where are you going? Ladies, stop right there." We speed up even more and disappear into the crowded trees.

We know it won't be long before they find us. We tell the others what happened, quickly gather our belongings, and prepare to leave. Dilveen suddenly screams and drops what's in her hands. I look up, and the three men are right there, silently observing us from afar. They slowly approach, their guns strapped to their backs, as if they don't intend to fire them any time soon. One of the men, the best dressed and probably in charge of the squad, looks at Dilveen and me but says nothing. He turns to my father and politely greets him.

They seem harmless so far, but Shireen isn't buying it. "Are you with the Chatta?"

The man who was pissing behind the tree earlier now holds a cigarette between his fingers and gives Shireen an angry look. "Yes, we are, but who are you to ask?" He plays with the strap of his gun, forcing us to give him our full attention.

My dad gets up slowly and tries to shake hands with them, but Shireen bares her venous fangs again. "You are traitors, and we don't trust you."

Dilveen yells at her to keep quiet, and my dad explains to them in an apologetic tone that we are headed to the border and stopped for a break. They instruct us to gather our belongings and to get going, ignoring Shireen's verbal battering. One of the men assists my dad while the other two lead the way. Following them, we wonder if they are going to hand us over to the army or help us cross the main road and into the restricted zone.

As we walk, Shireen says, "How do we trust you? You work with the government that's trying to kill us."

One of the men has had it. He turns around, and without stopping he heads toward her says, "Shut your mouth or I'll push it to the back of your head."

Long moments of silence pass as we walk past the farms and into the open land leading to the main road. Two of the men are now assisting my father as his limp has gradually worsened. Mistekhan is walking next to Shireen and grabbing her shoulder from time to time as a reminder not to open her mouth or do anything stupid. We spot military vehicles far away, but at this point they are mostly passing through. We finally reach the main road and stop.

The sun is directly above our heads, and I can't see a cloud in the sky. Father is very weak, his face soaked in sweat, and he asks for some water.

One of the three men hands him his water canteen. "Haji, we can't go with you past this point. You will cross the road on your own and can probably find some people near Hiror." They instruct us to stay low until they confirm the road is clear. They then give us the signal to quickly cross.

We thank them as they stand there observing us, mostly focused on my father's limp. Father turns to them and offers his warm thanks. "God bless you, son. We are very thankful to you."

Mistekhan offers her thanks as well and apologizes for Shireen's unpleasantness.

One of the men says, "No offense taken."

His partner lifts his hand in the air, motioning for us to stop wasting time.

When we reach the other side of the road, I turn around, and one of the three men is still standing on the asphalt, waving as he says, "Try to go as far as you can today. It is going to get bad here later." I hope Mother didn't hear that last part, but I already hear her sobbing.

We reach the outskirts of the empty village of Hiror late in the afternoon. Fatigue, exhaustion, hunger, thirst, and fear pull us toward the ground, but my father is still busy showing off his strength and power. I'm certain his body is falling apart, and if something were to happen to him here, no one could help us. We were fortunate earlier when God softened the hearts of the three Chatta men.

Out of water and food, we stop in the shade next to a

stream that cuts south through the village straight from the mountain top. This area is heavily planted and should provide some protection from planes flying overhead. We fetch some water from the cold stream and pass it around in the only canteen we have. The gushing sound of the water echoes in the abandoned village, reminding us that we're alone in this once-living village known for its generosity.

Father takes a sip of the cold water and sighs in satisfaction. He takes a few more sips, then hands the bottle back to me. He looks around and sighs again, this time in disappointment. "Oh, the memories I have in this village. As young boys we used to come here and hold a competition with the boys of this village. There is a pond up there near the mountain where this stream slows down. Villagers built a small wall from rocks and chunks of trees to further slow the flow of water where it is deep enough to swim in. We dared each other to stay submerged in the freezing water as long as we could. I don't recall ever beating the village boys here."

Mistekhan turns to my father and asks in a soft and broken voice, "Haji, what are we going to do? I'm worried about these girls, and you don't look good at all."

My father sits up and points. "Over there, across the mountain, is where we need to be. The border. I am sure there are thousands already there." He scratches his heavily bandaged foot with the tip of his cane. "We will rest for a few more hours and get going again."

"But it will get dark later," Dilveen says, "and we don't know the way,"

My father gives her a dismissive look. "You forgot I was a Peshmerga here for years?"

Dilveen blushes. "No, Haji, I didn't intend to question your knowledge and skills. My apologies."

We mull over our situation for the next ten minutes or so while Dilveen examines my father's foot and says it's time for a dressing change. I look in our bag for a clean cloth. The smell seems to be getting worse. We change the dressing, and I help Father lay back down. Within moments he starts snoring.

Mistekhan asks us girls to follow her to the village to look for some food. We walk along the direction of the creek until we reach the center of the village. No sign of anyone. We carefully enter the first house and inspect it thoroughly. Whoever lived here mopped it clean on their way out. Aside from some old blankets and worn-out kitchenware, there is nothing left. The next house doesn't look much different except for some dried food and bread we find in the living room. Sticking closely together as a group, the four of us proceed from one house to the next.

We find one that appears untouched. The beds are clean and neatly made. The kitchen is stocked with rice, flour, and sugar as well as thin Kurdish bread. Mistekhan grabs a dozen or so pieces of bread and rinses them with water. In a few minutes, the bread will be soft, and we will fold it and wrap it with a piece of cloth. From the bedroom, I grab some light blankets and hand them to Shireen to take outside. At the foot of the bed, I find a clean folded white sheet and put it under my left arm, thinking my father's foot will need a fresh dressing soon.

In the kitchen, Mistekhan and Dilveen are discussing whether to cook some rice for the journey, but they soon realize there is no oil. We settle for the simplest and most easily portable food, including preserved cheese, onions, and dried figs.

Then Shireen runs inside with a terrified look on her face. Still panting and obviously rattled, she says, "I think someone is out there." We all listen to her attentively as she continues. "I was checking one of the houses and noticed smoke rising behind it."

We investigate and find that the fire had recently been put out. Someone was definitely here not too long ago. A few cigarette butts lay on the ground next to the fire and an individual metal plate and spoon. We speculate it was one person. Military personnel usually don't travel alone, and we're too deep in the northern territories for an isolated soldier to be roaming around. It must be someone from the village. We look around, carefully inspecting every corner and shed around the house.

"You!" Mistekhan yells. "Whoever is out there! If you hear us, brave man, man of dignity and family, we are three ladies and one sick man in need of help."

The four of us continue shouting, but we hear nothing and decide to head back to our spot.

Father is leaning on his cane, his back to the tree. He walks toward us, and we tell him what we saw. He agrees that whoever was there earlier must have been from the area.

We gather in a circle to eat what we collected earlier. Afterward, Dilveen and I help my father to the stream, where we open his dressing. The smell is so foul that we have to cover our noses with our scarves. The wound now extends to the ankle, redness mixing with black layers of dead skin and dripping white and yellow pus. Dilveen pours a water jug on the wound while I gently clean it with a soap bar we took from one of the houses. My father barely flinches as we scrub the wound and pour water on it. It seems he can't feel anything. Not a good sign.

"I wish I could smoke a cigarette now," he says as Dilveen presses the dressing hard against his foot. Again, she doesn't elicit any pain. The only thing Father feels right now is nicotine withdrawal. But he's clearly exhausted, and he can no longer hide it. Sweat drips down his forehead and neck. We help him back to our resting spot while we pack and are startled by a voice from behind: "Is that you Haji Yasin?"

An older man in a brown shalwal and green shirt is standing next to a tree some twenty feet away, his gun hanging from his left shoulder.

My father quickly gets up and would have fallen over if not for the cane. "Tahir, it's you. My God."

The man, still a stranger to us ladies, runs towards Father and offers him a warm handshake, then greets us while placing his gun on the ground. "I heard your voices while climbing on the hill outside the village. You are lucky I heard you when I did or I would have turned the corner and headed into the valley."

Father introduces everyone to Tahir, then briefs him on our journey, mentioning little about his foot problem. Not that Tahir couldn't see it or smell it. Tahir politely asks my father to have a seat and rest, his eyes on the wrapped foot.

"When I returned from my Peshmerga mission, my family was gone, along with most of the village. Thank God my oldest son was around to help everyone cross the mountain. My wife and kids are at the border now. That is what my cousin told me."

"Do you have a cigarette?" Father says.

Tahir produces a half-full cigarette box from his pocket and takes out two. He hands one to my father and puts the other between his lips. He inspects his pocket and says, "Oh, I lost my lighter."

My father grabs a lighter from his own pocket, and with a smile of satisfaction, he lights Tahir's cigarette and then his own. "So why are you still in the village?"

Tahir and Father suck on their respective cigarettes like the world might end soon. Tahir coughs after a long exhalation and finally answers. "I stayed behind to ensure that everyone who left the village is safe, then helped a few families cross the road last night after word came that they were stranded with two infants."

My father pats Tahir's shoulder with pride and turns to us with a smile. "Tahir was always the first to the front lines and the last to leave."

At around five in the afternoon, we leave Hiror together. We make reasonable progress until the sun sets and leaves us behind when we're only halfway to the top of the mountain.

We hear several loud explosions from the other side of the main road far behind us. Tahir periodically inspects the surrounding area with his small military telescope. When night falls over the sky and the mountain trail is only faintly visible, we decide to rest at a flat spot near a tree. With our backs to the mountain, we sit in silence and look to the south and southeast. Patches of angry flames appear scattered over Metin Mountain.

Where are you Azad? You should be by my side, Azad, and help me carry this burden. My love, light of my eyes, who will stand by my side if I fall?

15

Azad

Metin Mountain, August 28, 1988

Haji Rajab is a man of destiny, always on the run. To follow him on a trail is to follow the wind. He catches every movement of his herd, and he instinctively knows when an animal is about to go astray. Jamil and I are barely able to keep up with him.

Yellow fields extend to the left of us with great opportunities for the animals to feed, but Haji Rajab is determined to push his herd away and toward the north and northeast.

After a few hours on the trail, Jamil sidles up to me. "This guy is not human. I haven't seen him drink water or eat anything since we met him."

We watch Haji Rajab throw a few rocks at a black goat about to pull out of the herd.

"Why do you care?" I say.

"I'm hungry, man. He has this large herd. What would it hurt if he slaughters one sheep or goat so we could enjoy some fresh meat?"

"Are you serious? You want to light a fire and barbeque meat when we're running for our lives?"

Jamil shrugs and kicks a rock. "If we are meant to die, there is no escape. At least we won't die hungry."

He picks up his pace, and when he's a good distance in front of me, he turns and gives me a wicked smile. "Let's see which animal I'm going to make this man slaughter for us."

Jamil catches up to Haji Rajab. I can't hear their conversation, but their body language is telling. Haji Rajab shakes his head and turns away, leaving Jamil in a cloud of self-defeat of his own making.

Jamil walks back empty-handed and full of rage. "This old man is as cheap as they get." He lights the last of his cigarettes and angrily throws the empty box over a rock. His defeated tone amuses me, so I remain silent and enjoy the rest of his rant until he takes the last puff on his cigarette.

Hungry and deprived of the fresh meat walking around us, we have no choice but to follow along with Haji Rajab. According to his estimates, it will take at least six more hours to reach BerAva, but with the evening soon upon us, he wants to stop and give the animals some rest. I insist that Jamil and I continue, but despite his dislike for our traveling companion, Jamil is convinced we must stick with him. Jamil is extremely uncomfortable with us taking this route at night and alone. I have always trusted his instincts, so I'm not about to question him now. Plus, he has a point. The old man helped us when we lost our way and could have walked right into army territory.

We descend toward the river and find a small, abandoned farm. We pick a watermelon and two cantaloupes and eat together next to the river. Jamil and I jump in the water to cool down and wash off two days of sweat and dirt. Haji Rajab's animals scatter around, finding resting spots as if they have known this area their entire lives. Throughout the day, my biggest fear was being spotted among this large herd by a helicopter and getting shot at, but we got lucky.

My wristwatch reads 10:25 P.M. Haji Rajab is finally reassured that his herd is settled, so he takes a spot next to Jamil and me and lays his head on his small wool bag. Looking straight into the sky, he addresses us with authority. "We will get some rest tonight, and before dawn we will hit the road. After another three or four hours, we will get to BerAva. If your folks are still there, we will pick them up and head to the border."

A few moments of silence pass as I wonder again if it's a good idea that we continue with him. "Just remember, my herd is my priority. I will not compromise their safety for anyone, and as long as you help me get them across, I will guide you along the best trails to Turkey. If any of my animals get sick, we will slaughter them and eat their meat. Otherwise, no one is touching my animals."

I expect Jamil to blurt out that he hopes one of them gets sick by morning, but he is already snoring. Soon, our peculiar shepherd drifts into a peaceful sleep as well.

Every time my eyes close, I'm awakened by the sound of an explosion in the distance or by morbid thoughts that something terrible awaits us.

STARGAZING WAS part of my childhood. When our father left us behind in the village for weeks at a time, performing his Peshmerga duties in the mountains, I often cried and asked Mother when he would be back. She always told me to look up at the sky and ask the stars. "Let the soothing love of the stars answer you in peace and tranquility," she said. So I squeezed my eyes shut and concentrated on one beautiful star, and the next thing I knew, the light of the day pierced my half-opened eyes.

Later, when I grew up, I realized what Mother was doing. When Father was forced into exile for years, Dilveen and Shireen often cried at night, demanding to see him. I lay in my bed on the roof in the summer and listened to Mother telling the two girls about her secret, silent communication with father through the stars. The girls immediately fell silent. While I stopped believing that story as I grew older, I always appreciated the silence of the moment and the ability to enjoy the peaceful sleep that it brought me.

Now, after many years and long distances, I find myself silently staring at the stars embedded in the dark sky as if they're embroidered into a large piece of fabric. With everyone around me asleep, I close my eyes and decide to sneak away from this place, this era, this world, and travel back into childhood, where I find the same stars in the same sky in defiance of time and place. With my heart already squeezed from worrying about my family, I shut my eyes and ask one of the stars to reassure me that they are okay, to offer a glimpse of hope. Is it too late to recover the illogical innocence of childhood?

The ground moves slightly beneath me. Unsure if it's a dream, I open my eyes and see a few bright lights moving across the sky above us. Our friendly stars aren't this mobile. The ground shakes again, this time hard enough to knock over a few of the nearby animals, and the roar of an explosion fills the air.

"They're here!" I yell and force Jamil and Haji Rajab to their feet. Haji Rajab frantically paces around, looking for his panicked, darting animals. He shouts in the darkness at Jamil and me to help him regroup his herd.

Jamil desperately tries to calm two sheep after another explosion not far from us.

"We should have left last night while we had the chance," I whisper. "The light will totally expose us."

A few animals lose their footing near the river, and moments later I hear a splash followed by the struggle of one of the animals against the moving water. I grab Jamil by the shoulder. "This old man will get us killed because of his animals."

Jamil runs toward the river and helps Haji Rajab pull the sheep out of the water. When he returns, he whispers, "We are not going to leave this man alone. He did us a favor, and we must return it. He could have chosen a safer route, but he came here for us."

As dawn breaks, and when Haji Rajab is reassured that his animals are accounted for, he announces that it's time to get going. We make our way through the rough terrain, Haji Rajab leading while Jamil and I follow behind the caravan to ensure all members of the herd stick to the trail.

"If my recollection is correct," I say to Jamil, "I believe there is a village behind the next hill."

He nods, panting and wheezing, then grabs my hand

and motions for me to be quiet. We both freeze in place, falling behind the herd as it continues ahead. I wave my hands, silently requesting an answer.

With his eyes closed, he listens attentively for a few seconds, then cries out, "It's a helicopter! I can hear it getting closer to us."

The sound is suddenly audible now that I focus. Seconds later, a whirring noise fills the sky as the dark-gray helicopter passes over us and into the valley before abruptly making a sharp turn and heading back in our direction.

Haji Rajab shouts at his herd to move off the trail where scattered trees make them less exposed, but there is no apparent escape. The helicopter slows directly above us. Sweat drips down my back, and my feet feel glued to the ground. I can barely hear Jamil crying out my name over the roar of the helicopter, and I think to myself, it's over. Bullets will pierce my flesh and bones before I advance one step.

It's time to stop running. Let it end here. I close my eyes, my body numb, my mind void. The sound shifts away again, and I'm certain it's me, that life is leaving my body. I must not have felt the bullet or the rocket. Perhaps it burned me instantly, sparing me the pain of slow death. But a hand violently pulls me away, returning me to my senses. My eyes are open as I stumble and nearly fall while Jamil pulls me behind him toward a nearby tree.

"Are you deaf or just stupid?" His voice is angry and impatient. I look up, and he points toward the valley. The helicopter is flying away from us. He takes a deep breath, but his face goes ashen with fear again when the sound of the helicopter grows louder again, followed by an explosion near the valley.

Haji Rajab yells at the top of his lungs: "Chemicals! Chemicals! We need to run up to higher ground."

The peculiar smell of rotten onions hits my nostrils. Jamil grabs his water container, removes the vest over his shirt, and cuts it in half. He wets both pieces of the torn cloth and hands one to me. We cover our faces and see that Haji Rajab is now rushing down the hill in the direction of his fallen animals. Jamil yells at him to come back, but he is not paying any attention.

Smoke rises higher, the rotten smell worse. The smoke turns greenish and causes our eyes to tear up. A violent cough overtakes us, and an invisible cloud of death passes through our lungs and momentarily brings us to our knees. I collect myself and slowly stand up, then pull Jamil to his feet as well.

After much struggle, I am able to fully open my eyes. The clouds of smoke are denser in the lower part of the mountain and the valley. We can't see Haji Rajab, but we hear his desperate cries for help. We call on him to come up to higher ground, but he yells back that he must help his animals. Jamil turns to run down after him, but I grab his arm and pull him away and up the trail.

Later, after the smoke clears and still struggling to keep our eyes open, we stumble across dozens of dead animals on the ground with white froth running from their mouths. Jamil and I duck under a large tree in a fetal position, our faces fully covered with the wet clothes. We call on Haji Rajab a few more times, but there is no answer.

16

Dilveen

Near the Turkish-Iraqi border, August 29, 1988, 3:00 P.M.

Does land belong to the people, or do people belong to the land? The question swirls in my mind as we walk away from our home, leaving behind its sacred soil for foreign land.

How can someone belong to a land when it is boiling under their feet? How can that land belong to them when with each step they take, they leave another foot of it behind them? We say the Kurds have no friends but the mountains, but I'm not even sure that's true. When you're running from death toward the unknown, you start questioning everything.

Even our hearts have turned against us. When we need

them to be strong, they break down and shatter. When we want them to be soft, they morph into rocks. Clouds dry up when we want rain and flood when we need calmness.

Everything is our enemy now. The sun is blazing stronger than ever, sucking the life from our thirsty and exhausted bodies. Even our tears, the last of what we own in this miserable world, have betrayed us. They disappear when we need them, and gush uninvited when we want them out of our sight.

You know what's the most eternal notion for the Kurds? That things will eventually get better. We have heard this all our lives. Father used to say it every time Mother complained that our lives were in disarray because of the Kurdish movement. "Things will get better, woman. Be patient."

But Mother also said it for years when we complained about our lives on the run. Mam Yasin says it. Every elderly person I know says, "Tomorrow will be better." Will it? How can it be better if we are dead before dawn?

Two days of walking this death trail feel like a slowly brewing divorce from the land of our fathers. Death is on our tail. My brothers are missing, vulnerable in the open for the monsters to grab. And here, Mother is a walking corpse with a bald blanket of sorrow draped over her distant face. We stand on the top of the mountain, our last connection to this country, to this land. I plant my feet down with force, and it feels as if the mountain is ordering its soil to loosen to accommodate me. Anything to show me that the mountain is still our best friend.

Before we begin our descent, I turn around and look in no particular direction. Somewhere across the horizon is our house, possibly bombed and uprooted by now. Somewhere in the distance we left behind my brothers, who are attempting to find a way to unite with us. I scan the long range of Metin Mountain and pray that there are more people on our side of it than are trapped in the merciless meat grinder of the Iraqi government.

This time, there will be no crying. I gently follow the rest of the family down into a new chapter of misery.

THE MOUNTAIN TRAIL drops into a valley divided by a river separating Iraq from Turkey. We stop for a much-needed rest, with the river barely visible behind trees.

We go through our last few portions of food. Water became a thing of the past two hours ago when Mam Yasin took the last sip from Tahir's canteen. Juwan sits next to her exhausted father and breaks down crying. I gently pat her shoulder.

"Stay strong, my sweetheart," I say to Juwan as I inspect Mam Yasin's forehead, which is burning with heat and dripping sweat. "Inshallah, he will be fine."

Juwan grabs his hand, which formed calluses during his life filled with hard work. She stops sniffling and draws a deep breath.

"How will he be fine when he hasn't said a word for hours? We have basically been dragging a corpse since the afternoon."

In the distance down by the border, masses of humans are scattered with no sign of movement across the river. It would be shocking if the Turkish authorities handed everyone a free pass. Not with the decades-long tension between the government and the Kurdish minority over rights and self-determination. A family passes us with two young men carrying an elderly woman on a stretcher made of wooden sticks. She is groaning in pain, her head shifting from side to side with every step the men take.

Mistekhan mumbles under her breath, "Inshallah, you will feel better, you poor lady. May Allah take revenge against whoever was responsible for this."

After a brief break, Tahir abruptly stands and instructs us to stay put until he returns. Before any of us says anything, he is already sprinting down the trail toward the river.

Some time passes, and I fall asleep after struggling to stay alert. I later wake to Tahir's loud voice announcing that it's time to leave. When I open my eyes, I find that my head is resting on my mother's right leg, the Quran in her hand as she reads in silence.

Tahir approaches us, leading a white donkey behind him. "It took a lot to convince one of my distant cousins to give up his donkey, but there is little use for it when the *Jandarma* don't allow anyone to take one step forward," he says as he sits next to Mam Yasin, studying his silent, pale body.

"So what are we going to do?" Juwan asks. "Maybe they will allow us to pass if they see how sick my father is?"

Tahir chuckles. "Forget about getting sympathy from them. Their hearts are made of stone."

Tahir stands up and gives Mam Yasin another look before turning to the donkey. "They shot and severely wounded two men down there, and they've been lying there bleeding since last night. The Jandarma won't let anyone near them."

Juwan puts another wet cloth over her father's forehead

and cries over his body. His chest softly rises with every muffled breath.

Mother inches toward Juwan and embraces her with her motherly touch. As if Juwan has been waiting all her life for such an embrace, she weeps hard.

"We are going to move eastward," Tahir says firmly, "and descend into a valley where the water narrows. There are no Jandarma points there. On the other side is a small village far away from the road."

He starts preparing the donkey. Seeing the puzzled looks on our faces, he pauses. "This is the best option if you want to save Mam Yasin's life. He will die down there by the river if we do what everyone else is doing. Plus, where we'll be headed, I know a man who does folk medicine."

Tahir gently helps Mam Yasin up and with our assistance lifts him onto the donkey's back.

"How about your family?" Mother says. "Are they down there?"

"No," Tahir says. "I was informed they crossed the border two days ago and are settled with some of our relatives on the other side."

"God bless you," Mother says. "I pray that Allah always brings good things your way and will take us to safety."

He guides the donkey from the head, and we follow behind, Juwan and I firmly holding Mam Yasin's shifting body so he won't fall.

Tahir turns to Mother and smiles. "Please don't mention it. I am doing what your husband or son would do for my family if the situation were reversed. Plus, this will give me a chance to cross the border and reunite with my own family."

Mother tears up with the mention of "husband" and

"son," but she covers her eyes with her white scarf to hide her reaction.

We pass between two heavy trees on a narrow trail and onto an abandoned farm with a torn and rusty fence. The refugees are out of our sight now, and the donkey is starting to pant. We walk beside the fence and turn into an open field. Behind us, the sound of a gunshot echoes in the distance.

Tahir sighs and mumbles under his breath. "They must've just shot someone else."

17

Azad

Metin Mountain, August 29, 1988

The last thing I remember is the colorless scent surrounding us. I slowly drift out of a heavy sleep to find Jamil face-down on the ground a few feet from me. All I can muster is shallow and careful breaths; the slightest chest movement feels like broken glass twisting in my lungs.

I slowly reach over to Jamil, terrified at his motionless body. I flip him onto his back, remove the piece of cloth still stuck to his face, and give him a few slaps. No response. I push against his chest and shoulders, but he remains still. I lean closer, finally relieved when I feel his chest rise. His cheeks and forehead have turned blackish-gray. Feeling self-conscious now, I run my fingers hesitantly over my face, feeling the sharp pain even the slightest touch produces.

We are engulfed in silence. My wristwatch reads 10:20 A.M. We must have been down for at least an hour. I shake Jamil's body again, eliciting a brief jerk followed by twitching of his blackened eyes. I look around, gradually recovering from the shock, and finally locate the water container. I drip some over his lips, and he finally opens his mouth, letting in some water as the rest spills over his right cheek and neck. It hurts when I smile, but I don't mind. Jamil takes a few more sips. He's slowly starting to come back. He is a fighter, and he won't go down easily. I help him sit up and rest against the tree while I walk around to inspect our surroundings.

Down the hill from us, masses of Haji Rajab's animals lie dead. I see no survivors. I see no sign of Haji Rajab either. I shout his name, but no answer.

Jamil is standing beside me now, still struggling to maintain his posture. "Where is Rajab?"

I start down the hill, and he follows me. A sheep is stuck between the edges of two large rocks, only one limb visible. Its head rests sideways on the left rock, only a matter of time before bugs and bigger animals start preying on its discolored face. My instincts direct me toward the animal in case it can be rescued, but the gruesome image sends me scurrying back, and I have to cover my face. A long violent cough hits me, bringing me to my knees for a good minute before I am able to stand again and catch my breath.

"Have you seen him yet?" Jamil says. "Is he OK?"

"I doubt Rajab made it."

Jamil, too, is hit with a cough, but his is heavier and lasts longer.

We soon find Rajab on his back with his head tilted sideways. His face is black and blistered yellow. His mouth is open and dry like a bone left in the sun. I wonder if he was crying for help or gasping for air in his last moments as he insisted on staying true to his love for his herd. Hopefully, they'll reunite peacefully somewhere where there are no helicopters.

Without tools to dig a grave, we pull Haji Rajab's body into a ditch and cover it with dirt, rocks, and chunks of trees so animals don't come for it. It's the best we can do under the circumstances. I consider placing Rajab's cane over his makeshift grave but decide to carry it.

We slowly head down to the river to wash our faces. And after we turn the corner at the edge of the mountain, I see a small village high on a hill. Columns of dark gray smoke rise from the few houses visible. There are no signs of life.

BerAva soon appears in the distance, surrounded by its apple farms. With our wounded lungs and weak legs, it will take us several hours to get there.

The trail leads onto a narrow dirt road that zigzags through the dry yellow field and disappears between two hills. Next to a large rock by the side of the road I notice an abandoned plastic basket lying on its side with a variety of fruits and vegetables scattered on the ground next to it. I stop and observe from afar. Jamil gently pulls my hand and motions in that direction with his head.

"I know," I say. "Someone left their food in a hurry."

"No, you idiot. Look over there." He pulls me harder this time, and we both stop.

I see a small red plastic shoe sticking out from behind the left edge of the rock. The image resolves as we approach. It's the perfect image of a family tragedy. The foot belongs to a little girl whose face is buried in her mother's lap. In their struggle to survive, the mother chose to leave her face exposed while guarding her child. The mother's belly appears pregnant. I can't help but wonder if the unborn baby struggled too. I turn to Jamil, who is weeping, and recall his excitement when he broke to me the news he was going to be a father.

A few feet away from the mother lies the father, flat on his back, his black face covered with bubbles and blisters. Inside his jacket on either side he has tucked two of his little babies, their bodies barely visible.

I can't hold back tears any longer.

"I think," Jamil says, "that BerAva is far away enough to not be affected by what happened here." He is pretending to be optimistic. The look on his face tells me his real thoughts.

Instead of moving farther on the dirt road, we cut across the open fields that appear to lead to large farms, where there should be ample covering and safety. I feel sick to my stomach, and every dry heave triggers another punishing cough.

Jamil stops abruptly and grabs my right arm, pulling me down to the ground with him. "There's a military car on the road behind us. Keep your head down."

A brown military pickup truck parks in the middle of the dirt road some three hundred or so feet behind us. Two soldiers are in the back holding their guns, getting ready to step off. We lie there motionless. If we get up, we could be shot at. If we stay here, we could be shot at. I hear yelling and shouting from that direction.

"What do we do, Jamil?"

He is breathing fast and blowing dust every time he exhales. "I don't know."

The voices grow closer, the shouting clearer, while we lie there motionless and confused. "Stay where you are, sons of bitches, or I will shoot your brains out." He's speaking Arabic.

Seconds later, two soldiers point guns at our heads.

They tell us to stand up, insulting and slapping us as we do so, and lead us back to the truck. The first soldier shoves Jamil onto the back of the truck, shouting, "What are you doing here?"

Jamil gives him a blank look as he reluctantly moves aside to give me space to climb in with him. The second soldier punches Jamil on his right thigh, repeating the question his comrade just asked.

I attempt to answer, but the soldier slaps my face. I want to explain to him that Jamil doesn't understand Arabic, but the soldier strikes Jamil on the face with the butt of his gun. Blood pours over Jamil's chin and shirt.

The two soldiers hop in the back and point their guns at us, waiting for a reason, any reason, to shoot us. The truck turns around and speeds along the dirt road. I can't tell if we are fortunate to still be alive. Time will tell.

18

Juwan

One kilometer into Turkey, August 29, 1988

W e reach the village at dusk. I don't know if two clay houses make a village, but they seem a lot more equipped than those in a big village. There are multiple farms scattered on the outskirts with storage facilities. A large black dog jumps from the corner of the fence, barking at us in an unwelcoming tone, but we are relieved when we realize the dog is chained to a metal bar. Tahir leads the donkey into the open field behind the bigger of the two homes. We sit down, totally exhausted.

Tahir calls on someone by the name of Subhi. An old man in dirty clothes and a long, messy beard emerges barefoot from the house. Whatever hair on his beard and mustache has not turned gray has been stained a dense yellow from lifelong smoking. He doesn't seem too excited to see us, and we are probably more people than he has seen in a long time.

Subhi reluctantly walks toward Tahir as Tahir slowly brings my father down from the donkey. The two men seem to know each other well, but their minimal exchanges are suspect. Subhi scans my motionless father with his curious eyes. "What happened to him?"

"This gentleman is sick," Tahir says. "He has the sugar disease and also a bad wound on his foot that's getting worse. He has been out since yesterday, and I need you to help him."

Subhi approaches my father, his eyes more curious now. He checks my father's neck for a pulse, then gives Tahir a nod. Then he walks to the fence and shouts at the dog, silencing it instantly.

Tahir notices our puzzled looks. "Don't worry. Subhi is a good guy. He has his own way, but he always likes to help. I have known him from previous trips when we came to buy food supplies from him."

Night falls, and we realize that Subhi is more caring and generous than he first appeared. He serves us a hot soup rich with meat. He shows us ladies the way to the house next door where we can get comfortable and rest. But our attention is solely on my father. Subhi quickly attends to him and says that his sugar levels must be very low, so he feeds him honey from some of the finest bees in these mountains. He also fixes some herbs and mixes them with a powder that he claims to be antibiotics and places it over Father's wound. Father opens his eyes at some point and takes a few sips of water. It tickles our hearts. He soon slips back into sleep.

Long past midnight, when everyone seems to be asleep in their sitting places, Subhi interrupts my sleep. "We have to get him to a hospital soon." Outside, a pack of wolves is howling, but thankfully Subhi's dog remains silent. "His foot is rotten, and this is a flesh-eating bacteria."

I imagine a three-headed monster grabbing my father's head, arms, and legs and taking him into dark clouds where the sun never shines and rain never falls.

Sleep and exhaustion finally take me, and I later wake to the sounds of Tahir and Subhi speaking outside. It is still dark. My father is soaked in sweat. I rub his forehead, and he opens his eyes slightly. From weak, shivering lips, he asks for extra blankets. Outside, the two men are discussing how to deal with my father's deteriorating condition. Soon, Mistekhan and Dilveen are also up, and judging from Mistekhan's preparations for prayers, I suspect we are approaching the early morning hours.

I rest my father's head on a pillow, add two more blankets, and go outside, where I find Subhi and Tahir sitting across from each other around a small fire. The cool night could easily pass for autumn back home rather than one in late August. Subhi and Tahir turn in my direction when I am a few feet away.

Tahir clears his throat. "We were discussing plans to take care of your father. As you can see, his condition is not getting better."

"He is going to get a lot worse if we don't get him out of here soon," Subhi says, his voice as blunt as can be.

He apparently has a wide network of people he deals with. "I have men who stop by almost every day, and their destinations depend on where they are coming from, Iran or within Turkey, and how soon they have to go back."

Reassured, I return to my father, who is only dimly aware now. Dilveen and Mistekhan help me prepare a small plate of honey plus a cup of water, and we try to get my father awake so he can eat.

There's a commotion outside now. The dog is barking, and I hear a third man's voice. Outside I see a young man standing next to Subhi. He appears to be in his early forties, with a short stature and a clean-shaven face. Subhi introduces him as Segvan. He smiles and greets me. Mistekhan appears and takes a seat next to Subhi by the fire, which is nothing but coals now.

I notice a small scar on the lower part of Segvan's right cheek. Dilveen and Shireen are soon outside, but they choose to stand far away.

Segvan lights a cigarette. "Subhi told me everything about the Haji who is sick. Is he your father?"

I nod.

"I will do my best to help. Subhi told me everything I need to know."

Next to the fence are eight horses with wooden boxes attached to their backs. Subhi grabs a box, walks past us toward the second house, and says, "Don't worry, Segvan will take care of you."

For the next few minutes, Subhi and Segvan unload the boxes and transfer them to the small storage room next to the second house. Tahir summons us inside the main house for a breakfast consisting of boiled potatoes and eggs and pieces of dried bread plus tea. We discuss a new plan as it has become apparent that our time with Tahir is about to end soon.

"Where in Turkey will you be taking us to?" Mistekhan asks Segvan, who seems more invested in breakfast than any of us.

Segvan sips from his hot cup of tea and answers nonchalantly. "We won't be going into Turkey."

The room falls silent. We're waiting for a follow-up statement or explanation of some sort. Segvan is staring at me, as if he's waiting for me to say something, but instead I stare at my untouched cup of tea, hoping for some clarity soon.

"Segvan moves goods between here and Iran, where he is from," Subhi says. "He is a good friend who is dedicated and trustworthy."

We all look to Segvan. He puts his cup of tea down and says, "I can take you all with me. I'll be headed back this afternoon, and I can get our sick Haji to a hospital as soon as we get to territories I have contacts in."

"Can't you take us to a nearby hospital in Turkey?" Mistekhan says. "Iran is very far, and we don't know anyone there."

"My contacts come and go on a regular basis," Subhi says, "but I don't know who will come when. Segvan happened to be here today. I don't know when someone from Turkey will pass by, but if you want to wait, you are welcome to stay here as long as you want."

"I don't think your father should stay here any longer," Tahir says, concerned. "His condition will continue to deteriorate, and I'm afraid I can't help if it does."

Segvan calmly pours another cup of tea for himself. The silence in the room is unnerving. Father groans in his sleep. My eyes are fixed on Mistekhan's, desperate for a nod, a word, any reassuring answer to a question only I can answer.

"Look," Segvan says. "I cross borders illegally and have no means of getting into any Turkish town or city. I don't have contacts on that side of the border. So if you need to go there, you'll have to wait. But like I said earlier, I will be more than honored to help you get into Iran and take care of you as if you're my own family."

I run my hand over my father's warm forehead and nod at Segvan and Subhi.

19

Azad

Metin Mountain, August 29, 1988

The truck shifts and turns on the rough dirt road, rocking my head and back against the burning metal of the truck bed. I keep my eyes shut during the twenty-minute drive. I don't want to see anything traumatic that I would carry with me forever. If the army decides to kill us, I don't want to see the bullets coming.

The truck finally comes to a stop, and the engine is shut off. I open my eyes and through sweaty eyelashes see that we're parked in the middle of an open field in front of a group of soldiers pointing guns at us. "Out of the truck!" one of them yells. "And no unnecessary moves, or you die."

They lead us through the dry, yellow field and between

two military trucks. Jamil looks pale and dehydrated. Keep it together, I say in my mind, hoping he can somehow understand me. Behind the trucks is a long row of thick, old trees with long, busy branches. Underneath are dozens of women and young children. I look around and don't see any adult men. Jamil and I exchange looks before soldiers shove us onto the ground not too far from the women and children. Some of the women mumble in a sad tone. Some of the children and infants are crying. Some of the mothers are as well.

Jamil and I lie on the ground, afraid to lift our faces off the burning dirt. Moments later, two soldiers kick us over onto our backs. The sun nearly blinds me through a cloud of dust above our heads. One of the soldiers shouts an unintelligible insult, and I hear a loud and desperate grunt from Jamil. A violent blow lands on the left side of my face. My head spins hard to the right, a ringing sound in my left ear. Another blow comes down on my left flank area, cutting my breath off for a few seconds that feel like an eternity. The sole of a large shoe slowly presses against my forehead.

"This is what you deserve, you traitors. Keep biting the hands that feed you and you will find your head under our boots."

The women are crying and squealing. More blows land on Jamil's body. A child begs the soldiers to stop. Finally, they do.

We lie there for a long time before gaining enough energy to move. Jamil finally reaches out to me. "Are you OK, brother?"

I am too weak to respond, so I wave my left hand his direction, indicating I am fine.

A shadow looms over me, blocking the sunlight. "What are your names, you bastards?"

I tell him between struggling breaths.

Another soldier demands to know where we were coming from, where we were headed, and what we were planning to do.

Jamil just lies there, motionless from pain and oblivious to what the soldiers are saying.

"Please don't hurt him," I beg, still unable to fully open my eyes. "He is my brother, and he doesn't understand or speak Arabic."

The shadow above me grows wider, and I can feel the angry breath in my face. He pulls me up by my hair. "Since your brother is a mule, I'll ask you. Expect yourself dead if you don't answer me immediately or if you even think about lying."

All I can do is mumble. And the world goes black.

I OPEN MY EYES. Night has fallen. Not far from us, three trucks have their engines running. Their headlights are pointed right at us. Several soldiers stand there, guarding the vicinity.

Jamil is next to me, resting on crossed legs with his head in his hands. When he sees that I'm awake, he runs his hand over the back of my head and says, "Hey, brother, are you OK? I was worried sick about you."

I try to get up, but every muscle in my body hurts and twitches. Children are still crying. A large cloud is moving slowly in the sky above us. I fight against the pain and slowly sit up with help from Jamil.

"What time is it?" I ask, my voice quivering.

Jamil grabs my hand and brings my wristwatch to his face. "It is a little after four."

I suddenly feel more pain as I realize how long I'd been out.

"You made a quick tour of hell and came back," Jamil says.

My throat is dry, and my head is spinning. "I'm thirsty, Jamil" I say, grimacing from pain as I shift my weight to a more comfortable sitting position.

He leans sideways and brings a small metal cup to my mouth. "Here, drink this water. I saved it for you."

I drink the whole cup in one quick swig. There wasn't much, nowhere near enough for my parched throat. I feel the disappointment in my guts, making me even thirstier.

"I'm sorry, Azad. These monsters wouldn't give us any more water."

Not far from us, a long and uninterrupted cough from a child breaks the silence. One of the soldiers shouts, "*Qurzulqurt!*" Death from poison. Soon, more children join the crying party. An infant has been wailing continuously for a good fifteen minutes, leading one of the guards to yell even louder while stomping the ground repeatedly, demanding silence from a crowd of hungry children who have been forced to sit still in an open field for hours upon hours. Somewhere else, another child is fussing, asking his mother for food while she desperately tries to hush him. She promises him warm bread later if he stays quiet now, but he is not buying it. Another child begs for food. "Please, Mama, I am starving."

One of the soldiers walks toward the crying children. Jamil uncrosses his legs and gets up on his knees. My mind is a dark place, awash in images of bloodshed, torture, and pain. The soldier stops near the women, one of whom apologizes on behalf of everyone crying. "They are kids and don't know better. Please, sir, don't hurt them."

All eyes are on the soldier. He reaches to his shoulder bag, takes out a few pieces of bread, and throws them toward the children. The headlight beams are shining straight on the soldier's back as he stands there motionless for a few seconds while the children jump on the pieces of bread in hysteria. One of the female voices urges the children to give their mothers a chance to equally distribute the bread to all the children. The soldier slowly turns around and walks back to his post.

With the commotion over the bread finally subsiding, Jamil turns to me and says, "I am dying for one piece of bread."

My stomach growls with lingering pain and persistent hunger as I mumble. "Food will only make you last longer to endure more pain."

AT DAWN, two military trucks turn in our direction from the main road. The darkness may have made us less visible to the soldiers, but daylight will remind them to abuse us. The two brown-and-green trucks park near the temporary post not far from us. A large cloud of dust slowly dissipates behind the trucks, and several armed soldiers hop off from the back of each. They join the rest of the men for a quick discussion, periodically turning and pointing our direction, then resuming what appears to be more than just a random chat.

Most of the children are awake by now. The fussing and crying resumes, which only terrifies the adults since we have been proven helpless to stop it.

Five armed men approach us with their guns drawn, ready to engage. Jamil and I shuffle our bodies in our seated positions, attempting to look and seem respectful to the authority coming toward us. Normally, we would stand, but any unexpected moves could rattle their nerves and provoke an entire round of bullets.

A soldier shouts orders. "Everyone, get up and move toward the trucks in an orderly manner. Now!"

I quickly rise to my feet, and Jamil follows suit. Soon the rest of the crowd stands as instructed. We slowly march toward the trucks, following the soldiers' orders as they randomly assign us to either of the two trucks. They push and shove us up and onto the back under a thick brown tarp. After some chaos and a mixed salad of insults, we're all loaded up, with two armed guards sitting on either side of the door of each truck.

The air reeks of gasoline, and I struggle to hold back a monster growling in my stomach. The ignition turns on, adding yet more noise to the din of crying and screaming children and women. The truck jerks backward, jolting us against each other. The two guards sit on the metal floor, their backs to each other, guns pointing directly at us. My eyes are fixed on the right index finger of the dark-skinned soldier right across from me. With each turn and bump, his finger could accidentally press on the trigger, shooting me directly in the face.

To my left, Jamil sits quietly, his face forever tired and pale. While most of our symptoms from the chemical exposure have subsided, lightheadedness and a persistent dry cough linger. To my right sits a young woman with an infant in her lap and a young girl leaning against her right shoulder, appearing to be asleep. The baby's face plunges in the mother's chest with each bump in the road. I study the sadness on the mother's face. She is sunburned, and her lips are dry and cracked. There are splotches of dried white vomit marks on her sleeves. Our eyes meet momentarily, then she gazes down on her infant child, as if asking me to observe her pain in the motionless ball of flesh and bone she is holding.

She looks up again, her eyes now full of tears. "They took my husband and young boy," she whispers, her gaze locked on me. I avert my eyes to the two soldiers, who both seem as tired as we are.

"They raided us after the morning prayer," the woman says, "and took all the men and young boys. They made us watch—"

A soldier kicks my foot and motions for us to be quiet. From the bag hanging over his shoulder, I suspect he is the soldier who distributed bread to the children last night. That's probably why he hasn't shot me yet.

The truck turns off the dirt road, and the drive is suddenly smooth. The thick tarp covers the top and sides of the tall metal box above our heads like a cage.

I hear the mother sniffle. I turn to her and whisper, "What did they do to you? To the men?"

She pulls the frail infant closer to her chest and sobs. "They gathered all the men and young boys in the middle of the village. They shot half of them in front of our eyes and took the rest away." She wipes her tears, but more pour down as she tries to clear her throat. She wants to talk. She is desperate to talk and say more.

The truck comes to a sudden stop, and we all shift in our seats. A few children are thrown to the floor. The teenage girl wakes up and pleads with a tired voice: "Mother, please stop crying. You will get sick." Her eyes are deep and beautiful, but they've seen things no child should even know exists.

I close my eyes and let my body shift with the movements of the truck as it takes us toward a place I am sure won't create any good memories for us. We make two stops on the way, but the guards won't let us out. The back of the truck smells of urine and feces, drawing numerous insults from the two guards. During the second stop, I steal a quick peek through the cloth and recognize the area: Zawita, a municipality on the outskirts of Duhok. We are parked on the road heading into the city. There is little traffic. Before we take off again, a guard pulls the back curtain aside and tosses us bread and insults.

Jamil and I jump at the bag, each grabbing a piece. Seconds later, a wave of embarrassment washes over me, and I drop the bread like it's a piece of burning charcoal. I hide my head between my knees. Never have I struggled for food or fought over it with anyone, let alone children. I want to raise my head and scream at the guard to shoot me. The one time in my life I wish to face a heartless man, I'm given a man who wears his heart over his gun.

Jamil breaks the bread into small pieces and distributes it to the children and their mothers. The mother sitting next to me tells him to take a piece for himself and his friend. I sit in silence and ignore him when he offers me a share of the bread.

~

AROUND THREE THIRTY, the truck turns onto dirt road for a few minutes, then comes to a stop. The afternoon heat has turned the covered truck into a steam bath. Most of the children have collapsed from exhaustion, thirst, and heat.

As soon as the engine is shut off, the two soldiers peel back the rear tarp, open the back door, and jump out. A short man with a thick voice in a formal military suit orders us out one at a time. I hop off before the young mother and assist her with her baby while Jamil helps her young daughter.

We're at a heavily staffed security checkpoint set up at the edge of a hill. Jamil and I exchange blank looks. We're in Duhok, in the city, for better or worse. In front of us is the Nizarki Fort, with its massive walls that extend in all directions. Numerous armed personnel walk toward us while the guards who accompanied us here attempt to maintain order by lining us up in a row.

The young mother makes a conscious effort to remain next to Jamil and me. When the soldiers start pushing everyone forward toward the fort, she carries her infant and grabs her daughter's shoulder, then starts walking timidly while talking to herself in an angry whisper: "Damn you, girl. Damn you for being alive. They killed your husband in front of your eyes and took your son, and now God knows what they will do inside."

One of the soldiers grabs her shoulder at the main door. He nearly hurls the infant from her grasp and orders her to shut up and walk.

20

Juwan

Turkey, August 30, 1988

Subhi and Tahir help Segvan load his goods on the horses. He dedicates seven of them for the supplies and prepares the eighth and biggest one to carry my father. It is apparent that Segvan is a smuggler, and a rather good one too. He takes out a worn map of the region and points at some markings on it, indicating to Tahir how he plans to get us across to Iran. We listen attentively, although all I care about is getting my father to a hospital. And from what Segvan and Subhi have indicated, it would be nearly impossible to sneak into a Turkish town that's big enough to have a hospital that can administer intravenous medicine or perform surgeries.

Tahir summons us ladies one last time to make sure we're still on board. Mistekhan is more concerned with his opinion of Segvan than his repeated apologies for not continuing the journey with us.

"Look," Tahir says, "I have never met him before, but I have met Subhi a few times, and he's a good guy. Subhi seems to know Segvan well, and honestly I don't want to get involved in whatever business they both are doing, but at this point we don't have many options." His eyes follow Segvan and Subhi as they load up the last horse.

"I won't be able to sneak you into any Turkish towns, and I'm afraid that if you wait here longer, your father won't make it."

I swallow hard as I imagine my father's corpse in this no-man's-land. "Can we please get going?"

IN THE AFTERNOON, we say goodbye to Subhi and Tahir, carrying whatever we can, mostly food and blankets, for the trip. Segvan takes the lead, guiding the first horse, which is carrying my father. Behind him are the other seven horses moving in unison, something they seem to have done many times. Father is out again, his body shifting without resistance with each movement the horse makes.

Shireen is ahead of us ladies, walking behind the horses, followed by Mistekhan, myself, and then Dilveen at the very end. After an hour or so of walking, Segvan turns around to see if we need a break. I immediately respond: "No, thanks!"

"If you get hungry," he says, "let me know. I have plenty of dried food in my bag. I didn't tell Subhi, so he won't be stingy with us." He giggles.

Maintaining a steady pace, we make it to the top of the mountain just as night falls. My father asks for water in a faint voice. I remove the jug strapped to my shoulder and bring it to his mouth, allowing him to take a few shallow sips before he closes his eyes again.

Segvan asks us to keep going to stay on schedule. I walk directly behind him, staying close by my father's side. The pathway barely accommodates one horse and one person side by side, and I can't see well anymore with the darkness settling in. Segvan holds a small gas lamp to guide us as we carefully make our way down the narrow trail, our pace considerably slower than earlier.

"So what's the plan?" I ask, panting as I struggle to keep up.

Segvan looks over my shoulder to make sure everyone is in line. He then looks to the front again, nearly falling when his leg catches on a branch of a dead tree. He cries out, and the horses stop. He moves the branch out of the way and shouts at the horses to get moving again. "We need to get to the main road before the sun is up tomorrow."

I look in the direction he is pointing. A few scarce lights move in opposite directions. Puzzled, I ask, "Why would we go there? I thought we were crossing through the mountains."

Mistekhan is now right behind me and listening in.

Segvan chuckles. "You said your name is Juwan, right?"

I don't answer.

"Did you think we were going to walk to Iran? If you want to walk for ten more days, be my guest."

Mistekhan, equally intrigued, joins the conversation. "What are your plans?"

I hear Shireen whispering something to Dilveen in the back. Probably another conspiracy theory.

We stop next at a flat area beside a hill. After checking out the area with a quick round on one of his horses, Segvan returns and sits a few feet in front of us. He lights a cigarette, takes a long deep breath, and points again toward what seems to be a road in the distance. "We will walk to the main road, where I have contacts that will take us in a truck all the way to the Turkish-Iranian border."

We sit in silence, absorbing his words while he works on his cigarette. Soon, he announces it's time to resume walking. He spends the next hour or so explaining our upcoming journey. We listen attentively, following him as we make our way down the mountain. He says the truck ride will take anywhere from seven to eight hours, depending on the military checkpoints, but he reassures us that this is nothing new for him and that he does this at least twice a month.

When we stop again, Mistekhan takes a quick nap, and Shireen pulls Dilveen and me aside. She grabs my arm, whispering, "Are you sure you want to trust this guy? We don't even know him."

I turn and look at my father, resting on the ground under Segvan's lantern. "We have no choice but to trust him." I turn to face Shireen again and add, "All other ways were pointing to the unknown."

"And this is not?" Shireen says.

Dilveen motions for us to keep it down, repeatedly turning around to see if Segvan is watching us.

Shireen takes a deep breath and points in the general direction of the road. "We should separate from him at the main road," she says coldly, "and seek help at a nearby village or town."

Dilveen slaps Shireen's hand and hisses at her. "Why are you putting doubts in our minds? Can't you for once shut your mouth and follow the people around you?"

"I can't take a chance with my father," I say. "He is dying, and we won't have a man with us if we lose him."

"I am only trying to be careful," Shireen says, "but let's do it your way."

Mistekhan is still asleep, something I have rarely seen since we left BerAva. I force my father awake to give him a few sips of water, and he falls asleep again without eating. Segvan is smoking another cigarette several feet away in silence, his back against a rock. The three of us settle down next to Mistekhan.

"I have no bad intentions," Segvan says. "If anything, you are more of a liability for me. Had it not been for Subhi's persistence, I would not have agreed to help you."

Speechless and drenched in embarrassment, I lie there motionless, eyes fixed on my father's resting body. I'm sure he overheard our conversation, and he can't unhear it. The awkward moment lingers. I wish I could disappear.

Dilveen does some damage control. "We want to thank you, brother, for all you have done for us. We have a world of worry in our heads, so please forgive us if we appear doubtful or unappreciative. It was not our intention."

Segvan gets to his feet, the tip of his cigarette glowing orange as he sucks in more nicotine. I am certain that this kind man has had it with us. We watch him inch closer to his horses, my mind already playing out the scenario where Segvan pulls his animals behind him and down the mountain before we can stop him or catch up with him. I lean closer to Dilveen, my heart pounding against my ribs, unsure what to do or say.

Segvan leans over my father's body, and in one quick maneuver, he pulls my father up and over the back of the horse. "It's time to get going, ladies. We have a timeline to meet."

In a matter of minutes, we are all on our feet, including Mistekhan, who seems to have finally gotten some rest, although she insists that we should have not let her sleep so long. A breeze softens the air, soothing my feelings as we embark on a mission of survival in mountains we don't know, with someone we don't know, and toward destinations we know very little about.

21

Azad

Nizarki Fort, Duhok, August 30, 1988

The Nizarki Fort sits in a large open field on the far eastern side of Duhok near its namesake village of Nizarki. Four circular corners round up the massive two-story structure. The outer stone walls contain hundreds of small windows lined by metal bars. Built in the early 1970s, the fort is a well-known military base, conveniently near the main road yet so terrifying that hardly anyone dares even look at it.

Guards lead us through the western entrance. Once inside, they separate me and Jamil from the women and children.

The fort has a courtyard in the middle flanked by two

long alleys of cells that run longitudinally in parallel, meeting at the gates. The two sides are mirror images of each other, with stairs leading to the second floor. The smell of feces and urine hits me as soon as we step into the corridor on the right. Dragging our exhausted bodies, we follow the tall, skinny guard through the hallway, catching glimpses of cells filled with male prisoners on our way. We stop halfway down the long hallway, and three soldiers instruct the women and children to follow them upstairs. The young mother turns when she reaches the landing, and our eyes meet again. The guard shouts, and she pulls her baby tighter to her chest, firmly grabs her daughter's hand, and disappears up the second set of stairs.

Two soldiers pull Jamil and me down the corridor, then stop in front of a large room with a metal door and several wide windows with bars. One of them pushes the door open and shoves us inside. Jamil falls face-down on the floor while I struggle to maintain my balance. I help him to his feet and notice pieces of feces in his hair. To say this room is unfit for animals is an understatement. Yet it is filled with dozens of men, at least sixty of them, lying on the bare concrete floor, some looking at us with interest while others remain adrift in sleep. I see no familiar faces.

Jamil and I slowly walk to the middle of the room and squeeze into the only available space, next to an old man who slides over a bit. He looks to be in his seventies and welcomes us in a sympathetic voice. "I am Haji Sharif." He points to a young boy to his right. "This is my grandson Raqeeb. He is only thirteen, but because he didn't have his ID on him when they caught us, they counted him with the men and separated him from his mother and younger siblings."

Haji Sharif seems eager to talk from the get-go, but there is not much to talk about other than pain and suffering. I want to ask where Raqeeb's father is but decide to let it go.

The scene is intimidating and humiliating. Every face looks tired, exhausted, and broken. The cell has small windows high above the floor overlooking the south side opposite the larger windows that open into the corridor. LONG LIVE OUR BELOVED SADDAM is scrawled on one of the walls. I turn to Jamil, and he has already fallen asleep on the concrete floor. Long live Saddam, and let the whole country pay for it with its blood.

We have been here for hours now with no food or water. The silence of the prison is periodically shattered by children and babies crying, soldiers shouting, and tortured screams through the walls. In the far back of the cell, a man continuously moans in pain while his neighbor attempts to calm him. Every sound and every movement of a guard keeps me alert, but Jamil somehow manages to sleep.

I try to reposition myself, and my hand falls in a pool of fresh urine. Somewhere else a man is suffering from explosive diarrhea, and whoever is next to him is mumbling expletives. I look at my electronic wristwatch, and the time is past ten o'clock. Haji Sharif is snoring, his shoulder pressed against mine, periodically twitching.

His grandson speaks for the first time since our arrival. "I'm hungry, Grandpa."

Now awake and leaning away from me, Haji Sharif whispers to Raqeeb to try and sleep, but that doesn't work. A monster in my own stomach wakes up the next time Raqeeb demands food.

Jamil is up now as well, and he leans forward to meet Raqeeb's eyes. "How long has it been since you ate?"

Raqeeb starts crying while twisting his body. Haji Sharif runs his hand over Raqeeb's head, turns to Jamil, and says, "Mamo, we have not tasted a drop of water or a bite of food since we got here two days ago."

Jamil rises to his feet. "Sons of whores," he whispers.

Haji Sharif shushes him. "One thing you will soon have to learn here is how to keep your mouth shut. Now sit down."

Jamil reluctantly sits next to me while Raqeeb continues to cry. The door suddenly opens, letting in bright light from a spotlight from the fort's opposite wall. All heads turn as a soldier walks in with heavy steps. In a split second, he kicks my forehead, knocking me to the dirty floor. Seconds later, I hear Haji Sharif groan and cry as Raqeeb is dragged outside the cell. The door is then shut, and the outside light is cut off. Jamil inspects my forehead, the pain of the impact still throbbing under my skin.

Outside, Raqeeb's cries grow louder as the guards beat him. Haji Sharif lays on his back in pain, shaking his head in desperation.

One soldier outside says, "He's just a kid."

We hear another slap followed by deep moans.

"How did you end up with the men, you bastard?" A different voice this time.

I imagine they'll take Raqeeb to the second floor with the women and children, but the voice of the angry soldier resumes. "If I hear you cry anymore tonight, I swear I'll pull your vocal cords out and stick them in your stomach so you never get hungry again."

Sniffles replace the crying and moaning. Good boy. Moments later, the door opens again, and Raqeeb is thrown on the ground. Haji Sharif quickly jumps and embraces him as sighs of relief and sympathy fill the cell.

Raqeeb groans and mumbles under his breath, "I am hungry, Grandpa," then falls asleep on his grandfather's knee.

Haji Sharif spends the rest of the night in silence. Later, I wake from a brief nap to the soft sounds of Haji Sharif and Jamil talking.

"They killed his father in front of our eyes, and now I have to care for him here while his mother and siblings are out there somewhere, maybe even dead by now."

"God is big and will help," says Jamil.

Haji Sharif draws a deep breath. "Indeed, He is great, but these men have defied the power of God."

I close my eyes, hoping for another merciful journey into sleep despite the toxic smell of feces and urine.

JAMIL WAKES me in the morning. "Hey, Azad, wake up" He taps on my shoulder persistently.

I struggle to open my eyes, a sharp headache dragging me down. The cell door is propped open, and two armed guards bark at us to get up. We quickly line up, except for one detainee, the same man who was moaning from pain all night. Two of his friends in the back force him to his feet, drawing even louder groans from him.

A soldier at the door hits us with a heavy plastic pipe as we exit the cell. The guards lead us outside into the courtyard. Once we are lined up, another guard paces before us, studying our faces as more men are led from their cells. The mixed noise of crying, moaning, and whimpering rises as the number of prisoners swells in the courtyard. Suddenly, a booming voice through a loudspeaker orders everyone to be quiet.

Behind us, two soldiers drag a man out of a cell as he screams, "Let me go, leave me alone!"

A third soldier approaches him and kicks him all over his body. We are not sure what he has done or why he is resisting.

Another guard appears in front of me and slaps me on the face. "Stand straight and don't look around, you donkey."

I look at the ground and apologize.

"You must be one of the new animals here? I saw you yesterday when you came in. Where's your ID?"

I sense nervous anticipation from Jamil as he slightly shifts next to me. The sun hasn't yet risen above the walls of the fort. I wish it were evening again so we could go back to sleep.

I manage enough courage to answer the soldier in the most apologetic voice I can muster. "Yes, sir. My brother next to me and I came together."

I reach into my pocket to take out my ID and ask Jamil to do the same. He quickly produces his, but I struggle to find mine. Fishing for my ID deep in my right pocket, I accidentally pull out the money my uncle gave me when he dropped us off. The soldier's eyes widen, his gaze now on the currency behind the ID in my hand.

"What are you doing with all this money, you bastard? Are you smuggling weapons to the traitors?" He grabs me by the hair and pulls me out of the line.

Jamil hesitantly takes a step forward, but another guard kicks him back into the line. The soldier pushes me to the ground in the center of the courtyard. Soon, a second man is pulled out of the line and thrown on the ground near me. Then a third and a fourth. Before long, there are more of us on the ground than are left standing. Jamil is among the fortunate still upright, but the young Raqeeb isn't. Haji Sharif begs the soldiers to let him take the boy's place, but they refuse. Raqeeb lies on the ground in a fetal position, his eyes shut, and his knees bound together tightly.

Two soldiers stand over our heads while we lie on the ground, unsure of what's next. With the rest of the detainees watching in silence, the soldiers order us back into our cells with firm instructions to clean the floors. "Clean your shit. We can't stand your smell."

They throw a bucket and a dozen or so pieces of cloth into each cell, and we go at it. No mops and no gloves. Lucky to still be alive, we scrub the floors with the clothes given to us, emptying the feces and other trash into the bucket. The smell is even stronger now than it was last night. I keep Raqeeb next to me and ask him to just hold the bucket. He is still shaking from fear.

Outside, soldiers get louder and rowdier with the rest of the prisoners, calling them "animals!" and "traitors!" I clearly hear sticks, pipes, and plastic wires striking the bodies of those men.

I can also hear a few women crying upstairs. I take a quick peek through the window to check on Jamil, and he is still standing. I sigh deeply, relieved. Behind Jamil, three soldiers are gathered around a young man on his knees, begging them to stop. This only encourages the soldiers to deliver more punishment. They seem to be asking him about something, and he keeps crying and denying it.

A tall, well-built officer in a dark-green suit emerges

from the corner of the hallway. He's carrying a large brick in his right hand. I give my cloth to Raqeeb and ask him to turn around and clean a urine stain. Everyone else in the cell remains still, looking out the window, as the officer stands behind the young man. With full force, he strikes the man on the head. Some of us in the cell jolt backward. The young man's body slowly drops forward onto the ground, nearly hitting Jamil behind his knees. The officer picks up the bloody brick and hits his victim on the head at least ten more times until his skull is crushed open, parts of white matter dripping down and mixed with the pool of thick blood.

I hear Raqeeb's hoarse scream. I turn and he is standing behind me, watching the officer kick the corpse a few times before walking away in silent pride.

Later, when we are reunited in our cell, Raqeeb runs to his grandfather and hugs him with tearful eyes. Jamil and I take our seats by the concrete pole in the middle of the cell while Haji Sharif and Raqeeb lean against the opposite side. Haji Sharif then walks to the window and screams at the soldier standing on the other side, begging for some food and water for his grandson. The soldier opens the cell door and hits Haji Sharif with a metal stick and instructs him to sit down or get ready to take a trip straight to hell. Raqeeb looks emaciated and dry, and some of us soon pass out from thirst and hunger.

Sometime in the afternoon, the door slowly opens halfway, and a guard throws several loaves of bread into the cell and leaves a bucket of water on the floor near the door. Chaos ensues. Haji Sharif urges the mob to spare a portion for his grandson. But what will a bite of bread and a sip of water do but tease our appetite and aggravate our pain and deprivation?

In the evening, most of us feel a little more energetic, but the humid conditions inside the cell make us thirstier. We finished the bucket of dirty water within minutes.

Cries of children from the second floor keep us awake. I hope they are getting more food than we are.

Haji Sharif asks a soldier standing in the hallway if he could bring some more water and food for his grandson. The soldier just stands there, motionless. I suspect he doesn't understand Kurdish, so I tell Haji Sharif to ask in Arabic. When the soldier continues ignoring him, Haji Sharif walks back and sits down again next to Raqeeb.

"Don't beg an enemy whose victory is displayed in your desperation," says Jamil, his gaze fixed at the ceiling.

"Would you please stop it with your idealistic shit?" I say.

The soldier disappears from the window for some time, then his shadow quietly returns. Leaning against the bars, he discreetly takes three loaves of bread from inside his jacket, slides them into our cell, then disappears. I carefully pick up the bread. Some of the men are asleep, but others are paying rapt attention to what's taking place. A few minutes later, the same soldier returns, passes two cups of water between the bars, motioning for us to come and grab them. Jamil and another guy take the cups from the soldier's hands.

We repeatedly thank him, and he whispers through the open window, "Stay quiet and get back to your places. Keep your mouths shut. This never happened, and it won't happen again. They'll throw me into the oven if they catch me."

22

Dilveen

The Turkish-Iraqi border, August 31, 1988, evening

After more than nine hours of travel, we finally come to a stop. We are fortunate that this part of the journey has been in the back of a truck. When we reached the main road earlier in the morning, Segvan met with an elderly truck driver near an isolated, old house off the road. He seems to have all his moves figured out.

They loaded up the horses first, then Segvan put Mam Yasin in the seat behind the driver and hopped in the back of the truck. Shireen and Juwan also sat in the back next to Mam Yasin, while Mother and I shared the passenger seat. The roads are small, rough, and zig-zagging. We have slept through half of the trip plus a few food and restroom breaks in the most remote areas. The driver hasn't spoken a word the entire time.

Finally we reach a distant area where the road splits. Segvan and the driver discuss something outside, then signal for us to hop off the truck. Something tells me this is not the first time the two men have worked together. They carefully unload the horses from the back, then take Mam Yasin out and situate him on the back of his assigned horse.

When the truck driver completes a brief financial transaction with Segvan, he drives away and disappears in the distance, leaving behind a cloud of dust and a group of travelers with more questions than answers.

The sun is starting to set, but darkness won't fall for another hour or so. Segvan insists that we keep moving. At a junction of two narrow dirt roads, Segvan leads the horses to the right. The road ends at the edge of a hill. Darkness has fallen now, and the sky feels foreign and dim. We are exhausted. We are scared. We are anxious about the unknown.

We walk another hour or so before stopping for a brief rest. Juwan insists on continuing, and I don't blame her. Mam Yasin's wound is starting to drip dark, bloody pus, and we can't wake him up. We gather our strength, take a few bites of bread and cheese, and get going in the dark. We are way out of view from any main road or even a side road.

Segvan stops briefly next to Juwan and points in the distance through the darkness. "We will head southeast and then eastward in the direction of the Turkish-Iranian border. Obviously we can't go through any official checkpoints, and the farther we are from inhabited areas, the better we'll be able to hide from the scattered Turkish military posts."

For Segvan, this is just another day on the job.

Shireen is walking next to me, and Mother and Juwan are directly behind the horse carrying Mam Yasin. We are barely able to see two feet ahead even as the trail is becoming rougher and narrower.

Shireen gets closer to me and whispers, "Do you see how this man keeps cozying up to Juwan? I don't like his moves."

I pick up my pace, ignoring her nonsense, but she catches up with me. "I'm telling you, this guy is not innocent. Why would a man go to all this trouble for us?"

"Maybe because there are still good people out there," I whisper back, panting as we try to catch up with everyone else.

"A smuggler? You want to trust someone whose job is sneaking back and forth between countries?"

I've lost count of how many conspiracy theories Shireen has thrown at us with Segvan as the star actor or perpetrator or criminal. She goes on and on, and I choose to ignore her, not necessarily because she doesn't make sense but because there is no alternative.

Juwan motions for Segvan to stop. We all catch up and huddle around Juwan as she inspects her father. Mam Yasin is feverish and unresponsive again. We help Segvan get him down and slowly lay him on a blanket on the ground.

This is the worst he has looked since we started our journey. Juwan rests his head on her knees while Segvan brings the water jug to his lips, but he doesn't move. Juwan becomes frantic and starts crying. Shireen gets on her knees and leans over Mam Yasin's body, her left ear on his chest.

After a few anxious moments, Shireen lifts her head. "His heart is still beating, but his breath is weak and shallow." We sigh in relief, though we're no less concerned than before.

Segvan instructs us to set up for the night despite Juwan's objections. I have to side with Segvan. He grabs his gun and two of our water jugs and disappears for a while, then returns with the jugs filled with water. The man knows this area.

Juwan and I check on Mam Yasin again. His body is cooler. Juwan turns to me and says, "His fever is gone, right?"

I can hear the concern in her voice, though she's attempting to disguise it.

She and I take turns watching him closely. Shireen falls asleep with her head on Mother's arm, who at some point also doses off with her back against a rock. Segvan is resting with his back against one of the horses with the gun secured in his lap like a mother would hold her infant. I am worried and scared. Worried about Mam Yasin and the long night. Scared about being in this open area among wild animals.

Segvan is chain smoking next to the lantern. A dog is barking far away, and I can see some distant lights.

"Get your rest and don't worry," Segvan says. "I have taken this route more times than I can count. As long as I have these two hands and the gun, nothing will happen to us."

A flash of silent lightning appears behind the clouds, and I close my eyes, hoping to drift away, even for a few seconds.

Sometime later, I wake up, startled by a violent scream from Juwan. I jump to my feet and rush toward her. Segvan is leaning over Mam Yasin's body, thumping his chest with his hands. Mother and Shireen wake up and hurry toward us as well. Shireen brings the lantern closer as Segvan desperately attempts to resuscitate a man who appears to be long dead. Mother says prayers in a nervous tone.

Segvan finally raises his head and turns toward the rest of us. "I am sorry, Juwan. God took back what belonged to him."

Juwan starts pacing around hysterically, slapping her face and crying out loud, causing the horses to jump to their feet. Mother and I attempt to calm her while Shireen follows us around with the weak lantern, but Juwan is inconsolable. Her cries fill the air as if the late sound of distant thunder from earlier has finally arrived. Drops of soft rain fall and mix with our tears as the soul of Mam Yasin mixes with the scent of fresh rain and slowly ascends. There is nothing we can do but watch the rain and listen to Juwan's cries.

With the light of dawn, Segvan gently places Mam Yasin's corpse on the horse, and we resume the trip. He says we are less than two hours away from the border, and once we get there, we'll be close to the first village on the Iranian side where he knows some Kurdish families that will help us give Mam Yasin a proper burial. After that, God only knows what we will do.

23

Azad

T hree days in captivity, and my pants are already loose. My skin is wrinkled from dehydration. Last night, someone gave birth to the most unfortunate baby, who opened its eyes to a world of deprivation and cruelty.

Judging from the cries of the mother, it was a long and painful labor. The guards screamed at her at one point, and a few elderly female voices begged for warm water, towels, and scissors. Things did not go their way. The guards just yelled insults.

Everyone in my cell sat in silence while the cries resonated through the walls of the fort. We were finally relieved when we heard the sound of a newborn crying. Since then, the crying has not stopped. I feel ashamed to say it, but I was actually hoping the baby would be born dead. How can a woman be a mother in this corner of hell? Jamil has been unusually quiet, probably thinking of his pregnant wife. I better not mention it.

The guards are allowing us in the courtyard now. Upstairs, children play in the hallways outside the cells, but they are not allowed downstairs. Raqeeb and I are sitting in the middle of the courtyard. His grandfather and Jamil are walking around, having a chat. Raqeeb hands me a small circular rock and invites me to play a game with him. He takes a small stone from his pocket and throws it on the ground across from me.

"Hit it with two tries," he challenges me.

I turn around and look for any guards nearby. To get a beating for being a patriotic Kurd is one thing, but to get it for playing a marble game inside a prison is stretching it.

Two guards are walking in the corridor with their guns strapped to their backs. One adjusts his military cap and looks in our direction momentarily.

Raqeeb grabs my hand and says, "Go, take your shot."

I inspect his stone and mine and see that there is a mismatch. I place mine between my right thumb and middle finger. The guard is watching me now. The hell with it. I aim and let it go. It is not even close. I reposition myself and throw it again. This time it lands at least a foot away from the target.

With a giggle, Raqeeb gets on his knees, and like a professional he takes aim. With one strike, he knocks my rock away, then he jumps up in celebration.

I look around, and the two guards are walking away and shaking their heads.

Raqeeb's victorious face lights up as we stand and join Haji Sharif and Jamil. Something about him feels familiar. It is as if I have met Raqeeb before.

The sun is above our heads, but its heavy heat still feels better than the shade inside the cell. Loud Quran recitations come from nearby mosques. It's Friday. Men must be headed to prayers. I wonder if people realize what is happening to us inside the walls of this fort. Are the children playing outside aware of what their fellow children from the mountains are subjected to inside the walls of this house of nightmares? Housewives must be preparing the best meal of the week for their husbands, fathers, brothers, and sons to enjoy once they return from Friday prayers. Do they know what's on the menu for the hundreds of wives, sisters, daughters, and mothers in here?

I spot two guards pulling a young girl by her arms on the second floor while the other females around her scream. I can't help but wonder what would happen if all the men from the surrounding neighborhoods of Baroshki were to raid this fort and help us escape. Could the soldiers resist thousands of men? I doubt they could resist so many even if the attackers were unarmed! I imagine a riot inside the fort, prisoners fighting back and bullets flying everywhere. A group of men bring down one of the main gates. Women storm down the stairs and drag the soldiers by their hair. Men outside drag more soldiers onto the streets beyond the fort, and an uprising starts. It rapidly sweeps through the city. I stand on the main street and watch it unfold.

Something hard hits me on the back of my head, and I

am suddenly back in the main courtyard. A guard orders me to get going. Donkey. Dog. Mule. He was barraging me with these insults and more while I was busy imagining the uprising a few streets from here.

The imam at the nearby mosque is concluding his sermon with prayers to the almighty God to protect our beloved leader Saddam and bestow blessings upon him.

THE NEXT MORNING, I hear a busy commotion outside, followed by the heavy shuffling steps of prisoners and periodic cussing by guards. One man in the back of the cell says he heard a rumor that we will be taken out of here soon and executed outside. When Raqeeb hears that, he moves closer to his grandfather. Jamil shouts at the man in the back to shut up.

Sometime later, I hear military trucks driving away. At least there was no gunfire.

A guard pushes our cell door open and orders us to maintain order and walk outside. In the courtyard are multiple bags of French bread and a few plastic buckets of dirty water. We all make a run for it, and everyone takes a drink of water and whatever is left of the bread while they can. This might be all we get for days.

Jamil and I sit on the ground across from Raqeeb and Haji Sharif. I am facing our cell, and above us on the second floor a few kids are looking down and giggling. Haji Sharif goes through his bread quicker than all of us. Raqeeb gives him a piece of his, but he declines and pats Raqeeb on the back.

"A good grandson and a good boy," I say, smiling at

Raqeeb. I offer Haji Sharif a bite of my bread, and he accepts it without hesitation.

"I haven't heard the baby cry today," Jamil says. "Have you guys?"

I look up at the second floor. Two kids are leaning over the wall and competing to see whose spit hits the ground first. I pray none of that spit lands anywhere near a guard.

Jamil and Haji Sharif discuss some farming topics that I have little interest in. I hear a voice calling Raqeeb's name from above. I can't see who said it. A few seconds later, I hear it again, louder and more persistent this time. Then I see her: a young girl leaning over the wall. She's screaming his name now.

Raqeeb looks up and starts running. Jamil and I follow him and stop right under the wall where the girl is looking down.

Raqeeb calls out, "Mother," and a young woman standing next to the girl answers him back. Her face is familiar to me.

More men gather around us as Raqeeb begins crying and Haji Sharif holds him tightly. The young woman is holding a baby and pushes her way in front of the girl by the wall. It's her! The young mother from the truck. At the sight of the young woman, Raqeeb jumps up and down with excitement. And as soon as he hears the woman's voice, he breaks down and screams while his grandfather tries to console him. Half a dozen guards attempt to disperse us.

Raqeeb sprints towards the stairway entrance, but the guards beat him to it.

"That is my mother," he says. "Let me go to my mother. Let me go!" He screams as one guard stands in his way while another pulls him by the collar onto the floor. We run behind them, but two more guards step in our way and point guns at us.

The guard stationed at the stairs shoves Raqeeb back onto the floor. He will not stop crying. I hear more crying less than twenty feet above us, and I'm certain one of the women crying is his mother, the very same mother we walked into this prison with.

Haji Sharif begs the guards to allow Raqeeb to join his mother upstairs, but they refuse, and one of them kicks him on his lower back, taking his breath away for a few seconds.

Within minutes, everyone upstairs and downstairs is forced back into the cells. The newborn upstairs, the one inmate who doesn't understand threats, begins another crying spree.

For the rest of the day and a good part of the night, Raqeeb retreats to his usual spot by the concrete pole. Never mind the torture and the insults; nothing so far has been more heartbreaking than the sound of Raqeeb singing Ayaz Yusuf's legendary song telling his mother to move the baby's cradle as the father is gone away.

When Raqeeb finally falls asleep, his grandfather sobs and repeatedly hits his head against the concrete pole. Men don't cry! That's what they always taught us out there in the real world, but all the rules of manhood have been violated inside these cells.

I am halfway asleep when the lock in cell door turns. Jamil and Haji Sharif are asleep, so I wake them up. Soon, Raqeeb is awake as well, and all heads turn toward the opening door. A guard stands there in full military gear while two others enter the cell, order us all to get up, and randomly hit us with wooden sticks.

"This can't be good," I whisper.

Raqeeb pushes himself against me as we all stand submissively. At first I can't tell if Raqeeb chose to lean on me or if he mistook me for his grandfather. He answers that for me when he whispers, "Please, Azad, don't leave me and my grandpa alone. Please help us."

Haji Sharif appears exhausted and drained, so Jamil and I help him to his feet. The soldiers soon have us all lined up in the middle of the cell.

"Indeed, it doesn't look good," Jamil agrees.

Reality sinks in. They are moving us out of this cell and most likely out of this prison. The men I'd noticed earlier who were missing from their cells after last night's commotion were also probably taken away. Jamil is standing behind me, Raqeeb in front of me, and Haji Sharif is in front of all of us. He turns to the guard and once more asks him to allow Raqeeb upstairs, but the guard shakes his head and motions for Haji Sharif to get moving.

"Please, he is a child. Just let him reunite with his mother. Do this favor for me, and may Allah protect you and your loved ones."

The guard briefly contemplates the request. Another emerges from the hallway, grabs Haji Sharif's arm, and shoves him forward and down against the dirty concrete floor. I watch in horror as his hat and scarf land a few feet away. Raqeeb moves to check on him, then I assist him back to his feet while Jamil grabs the hat and scarf. Guards shout at us to keep moving or we will be shot.

Hungry, tired faces fill the courtyard in the darkness. Soldiers order us to move toward the main entrance, where half a dozen Toyota busses are parked, their engines running. I check my wristwatch, and it's a little before midnight. Guards start loading us into the busses, and I try to stay close to my crew. A guard stands at the door of the third bus, inspects us, then orders us to board.

The city of Duhok is in deep sleep, the lights of its homes and streets reminding me that an element of life still exists outside the walls of the Nizarki Fort. We pass through the city center, and the market is dead. With the exception of a few police cars, there is no sign of activity. We drive past my uncle's market, and memories flash through my head. Every inch of that sidewalk has felt the soles of my shoes. Every bit of this street brings back memories.

Raqeeb is sitting right behind me. He keeps whispering questions to his grandfather, who keeps asking him to shush. So he turns to me. "Where are we going?"

I remain quiet, watching the guard and his gun in the seat next to the middle door. Raqeeb asks again and again.

Jamil has dozed off, and Haji Sharif whispers to Raqeeb again. "*Koro*, boy, stop asking questions. They will hurt us."

We reach the outskirts of the city. My school is so far away that it's not even on the horizon. My dream is slipping away from me. My future is falling behind quickly in the dark background.

A few minutes later, we turn at a main intersection and head toward Mosul. Raqeeb's inquiries have not stopped, and I'm impressed with the guard's patience so far.

I finally push my head against the headrest and whisper to him, "Raqeeb, you need to be a big boy, a young man, and be strong. You need to stay quiet for now until we get somewhere where we can talk, OK?"

"Will we be able to play marbles where we're going?"

"Yes, now just rest in your seat and try to stay quiet."

The guard is finally fed up, and he yells at both of us to shut up or he'll kill us.

The senior officer in the front passenger seat asks the driver to turn the radio on. A war song blasts through the speakers celebrating the victories of our great nation and its long-living leader. Long live Saddam! Long live Iraq! Death and humiliation to traitors.

24

Juwan

One kilometer inside Iran, September 4, 1988

My world has collapsed. The earth I walk on has shaken beneath my feet and swallowed me. One half of me is dead, the other half floating and burning. The sky has gone dark, and the color has left the flowers, their scent decimated.

My life was squeezed into a dark corner when yours was squeezed out, my dear father. Two days have passed since I saw them drop your body in the grave and throw dirt over you. I have not slept since the moment I found you dead. Not travel, not fatigue, and not sorrow have broken my will to stay awake and mourn you. I refuse to eat or sleep; once I do, I will have accepted your death.

THE VILLAGE of Rezanki is on a hill on the Iranian side of the border, though its two dozen citizens don't seem to have a preference for Turkey or Iran. It is the first place in the border region where Segvan seems comfortable with the villagers. They all appear to know each other well, and how would they not? There are only five houses here.

Segvan met with the men early in the morning and had a long conversation with them behind the house we're staying in, hoping that I couldn't hear.

We gather around a breakfast spread with yogurt, cheese, eggs, and hot bread. None of this looks or smells appealing to me. Dilveen prepares a small cheese and egg sandwich and forces me to take a bite. Segvan is sitting in the opposite corner of the room to give us some privacy, but his anxious demeanor shows a sense of urgency to discuss a pressing matter.

Everyone tells me I'll pass out if I don't eat, so I finally take a few bites of the sandwich with some hot tea. My head hurts, and I feel nauseated. I have been mentally out for days now; how much worse can it get?

It's time for us to leave. That much is clear from all the whispers and exchanges Segvan has been having with the men outside and with Mistekhan and Dilveen in here. He clears his throat, anxiously takes the cigarette out of his mouth and says, "Juwan, I know this is hard on you. It's hard for all of us to say this, but it's time we make a decision."

I set what's left of the sandwich—most of it—back on the plate and try to focus with whatever is left of my lost mind.

"My daughter," Mistekhan says, "this was the will of

God. Your father is with his lord now in a better place. You have a life ahead of you, and you can't do this to yourself."

Dilveen pushes the tea cup toward me and asks me to take another sip to open my head. I pick up the cup but don't drink anything. "I want to thank you for all you have done for us," I tell Segvan, "and for my dad in particular. I'm sorry about any delays we have caused you."

Shireen gently pats my shoulders, and I put my tea down. "I'm ready for whatever you all decide to do next. I can't think or make any decisions myself."

Segvan leans forward in his seat. "I have only done my duty to my fellow Kurds in times of need."

Shireen is silent. She won't look at any of us. I can't tell if she finally realizes she was wrong to be so suspicious or if she's imagining more conspiracies.

"I am headed back home to Hesenlu," Segvan says. "You are all welcome to come with me and be my guests—"

"No," I interrupt. "Please, we don't want to add any more burdens on you. Just take us somewhere safe, and we will manage from there."

There are a few moments of silence before Dilveen speaks up. "What are our most realistic options? Go back to Turkey or to a refugee camp in Iran? Which one is less problematic for you?"

Segvan rises from his seat and paces the room a few times. "Look, I'm willing to take you back to Turkey if that's what you all want. But the best option is to stay in Iran since we're already here."

We spend an hour deliberating and get nowhere, so Segvan repeats his earlier offer: "How about you all come with me to my town? The refugee camps are miserable. You can stay in my house until we find you a place to live. It will be fine. Plus, my wife loves guests."

We ladies exchange looks. Dilveen breaks the silence. "We've been enough of a burden already."

"Won't we get in trouble if we enter the city without proper paperwork?" Shireen says.

Segvan smiles and lights another cigarette. "You ladies, don't worry. I have a plan. Just give me your approval, and I'll take care of you like my own family."

I make one last trip to my father's grave. He is slipping further away from my life by the hour. While everyone else is packing and getting ready, I pick some wild flowers and place them at my father's head. The sun is stretching itself out from behind the mountains, quietly announcing another day, indifferent to sorrow and happiness.

25

Azad

Salamiyah, 260 kilometers south of Mosul, September 4, 1988,
4:20 P.M.

I 've lost track of the time. Lost track of how many
people have thrown up in the bus, through the
windows and onto the asphalt when we were lucky
enough to stop on the side of the road. Not once have we
been offered food or a bathroom.

We are passing through Mosul, the city I've always
adored for its vibrancy, and crossing the iconic bridge over
the Tigris. Hundreds of pedestrians are crossing the same
bridge connecting the historic side of the city to the modern
side. No one notices the bus passing through. They nonchalantly cross the streets, forcing the bus to slow down and the

guard to scream curses. What I would give to stop at one of the book stands.

Raqeeb points at various food stands on the sidewalks. An old man is pushing an old wooden cart and selling fresh nuts while another hustles between parked cars and offers fresh juice. We pass the main hospital, and I see a woman with a very pregnant belly getting out of a taxi and leaning against her husband.

"It will be OK, my brother," I say to Jamil and rub his knee. "Things will get better."

"God knows if I will ever be able to see my son," he says, wiping tears away with his sleeve.

I wonder why he thinks he will have a son and not a daughter, but don't most men assume that? I wonder if our ancestors preferred male children because they lived in constant fear of losing them in war.

Duhok slept as we passed through, and Mosul in its energy was oblivious to our existence. We are the outlaws, the unwanted sons, the overflow, and the leftovers.

We pass a road sign reading Salamiyah. I think hard but can't recall hearing about this place. I notice that the compass on the bus driver's dashboard points to the southwest.

Our bus is now circling a large, yellow, heavily guarded, concrete military base off the road. Behind it are three steel structures that look like storage units. The bus caravan stops near the first structure, and minutes later the officer up front asks the driver to shut the engine off. A wave of heat seeps through the open front windows. Men turn around in their seats, curiously examining what might be our new home.

The main side door finally opens, and the guard orders

us to hop off one at a time in an orderly fashion. He takes his gun off his shoulder and holds it in his right hand.

When the buses are finally unloaded and the prisoners lined up and accounted for, a military Jeep emerges from the base and parks in front of the first bus. An officer steps out of the passenger side and turns toward us. Huge sunglasses cover the top half of his face, a dark mustache the other half. With his arms crossed, he motions with his head to the guards to begin the process.

Each of the three storage units is at least a hundred feet long and thirty feet wide. They look freshly painted in brown. When the guards lead us into the units, the humid heat slaps our faces. There are no beds or mattresses, so we sit on the bare concrete floor. A few guys are retching not too far from me. An older man gets up and hurries toward the opposite hall, ignoring the two guards yelling at him from the front door to stop. I watch with tired eyes, expecting the man to be shot at any moment. He suddenly stops next to the wall, anxiously looks around, then pulls his pants down and expels diarrhea onto the floor. With sighs from the prisoners and insults from the guards, the hall erupts in chaos. The old man then stands, pulls his pants up, and falls backward into his own feces.

"He passed out," one detainee shouts.

Another gets up, but a guard orders him to stand still. A second guard tells his comrade to let the man help.

"All right, two of you clean up the shit, but if you do anything else, you will see your own blood beneath you."

The old man who fell is clearly unconscious.

Jamil volunteers to help. "Azad," he says to me, "please tell them he needs medical attention. I can't tell if he is alive or dead."

At least one of the guards understood. "If he's dead," the bastard says in Arabic, "even better. His road to hell has been shortened."

The old man seems to be moving his feet as he is slowly dragged from the pool of feces. The wretched smell irritates the guards, and they eventually order us outside and point us toward a water tank some twenty feet away.

The tank is a burning ball of metal in the scalding heat of the open desert. Its water is nearly boiling. Jamil and I hold the old man under the running water and clean him up with his clothes on. He slowly opens his eyes, immediately asking for water. We take turns drinking hot water from the rusted faucet, then spread out. The guards don't seem to mind as long as we finish cleaning the feces inside.

Soon, the men from the other two units are outside too and running for their share of the water.

Raqeeb approaches me with his grandfather. "Azad, where are we?"

"I don't know."

I can't see anything beyond this military post. Everyone seems to think I know every place and every person south of Duhok since I speak Arabic. We take a stroll around while several guards stand and observe.

"*Bapeer*, grandpa, come see this!" Raqeeb says.

He points at three dirty little shoes scattered in the dust between a few rocks. One is pink and the other two are blue. Jamil picks one up and inspects it. Not far away, Haji Sharif spots a wooden doll dressed in Kurdish clothes.

"Is this what I think it is?" Jamil whispers and places the little pink shoe in his pocket.

We walk back to the unit with the wind blowing hot

sand in our faces. On our way, Raqeeb asks his grandfather if he can ask the guards for some food.

Without hesitation, Haji Sharif walks up to a guard standing by the water tank and starts motioning with his hand and saying, "*Samoon, samoon.*" Bread, bread.

Haji Sharif points at Raqeeb and repeats his request. "Samoon, samoon."

The guard shoves Haji Sharif to the ground with the butt of his gun. Near the fence, an officer of a higher rank watches as Jamil and I help Haji Sharif up while he moans in pain.

We settle back in our spots on the floor inside the burning walls. Shortly later, another figure emerges at the entrance, and the two guards stand up straight and salute him. It's the same officer with the large glasses who watched us earlier, and he's carrying a large black bag. Everybody watches him anxiously, including the guards, as he quietly drops the bag. He nods without a word, then turns and leaves the unit. A dozen or so loaves of fresh french bread are stuffed inside. They're gone within minutes.

I hate to complain about being fed, but there's only enough food to arouse our monstrous appetites. It's more painful than raw hunger. It's like removing a scab too soon and irritating a wound all over again.

Later, at dusk, a voice through a loudspeakers tells us it's time to move again. "Everyone back to their bus and the same seats you were in before."

We promptly board the bus, avoiding eye contact with the guards. Jamil sits next to me and withdraws into silence. Raqeeb sits next to his grandfather, still asking questions and getting no answers. I gently ask him to stay quiet so the guards don't start yelling at us.

"Do you think they will take us back?" he says. "Maybe they realized they left behind the women and children?"

I look straight ahead as the guard pushes the door shut and takes his previous seat, scanning the prisoners for any unauthorized movement. The rough road feels even rockier at night. The base soon disappears behind us, and all light vanishes on both sides of the bus.

Raqeeb gently taps my shoulder. "Azad, I want to go back to my mom." I close my eyes, hoping to escape his voice, but he continues. "Please tell the guards to drop me off."

"All right, boy," Jamil says. "We're going back to Duhok, and then you can see your mother. Now sit back and stay quiet."

26

Dilveen

Hesenlu, Iran, September 4, 1988

We arrive by the minibus at the Iranian town of Hesenlu a little before sunset. The welcome sign at the entrance is faded. Small shops line both sides of the road, selling tobacco, ice cream, and groceries. I see a few scattered restaurants and a bakery. Some children carelessly cross the road, carrying all sorts of wood and scrap metal. An old man wearing Kurdish clothes is walking behind a long herd of cattle on the side of the road. Some shops are starting to close, while others are just now turning their night lights on.

The bus slows down and stops in front of a house with blue walls and a white metal door. Segvan hands the driver some paper bills and turns to us and says with a smile, "We have arrived."

We follow him out of the bus with our bags. A young woman in her late twenties or early thirties wearing a purple Kurdish dress with a red scarf tied halfway around her head emerges from the house.

"Shukriya," Segvan says, "I have guests with me."

He introduces all of us to his wife, and she gives us a warm welcome. Her Kurdish dialect is a little heavier than Segvan's but nothing we can't understand. She leads us into the guest room, two little girls walking closely behind us with shy and curious looks. The guest room is furnished with red sofas and decorated with a few black-and-white photos on the light yellow walls.

Once we are seated, Shukriya promptly returns with glasses of cold orange juice. Segvan reemerges later in new clothes and gently pushes the children out of the room, but they soon return with their mother to collect the empty glasses.

Over dinner, Segvan briefly describes our trip to his wife. Afterward, seeing the obvious exhaustion on our faces, she invites us to another room across the hallway where she has prepared our beds.

At the door, my mother turns to Segvan and says, "I know we have been a big burden on you so far, but Allah will reward you for it. I just have one more request." She mumbles a quick prayer. "My sons! We don't know anything about them. If you know anyone who goes to Turkey, please ask them to ask about my sons, Jamil and Azad."

"I promise I will check on them myself," he says.

Mother looks at Juwan and says in a broken voice, "Azad was supposed to marry her, and I did not get to see it."

27

Azad

West of the Tigris River, September 4, 1988

The guards drive us for two more hours, and at some point I doze off. I wake up when the bus comes to a complete stop and the guard opens the side door and steps out.

Jamil taps my shoulder and whispers, "Look over there."

He is looking straight through the front window. There are some lights moving back and forth in the distance, but we can't make out what they are or what's happening. A few minutes later, the guard returns and closes the door, then the bus moves again, but only for a brief distance. When it's parked this time, we are able to see the moving lights clearly.

There are several large bulldozers actively moving about and surrounded by several military vehicles. Two large lights are pointed in the direction of what appears to be piles of dirt. The prisoners whisper among themselves. Raqeeb is surprisingly silent. The driver steps out, leaving the bus running. A few minutes later, he returns and turns the engine off. Moments later, the guard steps out, leaving us behind in our thoughts and our theories.

"This is not looking good."

"We are doomed."

"I told you they were going to kill us, but you kept saying those days are gone."

Minutes seem to stretch into years as the bulldozers hover around a wide ditch.

Finally, a guard returns and orders us out. "Any movement out of order and you will be shot!"

We get off the bus and line up alongside it, as ordered. It's dark and hot, dry and scary. Memories wash over me. Was I right all those years to insist on staying in Duhok, away from my mother and sisters? Did I miss the opportunity to marry the love of my life and be happy? Am I here today instead of with my family because I was stubborn? They can't possibly be anywhere worse than here. No, no, no, I tell myself.

Raqeeb squeezes my hand. "Are you sure, Azad?"

"Am I sure of what?"

"That they won't kill us?"

I'm back to my senses now. "I don't know, Raqeeb, I don't know."

He pulls my hand once more, this time without saying a word.

A military SUV passes us on its way to the bulldozers, leaving behind a cloud of dust.

Raqeeb releases my hand and says without looking at me, "So they are going to kill us, aren't they?"

I close my eyes and listen to the machines from hell digging through the earth for the ugliest spots to hide away our sorry lives forever. We are not even worthy enough to lie dead on the ground in this country.

The noise of bulldozers suddenly stops, and I open my eyes to see at least five military vehicles parked near the work area. A dozen or so guards line up in front of us with their weapons drawn. They order us to walk toward the ditch in a single line.

Haji Sharif repeatedly stumbles in front of Raqeeb, and from time to time I attempt to pass Raqeeb to help his grandfather to his feet, only to be met by stiff orders from the guards to return to my position in line. I have already been called so many names from their dictionary of indignity that the next step is surely a bullet in my head.

With every step forward, reality settles in deeper. For years there was talk about the Anfal campaign in the Soran region and the thousands who went missing. We heard rumors of mass graves, but the thought of such extreme measures was always considered far-fetched until ... right now.

I am starting to feel dizzy, and my knees are buckling. Tired bodies walk the line submissively toward death. There must be at least thirty prisoners in front of me, with the first person in line now only a few feet from the ditch.

Suddenly the bulldozers' engines begin humming again. A dozen or so guards pull a bunch of men from the front of the line. I count to fourteen before the crowd grows too big and the scene turns chaotic. At first, everyone complies, but when the guards start pushing them in front of the bulldozers, some of the men start to plead to the guards while others resist.

I struggle to absorb what I'm seeing and to comprehend what's happening. Raqeeb turns to me frantically, but I avoid his gaze by closing my eyes. Raqeeb is right in my sight wherever I turn.

Haji Sharif is barely able to stand.

He yells in the direction of Raqeeb: "Do you remember how many times I told your hard-headed father that we should hit the mountains? He kept reassuring me that the Peshmerga would catch up with us and hold back the army. Well, some managed to run away, while idiots like us are about to be killed."

Jamil shakes his head at the atrocious timing of Haji Sharif's comments.

Another man turns and says, "Stop talking to the kid like that, man."

Haji Sharif directs his rant at no one in particular, and a commotion builds up not too far from us. The guards are getting louder. Two young men are on the ground, begging for mercy as the guards repeatedly kick and slap them. One of the bulldozers backs up, temporarily blocking our view. I hear the crack of rifles, and when the bulldozer is out of the way again, I see the two young men lying motionless on the ground. Several guards drag their bodies into the hole.

Then the guards pull more prisoners out of the line and throw them into ditch. I count nine men falling into the hole alive. The men beg for their lives; five guards standing above shoot them in an unorganized but quick fashion.

Raqeeb holds on to his grandfather's arm and starts

crying. I gently pat him on the back and ask him to stay quiet so as not to attract the attention of the guards.

I feel a hand on the back of my neck, and I lose my balance from fear. In my mind, I've already been tortured and killed.

It's Jamil: "What are we going to do now?"

I keep looking straight as the guards take another dozen or so men. Running would be suicide.

"What do you suggest we do?" I whisper.

He steps closer to me and whispers, "All I know is I'm not dying here. I have got to get back to my wife and baby. I don't care if the rest of the world burns!"

With the next round of men taken, our line now moves closer to the front. The cries of victims become even more urgent. Haji Sharif is still mumbling, and Raqeeb is standing on my foot as if to say you are not moving without me.

Another round of bullets, and another pile of bodies. Some of the men are breaking down in the back. The guards pull two of the men from the back and drag them by the arms past us. Another stops near Haji Sharif and motions with his hand, "Hey you, old man. You have been talking non-stop. Come out, let's go."

When the guard pulls Haji Sharif away, he loses his balance and falls on his face. His head is covered with sand and dust as the guard drags him away.

Raqeeb jumps and yells, "Bapeer, Bapeer!"

I hold him back while he continues to scream. "Let him go. Leave my grandpa alone. Let him go!"

Two soldiers start pushing us forward, and Raqeeb escapes my grip and runs towards his grandfather, catching him on the edge of the hole. Raqeeb jumps on Haji Sharif's body. One guard is holding Haji Sharif now while another attempts to pull Raqeeb away.

"You know what," says the guard pulling Raqeeb, "let's take you down with him. You almost dislocated by shoulder. You bastards can be buried next to each other."

"Please," Haji Sharif begs, "not him. Please spare him. Take me down, kill me, cut me in pieces. Just leave my grandson alone."

The guard violently throws Raqeeb to the ground. More guards arrive and fire at Haji Sharif, hitting him twice in the head and once in the thigh.

Raqeeb's screams fill the sky. The two men in front of me step out of the line and grab him. Guards swarm the area while more prisoners surge forward. The bulldozer drivers stop their machines and watch in shock. A guard attempts to pull Raqeeb away, but one of the detainees holds on to him. The angered guard shoots the man in the abdomen.

Another guard bumps into one of the large lights, knocking it down.

More shots are fired, and pandemonium ensues. Raqeeb is just standing there in shock as guards fire into the sky and demand order.

"Over there," Jamil yells and points toward a dark area behind one of the bulldozers. "Over there, let's go!"

Jamil starts running toward the bulldozer. I grab Raqeeb's arm and pull him with me, but he yells, "No, no, I don't want to leave Bapeer alone."

I ignore his cries and pull him behind me. It's dark as pitch past the bulldozer, but we keep running. More shots are fired behind us, but the sound grows more distant with each step we take.

I hear someone running behind us, panting and gradually closing in. Jamil and I zigzag our way through the darkness. We seem to be in an open area. Raqeeb is still screaming. Shots are fired in our direction. I turn and faintly see three men from the line right behind me. More shots come our way. Now two lights are shining behind us in the distance.

They've spotted us.

It's a military truck, and it's coming right at us.

We reach a small hill and run in separate directions. Jamil, Raqeeb, another man, and I turn left while the other two men head to the right.

More shots fired. One of the men to our right screams.

The military truck turns and follows us. I trip and nearly fall but maintain my balance as I give Raqeeb a push to help him catch up with Jamil. Behind the hill, the ground becomes clear again. I catch up with Jamil, and we both grab Raqeeb's hands and run faster, the other man staying right next to us.

The truck is close behind us now, and the soldiers keep firing at us. Raqeeb abruptly trips and falls, screaming from pain. I pick him up, and he screams harder. The other man drifts to the right as he continues to run, then falls with a loud cry.

"I can't walk," Raqeeb groans.

I lean over to inspect his foot, but Jamil picks him up and starts running again. I turn for a second and see that the truck has stopped near the fallen man. I take Raqeeb from Jamil, and we keep running across the open, dry land, leaving the truck behind us until its lights eventually drown in the darkness.

28

Azad

Somewhere in Iraq, September 5, 1988, 3:35 A.M.

We lose track of time and distance. There is nothing but fear and adrenaline. Every time we put Raqeeb down to take turns carrying him, he screams from pain. He won't let either of us touch his left leg. The distant light of the moon is our guide. Sometimes I wonder if it's also spying on us.

We stop to catch our breath. I look behind us and see no sign of headlights or anything moving. Jamil puts Raqeeb down, and we gently inspect his left leg. He screams when my hand finds a sharp piece of bone sticking out.

"We need to tie it," Jamil says, "but ..." He looks around. "I'm afraid he'll scream again."

I rest Raqeeb's leg on my legs, a move that proves painful to him as he tries hard to hold back another loud scream.

"You're a smart boy," I tell him. "A brave boy. A real man."

Jamil slowly rips Raqeeb's left pant leg, exposing the broken bone. I remove my shirt, rip off both sleeves, and hand them to Jamil as he gently presses on the broken bone. Raqeeb screams, kicks, pulls, pushes, and cusses as I hold him tight while Jamil wraps his leg to stabilize the bone. With the last knot, Raqeeb screams one more time before passing out, his face and neck drenched in sweat.

I let Raqeeb's head gently fall on my leg and lay my own head on a rock. Jamil walks around for a few minutes, takes a piss, then returns and lies down next to me.

We're both looking up at the stars now. "I don't feel good about staying here," he says. "We need to get moving."

But I am still panting. A warm breeze soothes us. Animals are barking in the far distance, probably just dogs but possibly wolves or other wild beasts.

"We can rest a bit," I say. "I think we ran far enough."

Jamil is already snoring. The sound of the dogs grows louder and rowdier until everything fades to dark and mute.

FAINT BARKING sounds in the darkness. Shadows hovering over me. Barely audible noises bubble up and vanish again. Bright lights now. Someone is shouting something in Arabic.

It must be them. They've caught us.

I don't want to open my eyes again. I press my eyelids

firmly shut. The Arabic voice is right above me now, asking me to get up. If I'm going to die, let me go with my eyes shut. Don't make me face my killers. Don't make me see what they've done to Jamil and Raqeeb in the night.

I hear Raqeeb grunt, and the Arabic voice asks him to drink.

I open my eyes and jump to my feet, still struggling to adjust to the shiny light of the sun. Raqeeb is lying on a blanket a few feet away from me, and a man in Bedouin clothes is standing above him and holding a water jug. Jamil is still asleep, so I give him a kick, and just like me, he's up on his feet.

The stranger is pouring water into Raqeeb's mouth. When Raqeeb finally lets go of the jug, the stranger turns to face us. He's tall and skinny with a long, wavy mustache and a spotty beard. His white dishdasha is mottled with yellow dirt, and he's wearing a thick, brown robe over it. He fixes the red headband over his head and approaches us with a smile.

"Welcome, welcome, brothers, welcome. I am glad to see you well. I was worried about you."

Jamil shoots the man a blank look. I clear my throat. He inches closer to me, but Jamil grabs the jug from him and starts drinking from it.

"I am Nabeel. Nabeel Al-Himood. I am your brother."

A young boy is running in our direction from far away. He is wearing a white dishdasha, which he has rolled up to his waist. He is waving a stick in his hand and calls on his father. "Yaba, Yaba, Mama said food is ready for the guests."

Nabeel introduces his son, Laith. The boy appears a little younger than Raqeeb but looks as confident as a thirty-year-old. He is the youngest of his seven kids, all boys, thanks to God, Nabeel says. I can't tell if Laith is deeply tanned from sun exposure or if he is just dark-skinned. I'm still taken aback by these two and their hospitality.

Jamil asks me in Kurdish, "Who is he? Is this real, or are we in a dream?"

It must be real because Raqeeb is now wide awake, grunting and moaning from pain.

Nabeel grabs my hand and says, "You are all my guests. Please follow me to my tent."

He attempts to pick up Raqeeb, but Jamil holds his hand in the air and stops him. Laith watches curiously and runs his stick back and forth on the ground. Jamil carries Raqeeb in his arms, I grab the water jug, and we follow a few steps behind the father and his son.

"My brother," Nabeel says, "you are my guests. You have nothing to worry about. You are under my protection."

He studies my face, unsure how much I understand Arabic.

"Shukran," I say in Arabic, thank you, and his face lights up with another smile.

"My boy found you lying here in the early morning as he was gathering our livestock. You are my guests, and you are under my protection. No questions asked."

Hundreds of sheep are scattered around a large black tent. Two big dogs circle the herd of sheep, maintaining order. I check my watch, and it's past eight o'clock in the morning. Nabeel and I help bring Raqeeb down as Nabeel's wife emerges from behind the tent with bread in her hand.

"Najma's cooking is legendary," Nabeel says. "She can cook for an entire village all on her own."

She invites us into the tent.

This is not a dream. There's a spread of yogurt, cheese,

eggs, and fried liver on the floor. Laith is serving us coffee. Raqeeb drinks some milk and falls back asleep.

"My brothers," Nabeel says, "my guests. It's our tribal rule that guests are not asked what brought them here. But I want you to know you will be safe with me."

It's clear that he has some idea who we are and that our situation is urgent. His wife returns with another pitcher of milk, offering a wide welcoming smile. Her wrinkled face is highlighted by traditional Bedouin tattoo dots.

Laith is outside singing an Arabic song for his animals. Jamil and I have maintained absolute silence, sweeping through every bit of food in front of us.

After breakfast, Nabeel puts his hand on my knee and says, "Kurds have done me favors I will never forget."

He offers us a refill of dark coffee. I take it, but Jamil declines. Nabeel drinks his with one gulp.

"As you see, I have a lot of livestock, and this has been my family's life for as long as we can remember. I have a house in the city, but Najma and I enjoy this life better. We are moving this cattle closer to a water source due to a drought in our area."

He stares at his empty coffee cup and smiles.

"This world is small," he says, still smiling as he seems to recall something from the past. "In the 1950s, we had a major drought here, and thousands of our animals died. My father made us move the remaining herd, several thousand heads, to Duhok. We stopped at a village called Mammani. Do you know where it is?"

I look at Jamil and give him a brief translation.

He nods and says, "Mammani, in the Doski region."

Nabeel resumes his story. "The sheikh of Mammani at the time, a kind and generous man, allowed us access to their area, and we stayed for an entire season. Years later my father was still talking about how the sheikh and his people saved us. We will forever be grateful to our Kurdish brothers."

Raqeeb moans in pain. Najma tends to his leg while we stand close by. He lies there in total submission as Najma removes the cloth and rubs his skin with warm water. When she finishes cleaning, she places four sticks over his leg, then wraps it with a clean piece of cloth. Surprisingly, Raqeeb is silent throughout the process, although his face is contorted.

"This is temporary," Najma says, "until we take him to the hospital tomorrow."

Nabeel excuses himself and leaves the tent. His wife follows and yells something at Laith. Raqeeb eats a few more pieces of bread, then falls back asleep.

"We need to get out of here immediately," Jamil says. He looks around and whispers. "I don't trust the Arabs. They will hand us over to the army. It's only a matter of time."

I don't see much use in arguing with him about that, but I agree that we need to leave. There are so many questions we don't have answers for. Where exactly are we? How will we get out of here, and where will we go? How safe are we out there in the open less than twelve hours after escaping a death sentence? If this family has bad intentions, what would stop them from holding us at gunpoint until a government unit arrives to arrest us?

Then there's Raqeeb and his injury, which will significantly hinder our ability to navigate any escape we might come up with.

Jamil and I are startled by the sound of a car approaching. Jamil stands, panic-stricken, and paces around the tent. "I told you. I told you they are not to be trusted. We will be executed soon."

I don't know which is more concerning, Jamil panicking or that I'm calm about what's happening.

The car comes to a stop, the engine remaining on. Laith yells something in Arabic, while Jamil and I remain inside the tent, listening attentively. My worried mind is at odds with my relaxed body. The car door opens and closes, and suddenly there's an exchange between Nabeel, his wife, and two men who speak in a similar Arabic tone.

"They're inside the tent," Nabeel says.

Sweat drips down my neck and back. Jamil was right. I imagine grabbing Raqeeb and running away again, but the scene in my mind doesn't end well.

Jamil grabs my arm and says, "Let's go. We can sneak out and run away before they catch us."

Nabeel barges into the tent with his entourage: his wife, Laith, and two tall, young men dressed similarly to Nabeel. They stand behind him as he introduces them to us as his two older sons, Mahdi and Falah. "They help me with transportation and supplies."

The two young men approach us for a handshake. I hesitantly extend my hand and say, "I am Azad, and this is Jamil, my brother. We are—"

"My sons will take care of all your needs," Nabeel says. That is one interruption I greatly appreciate. "Let's rest now."

"I want to thank you for your kind hospitality and what you have done for us so far," I say.

Nabeel gears up for another round of pleasantries, but I raise my voice a bit and continue. "We have a big problem that's hard to explain, but we urgently need to get going,

and if you could help us get out of this area, we will forever
be grateful."

Nabeel looks at his sons and then turns to me. "My
family loves the Kurds. You are our brothers. We share this
land, this soil, this air, and a lot more. I have a pretty good
idea how you ended up here, and you don't need to go into
the details."

I feel tremendous relief. If he truly knows why we are
here and hasn't turned us in, he is indeed a kind human. If
he has other intentions, we have no choice but to play
along.

"It pains us to see what the government has been doing
to your people. That's not something you or I can fix, but we
are here to help you in any way we can."

I translate for Jamil, and he slowly relaxes. Raqeeb is
awake now and asking for water. He is puzzled by all the
people around him but reassured when Jamil and I sit next
to him.

Over the next half hour or so, I discuss our situation
with Nabeel and his sons. We have made it clear to them we
need to get to Duhok for a chance at escaping to the mountains up north, but it will take a lot of time and effort if we
want to avoid cities and crowded areas. Nabeel suggests that
we stay with them and try to lay low, but Falah says they
passed through an unusually high number of military
checkpoints on the way here this morning. I want to yell at
Falah for not telling us earlier, but I remind myself that we
are their guests and that they are our saviors.

Nabeel draws some lines in the sand with his stick, indicating the main and secondary routes through the cities on
our way north. His sons conclude that they can drive us
about an hour northwest of here, but beyond that we would

be risking going through a checkpoint. We then would have to walk at least four hours to get close to the Sinjar area, and beyond that only God knows what would happen. The plan sounds good to Jamil and me.

But my eyes turn to Raqeeb. He can't even stand, and he obviously needs medical attention.

"What are you going to do with this boy?" asks Nabeel's wife.

Raqeeb realizes something is up, so he grabs my hand and asks, "What is this woman saying?"

Jamil and I explain to him that we must leave because the military is probably sweeping the area looking for us and whoever else escaped.

"Please don't leave me here. My father is dead. My mother and siblings are also probably dead now. I don't have anyone else. Please don't leave me alone."

I hug him. "Don't say that. Inshallah, your mother and siblings are safe, and you will get to see them one day." But I fail to convince even myself.

Najma takes a seat, gently taking Raqeeb's head in her lap.

"Sweet boy," she says. "I will take good care of you and make sure you are safe until your leg is healed."

I doubt Raqeeb understands what she's saying, but motherly touch is deeper and louder. It's clear that we're going to have to leave him behind, and it takes a lot of reassurance and tears before he eventually agrees to let us go.

Nabeel gives me his full name, shows me his ID card, and tells me where his main residence is. I exchange that for my uncle's information, including the address for his market in Duhok. He presses us to stay, but I remind him again that we must go.

Jamil is outside the tent now, anxious to leave. We bid a long emotional farewell to Raqeeb and promise that we'll return for him.

I pass Laith at the entrance of the tent. He follows me outside, holding his stick and shooting curious looks at us. Falah starts the car engine, and Jamil rides next to him. Mahdi hops into the back of the open pickup truck.

Najma hands Mahdi a satchel of food along and a jug of water. "This is for our guests."

I take off my wristwatch and tie it around Laith's wrist. He smiles wide in excitement. I'm sure his dad can afford things a lot more valuable than what I just gave him, but this is a family that cares about gestures.

Before I hop into the back, Nabeel slides some money into my pocket and says, "God be with you."

We do indeed need God to be with us.

29

Azad

Somewhere in Iraq, September 5, 1988

The truck shifts between paved roads and dirty side roads, passing through open and dry terrain until we enter a valley with a few small villages scattered about. At dusk we pass one with a large herd of livestock in the fields. The road then turns behind a hill and ends at an abandoned field. The truck comes to a stop just as night falls.

Jamil, Falah, and I carefully walk around, inspecting the area.

"This is the farthest we can drive while avoiding heavily populated areas," Falah says.

"Which direction is Duhok?" I ask, looking around.

He grabs my head and gently turns it to the right. "You are looking straight north. That should be roughly the direction of Duhok."

We exchange hugs with the two brothers, and Falah says, "Please be careful, and try to avoid the main roads."

"Our plan" I respond, "is to get to Sinjar where my uncle has a friend who may be able to further help us."

We grab our stuff, and they drive away after a warm farewell. A few seconds later, the truck slows down and backs up again, and Falah sticks his head out and shouts in our direction in the darkness. "Don't worry about the kid. We will take care of him like our own." The brake lights go off, and the truck drives away.

We aim for the bright flashing lights on a large tower toward the north for a few hours, stopping briefly for water and food breaks. "I wonder if Raqeeb is asleep now," I say. "He will definitely need surgery or at least a long rest period in a cast. Did we make a mistake leaving him behind? What kind of message did I give that young, traumatized kid about loyalty and friendship? What if we don't get out of this mess alive and he never makes it out of that place? What if we are never able to find him again?

"Would you shut up, please?" Jamil says. "I'm tired of your talk about this boy."

We finally get exhausted and stop for a longer break. The scattered lights of a village are near, and we take shelter next to the fence of a large farm. Our feet are barely holding us up. Jamil is concerned that someone may spot us, but I couldn't care less at this point. He rants about my poor choice of a spot, while I clean up my space and lie down to stare at the sky. Jamil finally lies a few feet from me.

"About earlier," he says and sighs. "I'm sorry about what

I said. Of course I care about the boy, but we just escaped the death squad and haven't even talked about it yet."

I feel numb. Staring at the blank sky, I ask Jamil, "Do you think they killed the rest of the men? And what about the women and children we left behind in the fort?"

There is total silence in the village ahead. And now Jamil is snoring. I can't stop ruminating about what happened. Thoughts and images tumble over themselves in my mind. It's going to be a long night.

I stare at the sky and think about how our lives have turned upside down in a manner of weeks. I think of the village and my days growing up there and my family's attachment to it, my mother, my sisters, and my beautiful Juwan. Images of innocent village people and their generous and welcoming nature flash through my mind. I missed out on life in the village while chasing my dream of school. With that thought, my mind travels to the city. To my school. To the streets of Duhok, where passersby amble in no particular direction, with only an urge to fill the streets and maintain the life of the city in both the heat of summer and the chill of winter. I close my eyes and see myself removing the veil of my bride, Juwan, on our wedding night and finally getting to see her beauty without the judging eyes of the villagers upon us and without time constraints limiting our words to each other.

A light crosses the sky, and with it my thoughts cross over to another side of our miserable world: men struggling to stay alive at the edge of the ditch as soldiers kick them, shoot them, and push them deeper down the hole before the bulldozers add the final layer of darkness.

I close my eyes and try to sleep. I can almost hear my mother's voice calling my name, asking me to leave the city and come back. She cries for Jamil and me to be safe. I am in a sea of thoughts and worries, shifting in and out of brief, shallow naps.

I awaken Jamil before dawn, and we find a small stream where we wash our faces and drink some water. We carefully pass the village, the pathway forcing us to remain within its vicinity. It's busier than I expected. An elderly woman dressed in all black is standing over a *tannour* clay pit oven and skillfully moving her hands in and out of it, producing large pieces of hot bread that she throws in a basket behind her. A young boy walks by, and she hands him a piece of bread, which he takes and runs away in excitement. My eyes are fixed on the bread.

I reach into my pocket and fetch the money Nabeel gave us. Fifty dinars can go a long way, but Jamil wants to keep walking and get away from this place. He has not been thinking rationally since we got caught. We need food. We need directions and assistance. One wrong turn and we could end up walking into a military checkpoint.

I examine my sleeveless shirt and realize I need new clothes as well. We observe the village a while longer and detect no military presence. I finally convince Jamil that it's a good idea to approach.

Um Abd is a sweet old Arab lady whose wrinkled face tells a story of struggle, though it doesn't make a dent in her smile. She isn't startled when we suddenly appear behind her uninvited.

She greets us with a wide smile and immediately calls on her son Abd to come. "My son, come here, we have guests."

She pulls out a hot piece of flat bread from the fire pit

and hands it to me. "Go on, my son, eat it. You must be tired and hungry from traveling."

This hajiya with her beautiful heart must entertain a lot of passersby. Perhaps we're just obviously exhausted travelers. I give half the bread to Jamil and work on my own half quickly as Um Abd watches with satisfaction.

Her son Abd is a large, dark-skinned man with broad shoulders and a belly that has seen plenty of greasy feasts. He wipes his mouth and mustache with his hand as he steps outside the house in a gray dishdasha with multiple holes in it and welcomes us with a firm handshake.

I introduce myself and Jamil and tell him that we miscalculated our way when we asked our ride to drop us off. Better to give him a story now than answer questions later or deal with assumptions. I resist his invitation to enter the house, emphasizing that we're behind schedule and need help getting back on the right track.

I don't tell him about our plan to meet up with Khairo, a Yezidi man in Sinjar who was a good friend of my father's. If he still lives in Sinjar, he can help us get to Duhok and meet up with my uncle.

I keep the exchange with Abd brief and to the point, emphasizing the need for a ride to Sinjar and some food for the trip. I produce the money from my pocket, drawing Abd's focused gaze. He says in a salivating tone, "Of course, my brother. I can secure you a ride plus enough food."

He leans closer to his mother's bread basket, grabs two pieces, and hands them to me and Jamil. "My cousin has a car, and I can talk to him right now. You can trust us." He nervously turns and walks around to the other side of his house.

Jamil looks anxious. "Did you tell him we don't have ID

cards? We won't be able to go through security checkpoints."

He's right, and I didn't mention it to Abd. Better to hold off now until we get in the car and leave this place.

A little while later, Abd returns and happily announces that a ride has been secured. His cousin should be here any time now.

As Abd packs some bread and vegetables for us, I remember my missing sleeves and say "Oh, by the way, is there any way I can also get a shirt?"

He looks at my shoulders and chuckles, as if he has only now noticed the missing sleeves. He disappears inside and comes back a few minutes later with two brown dishdashas. He hands one to me and the other to Jamil.

Jamil looks puzzled.

"You won't find modern clothing around here," Abd says. "Plus, I think you guys will have an easier time if you wear these over your current outfits."

Enough said.

The red GMC truck has seen decades of heavy work, and little of its original paint remains. Multiple fender benders and major accidents were repaired in the simplest ways possible. When it stops by Abd's house, the muffler makes loud choking sounds, then gives out.

Abd introduces his cousin Ali as our companion and driver to the promised land. Ali is probably in his late thirties with bronze, leathery skin. His white dishdasha is neat and clean. He introduces himself, and within minutes we are in his truck after thanking Abd and his generous mother and of course paying Abd.

Ali shifts the gear stick back and forth so many times that I start to wonder if he knows how to drive. Then the car suddenly jolts forward, sending us back against our seats. After a few hiccups, the run-down vehicle is alive. A few kids chase the truck as we cut through the old huts scattered on both sides of the dirt road.

Five hours and many shortcuts, long loops, and diversions later, Ali drops us off on the side of the road in a deserted area. If we want to enter Sinjar without going through a security checkpoint, this is the way to go, and Ali isn't willing to go any farther. We hit the road again, this time pretending to be Arab men walking in the middle of nowhere.

We reach the outskirts of Sinjar in the early evening hours. It's a large town, so there's more activity and a higher chance of running into trouble or being spotted. The area has a mixture of different ethnicities and cultures, so walking around wearing dishdashas doesn't increase the likelihood that we'll be recognized as strangers. The biggest issue is that we don't have IDs. So we decide to hold out until dark.

Another challenge will be finding Khairo. What if he doesn't live here anymore? That's the question Jamil keeps throwing at me. The closer we get to Duhok, the riskier everything feels, making Jamil more apprehensive.

We camp out and watch from afar until the town settles down with the onset of darkness, then we begin our manhunt. We approach one of the main streets, and a few young guys are having a heated argument over something. Best to pass by them without engagement. We then turn onto another street and spot a small market in a low-key corner of the neighborhood. An old man is sitting on a rock a few feet from the market's entrance. With a cigarette in his hand, he inspects us under the bright street light. I greet him in Arabic as we get closer to him. He shoots us a look and puts the cigarette in his mouth without lighting it. "Aren't you Kurdish?" he asks in Kurdish.

Jamil steps in front of me and immediately answers. "Yes, we're Kurdish."

I look at our dishdashas and then back at the old man.

"Then why," the man says, "don't you fools speak your mother language? Forgot your origin?"

Not quite the start we had hoped for. Jamil apologizes to the man, who is now moving the cigarette back and forth between his fingers and his mouth without having lit it yet.

I lean closer to him and ask, "Uncle, we are looking for a man named Khairo. Do you know him? Do you know where he lives?"

He stands up and brings his face close to mine. "Khairo is dead! He was like you. He forgot his origin and was sent somewhere the sun has never seen."

A voice comes from the market with a giggle. "Don't mind this old man. He is crazy and has lost his mind. Ignore everything he says. What can I help you with?"

The market owner calls several of his close friends and contacts and finally finds out that Khairo indeed is alive and still lives in Sinjar. We follow his directions half a dozen streets until we turn onto a well-lit street with larger homes. With further help, we reach a two-story house with red-and-orange walls and a black double-door entrance.

I ring the doorbell, and moments later a child opens the door and greets us in the Yezidi Kurdish dialect. I ask if this is Khairo's house, and the boy nods.

Khairo appears. He's tall, muscular, and has broad shoulders. His thick hands have performed a great deal of manual labor over the years. He doesn't seem to recognize us. He greets us under his thick mustache, and as soon as I tell him who we are, he lunges forward and gives each of us a warm and tight hug.

"Your father and I had a great friendship," he says, squeezing my hand firmly. He inspects me under the entrance's light. "Let me see your face closer. You take after your father, mercy on his soul. Come on in. My house is full of light now."

Khairo sits on the sofa with his head tilted back, his eyes red and watery as Jamil and I recount the events of our captivity and the circumstances that led us to his doorstep. At some point, he is so emotional that he can't get up to receive the plate of water glasses from his daughter at the door, so Jamil has to get up and take it.

We enjoy the luxury of a peaceful dinner at his house: rice and chicken with soup and fresh bread. For the first time in ten days, I get to take a bath. Khairo gets us a new set of clothes, and although the pants are a bit too long for me, they'll do. We are determined to leave at night, but Khairo knows better, suggesting that we instead leave in the morning when the laborers are out and about so we don't draw any suspicion.

Our beds are quickly set up, and Khairo tells us he has a plan in place and that we just need to trust him, my dad's *kreev*, the Yezidi best friend.

In the morning after breakfast, the three of us head out to the door, and when Khairo sees our shoes, he declares that we need new ones. This means stopping at a nearby store. He is determined to stick with us until our destination. He and his car, he says, are at our disposal.

What have we done to deserve this? What kind of bond did my dad build with Khairo for him to be so committed to us? His satisfaction in serving us is obvious in every step he takes and in every word he utters.

The plan, he tell us in a rather timid tone, is simple, although to my ears it carries layers of risk. "It is risky to go to Duhok under the current circumstances, so the safest alternative is Zakho. I know people who can take you there. I don't trust anyone to deliver the news to your uncle in Duhok, so I'll do it myself."

In the main market, he buys us new pairs of shoes and disappears inside a store for quite some time before stepping out with a medium-built man wearing a white dishdasha and a red-checkered scarf over his head. His distant cousin, as Khairo introduces him to us, has secured a construction contract outside Zakho and was scheduled to take several of his workers there tomorrow to start, but he'll gladly go today.

I don't like his cousin's body language—he's actively avoiding eye contact—but I decide to let Khairo take on that battle. I don't care as long as he gets us to Zakho with no questions asked.

Khairo whispers his instructions in my ear: stay calm at security checkpoints, and tell them you're laborers and forgot your IDs at home.

He takes off in his car and drives toward Duhok to tell my uncle we're coming while his cousin takes us through the busy market to pick up workers before heading to Zakho.

30

Azad

Zakho, Duhok Governate, September 6, 1988

Per Khairo's instructions, his cousin drops us off at the Zakho market and drives off without a word. Jamil and I soon disappear into the crowd and enter the market near the meat section. Fresh blood mixed with recently poured water runs down the middle of the worn-out concrete walkway. Earlier in the day, this market would have been packed with customers in pursuit of the freshest of meats, but right now one mostly sees lonely left-overs of beef and lamb hanging from hooks.

A friend of mine, Hisham, used to attend school with me in Duhok but moved to Zakho when his family was forced to relocate a few years ago over a tribal conflict. Since we plan to meet my uncle and his trustee Farhan after dark, we have some time to burn, and Hisham will take good care of us.

I see him at his shop wearing a blood-stained apron. He drops his butcher knife when he sees us and hugs me. I trust him enough to tell him a short version of our story, and he shares that some of his close relatives have also been taken from their villages, their whereabouts still unknown.

He sticks his head out of the shop, looks both ways, then returns. "Are you guys going to stay here or leave town? It's not safe to be walking around. If you get caught, you're dead." As if we didn't already know that.

We're hungry, so he hurriedly cleans his shop, closes it, and takes us to a small low-profile sandwich hut outside the market. After we eat, I stop Hisham near a stand that sells cheap electronics. I pick a simple black electronic wristwatch, search my pocket for my money, then realize I gave all of it to Abd.

A heavy voice behind me calls out, "Hey, you." My knees immediately feel weak.

"Hi, officer," Hisham says.

The world turns dark. Sweat drips down my forehead and underarms. I'm frozen in place as the same angry voice grows closer.

"You! How many times have we told you not to leave your stupid stand here and block the corner? Move your shit or we'll confiscate it next time. Got it?"

I muster enough courage to turn around. A middle-aged owner of a nearby stand begins packing his stuff. The two police officers in dark-blue uniforms walk away, and my lungs fill with air again.

Hisham quickly pays for the watch I'm still holding and smiles as he takes my arm and leads us away.

"Was it worth the risk?" Jamil whispers on our way out of the market. "I almost had a heart attack!" I look at my wristwatch again. We have somewhere important to be, and Hisham will be our safest escort to Farhan's house.

"It will be dark before we know it," Jamil says, anxious as ever. "We need to be off the streets."

I do my best to tell Hisham where Farhan's house is as told to us by Khairo.

Hisham nods. "I think I know where that is."

When we arrive at Farhan's house, my uncle's car is already parked in front of it. We thank Hisham for his kindness and especially for the watch as I look at it once more and appreciate how easy it is to shift between the time and date. Too bad it didn't also come with a compass. Hisham gives us each a warm hug and wishes us a safe journey forward.

He takes out a handful of dinars and starts flipping through them. "From a friend to a friend. We are what we are when we live for each other." He hands me a roll of bills.

I pat him on the shoulder and say, "You have already done a lot for us." I gently push his hand back, declining the money. He insists, but I give him another hug and say, "We will be fine. Trust me, I would have taken the money if we needed it."

Hisham says his goodbyes one more time and disappears in the dark alley. A few kids are still roaming around the dark street and bad-mouthing each other. Jamil turns to me to verify that we're at the right house, then rings the bell.

When we enter the living room, Mam Khorsheed jumps to his feet and embraces us with teary eyes and a broken voice. I finally realize the magnitude of what has happened to us and what may still be awaiting us. We've been in survival mode for ten days, and it shielded us from despair and hopelessness.

For the next two hours, Jamil and I recount the details of our captivity and escape. Mam Khorsheed's emotions settle down a bit. He fills his pipe with expensive tobacco, and the room fills with clouds of smoke as Jamil joins him. Mam Khorsheed listens attentively with special interest to every name we can remember from the fort, dutifully jotting notes down.

Jamil and I press Mam Khorsheed again for any information concerning the whereabouts of our family.

He shifts in his seat, fixes the hat and scarf over his head, and says, "I used all my connections to get some answers, but so far all I know is that some of the village people left for the mountains toward Turkey while others got trapped behind enemy lines." He sucks on the pipe. "I have not been able to confirm anything that happened in the Nizarki Fort."

"But we were there and would have seen our family if they were there," I say.

We discuss every possible scenario that could have led Mam Yasin and our ladies to make a desperate decision when we failed to show up on time. Our host enters the room with another round of tea. Who's counting?

"I've checked with my sources," Farhan says, "and most of the people in your area headed to refugee camps in Turkey near Mardin and Diyarbakir. Things are still not clear, but I know some of them have already arrived."

Jamil turns to Mam Khorsheed and asks, "Have they taken people anywhere else besides Nizarki?"

The answer to that of course is yes! The bigger question, for which there is no good answer, is where?

Mam Khorsheed stirs his cup of tea with a metal teaspoon, making the thick layer of sugar rise from the bottom like a tornado before dissolving in the dark liquid. It looks like how I've been feeling lately.

My uncle has never gone through this much tobacco in one night. We argue back and forth. We should remain in the area until things become clearer. No, we should cross into Turkey. Finally, Jamil stands and makes a decision.

"We are leaving for Turkey. I need to find my pregnant wife and the rest of the family, and that's not going to happen if we sit here and argue."

All eyes are on him now as he paces the room, clicking his fingers and scratching his hair. I think it's probably the right call, but I'm still not entirely convinced.

He looks at my uncle and says, "Mam, where else would they go? Our home region was empty when we saw it from afar, and they are too smart to sit there and get killed while waiting for us to return."

The entire room feels calmer now. It's as if everyone felt it was the right decision all along but didn't want to commit to it. So Turkey it is. That is where the family is. It's where we'll find Mother, Dilveen, Shireen, Mam Yasin, and Juwan. Turkey is where Jamil will reunite with his pregnant wife and see his son born.

The grandfather clock in the far corner of the guest room announces the onset of a new hour. It's midnight. Now we have to plan.

Mam Khorsheed takes out his notebook and starts drawing a rough map of the area deep inside Turkey. I have never been there, but Jamil visited once when we were a lot younger. Mam Khorsheed reviews the route we'll need to take and the alternatives in case we find trouble. Farhan recites the names of the villages that are known to be friendly and those that are hostile and known for Turkish Jandarma military posts.

All I can think about right now is our reunion with the family. I can feel my mother's hands in my hair as she pulls my head closer to her. Her black-and-white checkered scarf covers my face, announcing that I'm in my mother's world, safe, sound, and never to walk away again. Not for school. Not for the city. Not for anything. I kiss her hands, and they smell of onions, garlic, and every grain and vegetable she's cooked with thousands of times over the years.

Jamil snaps me out of my reverie by announcing it's time to leave. He is determined despite Mam Khorsheed's reservations.

Farhan's wife packs enough food for us to last several days, and Jamil and I divide it between two green military bags, each with a full canteen strapped to the side. I look at my wristwatch, realizing again how much I miss having a compass.

"One thing I want to make sure you don't forget about, Uncle," I say.

He sucks in a dose of lung poison, lets out thick clouds of smoke through his nostrils and says, "About that boy? What's his name? Raqeeb?"

Jamil is outside now and noticeably irritated, but I answer my uncle with a serious voice. "Yes, his name is Raqeeb. We promised that we would come back for him. In case something happens to us or we don't return, I need you to bring him back."

31

Azad

Iraqi-Turkish border, September 1988

B orders have never made any sense to me. On a map, a solid line seems to indicate tangible differences between countries. On the ground, though, aside from the border markings and the presence of patrols on each side, one would never be able to tell if this land is Iraq or Turkey. For two weeks, Jamil and I have walked this land in all directions, and only the actions of the people who live here seem foreign to us.

We finally reach a village that Farhan told us is friendly, and he was right. The village folk welcome us with open arms, and it soon becomes apparent that we aren't the only outsiders they've encountered lately. They feed us, allow us to rest overnight, and make no attempt to urge us to stay longer. They understand that we're running away from an enemy and searching for our loved ones. We gracefully replenish our food and water and head farther east, where we are told we'll see masses of refugees within a day's walk.

We are slowed in the afternoon by a Jandarma patrol that holds us at gunpoint for a few hours, then forces us to cross the Little Khabur River to the Iraqi side. There's no point arguing when communication is one way and guns are the language. Along the way, we encounter a family of ten, including two infants and an elderly man who needs help to walk. Jamil and I grab his shoulders, easing the burden on the two exhausted young men. We stop at the edge of the valley, which proves to be a mistake. The temperature drops like a stone after midnight, exposing our shortage of blankets and jackets.

The next morning, we share what is left of our food, and around noon we join thousands of other refugees scattered on the Iraqi side of the border. Eventually we lose the family we arrived with in the crowd.

Children are crying. Their exhausted mothers try to console them when hungry, reassure them when scared, and curse them when causing chaos. Jamil and I scan every face, every moving body, and every sound for any signs of our own family members. There must be at least ten thousand people on this side of the border with hundreds more on the opposite side being pushed and shoved by the Jandarma.

Jamil asks every man he comes across if he knows Haji Yasin. Many do, but no one has seen him. Jamil asks about his in-laws as we make our way down the hill toward the water. An old man carrying a load of wood shows little interest in helping us at first, but a cigarette gets him sitting on the ground and thinking harder. According to a man he knows, Jamil's father-in-law and his family were granted permission to cross the water earlier because they had a sick pregnant woman with them. That was last week. Jamil's jaw drops, and his eyes widen with interest.

The man demands another cigarette.

Jamil hands out cigarettes to the refugees like candy, but no one else has seen or heard anything about Mam Yasin crossing here.

We spend the next sixteen days among this mass of refugees, bouncing between the mountainous Iraqi side and the open fields of the Turkish side. Each time we cross, Turkish soldiers spot us and force us back.

Finally, the Jandarma open the border, and we join a flood of exhausted, hungry, thirsty, pale, and scared humans through the checkpoint. Once on the other side, we are forced to organize into lines and to sit down and wait for a few dozen trucks to arrive. When they do, the Jandarmas fire a few shots in the air and load us onto the backs of the trucks like cattle.

Our driver, a young Kurdish man, steps onto the top of his truck to adjust the antenna. "Where are they taking us?" I ask.

He takes a deep breath, his thick shoulders rippling with muscle as he fixes the antenna, dried white circles of sweat extending under his arms. "They have camps set up for you all. Thank God the foreign journalists and international community came. Otherwise, you would have died here."

"So where exactly are you supposed to be taking us?" Jamil says.

The driver steps down to the ground. He looks around to make sure no Jandarma are watching. "I'm not sure yet. We've been gathering refugees in this area for the past few days, and there are already some in Diyarbakir and Mardin plus a few other smaller sites. I'm really not sure, and I can get in trouble for talking too much."

We are all forced down against each other as the truck starts to move. The metal walls extend above us and create a rectangular window onto the sky. A large white cloud hangs above us as we bounce up and down on the rocky drive. It looks as if the persistent cloud is trying to bring down a piece of cotton to cover our wounds, but they're so deep that even we don't know where they are.

A little boy looks like he's going to throw up, so one of his idiot parents lifts him up so he can vomit over the side. The wind blows it right back at us, leading to angry rants and curses.

Jamil grabs my hand and asks, "Do you think we made a mistake coming with them?"

"What do you mean?"

"Well, we stayed here this long, and there's still no news of our family. Maybe we should have kept going."

With an empty stomach and a tired body, it doesn't take much to trigger me, and this conversation all by itself is enough to make me get angry at him.

"How many times are you going to ask me this stupid question, Jamil?" I bury my head between my knees and curse at no one in particular. "Look, with no food and water, we would have probably died out there. You heard the man earlier. Your in-laws went somewhere in this area."

Jamil shakes his head, beads of sweat running down his forehead.

"Who is to say that they aren't where we're headed?"

The truth is that I barely believe what I'm saying. Deep inside, I'm terrified to find out what really happened to our family. Jamil is looking for answers, but I'm avoiding them. Thinking about it makes me sick to my stomach.

The truck slows, and I find myself dry heaving. I stand up and stick my head over in case I vomit, but my empty stomach has nothing to bring up. We are passing through a village and notice that several women dressed in Kurdish clothes are busy baking fresh bread, not too far off the road.

As the trucks slow further, several village men and women throw pieces of bread into the backs of the trucks. I hear an old lady shout, "God be with you. May God claim your right from those responsible for this. Go. God be with you."

It's well past dark when the trucks stop again next to a wire fence that's still under construction. The driver opens the door in back, and it makes a loud crashing sound as it drops.

When we carefully step off, the driver whispers, "This will be your camp."

Jamil asks, "Where are we?"

"Just outside Mardin."

The Jandarma lead us past the fence and onto a large field where many tents are lined up. The night is chilly, and the children, now tired, scared, and hungry, are constantly crying. The trucks take off, and it's just us, the open land, the lonely night, the wind, and the Jandarma.

32

Juwan

Hesenlu, Iran, September 1988

Our first week in this town has been uneventful so far. Our hosts have been kind and generous. Shukriya is a sweet lady who has opened her heart for us. The house might be average in size, but it's bigger than anything we ever could have owned back in the village.

We have been staying in one of the bedrooms on the main floor, but Mistekhan insists that Segvan must find us a place, even if it's tiny, so we don't keep bothering them. Shukriya says she's against the idea, but we know she's just being a good host.

We can't continue to sleep in a room right across from

the hosts' bedroom. Segvan has been cleaning the storage room upstairs, and this sounds like a reasonable setup until we can stand on our feet. But for me, none of this matters. Life has no taste anymore. Not even with food, water, and a new life in a new country with new people who are kind and hospitable. I left my father behind several feet underground, deep in the mountains where his soul is surely lonely.

Mistekhan and the girls are hurting—I can feel it—but they don't want to show it. I feel everyone's eyes on me. Segvan always asks me how I'm doing before he asks the other three. He keeps reassuring me that if I ever want to visit my dad's grave, he'll take me, no matter what.

Another week passes, and we start to feel more comfortable as we settle in the room upstairs.

At dinner, Segvan sits across from us on the floor. Mistekhan finishes the small amount of food she put on her plate. "My son," she says, "you don't know how thankful we are for all that you and your wife have done for us. This is beyond kind."

Before Segvan answers, Shukriya puts a chicken leg on Mistekhan's plate. "You're family now, so please, enough with the formalities."

Mistekhan smiles, something we rarely see nowadays. "I know, I know. You are great people, but my son, Segvan, it's time that we try to take care of ourselves."

Segvan finishes his plate and rests his back against the couch. "I am here to help with anything. What do you need?"

"Can you find us jobs?" Shireen says. Her sharp blue eyes carry more seriousness than her words. She is firm and to the point, as she always has been.

Dilveen nods in agreement. I put my spoon down and reposition myself but keep my silence.

Segvan places a cigarette between his lips and motions for Shukriya to hand him his lighter from the table. "I've thought about this but wanted to wait until you all feel comfortable with it. Your status here is not legal, so we have to be careful." After a moment of silence, he adds, "I have a few places in mind that I will look into."

When we start to move the empty plates off the floor, he turns to me and says, "Juwan, do you also want to work? Perhaps you can rest a bit longer and then we will find you a job."

I leave the room without saying anything, but I hear Mistekhan say, "Maybe she needs to go out to feel better. She would benefit from a job too."

33

Azad

Mardin refugee camp, Turkey, early October 1988

It took Jamil and me over a week to settle in. We spent the first few days in the open in conditions worse than those on the mountain. Many people demanded to be taken back. Brand-new tents were folded near us, but the Jandarma wouldn't let us touch them. Then one day, workers came and put together the rest of the camp. Now it's properly inhabited.

Surrounded by barbed wire, it consists of long rows of large tents divided into two sections. Each tent is assigned to twenty to thirty people. Most families are large and have figured out arrangements, but conflict occasionally erupts when multiple smaller families with female members are forced to share the same section.

It's hot and sandy during the day and chilly and windy at night. Every day, more trucks arrive, unloading more people who look as exhausted, scared, and malnourished as we did when we arrived. Jamil and I have searched every occupied tent for our family, Jamil's in-laws, or any familiar faces. So far no luck.

The two of us share a tent with fourteen other men, all single or missing family members. We removed the partition inside the tent, creating more room to move around. We only recognize one of the men from the mountain, and none of our roommates are from the villages surrounding our home.

The city of Mardin is located in southeast Turkey about two hundred and fifty kilometers from Duhok. Although we are outside the city, we are in the "Mardin camp." We hear that there are at least two more refugee camps, one in Diyarbakir and the other in Mushe, giving us new hope that we'll find our family.

Over the next week or so, plumbing is installed for drinking and cooking water. A fight erupts when a few men approach the camp officials requesting private areas for bathrooms. The Jandarma fire shots in the air after we gather in protest. It pays off because the next day they start building a set of bathrooms, which always seem to be occupied.

Today, after lunch, we lie down in our tent, and Jamil says, "I want to talk to the camp officials about finding our family."

I laugh, but he gets up and starts pacing, restless and irritated.

"Jamil, look around you. How many people are here? Ten thousand maybe? At least. How many are missing a family member or relative? Do you think the camp officials know who we are or care what we're looking for?"

My words fly over his head. One of our roommates returns from the restrooms and notices Jamil's anxious demeanor. He makes a feeble attempt at humor, but I wave him away. In a nearby tent, a child is crying and a tired woman curses and says she wishes God had taken her life instead of bringing her here. A naked little boy rushes into our tent and immediately turns around and runs out when he realizes he is in the wrong place. Once outside, he starts crying.

I get up, but Jamil says, "Leave him. That kid is always lost."

I cross my hands under my head and close my eyes for some much-needed rest. Later, Jamil frantically shakes me awake. "Get up, Azad! Let's go!"

I open my eyes, then quickly jump to my feet. "*Bismillah*, what in God's name happened, man?"

He runs out of the tent saying, "I heard his voice. It's my father-in-law!"

34

Dilveen

Hesenlu, Iran, October 1988

Segvan knocks on our door around noon during lunch and calls out Mother's name. I open the door, and he is standing there with a wide smile on his face.

"I found you two a job," he says. "A good job."

I crack the door wide open as my mother invites him in. He passes by me without acknowledging my presence and takes a seat next to Mother. He seems a little too comfortable in our place. Yes, it's technically his place, but something about his demeanor today doesn't sit well with me.

"There's a poultry farm between here and Urmia," he says. "The manager is a good friend, and I've been able to get the two of you jobs there packaging chicken for restaurants."

I'm taken aback by how matter of factly he says only "two of you," but then I remember his previous discussion about giving Juwan more time to grieve and rest.

Mother smiles and says, "That's good news, my son."

Across the room, Shireen is throwing looks at me, and I immediately get her hint. "So this job is for Shireen, me, and Juwan?"

He leans against the wall and clears his throat. "No, only you and your sister. I thought Juwan needs more time to feel better."

"I think I'm OK now," she says. "I'd like to work."

"Yes, she needs it," Shireen says. "Can we find her a spot with us?"

Segvan thinks briefly, then heads toward the door. "I'm sorry," he says to Juwan. "I didn't know this was how you felt, but as of now they only need two. When I see the guy, I'll ask him about an additional spot."

Segvan steps out of the room, puts his shoes on, then sticks his head in again. "Please remember, your job is to go to work and come back with minimal interaction. I'll go with you tomorrow morning, so please be ready at eight."

The room is silent for a few minutes as we clear the dinner plates. Shireen avoids looking at me because she knows what I'm about to ask her. I stare at her, and she finally looks back at me.

"What?" she says. "Don't even think about asking me to be the one to stay home. I'll be changed and ready to go at fifteen minutes to eight. If you want Juwan to work so badly, you can give her your spot."

Juwan finishes stacking the plates on top of each other.

"You two don't have to fight over this. I'll look for a job if he doesn't find a spot for me. Please don't get upset over this."

She quietly walks out of the room with the plates, and mother immediately yells at Shireen. "Why do you always have to talk without any manners?"

I leave the room, too, and hear Segvan's voice downstairs. He's talking to Juwan, but I only catch the tail end of the conversation. "I'll find you a job," he says, then disappears outside.

In the kitchen, I ask Juwan, "What was he telling you?"

She rubs a sponge over a plate and says, "Nothing. He was just asking me if I really wanted a job, and I told him yes."

Moments later, Shukriya walks in carrying her youngest daughter, whose red cheeks scream illness. The poor thing stares back at me, unsatisfied with my curious looks, then pulls her head back into her mother's chest and closes her eyes. Juwan and I help Shukriya give the struggling child some fever medicine.

"Maybe you can ask your husband if the child needs a doctor," I say.

She laughs and leaves the kitchen, saying, "Like he cares about us."

I SUSPECT the neighbors know where we came from even though we're careful not to tell them. They seem okay with it, despite the dire picture Segvan has been painting for us. Segvan calls Hesenlu a town while Shukriya calls it a damn village. It has a population of around two thousand, maybe a little more, mostly scattered on either side of the main road not too far from where we are.

Most people I've seen so far wear variations of the Kurdish clothes we have grown up with, the men dressed in wide shalwal pants, shirts, plus or minus a vest, while women enjoy the colorful varieties of dresses and matching scarves tied to the back of their heads or under the chins. Farming is the main source of income here, which means a life of hard work and low economic status. We are half an hour or so from the legendary city of Urmia. A bus runs through here every hour during the day until eight at night and makes several stops between here and Urmia.

The poultry farm is halfway between Hesenlu and Urmia, just outside another town called Band. The farm is on the main road, and looking from outside, one can only see a small and narrow metal wall, but behind it is the farm with its massive, covered hall adjacent to a processing center.

Segvan accompanies us on our first day of work. We take the bus because he wants us to get used to the route.

"All you have to do is pay your money and sit on the bus and act like you've done it for years. When the bus stops at the poultry station, get out and walk to work." He looks calm, but I sense some stress in his voice.

The farm has a few dozen workers, mostly women. The men usually work the machines and other difficult labor. Shireen and I work in the coldest part of the factory alongside seven other women, packaging chicken in boxes to be taken to restaurants. After three days, we learn the job well enough that nobody needs to tell us what to do. We have the bus figured out, and we pay with exact change every time. We didn't need Segvan after the first day, and although we declined money from him, we borrowed money from Shukriya with a promise to pay her back once we are paid.

I keep to myself for the most part, but Shireen has already made a few friends, one of which is a middle-aged widow who's taking care of two teenage boys. Her name is Rasheeda, and she lives in Band, only one bus stop from here. Shireen already knows her life story. According to Shireen, Rasheeda lost her husband during the Iran-Iraq War, but his pension is yet to be approved because the government claims he is not dead but rather a prisoner of war.

A week passes, and Segvan still has no answer for Juwan about a job. He says he's spoken with our farm manager, but they don't need any more help now. Shireen thinks he's lying, but when has Shireen ever trusted anyone?

Just before Segvan leaves on his next smuggling trip, Mother begs him to ask around for news on Jamil and Azad. He promises us that he will. Juwan asks him again about a job opportunity, and he also promises that he'll address it when returns.

While Segvan is away, we are back to eating meals with Shukriya and helping her with chores. She's a beautiful twenty-six-year-old Kurdish woman from a small town northeast of Urmia. Her hazel eyes tend to look past me when I'm speaking to her, as if she's looking at something that isn't there. "After three children, I've gotten fat," she says, but I tend to think her new curves make her prettier.

Her father used to be a rich Persian rug merchant and exporter. When I ask her why there are no Persian rugs in her home, she says, "My husband is not the type of man who will spend on his house."

With Mother withdrawn to her room to read the Quran,

the rest of us four girls chit-chat over tea. Juwan pours some and asks Shukriya how she met her husband and if there was a love story involved.

Shukriya slaps her wrist and laughingly says, "At first, yes. I thought he was the knight who will take me to my dream land, but it didn't turn out that way."

"Isn't that the story of every Kurdish woman?" Shireen asks. "I've yet to meet a woman who is happy with her marriage."

"Stop being negative," Juwan says, "and let Shukriya finish her story."

Shukriya tells us about her youth and how she lived a luxurious life. She's the youngest of four children, the only daughter, and her father's favorite. Segvan randomly showed up in her life when her father hired him to work in his warehouse after he moved from another city. No one knew his origin, and he claimed that his folks had died in a fire when he was an infant, forcing him to move between foster families and orphanages.

"My father always admired a man who could stand up to hardship and refuse to be broken, maybe because he himself grew up in poverty."

We listen attentively as Shukriya tells us about the day her father told her that she would be marrying Segvan. She had little to say as she always looked up to her father and thought he knew what was best for her. Despite her older brother's reservations, her father insisted that she marry the man who had turned his life around and made something of himself when everything was stacked against him.

Her father passed away soon after her wedding. Conflict erupted between Segvan and Shukriya's older brother, who decided that things needed to be run differently in the business. They got into a fistfight, after which Segvan came home and demanded they pack and move away. There was no room for negotiation or even communication. Segvan was determined to move, and her older brother was not someone to change his mind or give in. This was more than five years ago, and Segvan hasn't spoken to her brother or visited the family ever since.

RASHEEDA PROVES MORE helpful than I gave her credit for. Although she's not able to get Juwan a job at the farm, she suggests reaching out to a Kurdish lady named Zozan in Band who teaches at the local school and needs help with household chores. Rasheeda arranges for us to meet Zozan at her house.

So one day while Segvan is away on a smuggling trip, we meet up with Juwan at the bus stop after work and ride with Rasheeda to Zozan's house. It's a two-story brick building with a layer of marble over the entrance door, the nicest house I've seen since our arrival, but Rasheeda claims her brother's house on the other side of town is even better.

Zozan is a slim, tall lady in her late twenties, elegantly dressed, and with the classy and calm demeanor of someone in her forties. We are served tea and cookies as Zozan describes her needs and asks Juwan some questions. Zozan doesn't seem interested in where we are from or even who we are for that matter. I suspect Rasheeda has already filled her in. Regardless, it works. Juwan will start in two days. She will work three days a week, on Saturdays, Mondays, and Thursdays, cleaning the house and cooking certain meals when asked. She will be paid for six hours no matter how long she stays. Juwan agrees with a wide smile.

On the bus ride home, Shireen says, "Hey, Juwan, did you even ask her about the pay?"

Juwan is looking through the window as animals, bystanders, electrical poles, and cars sweep by. Without looking away, she answers, "I didn't ask and won't ask. Whatever she pays, I will be happy."

At home, a thought suddenly hits me. "What about Segvan?"

"What about him?" asks Shukriya.

"We never asked him about this job. What if it ends up being a problem? What if he has another job lined up?"

Shukriya picks up her youngest daughter as she crawls toward the stairs. "Don't you worry about him."

35

Azad

Mardin Refugee Camp, Turkey, October 1988

Jamil's ears were not lying to him when he said he recognized his father in-law's voice. We spot Husain Ziway at the end of our row of tents, carrying a jacket in one hand and a ragged bag of clothes in the other. The excitement is instant. Jamil runs to his father-in-law with a long and warm exchange. We soon notice other members of the family emerging down the aisle and from behind another row of tents. They look tired and dazed, walking in a state of confusion and fatigue. Jamil runs in the direction of his wife, who breaks down crying and falls to her knees. More people appear, creating a commotion. I stand and inspect every face with focused eyes. Behind Berivan, her mother, her brother, with his wife and children, plus an older couple line up next to a tent, taking in Jamil's reception while I look around beyond and past them. I don't see Mother or my sisters or Juwan or Mam Yasin. My chest rises faster with every emerging face proving to be a stranger.

I barely manage to offer a greeting to Berivan and turn to Jamil, who now looks up at me and asks, "Do you see them around? Do you see Mother and the girls?"

His face quickly loses its excitement when I shake my head in silence. He turns back to his wife. She beats us to the question.

"Is your family here?" She drops the question, which casts a deep wave of worry on us.

"What do you mean? They would be with you, wouldn't they?" Jamil says in a rather angry tone.

Berivan lowers her head in silence, realizing that something has gone terribly wrong. Husain Ziway clears his throat a few times, and both Jamil and I turn around, a demanding look obvious on our faces.

He quickly narrates their story from the moments they left the village and their last encounter with our family. At this point, his words start to fly over my head, the only image hovering around my head is that of my mother, my two sisters, Juwan, and her father being stranded somewhere out there, where the possibility of survival is very low considering the circumstance under which they left the village and fell behind. We follow Husain Ziway's detailed narratives with our numb minds while Berivan stands next to Jamil, gently rubbing his arm, her eyes full of tears as her father continues.

"We were picked up by the Jandarma near a village

where some of our relatives were. Berivan at that time had recovered from some early pregnancy contractions or what a local midwife diagnosed as only exhaustion. Along with some hundred other refugees, we were trapped on the Turkish side for weeks until we were eventually picked up and brought to this camp. We did look for your family and continued to ask around. I assure you of that."

Husain Ziway's last words are pleas for us to believe him. All I can muster, though, is painful silence. I stand outside by the tent long after everyone around me eases into their respective places, refusing to give in to Jamil's request to come inside.

EVEN THOUGH IT'S the middle of October, the miserable heat feels like August. The camp appears to finally be at capacity, with more than half the inhabitants children and teenagers. Electrical wires feed a single light bulb in each tent. The ground is dry, and when it's windy like it was yesterday, waves of sand and dirt swirl and eddy through the air, blinding what's left of our vision and choking our sickened lungs.

Next to the camp in an open area, a group of men spent the last few days clearing the area of rocks and other debris. Now more than a hundred of us have gathered for the Friday prayer. A young man wearing a torn shalwal stands facing the direction of Mecca and calls for prayer. An elderly man confidently stands in front of us, assuming the role of the imam. He rubs his hand over his gray beard, and in a soft and confident tone reminds us that Allah is not punishing us, nor has he abandoned us. This is a test from the divine power. A test of our patience, our faith in his glory and wisdom, and our trust in our leaders. Few of us would dare question God, but I have no doubt there will be heated arguments over lunch about our leaders.

We sit there with pale faces and sad eyes, trying to hold on Mala's hopeful words. For most of the underfed and poorly clothed humans inside these barbed wire fences, hope is worth a fortune. For me, though, it dwindles every day. By the end of the sermon, sweat is running down my back and my armpits. The sun is still strong overhead.

We disperse and head back to our tents.

Last night, I woke up from a nightmare where my sisters and Juwan were burning in a valley raging with fire, screaming from the top of their lungs while Jamil and I wandered around in the mountains oblivious to what was taking place below. I was soaked in sweat when I woke, but as much as I hated the nightmare, I wanted to go back to sleep and return to that scene. I wanted to at least glance toward the valley to let my sisters and Juwan know I noticed them and heard their cries. Most important, I wanted to find out where my mother was. I pressed my eyelids shut, but sleep refused to touch them.

AFTER THEIR ARRIVAL, Husain Ziway and his family took a tent not too far from ours. Berivan looks as pregnant and as exhausted as could be. Jamil lets her stay with her family and near her mother, mainly because he is concerned she may go into labor at any time and also because we simply can't come up with a good enough system to share space and maintain privacy. He says he will not leave my side until we find the rest of our family. His happiness to be reunited with his wife, even under the worst of circumstances, makes it easier for him to make individual concessions.

Inside Husain Ziway's tent, we gather for Friday communal lunch. Typically, in the good days back home that now feel like a distant past, Friday lunch was the most celebrated gathering of the week. Families enjoyed a special meal while most businesses shut down. In this camp, however, we have only poor-quality rice, beans, and bread. I haven't seen any vegetables or fruits yet. We hear rumors that small stoves may be distributed later, but I'll believe in such luxury only when I see the long-promised shoes and clothing. Most children still walk around barefoot.

Over lunch, Husain Ziway tells us there are other camps in the area. A seasoned Peshmerga fighter, he has a network of people going back many decades. He knows most of the men in this camp, either personally or through their extended network of family and friends.

"Yes, uncle," Jamil says, "we heard that Diyarbakir is the major one."

Husain Ziway puts his spoon down, says a few prayers, then adds, "Yes, and the other camp is in Mushe."

Jamil turns to me and says, "OK, Azad, let's find a way to leave this camp and look for them."

On the other side of the tent where the women sit, Jamil's mother-in-law says in a loud voice we all hear, "Now calm down, you two, we can't believe we finally found you alive. My daughter went through a lot of misery and sleepless nights while we wondered about her man."

Husain Ziway repositions himself, extends his legs, and answers without turning to her. "Woman, you look here. These guys need to find their families as much as your daughter needed to find her husband. Stay out of this conversation, and don't put your nose where it doesn't belong."

A few awkward moments pass, and I say, "I think she has a point, Jamil. I'll find a way to go. You need to stay with your wife."

Jamil is visibly annoyed. "No way you're going alone. My foot on your foot, period."

We both look at Husain Ziway for further advice. "I think we should wait another week or so to find a safe way out of here, then we'll make a run for it. I know this area well, and we should leave before the November snows."

"Great," Jamil's mother-in-law says. "Now he wants to go too."

36

Juwan

Hesenlu, Iran, October 1988

My first day of work falls on a Saturday, only two days after we met with Zozan. I take the bus at six thirty and reach Zozan's residence a little before seven as instructed, before she and her husband head out to work.

Zozan opens the door with sleepy eyes. I hesitate for a few seconds, then follow her into the house as she hurries upstairs, leaving me behind and alone in the messy family room. I stand there motionless as her two children run up and down the stairs looking for books, pencils, socks, and other stuff they seem obviously stressed out over. A family portrait hangs on the wall leading to the family room. A man upstairs announces his presence as he clears his throat. He must be Zozan's husband.

A young, medium-built man, shaved and neatly dressed in a brown suit and white shirt, slowly and calmly comes down the stairs, the exact opposite of Zozan a few minutes earlier. Halfway down, he turns toward the second floor and shouts something in Persian before heading back down. He walks by me without saying a word. Zozan soon walks downstairs wearing a long brown dress with a white scarf.

She gently grabs my hand, pulls me toward the kitchen, and says, "As you can see, my life is a mess. Please start out by helping me put together a quick breakfast for my husband and the kids. Do you know how to make eggs?"

She doesn't wait for my response. Soon, the fridge door is wide open, and I am next to her preparing breakfast. Not the start I had in mind, but I will take this over a formal, bossy woman.

Zozan's husband, I soon learn, moved here from Tehran, where the two of them met during college. He was posted here last year as the principal of the newly opened elementary school, but he understands Kurdish very well, she has warned me. His family had an issue with him marrying a Kurdish girl, and they never fully embraced Zozan—even more reason for them to move away.

On my second work day, Zozan asks me to come four days a week when possible. My cooking is better than hers, she claims, and her house has never been this clean. I must admit that I have never had to clean toilets and tile floors before, and most of it is new to me, but Zozan wants her house's havoc undone when she comes home, and however I make that happen, she's happy. Her husband forced her to let go of the last three women, one of whom was Rasheeda, for different reasons, although it appears Rasheeda kept pushing Zozan's husband to go with her to various government agencies to ask about her missing soldier husband. I can't wait to tell Shireen about her best friend's adventure at Zozan's house, although I feel bad that she's in such a desperate strait.

Ten days after I started working for Zozan, I'm walking home from the bus stop around six in the evening. The end of October is near, and the days are getting shorter, but it's not dark yet. Kids are still playing on the streets, and a few shoppers are hurrying to get home in time for dinner preparations. Zozan paid me for the first time today, and I still have no clue about the currency here and whether or not she's paying me fairly. But she has been fair to me so far, and I can't imagine that she would cheat me.

I stop by the small market down the street from our house and put some potatoes in one bag and tomatoes and a dozen eggs in another. The owner is an old Kurdish guy, but I'm not interested in talking with him. I hand him all the money I have in my hand. He stares at me like I've lost my mind. Zozan must have paid me well. He takes one of the bills from my hand, then reaches into his drawer for some coins and hands them to me. I take my change and groceries bags and walk home.

I find Segvan standing by the door with his back against the wall. He is wearing fine jeans and a colorful long-sleeve shirt, his thick hair pulled back and shiny from a generous amount of gel. He stares at me, studying my bags as I greet him. I assume he has just returned from his latest long trip, so I welcome him back.

"Where did you go?" he asks in a firm monotone.

I'm uncomfortable with the ambush, so I silently head

to the front door. He throws his cigarette butt away and clears his throat.

"Where are you coming from, Juwan?"

I explain to him that I was able to find a job, and I tell him who I work for and where. His facial expression changes, and he remains quiet for a few awkward moments. I wish night had already fallen so I could hide my face from his unsettling gaze.

His oldest daughter runs back home from the street. She pushes the door open. I follow the child to the door, but he shuts the door in my face.

"But why did you do that?" he says and smiles rather awkwardly. "I told you I would find you a good job. You just had to wait for me to come back from my trip."

Stay calm, Juwan. Don't be alarmed. He's just trying to help. I muster enough nerve to answer him, still unable to meet his gaze. "I appreciate it. You have done a lot for us. This was an opportunity that came up, and I hope you're OK with it. Plus, I asked Shukriya, and she said that's a nice town to work in."

I watch his grip on the door slowly loosen, so I push my way inside and head quickly up the stairs without looking back. I will try and forget about this face-off. I certainly won't share it upstairs.

Later that night, while eating dinner in our room, I hear a loud exchange downstairs, the first fight any of us have heard. Shukriya is yelling obscenities, and Segvan shouts back with some words I can't make out. Shireen gets up and opens the door, and Mistekhan tells her to stay out of it. Glass breaks, and we all look at each other in shock. With the door open, the argument is more audible now.

Shukriya screams, "I'm not the one who found her the

job! They asked you for a job for her, but you couldn't find one."

A few moments of silence give us only temporary relief until more glasses shatter and the children start crying.

Segvan yells again, louder this time. "I told her I would find her a job when I get back! How hard is that to understand?"

"Why do you care anyway? The girl has a job and a way to get her mind off her trouble. Why are you so interested in her work and her life?"

Silence ensues for a few minutes, then the front door slams hard.

Shireen is still by the door, looking at me. "They're fighting over your—"

"Shut up and close the door, you nosy idiot," Dilveen says.

The four of us remain in the room while dinner sits there unfinished. I feel a knot in my throat. My stomach starts to gurgle, and I have a hard time keeping my balance even sitting down. I close my eyes, rest my back against the wall, and drift into my own world. I must've fallen asleep right there because the next morning I wake up in the same spot with a pillow under my head.

For two days after the fight, none of us says anything to Shukriya. We rarely see Segvan, and when he is home, he's in the living room watching TV and yelling at the kids. One evening I walk down the stairs to use the bathroom, and when I get out, I find Segvan standing right there. His hair is unkempt, and his face appears tired. I try to walk around him, but he blocks me.

He steps closer to me and says, "You're too good to be a maid."

I ask him to please get out of my way, but he comes even closer. His breath stinks of tobacco and alcohol.

"Juwan, I'm sorry if I made you uncomfortable the other day, but I don't know why you went behind my back and found a job."

I look around nervously, praying that no one is looking or listening. He seems oblivious to how this looks. Perhaps it's the alcohol.

"As I said," I tell him, "this was an opportunity I couldn't pass up. Besides, you've done a lot for us already." I take a step sideways and free myself from his suffocating presence and run upstairs.

He calls my name, and I freeze halfway up the stairs.

"Juwan," he says, "anything for you."

On my way up, I catch a glimpse of the hallway downstairs and see Shukriya standing there, frozen.

Upstairs, I find Dilveen standing outside, her back against the closed door, her arms crossed over her chest.

"What did I just see?" she asks, failing to hold back her shock.

I wish I could disappear into the floor.

She gives me a gentle shove, whispering in an angry voice, "Juwan, what in the name of God just happened?"

I push her hand away. "I don't know, what do you want me to say? You heard him. I'm tired. Let me go and sleep and maybe I won't wake up."

37

Juwan

Hesenlu, Iran, November 1988

Another week passes, and not a single word from Shukriya. Every time I see her black eye, I feel a load of guilt knowing she sustained it because of me, although I didn't actually do anything.

Mistekhan is mostly quiet as usual. Shireen, on the other hand, is as suspicious of Segvan as ever. As for Dilveen and me, we choose to give Segvan the benefit of the doubt and think of this whole drama as a misunderstanding. We finally manage to reassure Shukriya that we are not here to cause any problems or create conflict between her and her husband. She feels embarrassed and admits she overreacted. Her husband had returned from a long trip and ignored her, and she was already on the verge of exploding. She just needed a trigger, and she's sorry that I was it.

Segvan has been gone for days now, and I suspect he's on another smuggling trip.

He returns a week later, and things have settled down. He's friendly with his wife and kids, but whether that's his norm, I don't know and can't tell. He's also formal with the rest of us, which we don't mind a bit.

Zozan's house is a mess every day. I can't fathom how a small family can turn things upside down in one night. I doubt Zozan lays a hand on anything in the house, especially since I started working for her. Nonetheless, I cherish every minute I spend in her house, every corner of it, with the four bedrooms and three bathrooms to maintain. Their living room and family sitting area would swallow our entire house back in the village. The family uses three bedrooms upstairs, and the fourth one, located on the first floor, is off limits. It's where Mr. Hasan's school records, college papers, and other family documents are.

I move around the house noiselessly as if someone is observing and judging my every move. Colorful vases are placed at various corners in the kitchen and living room. Since my arrival, they have all gone from empty, misplaced, and dry to full of flowers and life.

I take out the trash and spot a young couple walking side by side. My thoughts travel back to the village, and I remember you, Azad. I remember your smile and the silent looks each time you visited the village on a school break. This couple could have been you and me, somewhere, anywhere, even under a wet tent or on a hard rock or inside a dark cave. You put school first, and we both paid for it. I hope you are safe and that you can find your way back to us.

Wherever you are, once we reunite, you will learn that my father is no longer alive. He can't put his hand in yours and declare me your wife in the presence of witnesses and a religious authority. Our lives have been shattered, but I don't regret waiting for you all these years. Just come back for me. Come back for us.

I FIND myself apprehensive every time I reach the front door. I expect Segvan to be waiting for me or that he'll emerge from somewhere behind me as I step off the bus.

One night, we deliberate after Mistekhan falls asleep. The thought of staying in this house haunts me the more I think about Segvan.

Shireen doesn't hide her radical views. "I think we should find a way to return home and leave this dump of a place."

Dilveen and I frown at her suggestion. Shireen is sitting there with her knees pressed against her chest, avoiding eye contact with us and apparently thinking of the next bomb to drop on us. "I don't trust Segvan, and I don't feel comfortable with his looks. We have no place here and no life. How did we end up here?"

Downstairs, another argument erupts between Segvan and his wife. Shukriya screams, then her voice slowly disappears somewhere.

Shireen sighs deeply and shrugs her shoulders. "There they go again. He probably dragged her back to the room by her hair."

Dilveen shakes her head in frustration. "It's not like Shukriya is innocent. Do you hear how she always answers him back?"

Shireen gets up on her knees and leans toward Dilveen, but I intervene before she can say a word.

"Why are we even discussing this? Let's focus on our own problems and what we can do about them."

"Yes, Juwan," Shireen says. "Let's think about our problems. The guy makes you uncomfortable, and his wife is having a breakdown over it, so what are you going to do about it?"

Rain patters on the metal roof, changing the vibe in the room. I remind the others that we're on foreign land with my father already dead and my fiancé unaccounted for. We have nowhere to go and no one to turn to. "We should get our own place."

We run the idea past Mistekhan, then suggest it to Segvan the next morning. We expect him to refuse. We already know that he doesn't want us to struggle to pay rent, nor does he think going to a refugee camp is a viable option. The nearest one is a good three-hour drive from here, and conditions are miserable at best.

"I am not going to leave you all alone," he says. "You are like family to me now." He turns to Shukriya with a smile, then continues. "My wonderful wife and I have discussed this already, and I have just the place for you to stay." Shukriya nods. "I am half owner of a two-story apartment building not too far from here. The first floor needs major work, but you all can use the second floor. It has a separate entrance with a decent room and kitchen." From Segvan's words, this seems like a perfect place. And it's within walking distance, close enough if we ever had an emergency.

A SMALL METAL door leads to a dozen or so stairs up to the second floor, where a narrow hallway ends at another small wooden door. Inside, the setup reminds me of the simplicity of village life. The small living room overlooks the street through the exterior hallway above the main entrance. Two of us barely fit inside the kitchen. The bedroom is decent in size, but the bathroom and shower seem designed as an afterthought. The walls are bare concrete, and there is no paint or finishing touches, but the apartment is still an upgrade compared to what we had in the village. Considering the circumstances, it's a golden opportunity.

Segvan offers it to us for free, but we decline and agree to pay him an amount that's manageable if the three of us contribute.

We buy four cheap mattresses and four sets of blankets and pillows. Segvan buys us a small gas burner for the kitchen and a portable electric heater. We promise to pay him back the next time we get paid. Shukriya gives us some kitchen supplies, and we sleep our first night like we finally have a home of our own even if it doesn't belong to us and even though it's in a foreign land where we feel more distant from home than the stars in the sky.

NOVEMBER COMES to an end and the weather turns colder, bringing the first wave of snow. One morning, we wake to a white blanket covering the town. I look out through the window and see a few kids playing in the snow. An erratic snowball lands on the face of an elderly passerby, and he nearly falls. He chases the kids away, but this time he slips and falls for real, landing on his back. It is still very early in the morning, and there is no one around to help him up. I observe him through the window until he finally gathers enough strength to get up and walk gingerly. I wonder why he's out so early.

In BerAva, our village, we had one or two major snowstorms per year. All major roads in and out of the upper Barwari region shut down for days, if not longer. Men panicked and removed snow from the rooftops so they wouldn't collapse. We poured fresh date syrup over plates of snow and ate it until we lost our voices. Then the annual snow fight took place, and everyone was a fair target.

It's my off day, but I'm up at my usual time. I kick Dilveen's and Shireen's feet to wake them, careful to let Mistekhan sleep. Soon, they're changed and ready for work.

I head back to bed once Shireen and Dilveen leave for work and wrap myself with an extra blanket. The small heater is quickly proving to be insufficient. I manage to fall asleep anyway and wake when Mistekhan calls my name in a broken voice. I jump to my feet and find her soaked in sweat, whimpering. Her face is pale, lips dry and cracking, as she holds her hand over her left flank area in obvious pain.

"Where are you, girls?" Mistekhan calls out. "Get me some water."

I examine her forehead. She has a fever. I remove the covers, then run to the kitchen to get her some water. I rush through the snow and grab some fever medicine from

Shukriya at her house, then return to see Mistekhan shivering. Intermittent fevers and chills persist through the day. When Dilveen and Shireen get home from work, she's visibly exhausted and barely able to talk.

We have known of Mistekhan's issues with kidney stones for a while. Dilveen says she always used natural remedies, but this time is different. We take turns sitting up with her at night to make sure she's okay. The next day, Segvan drives us to a local clinic, where a urine test reveals an infection and an X-ray shows a large stone. Mistekhan gave us a scare, but a week of antibiotics and aggressive hydration manage to turn things around.

Her silent demeanor, however, remains unchanged.

38

Azad

Mardin Refugee Camp, Turkey, January–March 1989

O ur camp has been tested by rough weather twice
so far. The first and worst time was in late
November when a sudden snowstorm hit us at
night. The snow didn't stick, but it left behind frozen tents
and nine dead, seven of them infants and newborns.

We protested in front of the camp's central building,
nearly freezing to death. Two days later we were handed
more blankets and some winter clothes, mostly for the children and elderly.

Then on the first day of January, the sky opened its
floodgates and dumped the kind of rain we'd never seen

before. At least that's what it felt like. Dozens of tents flooded, their contents violently washing away. We tried to dig trenches around the tents to divert the water, but the heavy rains overwhelmed us. We stood and helplessly watched the angry water sweep away shoes, silverware, toys, and countless other scarce supplies and materials.

The Turkish Jandarma didn't help. They seemed to have only one mission: yelling at us from afar and pointing guns at anyone who approached them.

There is little administrative structure, so members of the camp itself stood up as leaders, including Husain Ziway. Everybody knows him and likes him. He has a natural drive to lead, and he clearly enjoys the attention and power. Always dressed neatly even with old and worn-out clothes, his traditional blue-and-white *shal u shapik* set adds an element of authority to his stature, broad shoulders, and thick mustache. He served for decades as a Peshmerga and knows the ins and outs of the Kurdish revolutionary forces.

Today at sunrise, he runs through the rows of tents, hitting them with his cane and demanding that all young men come outside.

"The ground is finally dry, and we have work to do. Everyone out. Every man. Show me your faces, and don't make me bring you out with the cane."

On the ground, he uses his cane to draw the layout of a system of trenches behind the tents to drain water down and away toward the fence. Using every possible tool at hand, we dig all around the tents, a dozen or so men assigned to each row. The ladies take turns cooking warm food and making hot tea delivered by the young boys and girls. Our mood is finally positive! Jamil's father-in-law sure can be aggressive, but we needed the whip to get the job done.

We fall asleep in the early evening, exhausted but proud of our efforts. Sometime after midnight, I'm startled by loud cries from a nearby tent. Jamil jumps to his feet and run out barefoot, mumbling repeatedly, "It's my wife. It's happening."

Shortly before dawn, the midwife announces: "It's a boy!" The first camp baby of 1989. We all congratulate Jamil, his tired and long-worried face decorated with a wide smile.

THE JANDARMA finally allow a few men to leave camp and restock as long as they're back before dark. Initially they bring back food, supplies, and clothing, but later some are allowed to do day work for minimal pay, a golden opportunity. Local citizens of Mardin, most of whom are Kurds, show solidarity and support, a glimpse of hope and love when otherwise surrounded by hate, discrimination, and psychological torture.

One of the first items brought back from outside the camp is a cradle for Jamil's baby, Wahid. Jamil knew all along that he would name his baby after my father if it was a boy, but he never mentioned it to me. I guess he didn't want to hear me ask, "What if the baby is a girl?"

While I appreciate that Jamil is keeping my father's name alive, every time I hear it I remember the last image I have of my father: his lifeless body dangling from a pole in the center of Duhok surrounded by hundreds of pitying onlookers. I have yet to garner the courage to carry the newborn.

Now that Jamil's wife has given birth, it's time for us to get back to the real business at hand: finding the rest of our family. This time, his mother-in-law, Seti, will not get in our way.

39

Azad

Turkey, March 1989

In 1969 and 1970, the Kurdish liberation movement sustained a major hit, and its fighters scattered into the mountains bordering Turkey and Iran. My father and a few dozen of his men crossed the Turkish border and hid in the rough terrain as the Iraqi army chased them to the very edge of the Iraqi side. Three of his men were injured by shells, and my father supervised an operation to sneak them into Turkish towns for medical treatment. Over the course of a few weeks, they moved between Mardin, Batman, and Diyarbakir, securing medical supplies and weapons, then returned to BerAva when military operations were called off.

Husain Ziway was one of the men with my dad during that operation. And now he's made the unilateral decision to accompany Jamil and me on our mission. He knows the area well, and he will not let us go alone. Despite Seti's frowning disapproval, he is more excited than we are to leave the camp.

We have made arrangements with a Kurdish driver, and Diyarbakir, less than a hundred kilometers from here, will be our first destination. Afterward, we'll head to the Mushe refugee camp, which is a lot farther. Our driver demands the entire payment in advance, and while Jamil and I protest, Husain Ziway pays him on our behalf, mainly because no one else will take us.

We reach Diyarbakir a little before noon. A few white clouds move slowly above us as temperatures rise precipitously, just in time for a good day in early March. When our driver stops at a small electronics store to drop off a package, I observe the pedestrian traffic through the dirty rear passenger window. A sudden knock on that passenger window scares the daylights out of me. I turn to the side, certain I will see a loaded Jandarma gun. Instead, an old woman is standing there and mumbling something I can't make out. The driver returns, and as soon as he spots the lady, he glares at her with an angry face and waves her away as if dealing with a stray animal. "These beggars will chase you until they strip you of every bit of money and still say they're hungry. One should never give them face."

He gets in, slams the door shut, and grunts as he turns on the engine. I turn and look through the rear window as we speed away. The lady is still standing in the same place and surveying her surroundings. She could be looking for her next victim, or maybe she's wondering how on earth she ended up where she is now, much like Jamil and me.

Diyarbakir is larger than I expected, its vibrant streets making me wonder what life might have been like back home without war and oppression, but we soon leave the city behind, the road opening up with an additional lane in an area with few trees and little scenery. With Jamil snoring next to me and the driver bemoaning how mistreated the Kurds are, my gaze drifts to the road ahead.

A column of dark smoke rises above an old factory off the highway on the right. An old truck emerges from the field in front of it and turns onto the road without any warning, forcing our driver to pump the brakes. The car swerves to the left and nearly hits another car.

Jamil wakes up to a heated exchange of obscenities between our driver and the truck driver, then shakes his head and drifts back to sleep.

We reach the camp around noon. There are no tents, only buildings, and the driver reads my mind. "This camp is different from yours." The three of us listen with interest. "Let's just say the refugees are lucky to be here. This used to be emergency government housing. It was built to house victims of earthquakes, but the local authorities decided to house the refugees in it."

A barbed wire fence stretches for nearly a kilometer. Two soldiers stand on both sides of the main gate and force our driver to park far away. He turns to Husain Ziway, as if silently asking him to step out, but he knows better. He agreed to drive us and help us with security and official procedures.

Husain's rigid body language is a silent reminder, so the driver steps out of the car and says, "Stay put until I return."

He walks to the gate, where one of the two soldiers meets him by pointing his hand in the air in a firm gesture. Not a good start. After an animated exchange, the driver is finally allowed through the gate. At least fifteen minutes pass while we anxiously sit and wait.

"We should have expected this," I say.

Jamil glares at me. "Expected what?"

"Why did we think it would be so easy to drive up here, show up at the gate, and just walk on in? We didn't think this through."

"It was your idea. You forgot?"

"Settle down," Husain says. "We knew it would be hard. Let's see what happens. Be patient."

A dark cloud looms overhead, adding to the dim mood. We'll almost certainly have to turn around if we're lucky enough not to be arrested.

"There he is!" Husain says.

The driver returns through the gate and walks slowly to the car, his eyes at his feet. A few more seconds and my fears will be proven right. "Give me your camp-issued IDs," he hurriedly says, his body halfway inside the car through his driver-side window. His urgent tone is completely at odds with his relaxed body language. When was the last time anything made any sense?

He returns to the gate and minutes later waves at us to come out. A soldier directs us to a concrete stand nearby. Our driver says something to an official in Turkish, his facial expression tense and serious, then turns to us.

"They've given you permission to visit the camp for a maximum of twenty-four hours, considering your circumstances. I had to explain to them you will only be looking for your missing family and guaranteed that you won't cause any trouble. In return, they will take a written statement from me." The driver pauses, as if expecting thanks for his major accomplishment, then points to the first building. "See there? You'll have to search through dozens of buildings. You're on your own. I'll be back tomorrow at noon sharp. If you aren't at the gate, I may go to jail."

The driver walks off and retrieves his ID card from the soldier, leaving ours with him.

What a stark difference between our camp and this one! Dozens of concrete buildings are lined up in rows. It looks more like an organized residential complex than a refugee camp. It includes a large field that has been divided into several soccer fields and a few volleyball courts.

Just like at our camp, everyone here seems to know Husain. "Is that you, my dear friend Husain?" says an old man with a deep voice. "What a coincidence. It is so good to see you. Thank God you are alive. Welcome here. Welcome."

The man embraces Husain warmly. More men wander over and join him, paying no attention to me or Jamil until Husain Ziway introduces us.

"Who doesn't know Wahid Barwari?" the man says, referring to my father. "This place is blessed by the arrival of his sons as great guests."

The old man, now our proclaimed host, invites us to his home, pointing to the third building down from where we are standing.

A young man with nice clothes and neat hair pulls me aside with a focused look. "I heard you have come from the Mardin camp. Can I ask you about some relatives of ours who were taken there? My aunt—"

Jamil pulls me away before the young man can even finish his question.

The concrete building has three stories, each with two units. Each unit houses a minimum of forty people in three bedrooms. Our host sits across from us on the floor and says in an apologetic tone, "Please excuse our place. As you can see, we don't live in the best of conditions."

I look around and see painted concrete walls with intact windows, rows of mattresses, and faces that look well fed. You think *you* don't live in the best of conditions? How about coming and visiting our camp?

When lunch is served, I look in shock at the plates of rice, bowls of chickpea soup, and fresh loaves of bread. Jamil's eyes turn to saucers when a plate of chicken arrives.

Minutes drag on slowly, and I seem to be the only one with a sense of urgency. While my mind is fixed on finding my family, everyone wants to talk about something else, anything else. Jamil appears relaxed, even in moments of serious talk. He's happily enjoying tea and high-quality cigarettes.

Finally, Husain Ziway reveals the purpose of our visit. I hold my breath while he tells everybody our story. Continuous silence from everyone else suggests—correctly, as it turns out—that nobody knows anything about Peshmerga legend Wahid Barwari's family. Our host, disappointed for not being of any help, repeatedly praises our father's accomplishments. Of course, this adds nothing to make me feel better and definitely nothing to take away from my emotional letdown.

When we leave the apartment building, I'm drained of hope. Jamil follows me with hurried steps. "Wait, brother, where are you going? Don't be upset, and don't lose hope. We will find them, Inshallah."

The young man from earlier appears again, and I apologize for brushing him off earlier and inform him that we'll help him find his aunt if we can. He offers to guide us to each building at the camp. An hour later, still nobody knows anything useful.

We fare no better at the Mushe camp.

After what feels like a failed mission around the globe, we return to our own camp with arms longer than legs, as the Kurdish proverb says. I head for the tent and hide under the covers just as night falls, hoping the nightmares of Nizarki will return and take me this time for real since there's nothing is left to live for.

40

Juwan

Hesenlu, Iran, March 1989

Spring follows the crippling grip of a long and brutal winter. A series of heavy rains plus two snowstorms caused the water levels to rise, and judging from the body language of farmers, it's going to be a good season for crops. No matter how dark the nights are, the sun always rises in the morning, regardless of who was able to sleep and who couldn't, and regardless of who wants the darkness to continue and who prays for it to evaporate. Green shoots appear in the fields in defiance of sorrow and pain. Is it unfair that the world continues to play its own music while some of us scream from pain?

I sit by the small window in the kitchen and look onto

the street as the sun heads down toward the western horizon. Dozens of simple-looking men and women sit on the sides of the road showcasing their varieties of wild greens and vegetables. It takes me back to our days in BerAva when we made all-day trips to the edge of the mountain in search of the same wild plants. The sound of a flock of birds flying freely over our apartment makes me curious how far they have traveled to get here, and I wonder how and why we ended up in a place so familiar and yet so far away and so foreign. Knowing the answer yet still asking the question is more painful than holding on to an unanswered question deep down.

Mistekhan fell ill for a few days last week with what appeared to be lingering effects from another infection. Upon her request, we were able to secure her special herbs plus fine tobacco. She still insists it's the high-quality tobacco that saved her. For her and many other women her age, nicotine isn't delivered by tobacco smoke. They prefer to grind the tobacco into fine particles and sniff it through each nostril. They say the soothing relief is nearly instantaneous. I'm not sure where this tradition comes from, but Mistekhan has drifted back into the habit after giving it up for a long time, probably because she is stressed.

Segvan has been gone for almost two weeks, and during this time we've paid Shukriya several visits. One particular TV drama show has stolen Shireen's mind, and I believe it's only a matter of time before she walks into the apartment carrying a TV set. On her request, we stay with Shukriya for a few nights until Segvan finally returns. For better or for worse, we wrap up our visit within an hour of his arrival. Before he is out of the shower, we are out of his house. It felt a bit awkward, but it reassured Shukriya that we were there for her company and no other reason.

The next morning, I'm getting ready for work when I hear a knock on the door. It startles me, and I twitch and drop the comb on the floor. We never expect unannounced visitors, especially not so early in the morning. And Segvan has filled our heads with fear that the local police may snatch us and take us to a refugee camp at any time.

Dilveen walks past me, opens the door, and invites Segvan in. He greets me and proceeds to take a seat in the far corner of the room without looking at me. It's too early in the morning for a regular drop-in. Mistekhan soon returns to the room to offer our guest welcoming remarks.

Minutes later, Shireen is serving hot tea. All eyes and minds are on me. I know it. Any second now, Segvan will bring up his encounters with me and the way his wife handled it. I dread even thinking about it let alone talking about it.

He fidgets and avoids eye contact. We wait in silence for him to tell us why he's here so early in the morning. A breeze chills the heated silence through an open window. I hear two men outside arguing over territorial rights for street stands, one claiming that the other has taken a spot he has used for years.

Segvan clears his throat, takes a sip of his tea, and begins. "I returned from my trip yesterday, but you all left before I could talk to you." Mistekhan fixes her white scarf as Segvan downs the rest of his tea. "As you have requested since your arrival, I've been asking about your sons during my last two trips."

His gaze is fixed on Mistekhan. "And what did you find out?" she says. "Please tell me."

Segvan hesitates for a second. "I'm afraid the news is not good."

The three of us lean forward. I swallow hard and scan the room with narrow eyes, hoping I misunderstood him.

His words drop like a bucket of ice: "I ran into some men who said most of those captured by the army were executed."

Dilveen gasps, and I sink into a hole where I can't muster any energy for a follow-up question. Mistekhan sobs, hiding her face in her scarf.

Shireen rubs her hands against her mother's and says, "But Jamil went to Duhok to get Azad. How do we know they even got out of the city?"

"The thing is," Segvan says, "I went all the way to the border across from your home region. I asked around until I met some men who had swept through your village and some other neighboring villages."

With every word, my heart sinks deeper.

Mistekhan asks in a cracked voice, "Please tell me what you found out. What did they tell you about my sons?"

Our anxiety is palpable, but Segvan is not finished yet. "I am sorry, Aunt Mistekhan, but I'm afraid both were killed during the raid on the village."

He gets up and leaves hurriedly, bumping into Shireen, who is now up and rushing to the kitchen to get her mother a glass of water. Mistekhan emits a deep, wounded cry. Segvan closes the front door behind him, and the entire room bursts into tears. Mistekhan slaps her own face as she continues to sob.

∾

EACH ONE OF us is taking the shock differently. Mistekhan has fully withdrawn. She refuses to eat or drink. Dilveen and I sit across from each other and share blank looks with teary eyes. It feels like we are in a prison inside a prison. The bathroom is my sanctuary now. It's where I cry and cry and cry and then cry some more. It's where I ask questions there are no answers to. Why do I have to endure the loss of two loved ones in a matter of months? Why is this happening to us? How much more can we take? What's left to live for in the absence of the two most important men in my life?

Shireen immediately blocks out the news and its emotional burden and goes back to work the next day. No power will stop her. A few days later, Dilveen and I follow suit. On my first day back at Zozan's house, she is angry, agitated, and apprehensive. I didn't show up the previous day, plunging her life into havoc. She walks back and forth past me, dumping baskets of dirty laundry, shoving pieces of furniture around, and putting dirty plates back in the sink for me to wash.

"The house is a mess. I left everything thinking you would be here. I can't stand this mess. How can you do this to me? If you are not going to show up, at least let me know."

I do my work, silently absorbing her verbal abuse. I wait for her husband to take the kids to school, then drop it all on her without any buildup. "I just found out that my fiancée and his brother were killed during a raid on our village after we left."

She stops at the living room door, her blue purse tucked under her arm. A hush settles over the house. The clock on the wall emits a single gong, indicating half past seven. She slowly turns and faces me, her face blank and her mouth open. "What did you just say?"

I can't say it again. I can't say anything. My tears do the talking, and she embraces me in the hallway.

She is late for work and must realize that discussing this will take an entire day. She finally lets go of me and dashes out of the house, sniffling and wiping her eyes.

It takes a few days before I can fully open up to her, and not only does she want to listen, but she also has a lot to say. Apparently she has no friends in town she could open her heart to. Now she claims that she does.

41

Azad

Turkey, April 1989

I find myself swinging from anger and sadness to anxiety. The nightmares are longer and scarier. They follow me when I'm awake, pouncing on me and leaving me exhausted and shaken, sometimes driving me back to bed.

Soldiers shoving me into a military car. Dragging me face-down into a pool of blood. Unseen forces emerging from the darkness and snatching me into a ditch. I watch myself buried in the dirt of my own country.

I can hear my sisters, my mother, and Juwan crying in that darkness. I can't see their faces, but I feel them slipping away as I struggle to breathe, struggle to scream, until I finally scream myself awake.

Every day I see sympathetic faces in the camp. They have heard my screams at night firsthand or heard of my miserable and sorry story through others. They know what I'm going through.

"Stay strong." "Keep your faith." "No doubt your family is waiting for you in a safe place." They say the right things, but I avoid anyone and everyone.

Every morning, I take my tea and sit next to the barbed wire fence at the far edge of the camp and review my life like it's recorded on a broken tape. There are so many ifs, whats, and whys that my exhausted mind turns on itself until something snaps me back to reality: the cry of a baby, the fight of some boys over soccer, or simply Jamil grabbing my shoulder and pulling me up. Even he feels distant, although he seems to be everywhere I go. He is busy with his infant, and every time I see him enjoy a moment with his wife or son, another mile of distance stretches between us. Deep down, I know I am being unfair to him and to everyone around me. Perhaps I should slip out of camp one day and never return. It may be the only way Jamil can live his life properly.

42

Juwan

Hesenlu, Iran, May 1989

Mistekhan is shrinking like a rose cut and left in the heat. What started as intermittent pain from an apparent kidney stone has turned into unbearable and persistent pain. She is the sickest we have ever seen her.

Shireen rushes to get Segvan, who is luckily in town. At a nearby clinic, a battery of tests plus an X-ray, all paid for by Segvan, reveal another urinary tract infection plus a large stone on the left side. We return home with antibiotics and fever-reducing medicine.

Over the next two weeks, her condition waxes and wanes but still requires attention around the clock. Dilveen is forced to quit her job because the factory won't allow her to consistently miss work days. Late one evening, Shireen screams and brings us to our feet in terror. "She's not breathing!"

Dilveen rushes to her mother's side. "Juwan and Shireen, go get Segvan right now!"

She and I run through the empty streets under the faint street lights, nearly tripping over various objects kids left out after their games and street competitions. It must be near midnight. Shireen heads straight to the door and knocks without stopping until a light turns on in the hall-way. The door slowly opens. Segvan is there in his pajamas, his eyes swollen and his face flushed. I explain what's happening while Shireen struggles to pull herself together.

"OK," Segvan says, his eyes wide, "you two go back home, and I will hurry and get the doctor." He disappears in the hallway while finishing his statement.

When we return, Dilveen is holding Mistekhan's head on her knees and slowly pushing some water into her mouth with a spoon as she struggles, coughs, and moans in pain.

Sometime later, Segvan arrives with a young doctor, who gets to work examining her. "I'm afraid she is extremely ill and needs to be taken to the hospital immedi-ately." He turns to Segvan. "We should take her to Urmia."

Dilveen cracks her knuckles. "But we can't afford—"

"I will take care of it," Segvan interrupts. "We will take care of it. We will take my car."

We carry Mistekhan downstairs and out to the car, and she collapses on the back seat. Segvan gets behind the wheel, the doctor rides in the passenger seat, and Dilveen rests her mother's head on her leg.

"We have limited room," Segvan says.

Shireen slides by me and sits by her mother's feet anyway. "I'm coming too." She slams the door shut.

There's definitely no room for me. "I'll let your boss know," I say to Shireen just before the car speeds off, its taillights slowly disappearing in the darkness.

I head to Segvan's house in the morning, my heart pounding from worry. I knock on the door, and Shukriya hugs me and invites me in. "I am so sorry to hear that Aunt Mistekhan is ill again. Segvan just left."

I follow her to the living room.

"Segvan says she's in critical condition and probably needs major surgery."

I feel sick to my stomach. Critical condition? Major surgery? What kind of surgery? How bad is it? Is it going to require a lot of money?

Shukriya is sympathetic but also apologetic for not having answers to my questions. But Segvan later shows up at the apartment wearing an awkward smile.

"How is she?" I ask immediately.

He takes one last puff from his cigarette, then puts it out under his shoe. He steps forward, but I keep my grip on the door. No invitation has been offered.

"Hi, Juwan. I saw you leaving our house and tried to catch up with you."

I pull my scarf down over my head and ask again, without looking at him. "What happened to Mistekhan? Is she going to be alright?"

He realizes I'm not about to let him in, so he shifts his body against the metal door. "To be honest, her condition is potentially life threatening if not treated."

I look straight at him.

He blinks and avoids my gaze. "The doctors did an extensive workup. Mind you, I had to jump through a lot of hoops to sneak her into the main hospital in Urmia."

My hand starts shaking against the door as my grip loosens.

He clears his throat and continues. "They say she has a large stone blocking the left kidney, and it's caused most of the kidney to rot."

I close my eyes, struggling to maintain my balance. Without opening my eyes, I say, "I need to go there. I need to see her."

I hear him walk away and open the car door. When I open my eyes, he's motioning for me to get in his car. "I'll take you there."

I jump in without thinking, and before I know it, we're turning on the main road. I hand Segvan two week's pay in cash that Zozan gave me. "Here, take all of it. Will this help cover the treatment?"

He shifts the gear, his hand nearly touching my left knee. The car picks up speed, and he chuckles as he pushes my hand back toward me. "This won't even cover one day of the hospital expenses. Please keep the money. I will try and find a solution."

I place the cash on the dashboard.

THE HOSPITAL SMELLS of illness and disinfectant, and I want to throw up. I'll never forget the first time I went with my father to Saddam Hospital in Duhok right after it opened. My dad needed follow-up for his diabetes, and Azad took us. I walked as close as possible to Azad so the smell of his cologne would block the nauseating stench of the hospital rooms and hallways.

I follow Segvan down the corridors and up the stairs to the third floor, staying at least a couple of steps behind. A security guard stands at the corner of the hallway next to a room where a few nurses are sitting casually. I hold my breath and rush to catch up with Segvan, worried the guard may stop and question me. We turn the corner into another hallway, and I sigh in relief. Each room has large glass windows, some darkened with blinds and others open for spectators.

We reach the next-to-last room on the left, and Segvan stops at the door. The second bed is surrounded by a dirty yellow curtain. "I can't go in with you. It's only for women."

I step inside the room and slowly walk through the curtain, doing my best to ignore the cries of the elderly lady in the first bed. Dilveen is asleep on a small plastic chair next to the window.

Shireen is at the edge of the bed, motioning for me to keep my voice down. "They gave Mother some pain medicine," she whispers, "and she's finally resting. Dilveen fell asleep a few minutes ago."

A plastic bag of fluids is hanging from a pole next to Mistekhan's head and flowing through a tube in her arm. There's more color in her face now, and she's breathing more deeply. Shireen softly tells me that Mistekhan will need surgery to remove her left kidney in a day or two after the infection settles down. There is a lot we don't understand, so we dive into the most pressing matter: money. How much is this going to cost, and how on earth will we pay for it?

Shireen has to work tomorrow, so she leaves with Dilveen, but I spent the night in the hospital.

Segvan and Dilveen return in the morning with breakfast and tea. The doctors are happy to see that Mistekhan is more alert and no longer has a fever.

"The doctors will most likely take Mistekhan into surgery tomorrow or the next day," Segvan says. It's clear that he can see my thoughts on my face because he adds, "Don't worry, there's a solution for every problem."

Later in the day, an obese, elderly nurse comes into the room to change the fluid bag and declares in a deep voice, "Only one person can stay with the patient at night."

Shireen gets into a heated exchange with her and the nurse finally agrees to let both sisters stay, but not me.

"Can I just find a place to sit outside or in the hallway?"

The nurse hisses at me and points outside with her thick finger. What a pathetic human you are, I think. I gently pat her shoulder and attempt to plead my case, but she pushes me away and yells for me to leave.

I again find myself following Segvan down the hallway, the hospital smell stronger than ever when mixed with my anger and frustration. In the parking lot, Segvan's car reeks like an ashtray. I roll down the window so I can breathe, and I shudder to think what will happen if Shukriya finds out I rode with Segvan alone, even if I don't say a word. Note to self: Coordinate with Dilveen and Shireen to travel by bus from now on.

Segvan suddenly stops in front of a small restaurant. "Hungry?"

The aroma of chicken hits my nostrils and reminds me of the time Azad took me and my father on a walk through the main market in Duhok after a doctor's appointment and treated us to tasty chicken sandwiches. Even so, I blurt out, "No, thank you. I'm not hungry."

But Segvan steps out of the car and disappears inside the restaurant. I can't tell if I feel more uncomfortable with him next to me or sitting by myself in the darkness. He finally returns with a paper bag in his hand and sets it on the dashboard. "Best sandwiches in all of Iran."

The dashboard clock reads 9:35 P.M., and I scream inside for him to hurry and get us back home, but anxiety stops my voice at the top of my throat. As if hearing my hidden cries, he takes off on the road leading away from the center of the city.

After some time, he makes a few turns, and we are suddenly on a dark and narrow road with little traffic and no houses in sight. Then he parks on the side of the road.

I turn to him with a puzzled look, but the darkness swallows my body language. I feel my heart raging inside my chest, and the lump in my throat nearly chokes me. A car passes us going the opposite way, briefly illuminating Segvan's eyes. He turns on the overhead interior light. Suddenly, I miss the lonely darkness from earlier.

He reaches into his jacket and produces an envelope from his pocket and gently drops it on my knees. I flinch and push my back deeper into the seat.

"Open it," he says. "It's the money that will pay for Mistekhan's surgery and hospital stay."

I want to pick it up and thank him, but it doesn't feel right. Why now, and why here?

I fix my eyes on the envelope. I can't see much in the dim light, but I feel Segvan's eyes on me. "Where are we?"

"You know she will die if she does not get that surgery. At best, the infection will return as soon as she leaves the hospital."

"Thank you for all you have done for us, and this is very generous of you." I intentionally rush through the last few words, hoping to end this moment as quickly as possible. Please move, I silently scream at him again. "Can we go now, please?" It's all I can manage to say.

He slides toward me and places his arm around my neck.

I scream and pull away so hard that my head hits the window.

He withdraws his arm and waves the envelope in my face. "I've done a lot for you. I'll do all of this and more to get your approval. You don't know how—"

"Take me home!"

He brings his face closer to mine, the stench of cigarette smoke on his breath. "Look, Juwan, I really like you. I liked you the moment I saw you. I know you like me too."

I push my face farther against the window. "Please stop. I have never looked at you as more than a brother and a fellow Kurd standing by people in need."

I want to scream at him that I am engaged. I want to slap him, punch him, and gouge out his eyes, but the mere thought of touching him, even if it's because I'm putting a beating on him, overwhelms me with disgust.

He withdraws and says, "I'm sorry, Juwan. I didn't mean to scare you."

He's lying. I know he is. There is no remorse in his words.

"I really like you, and I'm sure I can fill your life more than Azad ever would have. Just let me take care of you."

I wish I could bring up all my guts and spit them at him. Instead he pushes his face against mine and violently kisses me. His hand presses firmly against my neck, squeezing my throat shut.

I kick against the glove compartment and jerk my head back and forth, managing to hit his nose with my forehead, freeing my face from his grip for a few seconds, allowing me to scream at the top of my lungs.

He immediately recovers and wraps my face with his palms. "Kick and scream all you want. If I want something, I get it, and right now I want you."

He's breathing faster now, and the intensity in his voice rises. "I can drop you off here and forget that you and Mistekhan even exist, or you can give me what I want and things will be better than you ever imagined."

Another car is approaching. I grab the door handle. It would be so easy to get out and get the attention of whoever is coming. But the car makes a turn, and its lights disappear. My throat is already hoarse from screaming, and I can't muster any more energy to think or act.

Segvan becomes quiet for a few seconds while I struggle to catch my breath. I'm afraid to talk, turn, or even move. Anything could elicit another reaction. Turns out that even silence will get the job done. In a split second, he attacks me with his hands and forces me toward him. His face violently brushes against my neck and chest, and I feel his hands touching me in more places than I can react to.

"Please stop, please. Wait. Please don't do this to me. Don't let me live the rest of my life with the sin of adultery.

Take me as your wife until you do your thing, and then let me go."

He withdraws and silently contemplates my words.

"Don't play games with me," he says calmly.

"I'm not. Just don't rape me. Give me a little dignity if you're going to be an animal."

He chuckles. "Are you serious about this?"

I say nothing.

"OK then. We'll do it your way. But I swear if you do anything stupid, you'll disappear, and no one in this land will even think of you again."

He turns the car on again and makes a U-turn toward the city. I close my eyes and pray this is a nightmare. I keep my eyes closed with my head against the window. With each bump, I feel my heart shatter into a hundred pieces.

I open my eyes again when the car comes to a stop. We are on a narrow street in a dirty neighborhood with trash piled in front of and next to houses. The street lights happen to be functional, so they're illuminating all the signs of miserable human life in this part of town.

Segvan steps out and instructs me to stay in the car. The walls in front of the nearest house are covered in war graffiti.

An elderly man opens the door and seems to know Segvan. The two engage in a discussion in Persian as Segvan periodically points in my direction. The man disappears inside for a few minutes and returns with a set of keys and casually hands them to Segvan.

Segvan returns to the car and drives down the road and then stops again, this time in front of a house that looks even more unkempt than the one we just left. The street is empty and darker. Where are the children defying social norms by playing until late hours of the night? Where are the men who always like to hang outside, smoking cigarettes and discussing their miserable marriages? Where are the police? But then, what would anyone do for me at this hour? I could very well end up with a gang of monsters instead of just one.

I desperately reach into the space between the seats and over the dashboard, hoping to find a sharp object, but there's only the bag of sandwiches.

Segvan orders me out and warns me not to make any noise. My hands shake, and I can barely maintain my balance as I follow him to the porch. He unlocks the door and motions for me to go in.

"In a few minutes, my friend will bring a religious man and some witnesses, and you will officially be declared my wife. Just as you requested." He says this with pride, as if I'm supposed to be impressed.

I sit across from him on an old wooden couch with worn-out red cushions, keeping my eyes down and my hands crossed on my lap. He takes out a Swiss Army knife and cleans dirt from under his fingernails, making sure he has my attention. I hear the knock on the door, and tears start to fall on my hands.

THE WEIGHT of his body on top of me feels heavier than a mountain on the bottom of the sea. His hot breath against my face is like that of an animal that finally managed to grab its prey with its claws. I lie there under him, squeezing my eyes tighter than I ever have in my life. I kick a few times in a final attempt to free myself from him, but his weight only grows heavier.

He slaps me, groaning in anger. "Open your eyes and look at me."

Our eyes meet momentarily, mine full of fear and his full of lust and hunger.

I scream as he takes whatever is left of my life, my voice feeble against his gigantic, sweating body. His eyes are closed now and his face red, and my cries are answered with slaps. He groans and roars like a wounded animal until, suddenly, the weight of the entire earth lifts off me.

I PULL my dress over my shivering body. The ticking wall clock is louder than ever. Segvan is outside smoking a victory cigarette. Nothing makes sense anymore. Nothing means a thing.

When he returns, I'm fully dressed and sitting in a fetal position in the far corner with my head between my knees. He slowly approaches and gently places the white envelope next to me. My gorge rises, and I violently fall sideways to the floor, vomiting and retching.

Segvan leans over me, my face covered in vomit, and says, "Look, Juwan, I really like you. I can treat you like a queen. But by God if you say anything, I know people who can throw you and your companions behind the sun."

43

Dilveen

Hesenlu, Iran, May 1989

After a one-day delay, Mother's surgery finally goes through. The next morning, Segvan shows up and says it's fully paid for. We are forever thankful to him. But where is Juwan? We haven't seen her for two days. Segvan says she's at home with a stomach bug and unable to stand up.

She arrives with Segvan on the third morning, her face pale, sick-looking indeed, and she breaks down crying as soon as our eyes meet. Mother is awake now and calls Juwan's name as soon as she hears her voice.

Before we leave the hospital, the doctor tells us the recovery could take time, but more importantly there are a few stones in the right kidney as well, and even though they aren't causing an obstruction, Mother will need to follow up. We leave the hospital with medicine to prevent new stones and clear instructions that she should drink plenty of water.

SOMETHING'S WRONG WITH JUWAN. She won't look anyone in the eye, and she spends long stretches of time in the bathroom, her eyes red and puffy when she finally emerges. She skips two consecutive days of work at Zozan's house, spending the majority of the time sleeping or doing chores —anything to avoid talking to us.

When Segvan drops by to check on Mother, Juwan happens to be the one who opens the door for him. They exchange a few quiet words before Segvan comes up the stairs, followed by Juwan a few minutes later. I quickly forget about it, but only briefly.

The next day, Segvan visits twice. The first time, in the morning, he asks about Juwan, and I tell him she's at work. He returns early in the evening with a few bags of fruits and vegetables. Juwan leaves the room as soon as he sits, and when he's ready to leave, he asks to speak to her. Shireen rolls her eyes. The ceiling fan whirls overhead at high speed, at times roaring as if it's about to fly off. Segvan's awkward request adds more heat to the room. Mother is sedated by painkillers, and I'm thankful she isn't awake. I call Juwan a few times with no response. I motion at Shireen with my head, and she rises from her seat and leaves the room.

Juwan returns minutes later behind Shireen. They both

take seats next to each other on the opposite end of the room from Segvan. Juwan won't look at him. He finally asks if they could talk outside.

He follows her out the room, and they disappear down the stairs. Shireen and I carefully walk to the window and steal a glimpse of their upper bodies by the closed front door. The two seem to be having a heated exchange. My curiosity has turned to worry, and I decide it's time to hear the inaudible. I leave the room and stand at the top of the stairs, the two of them too tense to notice me standing there.

Shireen approaches and says, "What's going on here?"

Now we have their attention. Juwan looks in our direction with a worried face and says in a desperate voice, "Please tell him to leave me alone."

I slowly descend the concrete steps, the weight of Juwan's words pulling me stronger than gravity. She's pacing nervously and cracking her knuckles.

"What do you mean leave you alone?" Segvan says. "I have a right to ask you whatever I want."

"Will one of you just tell me what in the name of God is going on?" I blurt out angrily.

Juwan points an angry finger in Segvan's face. "You promised you would let me go. Go on. Divorce me as we agreed and leave me alone."

My jaw drops. Shireen looks even more bewildered than I feel.

"What did you just say?" I say, inching closer toward Juwan.

Juwan chews on her nails.

Segvan looks like a wounded beast contemplating an attack. "Go on. Tell them you are my wife and that I have access to you whenever and however I want."

I slowly sit on the concrete step, silently begging Juwan to slap Segvan and shut him up, but she says nothing.

"You whore!" Shireen says. "You couldn't even wait a few weeks since finding out my brother is dead! You worthless traitor."

I scream at Shireen, and she turns and disappears inside. I take a few wobbly steps back toward Juwan. She's hiding her face in her hands and sobbing. I gently grab her arm, but she pulls away from me.

"You need to tell me what's going on, Juwan. I don't know what to think or believe." I turn to Segvan, my voice shaking. "Did you mean what you just said? Is it true?"

"Yes, we are married," he says, his voice dropping on me like a bucket of cold water. "We got married in a religious ceremony. Now, would you give me some private time with my wife?"

"I am utterly disappointed in you," I say, not sure which of the two will find my words more fitting.

A plastic bag full of clothes flies down the stairs, landing at Juwan's feet. Shireen is back. "We don't want you here. Take your shit and leave with your lover."

"Let's go," Segvan says. "You deserve better than this. And by the way"—he's looking at Shireen and me now —"don't forget this is my place, so don't get pretty with me."

"Don't forget," Shireen says, "we're paying rent."

I rush up the stairs and push Shireen into the room. Mother is awake now, calling my name. When I return to the stairs, I find the front door open and both Segvan and Juwan gone, along with the plastic bag.

PLEASE GOD LET this all be just a dream, a nightmare, anything but reality.

My head is spinning. I run to the kitchen and sit on the floor with my back against the refrigerator while Shireen prepares dinner in the coldest of ways. She goes back and forth between the kitchen and our room, attending to Mother's needs as she slowly sits up. What will I tell Mother when she is fully alert and asks about Juwan?

My body jerks at the sound of repeated knocks on the front door that sound more like kicks.

It's Shukriya. She barges into the room, her sleeves rolled up, her scarf half-tied behind her head, her gold bracelets angrily hitting each other as she raises her hand and waves at no one in particular. "Damned be the day you came into my life! I've had nothing but trouble and headache from you in return for all the kindness I've shown you homeless, helpless, and miserable souls."

Mother looks every bit confused. She must think this is a dream or a side effect of the pain pills. No one has told her anything yet. "What's happening, girls?"

"What's happening," Shukriya says, "is that your so-called future bride has been secretly working to steal my husband away from me."

Mother turns to me, and I look away.

"You aren't the innocent people I thought you were," Shukriya says.

My mother groans from pain as she tries to stand up. "Dilveen, what's happening? What's she talking about?"

Explaining to Mother what I witnessed earlier feels like a taller climb than any mountain we crossed to get here.

I take Shukriya back to her home in hopes of figuring out exactly what happened. Segvan receives us in the hallway and wraps up the whole matter with some well-rehearsed words. Juwan is his wife, they are lawfully married, and there's nothing anyone can do about it. It's his legal right to get married a second time. Juwan will live in his house like a queen, and anyone who doesn't like it can smash their head into the nearest and thickest wall.

He wouldn't allow us to enter the second bedroom, where Juwan has locked herself in. It's where we slept during our first week here, which makes matters even more awkward.

After a heated exchange between Segvan and Shukriya, Juwan steps out of the room, her eyes bloodshot. "Please, everyone stop fighting or I'll kill myself right now." She turns to me with pleading eyes and says, "It's not what you think. Please believe me."

Segvan nonchalantly walks to his new bedroom.

"Just answer me with a yes or no," I say. "Are you married to Segvan? Yes or no!"

She looks down and nods, then runs back to her room sobbing. I turn around and head for the front door as Shukriya and Segvan get back at it. When I step outside, I can hear Shukriya screaming and what sounds like slaps. I pick up my pace. The sooner I no longer hear it, the closer I'll be to a new chapter where somehow Juwan magically slips away. I don't know what to think, but I only have a few minutes to figure out what to tell Mother.

OVER THE NEXT couple of days, we struggle to process the shock. I can't figure out a reasonable explanation for any of it, and having Shireen around doesn't help either.

A week or so later on a hot and grinding morning, Juwan shows up at our door. She begs to come in, and of course I let her. She is still part of our family, regardless of what happened. At least that's how I think. Luckily, Shireen is at work, or maybe Juwan timed her visit right. She rushes upstairs and sobs for a good few minutes until Mother pulls her head to her chest. I expect Juwan to walk us through exactly how and when she got into this mess with Segvan, but instead she cries, "It was beyond my control, I swear. I'm afraid to talk. This man is dangerous."

Mother gently pushes Juwan's head away, then rests her back against the wall. "My son is gone, and nothing will bring him back. What else matters beyond that?"

Juwan resumes crying and looks at me in pleading eyes.

"Juwan," I say, "how do you expect us to swallow this news if you don't give us any details?"

I expect her to interrupt me, but my disappointment grows when she maintains silence. She's not even crying anymore.

"I'm sorry, but this is all too much for us. Be thankful that Shireen isn't here."

"You won't understand. It's beyond a simple explanation!"

"Try me," I say and shrug. "I have all day."

"I'm scared. He'll hurt us!"

Mother wipes away her tears and asks me to fetch her Quran and turns to Juwan with twitchy eyes. "Go on, my daughter. Go back to your new home, focus on making yourself happy, and don't worry about us."

I follow Juwan down the stairs, and halfway down I grab her shoulder with a firm grip and hiss, "You are not going to leave like this without telling me what happened. At least me! You understand?"

She looks up at me, her eyes shiny from tears, her lips dry and cracked. "Segvan forced me to do things you won't believe. Things, I can't tell you. He threatened to hurt me if I told anyone."

I sense the sincerity in her words, but she's only adding to my frustration.

I shake her shoulder again, unsure what to say.

"And if you think for a second that I betrayed you, I have nothing else to say. The sooner you all believe me, the easier it will be for us to figure out a way out of this mess. Because he no longer wants me to contact you. And you tell that big-mouth sister of yours to never run her mouth at me again or I'll rip it clean off her face."

44

Azad

Mardin Refugee Camp, Turkey, June 1989

Summer drops its burning wings on the camp with unbearable heat, a dry spell, and yellow dust that hangs in the hair for days. We've grown accustomed to life in this confined space and do what we can to improve conditions even though food rations are still limited and the water supply is unreliable. Clothes have only been distributed a few times since our arrival last year. Dozens died during the winter from illness and cold. Despite all this, men and women roam the camp finding creative ways to fill their days. With fewer restrictions on travel outside the camp, most families found ways to earn a bit of money to add to their collections of food and cooking supplies.

Most families now have a TV set, a radio, or both. Young boys cleared a large area near the fence into a soccer field. No metal posts? No problem. A few kids showed up one day with four wooden poles and installed them in the ground. They probably stole them, but no one wants to talk about it. At any time of the day there could be a soccer match or a fight in that field, but the girls enjoy their childhood in a much more civilized manner.

On the days I don't work outside the camp doing random jobs, I stay inside the tent, mostly sleeping or pretending to be asleep. Jamil has joined a group of nationalistic ex-Peshmerga who call themselves the Sons of the Land. Traumatized, confined to this camp, and bereft of money and weapons, mostly they just talk and argue.

When I'm sleeping, nightmares recur regularly no matter which direction I go: a military car chasing me, a plane dropping bombs, a prison guard dragging me away. When I'm awake, I'm haunted by images of my mother, sisters, Juwan, and her father running away from the army or being dragged into a hole as bulldozers cover them with sand and rocks. Who is responsible for their disappearance? No one else but me.

A million what-ifs swarm my head as I reflect on all the things I could have done differently. What if I left school earlier and joined my family in the village when we saw trouble on the horizon? What if I stayed in the village after Jamil's wedding to see how things would unfold? What if I married Juwan and somehow forced my mother and sisters to move in with us in Duhok? As farfetched as that possibility would have seemed back then, I should have at least tried.

JAMIL HAS GONE to yet another one of his meetings. My two other tentmates are working in the city today, and the afternoon is just starting to taper down its suffocating heat when something hits the back of our tent a few steps from where I'm laying down. I spring to my feet and rush outside to check it out.

A young boy with a faded blue soccer jersey and worn-out pants is sitting in the shade between our tent and the neighboring one. He looks up at me, squeezing his eyelashes against the shining rays of the sun. "I'm sorry, uncle. I tripped and fell. Sorry if I bothered you."

I step forward, now standing right above him, blocking the sunlight. His sharp eyes are now wide open and confident. On the ground between his knees is an old notebook filled with scribbles.

"What's your name?" I ask.

He writes something at the bottom of the page and without looking at me says, "My name is Ali."

I lean over, annoyed at his casual response, and grab his notebook. I quickly flip through the pages. "What is this?"

He stands up, anxiously moving the pencil between his fingers and answers, even more confidently, "It's the alphabets. I'm trying to catch up on my studies." He holds his arm out, asking for his notebook back.

I hand it over and ask, "How old are you? What grade were you in before coming here?"

He appears excited at my questions and looks straight into my eyes. "I'm nine. I was in third grade. How about you, what grade were you in?"

I'm taken aback by his boldness, but I chose to go down

this route. I tell him about my school, and he listens attentively, his notebook tucked tightly under his arm. Ali stares at the ground next to his torn black plastic shoes, thinks for a few seconds, then looks up. "Will you teach me?"

I'm impressed but also annoyed. "No, I don't have time to teach you. Why don't you go somewhere else and do your writing?"

He doesn't flinch or even blink.

"I need to rest, so I better not see you near my tent again."

I walk back to the tent, and just before I step inside, I turn around for one last look. Ali is still standing there, his notebook silently beckoning me, his sharp brown eyes even more daring. I step into the tent, walk straight to the small metal box where Jamil keeps his cigarettes, and light one for myself, my first in a long time.

How did this kid end up at my tent? Who sent him? What does he see in me that suggests I might teach him? I sit and think without taking any puffs from the cigarette as it slowly burns away between my fingers. I suddenly find myself on my feet, almost against my will. I run outside, but Ali is gone.

For the rest of the day, I can't stop thinking about Ali. I ask Jamil about him, but he swears he didn't send the kid over to me, nor does he know who he is. There are probably dozens of kids in the camp named Ali.

"Why are you so curious about him?"

The truth is, I don't know. I don't even know what I'd do or say if I were to find him again.

And yet I go looking for him. I search the various corners where kids often sit and play cards. I take a casual stroll down the long rows of tents, looking right and left. No sign of Ali. I ask two boys if they know a kid named Ali, and they laugh and point at each other. "We're both named Ali."

At night, I lay in bed, staring into the darkness while my tentmates snore through deep sleep. I inspect my wrist-watch, and it's past midnight. Somewhere in the back-ground, a child is crying, and elsewhere a few men are laughing out loud over God knows what lame joke or story. A few women pass by our tent headed in the direction of the restrooms, one of them quietly telling another, "Did you know Salwa is pregnant?" Their faint voices quickly disap-pear as they continue to walk away. How people find a chance to make babies in this camp is beyond me, but it's the least of my concerns now. Jamil and I have to be at a construction site early in the morning, but Ali won't leave my mind. Despite my resistance, my eyes finally give in to sleep and another nightmarish journey.

In the morning, Jamil and I eat breakfast and quickly get ready for work. I grab my heavy-duty gloves and step out of the tent ahead of Jamil. And there he is, standing by the corner of the tent, Ali, still wearing that blue jersey but a different set of pants, notebook in one hand and pencil in the other. He stares at me without uttering a word, our eyes fixed.

Jamil follows me outside. "Who is this kid?"

I want to shout, "Go away and enjoy your childhood like the other kids. Don't make yourself the prisoner of some-thing you may never be able to achieve while on the run for your life as a refugee in a land that doesn't even want you."

Jamil grows inpatient as he stands there waiting for me. Ali blinks a few times, then turns and starts to head away.

I hand my work gloves to Jamil. "Find someone to help you today. I have something important I need to do."

I leave Jamil with a confused look and run behind the boy, yelling, "Ali, wait!"

Ali turns with a smile, as if knowing deep inside that he had me from the first glance.

I hear Jamil mumbling a few cuss words while I take Ali's hand and say, "Let's go find a place with some shade and start our first lesson."

Two weeks later, I have more than seventy students.

IN EARLY JULY, the heat of summer reaches its peak. We drink water piped to metal faucets over hot ground and stored in handmade clay water pitchers in the tent so it can cool down. Some of the few well-off families have managed to buy small refrigerators, at times allowing us to place ice cubes in yogurt drinks.

It's Friday, and the prayer has just finished. People usually disperse quickly to escape the heat, but today there is a feast held by an elderly man who finally located his missing teenage son in one of the villages near the border. The mother vowed to slaughter three sheep if her son ever returned to her by the grace of God. The poor father had to work extra hours, borrow money, and use all his savings to satisfy his wife's promise. And so today, everyone sticking around will be treated to fresh meat with rice and a soup of some sort. Jamil and I decide it's not worth getting a heat stroke for meat, so we head to his in-laws' tent to eat whatever Seti and Berivan have prepared for us.

By early evening, dozens of people fall sick with vomiting and diarrhea. Mostly men and young children, they line up by the bathrooms in desperation and with pale faces. Cries erupt across the camp as some of the sick pass out from dehydration. I know there's a small clinic, but I've never even seen it or thought about getting within ten feet of it. Panic sweeps through the camp as the sun starts to go down, with dozens of people being hurried to the small infirmary.

A lady steps out of a tent and screams, "My daughter is dying, please help!"

I rush inside the tent and see that her daughter is one of my students. Her face is pale, and she's barely responsive. I carry her on my shoulders, her head swinging back and forth with no sign of muscle strength.

We reach the infirmity, where a mass of people have already gathered. Two Jandarma men only allow the sick inside.

Someone keeps calling *dikhtor, dikhtor,* where is the doctor?

I look around inside the clinic, which is the size of a bedroom with a single rusty examination table. A lonely oxygen tank sits in one corner next to a small plastic storage box. There are no nurses around, but finally the dikhtor shows up.

Dildar is a tall, thin, middle-aged guy from the village of Hiror on the far northern side of our region, all the way near the border. I have never met him, but Jamil seems to know him well. He was supposedly a doctor's assistant a long time ago before he joined the Peshmerga and became their "doctor." He is quick, efficient, a no-nonsense guy. Alarmed by the dozens of sick patients all over the camp, Dildar yells at the guards to call for medical support and ambulances, but their body language suggests anything but urgency.

Two hours later, my count is at seventy-two patients. An elderly man was dead when his family brought him in. Two more die inside the clinic, and the conditions of the rest range from mild to critical. When a medical team finally arrives, two young male doctors and a female nurse quickly set up their stations inside. They shout in Turkish, and no one, including Dildar, seems able to communicate with them.

I step closer to one of the doctors as chaos ensues and ask him, "Speak English?"

"Yes!" he says and points at an elderly man who's resisting a jab in his arm for fluids.

I spend the night translating as best I can. By early morning, we have three dead and four of the critically ill taken to the hospital while everyone else seems to be recovering.

The massive food-poisoning incident highlights how miserable the medical care is in this camp, which leads to the permanent assignment of one trainee doctor and a nurse on a daily basis from morning until late afternoon.

I have a new friend now in Dildar. I also develop close ties with the young Turkish student doctor who is assigned to the camp and who pushes to get a job for me in the infirmary as an interpreter. It's through this new window of opportunity that I'm able to purchase a portable cassette player and a set of English lessons on tape for myself and some posters for basic English-language lessons for my students. If Dildar is called a doctor, I might as well be called a professor.

45

Dilveen

Hesenlu, Iran, June 1989

I stand in front of the mirror as I often do, and if not for the scar, I would have not recognized my pale, shrunken, and aged face. There was a time when I would stand in front of the mirror and reflect on the only thing I found wrong: my scar. But now I can't tell what hurts more, the scar or the fact that I'm a hopeless refugee who's no longer able to work because I have an ill mother who is still silently mourning the loss of her sons. On top of all that is the shock of Juwan's sudden marriage. I look deeper in the mirror, wanting to only see the familiar scar, but I see an abundance of invisible scars, scars carved by fear and hopelessness. Scars as heavy as mountains and made from the same heavy, rough, and stubborn material.

With Shireen at work, I try hard to get Mother up and around, but she won't even sit outside, preferring to spend most of her time consumed in silence. I decide to go out for a stroll and to stock up on food. I wait until late afternoon for the temperature to cool down, but the heat is relentless, so I finally summon my courage and head out. The asphalt is blazing with heat. Each step feels as if the ground might swallow my feet.

I look in the direction of Segvan's house. Or should I say Juwan's house now? I contemplate walking up there for a frank confrontation, but what good would that do? She has made several attempts in the past two weeks to talk to us, but Shireen refuses to see her, and I'm afraid another confrontation may give my mother a stroke. And there's no telling how Segvan would react if there's another fight with Juwan.

On my way back home, Segvan suddenly appears behind me, his voice sending a jolt through my spine. I have a feeling he's been following me since I left the market. He accompanies me all the way to our place and detains me at the door for a long time, relaying to me his struggle in getting Juwan to adjust to the marriage as if I am to be blamed for it. I diplomatically tell him we're all trying to move past it.

"You have to solve your marriage issues by yourself," I say, mustering the courage to look him in the eye. "We're out of the picture."

His gaze only grows sharper and more serious.

I shift my weight from side to side, trying hard to look anxious so he'll leave, but he seems to realize the close bond

Juwan and I have—or rather had. I maintain my silence as he prattles on about being the oppressed victim in a conflict he started on a battleground he owns and with terms he dictates. *Please leave before my sister comes home.*

My fears come true when Shireen suddenly emerges from around the corner on the street. I can already guess that she's in a bad mood after a long day at work. And with Segvan's presence, a bomb is ready to go off.

She approaches me directly, totally ignoring Segvan. "What's he doing here?" she asks, cold as can be.

I can sense the tension rising. I want to remind her that this, after all, is his place.

But before I can utter anything, Segvan says in a hesitant tone, "I'm hoping there won't be any hard feelings between us. Also, Juwan is still isolating herself, and I was thinking that if you all avoid communicating with her, she might get used to her new life with me."

Shireen, please go inside. Please don't respond. Please let me handle this. But I know my sister.

"Listen, man," she says. "We don't care about you or your whore of a wife. You can keep her. As long as she stays away from us, we'll be happy."

She storms through the door, and I'm fully prepared to slap every inch of her face if she comes back out and says anything else.

Segvan is already leaving. I want to run up there and pull Shireen down the stairs by her hair, but I know that as soon as I'm next to her, she'll shut me down. It happens every time.

The next day, Segvan shows up again early in the morning. "Pack your stuff, it's time to go. You're not staying here anymore."

My jaw drops, and my eyes widen in shock. He barges in and storms up the stairs. With total disregard for our privacy, he walks through the place, gathering whatever belongings he can get his hands on, repeatedly complaining about how disruptive we've been and how ungrateful we are for everything he's done for us. Even Shireen is speechless.

Mother finally confronts him, but he's having none of it. "Look, it won't work out for you or for us if you stay in this town. I don't have anything against you, and I want to help you, but you just can't stay here. And you"—he turns to Shireen and narrows his eyes—"you have a tongue longer than a tree, and at some point it will need to be cut."

Mother steps between them. "Please, my son. We don't want any problems. You have done a lot for us, and for that we are thankful. And whatever you had or have going on with Juwan, it's not our business as she is your lawful wife."

He seems to have it all planned out. "I found you a small apartment in Urmia and a job for the two of you. I've paid your rent for two months, and by my mother's grave, if you ever contact Juwan or try to ruin my life, I'll have the police arrest you for being here illegally." I've never seen him look more serious or sound so determined.

We pack our essentials and ride in the back of his car in broken silence. I refuse to look back. I yearn for a tall, thick wall to fall behind us, separating us from everything that is Hesenlu. Segvan drives through the busy streets of Urmia, maintaining silence while filling the car with cigarette smoke. He hasn't said a word since we left Hesenlu.

We enter a heavily populated area with old buildings stacked next to each other in a disorganized manner. All sorts of trash is laying on the streets. We turn onto a narrow street that barely fits one car. At the end of the street,

Segvan stops the car and lowers his head over the dashboard. We're looking at an old multistory brown building with laundry draped over its balconies and windows.

He fetches a set of keys from his pocket and waves them at us. "This is it. We're here."

He steps out and opens the trunk, then motions for us to get out. I catch Shireen wiping tears on her cheeks. She looks away as soon as she notices my glance. It's the first I've ever seen her cry.

The front door to the building is missing. We climb up the stairs behind Segvan, carefully avoiding piles of fresh and old trash scattered everywhere. The walls are covered in writing and stains. A thick layer of humidity lingers in the hallway, adding more heaviness to the smell of rotten material and cooking.

On the second floor, Segvan stops at the third door on the left. We pause in the hall, observing him as he inserts the key into the lock and turns it without the slightest hesitation, quickly disappearing inside. The three of us drown in silence, then Segvan's voice calls us in a surprisingly gentle and inviting way.

He extends his welcoming arms in the middle of a tiny living room with one old sofa. The bedroom is empty, but he promises to return with our mattresses from the other apartment. The small kitchen comes with a two-burner stove but no refrigerator. That issue, too, he says will be solved when he comes back with the small refrigerator we left behind in Hesenlu. We have a hundred problems, but lacking mattresses or a refrigerator isn't one of them.

"So this is going to be our place?" Mother says. "We're going to live in this area now?"

As if it's not obvious! I know Mother is trying to appeal

to Segvan's emotions so he might change his mind, but the look of determination on his face says the contrary.

Why is he still helping us? Is he trying to redeem himself after taking Juwan away? Or maybe in his mind he still thinks he's going above and beyond! But on second thought, what's stopping him from throwing us onto the street and telling us to go to hell or simply calling the police on us as he has repeatedly threatened? I cringe at the thought.

He stands at the front door and clears his throat. "I hope you like this place."

"What about our jobs?" Shireen asks.

He pretends to be in a hurry, but I know Shireen, and she's not going to let him leave without securing this important piece first. She repeats her question while he anxiously kicks the edge of the door with his foot. Finally, after a deep sigh, he says, "OK, if you insist and are not tired, I can take you to your new place of work now and introduce you to the owner."

We leave Mother in the apartment, lock the door, and follow Segvan out. It's a good fifteen-minute walk, he says, but he prefers walking over taking his car. This way we'll learn the way to and from work.

We zigzag through a few dirty and haunted-looking alleys, then turn onto a large multilane industrial street full of mechanics and tire shops with a few small restaurants scattered here and there. At the next intersection, we cross and turn right onto another street that has significantly less traffic. Segvan slows his pace, studies the first few buildings, and then points to the third one on the right. It's an old two-story brick building with spotty and worn-out yellow paint. A broken rectangular sign hangs in front with a picture of a sewing machine on one side and some words with missing letters on the opposite side.

Segvan tells us to wait outside as he enters through a solid white steel door. Shireen and I wait by the wall, nervously noticing the scarce foot traffic around us. He returns a few minutes later accompanied by a tall and skinny old man in a brown suit. The man inspects us through his thick glasses. Segvan doesn't introduce him to us, and the man doesn't say his name, but we silently follow them in.

Inside is an open rectangular warehouse with numerous sewing machines against the walls. The humming of the machines is mixed with the roar of a huge circular fan hanging from the ceiling. More than a dozen women, young and old, work without even noticing our presence. At least six machines are unattended to. In one corner of the warehouse are rolls of fabric of various colors. The old man points at a narrow set of stairs and says, "That's our second floor, where we do automated machine sewing. Our ladies cut them here, and I have a few part-time men who move packaging between here and upstairs." He yells upstairs: "Ramo!"

A chubby young man with deeply tanned skin and thick hair rushes down the stairs. He wipes his greasy hands on his pants and wears a distinctive smile on his face.

Ramo is also Kurdish, and he has a variety of duties, including mechanical repairs and troubleshooting. He greets Segvan and sizes us up before turning to his boss for orders. The old man tells him to pick us up on his way to work the next day, to which Ramo nods and further widens his smile.

We follow the owner back to the main entrance, my

heart pumping with excitement knowing that our employer is Kurdish. He turns to us and says in a gentle tone, "We'll get you busy with various tasks while you learn how to operate the sewing machines. As you can see, that is where I need the most help."

We can start the next day if we want, he says while looking at Segvan as if asking his permission. On the way out, I turn behind me to absorb the feel of our new adventure. Ramo is still busy cleaning his hands and staring at Shireen. She returns the look, then hurries to catch up with me and Segvan.

IT's EARLY JULY, and we've been in this apartment for exactly two weeks. Time seems to be moving fast. We're used to the place now, we've learned our way around the area, and we finally feel comfortable enough with our jobs that we don't worry we'll get fired. Even Mother has attempted a few short walks around the block while we were at work.

During the first few days on the job, Ramo accompanied us to and from work. And on those trips, we learned some things about him. He shares an apartment with two other guys not too far from our place. His folks live in a village about an hour or so from Urmia. He attends a technical institute where he's studying to be an electrician and divides his time between the city and the village.

But one thing seems to have happened too fast for my liking: Shireen and Ramo have grown awfully comfortable with each other in the short amount of time we've been here. I am no fool. I see the way they look at each other. I notice the silent language.

Mother has a fever again this morning, forcing me to stay home while Shireen—gladly, I'm sure—goes to work. In the evening after Mother finally sleeps, Shireen goes on about her day at work. Of course Ramo's name comes up repeatedly. I give her a look, and she smiles, defiantly refusing to look away.

She pours two cups of hot tea for us while I empty a bag of roasted sunflower seeds in a plastic cup and place it between us on the sofa. I corner her about Ramo and how it's even more obvious that the two feel something for each other.

Shireen chuckles dismissively and says, "Why don't you put that nonsense aside and listen to what Ramo told me today."

I take a sip on my tea, then grab a handful of roasted sunflower seeds, stretch my legs, and raise my eyebrows in anticipation.

"Segvan has been misleading us about the seriousness of our illegal status here." She says it matter of factly. I open my eyes wider in surprise while she continues. "Ramo says there are thousands of people like us roaming around the area without any problem."

I keep cracking the seeds and spitting the shells in the trash bag and take the last sip of my tea and maintain my focus on Shireen's words.

"So he really doesn't have anything against us or on us, but ..."

I knew there was a *but* coming. Shireen pours another round of hot tea for both of us while I glare back and ask, "But what? Continue."

She knows I will be skeptical, but still she continues. "Ramo did agree that Segvan seems well connected and can easily get us in trouble with a simple accusation with his police friends."

I take a deep sip from my tea and shoot her a dismissive look. I won't even entertain the idea of opening another skirmish line with Segvan or stepping outside the boundaries of our new little world. Not with our desperate financial situation, and certainly not with our mother on the verge of a major illness.

ANOTHER BOUT of illness hits Mother when we wake up one morning and notice her flushed face and bloodshot eyes. Soon after she's up and walking, she complains of a severe headache. It's Friday, and most places will be closed. Shireen and I are both off, but we don't know our way around well enough to find a clinic or a hospital—not that we would take her alone anyway.

We convince Ramo to come in the afternoon and help us take her to a small neighborhood clinic, where a physician assistant checks her out. "My God," he says, "her blood pressure is very high. She's lucky she didn't have a stroke and die in her sleep."

My blood pressure must be high now too. This is one time I wish he did not speak our language. He gives my mother a few pills, we wait for another hour or so, then he checks her blood pressure again. This time, he's much less alarmed as he smiles and says that her blood pressure numbers are better than earlier but still not where they should be. He gives us a few boxes of medicine, which Ramo insists on paying for, and we leave the clinic.

On our way back, I hold my mother's hand as she walks gingerly while Shireen and Ramo talk about work. I feel alone and lonely. Distant and lost. Where are we headed? How much longer are we going to be walking, talking, and breathing liabilities on other people? Ramo is not Segvan, and he surely can't help us financially.

46

Juwan

Hesenlu, Iran, June 1989

I'm wearing the white dress and high-heel shoes Azad bought for me at a fancy store in Duhok. Our wedding lasts three days and nights, filled with traditional Kurdish dancing and magical folk songs sung by beautiful voices. On the first morning, breakfast is a feast second to none: all types of cheeses, eggs, meat, yogurt, honey, and high-quality nuts like almonds, walnuts, and hazelnuts. Tea is served dark and with dense layers of sugar in round after round until men feel enough energy to get up and dance again. I enjoy being the center of attention among the women as the bride of the son of the village whose ambition to reach college has finally been realized.

And while women dance and sing around me, all I can think of is Azad, my dream, my love, the man I waited so long to be reunited with.

This has been my dream every night for weeks, but I wake every morning and find myself married to a man I barely know. A predator who calculated his every move and measured every step before he cornered me and snatched me into his cage. No matter how and where I turn, I find countless ways to convince myself that it's my fault. The physical prison of being confined to this house and not allowed to contact the only family I have left in this lonely world. The emotional prison of facing Shukriya and her accusatory looks day in and day out.

I'll be honest: I spent the first week locking myself in my room when Segvan wasn't around, watching my back every time I moved around the house. I expected Shukriya to attack me from behind at any moment. I woke up a few times from a nightmare of her angry face hovering over mine as she squeezed the life out of my already-dead throat.

I hid a knife under my bed for a while.

The first week passed with Segvan spending most of his time at home and around me. He bought a brand-new furniture set for the bedroom. He screamed at and punched Shukriya. She took the kids and left for her brother's house only to return the next day broken and subdued. Then things calmed down between them as Segvan started to go out more.

During the second week, he spent most nights with Shukriya, which gave me the luxury of darkness and silence as I lay in bed reflecting on the mess I fell into and wondering how to climb out of it. I sneaked out of the house a few times to appeal to Dilveen, Shireen, and Mistekhan only to find myself lonelier and more estranged.

SEGVAN SHIFTS his weight and lays next to me, his heavy breaths like doses of death. I press my eyelids against each other as if that might somehow make him disappear, but he's still there. He's everywhere. He says something between his now-slowed breaths, but I can only hear background noise.

He gets up and turns the light on, forcing me to close my eyes tighter. He returns to bed and lights a cigarette. The cigarette sizzles as its tip burns. He shifts his body toward me, running his fingers through my hair, now wet from tears. The mere thought of him choosing to stay next to me after devouring my body again makes me sick. Sick to my bones. I'd rather he leave me behind like a piece of dirt.

"Why me?"

I hear him exhale deeply after another pull on the cigarette. Every moment of lingering silence infuriates me.

"Because you're pretty. The prettiest woman I have ever seen in my life."

Feeling even more violated, I ask him again, facing the ceiling with my eyes shut. "Why did you pick me? Aren't you satisfied with your wife?"

He chuckles. "Yes, I am ... with my new and my real wife."

I want to jam the cigarette down his throat and scream in his face. I want to slap him over and over and press my nails through his skin and into his eyes. Instead I take a deep breath. "Please tell me why. You already have a wife and kids. Why did you do this to me?"

He seems irritated now as he lights another cigarette. The heat mixed with the smell of his sweat and the nauseating smoke of his cigarette are nearly enough to make me pass out, but he has my full attention when he aggressively clears his throat. I open my eyes so I can see his face when he speaks.

"I chose you because my first wife is crazy. She doesn't understand how to be a wife and behave like a woman."

He turns away from me and stretches his legs in bed. "Shukriya is a different person each day. I can't take it. She's ruined my life and my marriage."

You are talking about ruining lives? You bastard!

He suddenly turns and leans over me, his breath violating mine, and says "I don't know why I chose you, but I know you are a beautiful and amazing woman. I can't get enough of you."

I shut my eyes again and wish to disappear deep into the ground underneath the squeaking bed.

IT'S BEEN THREE WEEKS, and I can't take it anymore. Unable to see Dilveen and surrounded by the walls of my haunted bedroom, I can't go on. Segvan is getting ready to leave for his first trip in nearly two months. I have to find a way to get him to allow me to visit Zozan, whom I haven't seen since the day I collected money from her on our way to the hospital. It takes a little bit of smiling and sweet-talking to get the OK from him, but he makes it clear that he is not going to allow his wife to work as a maid but that I can visit her as a friend if I want.

I head over there as soon as he leaves the house. School is out for the summer, so I expect Zozan to be home. After a few rings, she finally opens the door and gasps when our eyes meet.

"God, help me understand where this woman has been all this time!"

Luckily, her husband isn't home and her kids are playing outside, so I spend more than two hours catching her up on every detail since we last met. She cries with me and tries to console me in her soft yet anxious tone. Her children storm into the house and grab ice cream cubes from the freezer, then run outside despite their mother yelling at them to stop.

"You see?" she says. "No one has a happy life. My life is a mess, as you can see. We must accept our *qadar*, our fate."

I chuckle at her ridiculous comparison, but she adds, "You were forced into a marriage that you think is not good for you, but you never know. Look at me. I chose to marry my husband whom I got to know during our teacher training, and I broke my family's word by marrying him. Sometime after our wedding, I discovered he has schizophrenia and is medication-dependent."

I'm grateful that she's managed to distract me from my own problems, even if for just a few minutes.

She sighs deeply and places a piece of cake on my plate, which I totally ignore. "He sees things and hears voices that don't exist. It's scary and sad at the same time. He's stable and good when he takes his medication, but every once in a while he feels like he doesn't need the medicine anymore, and things fall apart like a train derailing at full speed."

My own train derailed ten months ago, then caught on fire.

I leave Zozan's house feeling worse than before.

It's time to confront Shukriya, and whatever happens, happens. And there's no better time now that Segvan is away. If it comes down to fighting, so be it.

In the evening after I return from Zozan's house, I fix dinner and tea for myself, and on my way to my room, I notice Shukriya in the living room struggling to feed her children. I step into the room and sit across from her. I put my plate next to hers and carefully drink my tea while watching her through the tip of the glass. She doesn't acknowledge my presence. No verbal or physical abuse from her yet. Victory for me so far.

I clear my throat and hesitantly say, "I just want you to know, I—"

"Yes, I know. You didn't plan it. It just happened. Spare me that shit."

Minutes pass in silence as we ignore each other.

She flips through the channels on the TV, paying no attention to what's on. "Was it your idea or his to get married?"

I expected that question, but somehow it still takes me by surprise. I stare at her with a blank face.

"Oh, come on. I knew he had his eyes on you from the beginning. He's my husband. I know him. I just want to know if you begged him to marry you after he got what he wanted or if it was his idea?"

Her insight shocks me. But at the same time, it doesn't. I

hesitate for a moment, but decide to plead my case, hoping that she'll feel a connection with me once I've revealed the most intimate aspect of my tragic marriage to her husband.

Her face remains unchanged as I tell her. Her eyes are at her knees, avoiding my gaze while I'm begging deep inside for a single sympathetic look.

When I finish, I expect her to say I deserve it and that I'm a whore. Instead, she looks at me and says, "I don't really care that you married him. In fact, I wish he would spend every night with you and keep his stinky breath as far away from me as possible."

Shukriya is smart and intuitive, with a mind of her own. For better or for worse, she can read the questions on my face, and she answers first with a nod. "Why did I marry him? And why am I still with him if he's so evil-hearted and abusive? For starters, marrying him was a mistake, and I'd rather not go there. Damned by the stupidity of youth. As for staying with him, well, where would I go? My brother refuses to understand me. He says I deserve all my misery for not listening to his advice from the beginning. For honoring my father's word? Segvan is a great manipulator. I could easily find myself on the street and without my kids if I headbutt him."

I'm confused. What about all the name-calling she spits at him on a regular basis?

"I'm sure," she continues, "that Segvan will portray me as the crazy wife who doesn't know how to make him happy. I feel bad for you because you're still innocent and fresh. He'll abuse you just as he does me, but I don't care."

She gets up and leaves her plate for me to clean. At the door, she turns and taps her finger repeatedly on her chest. "Let's get one thing clear here. I'm the boss in this house, and you will stay out of my way. I still hate your guts, and the last thing I want is for you to try to get close to me."

OUR ROOMS ARE RIGHT across from each other, and to know that I could step out of my bedroom at any time and find my nemesis standing in front of me—or more accurately, she'll see her nemesis stepping out of her room—feels rather unsettling.

But she's back to ignoring me now. And while Segvan is away, I make daily trips to Zozan's house and insist on cleaning just like before, mainly because her house remains a mess. She insists on paying me for my time. The latter part of the deal must remain a secret or I'll lose my privilege to visit.

On a hot afternoon in late June, I step off the bus, and as usual I stare at the intersection that separates our street from the one Dilveen and the rest of the family live on. I stand there for a moment, then decide to walk over there. Dammit! Segvan is away. And I don't care what Shireen says or does. Dilveen will never kick me out. I'm going. I'm going to lay it on them, exactly the way it happened, whether they believe it or not. And when I finally empty my plate, we're going to figure out how to escape from this hell.

I walk slowly toward the building, trying to gather my thoughts and my courage. When I finally get there, I notice a few men carrying buckets of concrete mix up the stairs while another stands on a wooden ladder against the main outside wall. I gently push against the half-open door.

"What are you doing here?" a man's voice calls from upstairs. "Are you lost?"

The men outside are yelling at the men working upstairs.

"I'm here to visit my cousins," I say, timidly stepping closer to the door.

A man with hair speckled with bits of fresh wet concrete steps outside swinging an empty bucket. "Oh, you must be lost. Nobody lives here. We've been working on this apartment for over a week now."

Segvan, what on earth have you done?

47

Juwan

Hesenlu, Iran, July 1989

Did Segvan have something to do with their disappearance? Did they decide to go and pursue life in another town or at some refugee camp? Did they return to Iraq and leave me behind? But how, when they don't know anyone? With Segvan still away, I mull these questions over and over, each time feeling more puzzled and more worried.

On July 12, Segvan finally returns from his long trip. He looks exhausted and worn out, yet he takes me by the hand into the bedroom and hugs me like a child. It disgusts me. He doesn't smell of alcohol, so I know he's in his right mind.

With his body still attached to mine, I ask, "What happened to Mistekhan and her daughters?"

He takes a deep breath and lets go of me. I am prepared for rage, and his calm demeanor surprises me. He gently opens the dresser drawer and grabs a large towel before heading to the shower.

"I'm sorry, Juwan. I meant to tell you before my trip." He sees my shocked face, then adds, "I went by one day to check on them, and they were gone. Totally gone and with no trace. I asked around, and the neighbors said they saw them leaving with some of their belongings."

On his way to the shower, he turns to me again and says, "I'm sorry again, my love. I thought I had told you. I'm sure they'll show up again or settle somewhere much better. I tried to help them. I really did."

Over the next two days, he ignores me while cozying up to Shukriya. This in itself doesn't bother me even a little bit. I don't want him within ten feet of me. But his obvious dislike of my bringing up my family is as unsettling as it is puzzling.

Segvan decides to take Shukriya and the kids to the city to shop for Eid—a rare occurrence. I wait for them to leave, then get dressed and head to Zozan's house. Although not a scheduled work day, I figure with Eid being the next day, she must be on the verge of a nervous breakdown preparing her forever-messy house for the holiday festivities.

Zozan's husband, whose name I still don't know, went shopping for sweets and took the kids with him. Zozan's rundown of her day's events is frantic as usual. While I clean the kitchen, she yells from the second floor, describing her recent fight with her husband about whether they should go to Tehran to celebrate Eid or stay here.

I yell back. "Why don't you go? You don't want to see his family? Is that why?"

She is now mopping the stairs, and between her gasping breaths she says, "Oh no! It's him. He doesn't want to go."

She still refers to her husband in third person, and I have no plans to ask her what his name is. She goes on a rant for a good ten minutes. She wants to go to Tehran to escape the depressing environment here, but he wants isolation. Plus, according to her, his family has never been to their house, so it's their turn to pay some respect. What a strange world we live in. Some women can't stand seeing their in-laws, and they go to war with their husbands over it. Others, like Zozan, are ignored and neglected by the in-laws, and yet *she* wants to visit them for Eid and *he* refuses.

We are almost done cleaning when her kids storm into the house, followed by the dad, who looks distant and far away but manages to say hi this time. I excuse myself and tell Zozan it's time for me to go before Segvan gets back. Also, I don't want to witness another nervous breakdown when her children create another mess. I keep the latter thought to myself.

She walks with me to the main door and says, "Oh my God! I totally forgot. Your girl Dilveen showed up at my door the other day and asked me to tell you they are safe, but they desperately need some money for their mother's medicine."

I'm halfway out the door when I hear this. "What? Are you serious? And you didn't think it was important to tell me when I first got here?"

She taps her fingers nervously and shifts her weight from side to another. "I'm sorry, Juwan. I totally forgot. You showed up out of nowhere, and we got busy talking."

I'm not as angry at her as I am worried about the fact that Dilveen came to Zozan's house instead of to me.

I grab her shoulder and ask, "What did she say? Where are they? Zozan, you could have at least tried to contact me." I realize I've been shaking her with every word, but she takes the abuse without moving a hair.

"I'm sorry. I really am. I feel terrible. She looked distraught, and I tried to calm her down and find out more details, but she was in a hurry and gave me a number to call. She said it's a clothing factory she works at. Let me get it for you."

She escapes from my firm grip and disappears inside. None of the scenarios that come to mind are good. Zozan returns with one of her kids crying behind her and holding his brand-new Eid shoes and asking her to undo the tied laces. She ignores his cries and produces a piece of paper with some digits written on it.

"What will I do with this? I don't have a phone. Please, what else did she tell you?"

She studies the numbers again and says, "I'm really sorry. She came the day my husband and I had a fight." She is whispering now. "And I don't know where you live, so how could I communicate with you?"

Zozan fetches the paper in her palm and says, "Tell you what. I'll find a way to go to our school today and use the phone to call this number. I'll tell her to come and meet you here after Eid. I promise you, I'll do my best to get her back here. I'm sorry again. I wish we had a phone. If my husband weren't so laid back, he would have pushed the school district to install a line at our house by now."

I walk away from her house and toward the bus stop, my head buzzing.

~

SEGVAN SLOWLY RETURNS to my world. On the second day of
Eid, he takes Shukriya and the kids to visit her brother early
in the morning. She wants to stay a few days, so he asks me
if I want to visit Urmia. I shiver at the thought and immediately say no. I can already picture the silently intimidating
room with the old bed and worn-out window shades. I can
smell his suffocating breath and feel his body pushing
against mine, pinning me deeper into his control as I lay
there helpless.

I feel every bit of my breakfast rising in my stomach like
a sour and bitter volcano, which erupts as soon as I reach
the bathroom. I don't recognize myself in the mirror. I see a
faceless body, lost, useless, hopeless, regretful, and guilty.

Segvan knocks on the door, mumbling something I can't
quite make out over the loud faucet. I collect my thoughts,
regroup, and get out of the bathroom. I must change the
scenery and make him think about himself instead of me. I
need him distracted and at ease if I'm going to have any luck
getting back to Zozan's house as planned. I tell him a candy
or sweet I ate at Eid festivities probably didn't sit well in my
stomach.

I can't let him think that the name "Urmia" had
anything to do with my sick stomach. If that means I have to
force myself to go to Urmia with him, so be it.

Two hours later, we're driving around Urmia's crowded
streets, this time on the opposite end of the city, where
beautiful houses and well-dressed people give me a whole
new impression that isn't likely to trigger me.

I pretend to be interested and excited to be with him.
He's thinking about me now and a little short-term fun, but

my mind is far away from him, imagining a future where he doesn't exist. Whatever it takes for that to happen.

We shop at various high-end stores, then eat an early dinner. We grab ice cream on the way back, and it's scary how I'm able to be so miserable on the inside and seemingly content on the outside. I can't tell who I am anymore! What I know pretty well, though, is that the man sitting next to me and driving us home is not someone I could ever love or acknowledge, no matter how much he claimed to love and adore me.

On the fourth day of Eid, Segvan leaves to pick up Shukriya and the kids. It's my best and most likely only opportunity to make a move. I head to Zozan's house filled with anxiety and anticipation. Her husband opens the door and looks perfectly welcoming. He invites me in, but I kindly decline and ask to speak to Zozan. He disappears inside the house, and she emerges a short time later. Before I explain to her that today was my best chance at leaving the house, she pulls me inside by the hand and closes the door.

"Listen, I reached Dilveen after multiple attempts." My eyes widen with interest. "She said she can't come because her mother is too ill." Zozan can read the disappointment on my face, but she smiles and says, "Look, she gave me an address. It's the warehouse where they work. I have it written down. One moment."

She rushes back inside and returns with a yellow piece of paper, which she hands to me. She points to the address and the name of the factory. Underneath, she has written the bus route to get there.

"I really want to come with you," she says, "but I'm expecting my in-laws today, and I have to cook and get ready. And here, take this." She hands me a wad of cash.

"It's the money I owe you for your help plus some extra as a gift for your family. Please accept it as a token of our friendship."

I timidly accept the money and head to the bus stop, this time crossing the street to go toward Urmia instead of taking my usual route west back home.

I STAND at the door for what feels like eternity, knocking repeatedly and waiting for someone to answer. I pull the door gently, and it opens, but I quickly shut it again, unsure if I'm in the right place or what to expect inside.

A voice yells behind me. "Hey, what are you doing there? Move away, we don't allow beggars here."

I freeze in my place, too scared to turn or even flinch. A young man carrying a large roll of fabric over his shoulder passes me and heads to the door. "Are you deaf? Didn't you hear me? Go away!"

"I ... I'm sorry. I am not here to bother anyone. I just need to—"

"Go away," he says. "You're lucky the owner isn't here today, or he'd be chasing you with a mop stick."

I grab hold of the door just before it closes and yell behind him, "Please, I'm looking for a family member."

Loud machine noises come from all directions inside, making me more anxious. I keep my hand on the door and watch the young guy drop the fabric roll on the floor. He yells at me again, but I insistently walk toward him.

Then I hear my name called, and Dilveen emerges from behind a wall, yelling at the young man. "Ramo! Ramo! Leave her alone. She's my cousin."

She throws herself into a tight embrace with me while the young man looks on in disbelief.

INSTEAD OF MEETING with smiles and excitement, we meet with tears and disappointment. Instead of sitting and catching up over tea, we stand by a corner of the noisy warehouse and regale each other with the new chapters of sorrow in our lives. But I'm glad to hear they're safe and have a place to stay, and I'm glad Shireen isn't at work today. The last thing I need is her attitude. She and Dilveen have been alternating work days the past week so that their mother can be attended to at all times.

We don't broach the subject of my marriage with Segvan and the drama that surrounds it, although it's the deep and rotten root of our problems and the distance between us. I decide to save that for another time. Now, I must get home before he returns, so I place the money in Dilveen's hand and excuse myself, promising to follow up later.

She gives me their address in case of an emergency, and before I can leave, she grabs me by the shoulders and says with tearful eyes, "Thank you, Juwan. I don't know what we've done to deserve all this punishment, but please don't leave us alone."

But I'm the one living inside the lion's den. I'm the one who has been left behind. I am the one who is being punished!

48

Juwan

Hesenlu, Iran, July–August 1989

The nausea continues. The very thought of food gives me dry heaves. Earlier, Segvan asked Shukriya and me to fix dinner together, and I was surprised when she was willing to sit with me in the same room to have a meal, a rarity since our one-sided rivalry started. As soon as we put the plates down in the center of the living room, another wave of nausea hits me. I rush to the bathroom and vomit profusely.

They must think I don't want to sit with her. To debunk this theory and to avoid yet more drama with Segvan, I force myself through two rounds of hot tea and cut a fresh water-melon as Segvan tries to lighten the mood. He appears sober for once, and forcing myself to sit with Shukriya in peace is better than another intoxicated showdown.

Our lives under this roof are unpredictable and contradictory. We never know which version of the beast we're going to get. Everything could be rosy one moment and then turn into hell for the silliest reason or even for no reason. He claims to love me, yet he's stripped me of every last hope. I hate him, yet I find myself glad to see him safe and sound after each trip. Why? I don't know. I really don't. Maybe because I've lost my connection to any alternative, and to lose him would mean I can't backpedal. Somehow, deep inside, I seem to have convinced myself that in order for me to be able to leave, I must have him in front of me or I'll doubt my every step, worried that he could be anywhere, unseen, hiding, and plotting. Sometimes I get the urge to ask him to check just one more time if his news about Azad and Jamil's disappearance is true. Then I scold myself for being so stupid. What would I expect to hear back?

He inspects a large piece of watermelon, then takes a bite from it. "This watermelon is as red as an apple from heaven but as bland as a tree from hell."

He throws the rest of the watermelon piece back on the plate and picks up a yellow apple. He looks at me and then Shukriya, both of us keeping ourselves busy eating, then he takes out his Swiss Army knife and meticulously peels the skin off the apple until it falls onto the plate as one long piece. He slices a thin piece, stabs it with his knife, puts it in his mouth, and smiles. "Now I know why Adam was tempted to eat the apple. God hasn't created anything better than apples."

He chews through the rest of the apple, flecks spraying from the corner of his mouth. When he's done, I pick up the fruit plate, and he says, "Tomorrow I'm going on another trip that just came up, and I hope you two build a nice relationship with each other while I'm away."

I leave the living room when he finishes speaking, and seconds later I notice Shukriya storming out as well, her heavy steps speaking for her.

In the morning, I lay in bed while Segvan gets dressed. Even the sound of him combing his hair triggers my nausea, so I pull the sheet over my head and fight the urge to vomit. He repeatedly tried to get close to me last night, and I threw up once when he got close enough that I could smell his cologne. He then left my room and returned later, angry and cursing, when Shukriya wouldn't open the door for him.

"The bitch is pretending to be asleep," he said as I forced myself through dry heaves. "I know her."

There is some commotion between him and Shukriya over breakfast, and then it's all quiet except for the sound of the kids running around. The heat of July has only intensified as we approach the end of the month, and the ceiling fan doesn't help my nausea, so I head to the kitchen to fix myself a cup of tea with honey. I stand facing the front door as I sip the tea and reflect on all the times I passed through that door. What if we had never come here? What kind of world would await me if I decided to run through the door one last time and never look back? Where would I go? What would I do? Would the only real family I have here accept me? And how far would Segvan's octopus arms reach? Does he actually love me, or is this some sort of a mind- and body-control game?

I take another sip as Shukriya's familiar dismissive voice

comes from behind. "It must be nice to pretend to be sick so you don't have to wake up and make him breakfast."

A street vendor outside is yelling about the best kitchen-ware that will outlast even a house.

"Are you pretending to be deaf now?" Shukriya says.

I tap my tea cup with my fingernails, doing my best to appear nonchalant, then answer without turning to her. "I don't need to pretend anything, and I certainly don't care for your comments."

She is standing a few feet behind me now. "If you're going to continue to live here, you will have to do what I say. I rule in this house."

I turn around and walk right past her without acknowl-edging her presence, head to my room, put on my dress and abaya, and walk past her again. Right at the door, I turn and say, "I will do what I want, when I want, and you can do whatever you're capable of." I slam the front door behind me.

I reach Zozan's house and hear her on the other side of the door splashing buckets of water on the tile floor in the garage. She violently pours another bucket, and water flows under the metal door.

I knock once and say, "Hey, Zozan, open the door, it's me."

Her husband is home, but he pretends to be busy and heads upstairs as soon as I get inside the kitchen with Zozan. I follow her around the first floor as we clean up, organize, and catch each other up with our news.

"Are you alright?" she says. "You look pale and sick"

I'm taken aback by her question but decide to blow it off. "I'm fine. I'm just exhausted."

"Listen, my kids love the bean soup when you make it.

And you won't believe it, but my husband just asked me if you could make it for us. Can you?"

I smile and say, "Certainly!"

At one in the afternoon, we're ready to prepare lunch. I add fresh water to the bowl of beans and set it on the stove. When it's time to add oil and tomato paste, the smell sets me off. I barely manage to get to the sink before violently throwing up. I lay on the floor with dry heaves for a few minutes while Zozan repeatedly asks if I'm alright. Some time passes before I'm able to stand again, and Zozan helps me back to the sofa.

"I'm fine. I must've eaten something that didn't sit well in my stomach."

She looks down at my stomach. "When was your last period?"

I flinch in pain and barely register her question. It's not until after her follow-up question that I realize what she's asking me.

"Have you seen any blood lately?" I shoot her a desperate and pleading look as she continues. "Honey, I think you might be pregnant. Actually, I'm pretty sure that's the case. Tell me, when did you last see blood?"

How stupid! The possibility hadn't even occurred to me. I'm instantly up on my feet. "No, no. This can't be it!" I clench my fists until my knuckles feel like they'll pop off my hands.

I can't make out anything Zozan is saying. The room has turned dark. I only sense her presence behind me as she stands there, helpless, watching my nervous breakdown. I grab my purse and storm out the front door, ignoring her pleas for me to stop.

I SPEND the next four days going back and forth between my room and the bathroom. On the fifth day, I wake up determined to do something about it, to translate my anger and fury into action.

I walk to the concrete stairs up front, careful not to make any noise from my plastic flip-flops. I stop on the third step, look down, and jump. I climb up again, one step higher this time, and jump down again. I do it over and over again, each time landing on my feet, struggling to maintain my balance. Dammit! A pregnant woman in our village once lost her pregnancy after she tripped over a chunk of a tree and fell face-down. She didn't even bruise, but later that night learned that she lost the baby. I knew another young bride who went through her entire pregnancy refusing to carry a single pitcher of water, claiming she may lose her pregnancy if she lifted anything heavy.

Shukriya's voice cuts my thoughts off. "This is not how you end a pregnancy."

I freeze. She's standing by the corner of the bathroom wall. How long has she been there? More importantly, how in the world does she know I'm pregnant or what I'm trying to do?

"What did you just say?"

She smiles. "You heard me right."

I sit on the stairs, feeling pins and needles in the soles of my feet. Shukriya, with her gaze fixed on me, doesn't move.

I rise and walk down the stairs toward her. "Who says I'm pregnant?"

She chuckles and says, "A pregnant woman can smell another pregnant woman from a mile away."

"You are?"

"Yes, just like you."

"Why is this happening to me, God, why? What have I done to deserve this punishment?"

She follows me into the house. At the door of my bedroom, I sense her right behind me, still silent.

"Leave me alone! What do you want from me?" I blurt out.

"You are my rival, and I still hate you. And I'll always blame you for things that are your fault and even for those that are not. But you have to understand, I'm not your enemy here."

None of that makes any sense. I struggle to hold back tears as she takes my hand and leads me into the living room. The two of us sit opposite each other, separated by a few yards, although the space that matters extends for miles.

"What changed for you to decide to talk to me?"

"Look, honey, we're not friends, and we never will be. We have one thing in common, being pregnant by the same animal. That's all."

"Why do you stay with him? He beats you up, abuses you, and neglects your children, so why stay?"

She chuckles and shrugs. "Why do you stay with him?"

I look at her, insulted by her notion that I have a choice. "You're crazy if you think I wanted this or want to continue. I have no one left in this world to help me or protect me. I wish I was dead."

I feel nothing but sympathy for her as she tells me about her own struggle without any real family support. And in this society, divorce is nearly impossible for a woman. Behind her dismissive tone are cries for validation.

My nausea returns. "Well," I say as I get up, "I know one thing for sure. I'm not keeping this pregnancy or continuing to live this life. It's only a matter of time."

What she says next stays in my mind for days: "You have no idea who you're dealing with. This man is not just a smuggler. Have you ever wondered why he makes all these trips and has so many connections with the police and God-knows-who-else in the government? Think about it before you do anything stupid."

NUMB from the looming pregnancy and tired of spending my days camped inside my room, I decide to go back to Zozan. This time, though, I ask her to accompany me to Urmia. I want to see Dilveen, and since it's Friday, I figure she'll be off, so I hand Zozan the piece of paper Dilveen gave me and demand that Zozan help me find the address.

She gets dressed quickly and brings along her older son. We get off at the wrong bus stop and end up walking five or six blocks before a man points us to the heavily populated housing complex we're looking for. I try my best to ignore the trash on the street and the chaotic streetscape. Zozan, on the other hand, pinches her nose in disgust. She says she and her son will wait for me at the market down the street.

As much as I wanted to avoid seeing Shireen last time, this time I'm glad she's home. They're all home.

"You all have to hear me out," I say, "whether you like it or not. And if you don't believe what I'm about to tell you, you'll never see me again."

I tell them everything. Mistekhan quietly sobs. Dilveen nods her head as if indicating she knew there was more to the story all along. Shireen tries to interrupt, but her mother motions for her to shut up.

Dilveen hugs me tightly, then I gently push her away. "Look, I have no place with Segvan. And we have no place here. We have to stick together and find a way out."

"And go where?" Shireen says. "Do you have a magic stick you can take out of your behind?"

I slap her on the cheek. "I will not take any more abuse from you. You'll never understand what I've been through." I point toward my belly. "Do you have any idea how much trouble I'm in? Do you?"

"Look, Juwan, we all have more weight on our shoulders than we can carry," Dilveen says. "We don't want anything from you, and we're certainly in no position to judge you. Just help us with money whenever you can so we can pay for Mother's medicine and treatment."

Unsatisfied, I say, "You know I'll never shy away from helping you, but that's not the point here. We have to do something."

Dilveen interrupts me with a soft tone. "We are hopeless, helpless, and powerless. Please go home, and don't make this any harder on you or us."

I am angry, enraged, and unsettled. I leave the building, determined to confront Segvan as soon as he's back.

I RETURN home before sunset and find Segvan's car parked by the door. I hold my breath and collect myself as I enter the house. I've never been out alone this late, never pushed Segvan to this limit, and I should have thought about how he randomly returns from his trips unannounced, usually at the wrong times.

I find him sitting in the living room eating dinner. Shukriya is busy feeding her children. He sets his cup of tea down when he sees me. I try to maintain a straight face as I greet him. He's obviously angry, and I only pray that he isn't drunk.

We immediately get into a heated exchange, with him questioning my whereabouts and refusing to believe I was with Zozan the entire time. I turn to Shukriya and wonder if she's happy to see our downward spiral or if she has any sympathy for me.

Segvan blames her for letting me leave. I sense the rapid rise in tension and pray that Shukriya doesn't scrap with Segvan, who's now obviously intoxicated.

I keep quiet as he unleashes a barrage of insults at no one in particular.

When Shukriya picks up the dinner plates, she does what I'm silently begging her not to do: she talks back. "Why do you always blame me for everything?"

It's not what she says but how she says it. Or maybe that doesn't matter. Maybe what's about to happen was determined the moment Segvan stepped inside the house.

He kicks her left knee, throwing her against the TV. The dinner plates fly in the air, their contents scattered all over the floor. Shukriya gasps, visibly in pain as she holds her flank area and tries but fails to stand up.

I help her to her feet, but she pushes me away and says, looking straight at Segvan's red face, "You bastard! You haven't been here an hour, and you already want to show off your manhood."

Please stop it. Please stop talking. Shukriya, though,

won't back down. Segvan slaps her face, forcing her scarf off her head. He walks toward the door as I stand there motion-less, terrified, and wondering what's stopping him from laying his hands on me.

Shukriya runs her hand over her face and mumbles some insults. Segvan turns around, now right behind Shukriya, and shoves her face-down into the sofa with his foot in her back. As she extends her hands to protect her face, her chest hits the arm of the sofa and her belly hits its wooden edge.

I gasp and scream, "No! Please no. She's pregnant!"

Shukriya's kids aren't around, thank goodness. I run to her side, and she groans in pain with the slightest attempt to stand up.

Segvan stands at the door, chuckling. "Pregnant? This rabbit doesn't know anything else. Who said I want kids from her?"

Shukriya is finally able to sit on the sofa but still too weak to talk.

"Will you stop it? Stop being a terrible man, a terrible husband! Go ahead, hit me too. Go ahead! I'm pregnant too. Hit me, go ahead!"

Segvan's face drops. He approaches me and Shukriya, but I push him away, and he soon heads out of the front door.

Don't return. Inshallah, I think to myself, you leave and never come back.

I WAKE EARLY in the morning with Segvan dead asleep next to me. I hear Shukriya moaning in the hallway, and I immediately jump to my feet. I find her sitting in the middle of the hallway, crouched and groaning from pain. There's a trail of blood all the way to her bedroom door. I consider calling Segvan, but what good would that do?

I rush outside and summon Khateen, a middle-aged, heavy-set woman who has the look, personality, and deep voice of a man. She's the neighborhood's midwife. Since my arrival here, I've avoided making friendships and have had few meaningful encounters beyond the exchanging of pleasantries, but Shukriya told me about Khateen a few days ago and urged me to go see her.

She looks sullen when she opens her door, her hands covered with fresh dough and her face covered with flour. I tell her it's urgent, and she follows me to the house a few minutes later.

When we get inside, Segvan is on his knees next to Shukriya, and she's pushing him away with shaking hands. Khateen and I help Shukriya to her bed, where Khateen can examine her in peace. When she's finished, she curses and walks outside to face Segvan.

"Why do you keep doing this to her? What is it with you? The whole street can hear your fights. You nearly killed the woman after you killed the baby inside her. Fear Allah."

She's much taller and better built than he is, and I wish she'd knock some of his teeth out. She kicks him out of the house instead. A victory! I'll take it even though it is small.

After taking care of Shukriya, Khateen examines me too. The look on her face as her hand moves inside me says it all. I refuse to cry. I refuse to look weak. What I would give to be in Shukriya's situation right now.

I refuse to believe Segvan later that night when he

swears he did not mean to hit Shukriya. And when he tries to get close to me and celebrate "our baby," as he wants to label it, I confront him about what he did to Dilveen, Shireen, and their mother.

His face turns red. "How did you find out about it?"

"What do you *want* from me?" My lips shiver in anger.

Deep down, I want him to get angry and hit me. I want him to drag me to the living room and do to me what he did to Shukriya. I want to scream at him, tell him I hate him and the very thought of having a part of him growing inside me.

Instead, he says, "Juwan, I really love you. I want to build my life with you. If you think I'll divorce you or let you go, you are mistaken. I won't give up on you."

I bury my head under the pillow and ask, "Why me? Why are you doing this to me?"

He lights a cigarette and answers in the calmest voice he has. "I also wish I knew why I want you, but maybe the moment I do, everything will be ruined and you'll be just like Shukriya."

49

Dilveen

Hesenlu, Iran, August–November 1989

The owner of the clothing factory, Saleem Agha, is a kind-hearted Kurdish man who has been nothing but accommodating since we started working here. He has never asked about our lives or questioned us on our whereabouts.

Ramo told us all about him. He started this business with his wife in their basement over four decades ago. Eventually, the second floor of this building was buzzing and humming nonstop with machines, producing hundreds of boxes of clothing a day until Saleem lost his only son in the Iraq-Iran war a few years ago. Things went south after that, and he slowly lost interest in the business. The machinery stopped for a while last year when his wife started losing her memory and her ability to continue to function in the factory.

Now the poor man spends his time between the factory, where his memories have been embedded, and his home where his wife' memories are voided. Despite all this, Saleem Agha always comes dressed in a suit and with his grey hair neatly combed. He's always cleanshaven, but otherwise he looks lifeless. He never asks who's working and who's absent, and if not for Ramo, things would fall apart.

When Mother is feeling well, Shireen and I show up for work at the same time, and today is one of those days. Lately, she's been complaining of headaches again, and sometimes she can't use her left arm for a while. She refuses to see a doctor, and quite honestly I'm not sure we could even afford one. We haven't seen Juwan since her last visit to our apartment.

Saleem Agha is already in his small and clutter-filled office when we arrive. Ramo is upstairs moving some stuff around, and he comes down and greets us. I see the looks he and Shireen exchange every time they see each other.

Ramo appears to be Saleem's right hand. When I walk across the warehouse to grab a roll of fabric, I see Saleem hugging Ramo in the office and sobbing. I immediately look away, but Ramo notices me.

Later when we close and leave, Ramo accompanies me and Shireen as he so often does. "You're probably wondering why Saleem Agha was upset earlier today."

"I don't care," I say. "I just want to work and get paid."

"Today is August 16," Ramo says. "It's the anniversary of the day he learned of his son's death in the war three years ago. He has a nervous breakdown every time. I was hoping he wouldn't come to work today, but I guess he had to share his emotions with someone. He tells me I remind him of his son. It really breaks my heart."

"Maybe," Shireen says, "he'll pass the factory on to you."

Awkward silence.

"Stop being an idiot," I say.

Ramo parts ways in front of our building, and as I walk up the stairs, I can't help but feel jealous of the connection my sister has with him.

At the door, I slap Shireen's wrist. "Hey, tell me what's going on between you and Ramo? You better not get us into any trouble."

She shakes her head and says, "Don't worry. Our life can't get any shittier than it already is, so what's another problem to add? Plus, why do you care if I finally have a little life after all the hell and drama we've been through? Don't stand in my way!"

She walks past me and into the apartment. Thinking about it, I admit that I'm more jealous of the attention she's getting than worried about a potential problem. Why would a guy take a pass on me for my sister while another man, albeit an evil animal, is interested in Juwan instead of me even though he knew she was taken?

It has to be the damn scars. I know I shouldn't be thinking about this right now, but I'm human. I'm a woman with feelings. And these scars seem determined to hold me back, to torture me, and to sink deeper into my skin by the day. The damn scars!

∾

I DON'T KNOW how much longer we can continue. We're hardly able to make ends meet, Mother is barely mobile and has no interest in eating or anything else, and we're in limbo with Segvan and Juwan. Although we don't speak of it, we know those two are headed toward an explosion.

The best thing that has happened to us lately is Ramo, even though I resent feeling unwanted. He talked to the building owner, an old lady who lives on the first floor. She's not the type to let anyone squeeze by if they owe her anything. Ramo says Segvan paid her until the end of this month, but she's been demanding September's rent for days now.

Ramo asked us to avoid interacting with her to avoid unwanted attention. So Segvan was right: we're better off laying low.

I don't know what to believe anymore.

We don't hear from Juwan for weeks until one day in early September. Shireen and I walk back home as usual with Ramo. This time, we invite him to join us for dinner. Halfway up the stairs, we find Juwan sitting by the door of our apartment. If she weren't well-dressed, she'd pass for a beggar. She quickly gets to her feet when she sees us approaching her on the stairs.

"Thank God you came. I've been waiting for hours."

She looks tired, her face pale, and dark lines have formed under her eyes. She definitely lost weight since we last saw her, and I can't help but sneak a peek at her belly even though I don't even want to think about her pregnancy.

Shireen walks past her to unlock the door.

"Why were you sitting here?" I say. "My mother is home. Why didn't you knock?"

Juwan stretches from the fatigue of sitting on concrete and says, "I knocked a hundred times. No response. I came three days ago, and the same thing happened, but this time I'm not leaving without seeing you. I can't keep making this trip."

Three days ago we took my mother to the doctor, so that would make sense, but today? A wave of anxiety passes through my chest, and my heart pounds when I hear Shireen scream from the living room. We all rush through the door to find Mother laying on her side with her head on the hard floor.

Surely she's dead.

I drop to my knees and start slapping my legs and thighs.

Ramo and Shireen attend to Mother and gently move her over.

Ramo says, "Her chest is moving, thanks to God."

She opens her eyes, and I let out a hysterical cry. Juwan stands timidly behind us, unsure how to react. She looks around with a sense of nonbelonging. When Mother attempts to talk, her mouth droops, and the left side of her face appears draggy. I grab her left arm and lift it up, and it's as heavy as a large stone. As soon as I let go, it drops back next to her thigh.

I lose track of time while we get her situated, and I snap back to my senses when I hear Shireen yelling at Juwan. "Why do you keep coming here? You have the feet of bad luck. Look what happened to Mother the day you decide to show up. Go! Leave us alone. Enjoy your life with the knight of your dreams."

Ramo just stands there, silent, while Mother is looking at us, trying and failing to say something.

I turn to Shireen and scream, "Stop it! I told you to stop talking to her like this. She's not the reason this is happening. Shut up!"

Ramo intervenes now. "OK, ladies, this is not the time. Your mother is ill. That's all that matters." He then turns to Juwan and politely says, "My sister, maybe it's a good idea to keep some distance until things settle down."

Juwan shakes her head. "I'm not here because I need anything. I'm here as a family member. We have a common enemy who's put us in this position. I won't let you stop me from coming here. We have to find a way out of this hell."

Her face is now swollen and red, and she storms out the door. Soon, Ramo is gone, too, and I find a small stack of paper bills on the couch.

I wave the money in Shireen's face. "Do you see this? Is this what you're angry at Juwan for? You stupid idiot. I swear by the name of Allah, I will cut your tongue if there's no other way to stop you from talking."

THE NEIGHBORHOOD DOCTOR, an old, friendly nurse turned expert, comes to our apartment the next day with Ramo. After examining Mother, he determines that she had a stroke and may or may not recover her ability to speak or move her left side. "You can take her to the hospital and run some expensive tests, but the doctors will tell you the same thing."

Ramo shrugs. "Well, we trust our doctor, and he's rarely wrong." I have a feeling Ramo doesn't want to be dragged into a financial swamp.

We agree to watch her for another week and then revisit

the situation. Ramo pays the doctor, and when I ask him about the expense, he adamantly refuses to even discuss it. "You're family now. How dare you speak of money?"

He won't say he's like a brother to us because he's not. At least not to Shireen. Can I blame her for falling for such a great guy? What more can a vulnerable girl in a foreign land ask for?

It suddenly dawns on me that a year has passed since we left home and lost our hearts and sense of identity. Oh, Mother. What were you thinking about when you fell on your face and lost your speech and strength? What did you imagine had happened to your sons before your mind could no longer take it?

Three days pass, and Mother's condition remains the same. She requires help in the bathroom, to get up, and even to sit in the chair. She chokes on food if it isn't liquid.

I'm busy at work sewing a red dress when Shireen rushes into the warehouse and whispers, "That thug Segvan just left our apartment."

I take my foot off the machine's pedal. "What? What did he want?" She and I move to the hallway where we can talk more freely, and Ramo follows.

"Segvan came by very angry. He didn't even care when he saw how bad mom looks. Apparently, he and Juwan had a fight. He's furious that we're still in contact with his princess and ruining their marriage."

So nothing new. A couple of the ladies in the warehouse see us talking and stare at us.

"Ladies," Ramo says, "get back to work. What? You've never seen humans talking before?"

"This time," Shireen says, "he said he'll make sure the authorities handle us."

"Let him eat shit," Ramo says. "He's bluffing."

Shireen mumbles under her breath, "You don't know this guy."

As much as I hate Shireen's in-your-face attitude, it's unsettling to finally see her intimidated.

When Ramo is off attending a malfunctioning machine, Shireen asks me, "So what are we going to do? I keep telling you that Juwan's dumb face shouldn't come to see us. She brings us nothing but trouble."

"And she also helps us with money we desperately need."

Hearing myself say those last words makes me feel selfish for taking money from Juwan while giving her no space in our lives. But which life are we talking about? Life in a cramped apartment that smells of old paint, humid walls, and exhaust from the street? Life on the run, not knowing what to expect or where to go or what might happen next? Do we owe Juwan anything? Maybe? Maybe a lot more than we're willing to admit. Definitely more than Shireen will ever realize.

But at the same time, are we obligated to put our survival on hold while we sort everything out?

MOTHER IS no better next week. When the doctor returns to check on her, he offers little hope in terms of improved prognosis. Then things take a sharp turn for worse when Ramo shows up early one morning, frantic and terrified, while we're eating breakfast and Shireen is already dressed and ready to go to work.

"Get your stuff ready!" he says. He pants repeatedly and catches his breath, then continues. "You have to leave."

"What do you mean?" I say.

He gulps an entire cup of water at once and wipes his lips with his shirt.

"This morning—a police car was parked in front of the building when I arrived. They stopped me and asked if I knew two girls working there illegally. They didn't mention your names, but who else would it be?"

I notice that the front door is still open, so I ask Shireen to close it and lock it.

"The look on their faces was serious," Ramo says. "They said someone tipped them off that two girls left the refugee camp and never went back. That bastard actually did it."

Mother is listening attentively, and I can see her face wrinkle as she struggles to speak.

I say, "Mom, don't worry. Just relax. We'll take care of this." I then turn to Ramo and use the calmest tone I can muster. "So then what happened? Are they here?"

"I told them how you two were recommended to Saleem Agha by another person, and being the nice guy he is, he said okay without requiring any documentation. They're still parked next to the building, most likely waiting for you to arrive so they can arrest you and God knows what else."

We scramble to get our stuff ready, and when I return from the kitchen, Ramo is gone.

"Ramo went to get a taxi while," Shireen says, hustling around the apartment for whatever valuables we can't leave behind.

I suddenly realize we have no idea where to go. But Shireen answers my question before I can ask it when she tosses a bag of clothes at my feet. "Ramo said he'll take us to the village where his folks are, away from attention."

I don't feel comfortable with his unilateral decision, but what choice do we have?

THE DRIVE TAKES NEARLY AN HOUR, including some traffic delays, with Ramo instructing the driver to use back roads as much as possible. No questions asked. The driver spends the majority of the time listening to the radio, switching back and forth between various stations, all in Persian. After struggling to get comfortable in the car with the three of us in the backseat, Mother is finally able to nap as we drive through the countryside, much of it yellow as we approach mid-September.

Ramo points to a hill about half a kilometer away from the main road and tells the driver to drive around it. His folks live in a village on the other side in a large stone-and-clay home with a massive farm next to it. The rest of the homes are located on the opposite side of the hill.

The remaining doubts I had about Ramo dissolve when we meet his parents and his two wonderful grandparents. They're all lovely, welcoming people. And either their son has already told them a lot about us or they're the type of hosts who don't ask prying questions of guests.

We spend a week slowly adjusting to a new place and yet another trauma. After leaving our jobs, we have no financial support. At first, we were worried about Ramo getting in trouble, but to avoid raising suspicions, he immediately drove back to the city after dropping us off. When he returned two days later, we were relieved to learn that the police never returned to the factory. But when Ramo stopped by the apartment, the door was open, and the place was empty. Segvan was serious. And it's not safe to leave trails that may lead him to us.

With Ramo gone the majority of the time, we grow accustomed to the new family, which has provided us with one of their three bedrooms. It must have belonged to Ramo prior to our invasion.

I wonder if we could find a way for Juwan to join us here, but the mere mention of it sends Shireen into a fury. She threatens to run away if Juwan ever learns of our new place. She makes sure Ramo knows that as well.

I have to admit that I'm siding with her this time. It's no longer about our relationship with Juwan. We can't leave a door open for Segvan.

Perhaps we can develop a plan during the winter to return to Iraq or go to Turkey when springtime arrives. And maybe Juwan could join us then. But then I imagine her very pregnant belly and the rough terrain.

Shireen and I help the family with farm work, and in the mornings we often bring Mother out to sit in a chair facing the open fields. Back home in BerAva, this was the time of year when the villagers started preparing for winter. Once October arrived, cool breezes warned of the cold to come, and the trees let go of their leaves. Now here, so far from our village, we desperately look for any resemblance of home but don't see it. Even the trees look less inviting, the cattle wilder, the water less soft, and the sky uninspiring.

It's a cold and foggy morning in early November. Mother opens her eyes after nearly a full day of sleep and motions for some water, which she is barely able to drink. Her lips are dry, her face anemic, and her eyes weak and twitchy. Mother, the woman of God, the mountain of patience who stood strong against waves of tragedy, has finally raised the white flag. She is not about to go in her sleep. She is going to give us one last chance to talk to her, to feel her warmth, and to reassure her that we will be fine, although we have no way to deliver on that promise. I refuse to make the last sight of our faces a tearful one. Instead, I rub her sunken cheek as her head rests in my lap and remind her how strong a woman she is.

She twitches while taking her last breath and raises her index finger to the sky. I actually see her death. The death of her sorrows and miseries. The death of her despair. The death of hopeless moments of waiting. Mother always told us that with each soul leaving this earth, new ones are created and born. So with Mother's death, there is birth but also another burden of loss on my shoulders. Another scar made from mountains. And so mother leaves us and departs a world where she has seen more cloudy and rainy days than sunny and peaceful ones.

With the help of a few ladies in the village, we wash our mother's body and properly prepare it for burial. By early evening, light rain falls as we lower her body into the ground. "All glory to Allah," one lady says to another, "she is buried on a Friday, and the rain proves she was pious." Only if you knew!

50

Juwan

Hesenlu, Iran, November 1989-February 1990

The world is merciless. Brutal. It could not care less who falls while it continues to spin.

Children are playing as they always do out the window as my belly continues to stretch in defiance of my will. It's cold outside. The rain comes down harder, forcing the kids to abandon their soccer match and head home.

I felt the baby kick earlier this morning, but I ignored it. I do not wish to be reminded of its existence. I'm certainly not looking forward to its arrival.

I envy Shukriya. She lost her pregnancy, but Segvan scarred the inside of me. I run my hand over my belly and wonder if babies can sense how their mothers feel about them. I spend the rest of the day waiting for another kick, but it doesn't come. Maybe babies can feel rejection.

I have called Dilveen at the factory three times from the phone at Zozan's school with no luck. Every time, a man says the girls no longer work there and hangs up.

Once, however, I recognize Ramo's voice on the other end of the line. When I introduce myself, he goes silent for a few seconds and then says, "Don't call here again."

When the first snowfall clears in mid-December, I take advantage of Segvan's growing excitement with the pregnancy to ask him to take me to Urmia to shop for baby clothes.

"Absolutely," he says. "Spend as much money as you want on whatever you find for him."

Him? So he's already expecting a boy. Disgusting.

When we finish shopping, I ask in a begging voice, "Please, Segvan, let me check on Mistekhan and her daughters. I just want to see if they are OK."

I expect him to raise hell, to get angry, to fume, or to at the least ignore my request. Instead, he calmly says it's okay.

But I should have known better. When we reach the apartment, an old man opens the door. He's irritated that we made him come out in these freezing temperatures. Yes, he lives here with his wife. Yes, they recently moved in. No, he never met the previous tenants. Then he shuts the door in our faces.

Segvan, I know you had something to do with it! You can't fool me by acting surprised. You can't make me fall for your lies anymore. And no matter how much you try to keep me within the walls of your house, I will find out exactly what happened.

WINTER IS hell in this house. With his smuggling season still off, Segvan is around more often and always fishing for a fight. He lays on the living room sofa for hours, demanding total silence in a house with little kids. On the days he goes out, he usually comes home intoxicated, angry for losing money in a card game, or both. Iran's strict laws against alcohol, gambling, and other social sins seem to have been written with carveouts for Segvan.

One day he comes home and announces that he's having friends over for dinner. Shukriya and I have less than an hour to prepare. They're important guests, he says, and two of them are police officers, so he brought two bags of meat and three chickens.

Shukriya questions him about the timing, so he ignores her and turns to me. "Will you please cook us dinner since this cow over here seems to have forgotten how?"

"Your princess can cook shit for you and your guests," she says. "I'm going to my room."

He grabs her head and pulls it toward him in one forceful move, throwing her to the floor. Once she's down, their eyes meet, he standing above her and she on the floor. He leans and punches her in the face. Her older daughter, standing in the hallway, adds to her mother's painful groans with cries of her own.

I grab his arm and push him out of the way. Before he can storm back at her, I grab a large knife, step between them, and point it at my belly. "If you touch her, I'll kill myself."

He freezes. His eyes fixate on the blade and then move down to my belly. I silently dare him to move forward and give me a reason to end the misery. I walk toward him, the knife still at my belly, and he starts to retreat.

"When I get back in an hour, dinner better be ready." He stalks off in defeat.

Five hours later, his guests are still in the living room, smoking, playing cards, yelling, and hurling obscenities at each other. Shukriya is sleeping in her room with a swollen cheek while I try to find ways to entertain myself and the children.

A FEW DAYS LATER, while Segvan is out, Shukriya approaches me in the hallway. "Let's go check on your family."

I stare at her, puzzled.

"I heard you arguing with him about Dilveen and her family, and I want to help you."

The ground is still wet from yesterday's rainstorm, and Shukriya's kids enjoy jumping into several small puddles as we walk to the bus station. Schools are out as the country observes a national holiday of some sort, so we hope to find Zozan at home. Shukriya initially declines to go inside, but after much insistence, she reluctantly joins me with her girls.

A nice new-model gas heater sits in the middle of the living room. Zozan's kids are fixed on the TV screen and watching a cartoon featuring heroes fighting some sort of dinosaurs. Shukriya's kids join the TV party while I introduce her.

Zozan looks at her for a few awkward moments before catching herself and saying, "Oh, I'm sorry. We haven't met!

I was wondering why I didn't recognize you. Welcome to my house."

I move beyond the pleasantries and awkwardness and ask Zozan for help accessing a phone, then I remember that the schools are out for the day. "How stupid of me to pick a day like this to look for a phone."

"You are so in luck. After more than a year, they finally installed a phone line for my husband. We've barely even used it."

It's on the desk on the opposite side of the living room. She hands me the receiver and helps me dial the number to the clothing factory. It rings at least seven times before an old man answers. I recognize the same unwelcoming voice that had told me Dilveen and Shireen no longer worked there. This time, I hang up before saying a word.

I try a dozen more times until I finally get the familiar young voice. As soon as he says hello, I introduce myself and beg him to please not hang up on me. I just want to know if Dilveen, Shireen, and their mother are safe.

There's a long pause on the other end, followed by a deep sigh. I know Ramo didn't hang up because I can hear machine noise in the background.

I beg him again, and he finally says something. "Please let this be the last time you call here. You're going to get me in trouble. The short version is their mother passed away. They don't want to meet you or talk to you. Got it? Now please go away."

An angry click and the machine noise is gone.

∽

IT HAS NOT STOPPED SNOWING since last night. My painful contractions have picked up since last evening. They bring me to tears every time.

I'm scared, lonely, and above all unprepared. Last night the contractions were so severe that Shukriya asked Segvan to go and get Khateen. But she said, "Let her get the screaming and pain out of the way. The baby won't arrive until morning."

After his third attempt to summon Khateen, Segvan gets angry and goes to sleep with the kids in the other room while Shukriya stays with me in my room.

Shukriya opens the window blinds. "It looks like three feet of snow out there. Every year we get a storm in February, but this is the worst I've seen in years."

Three feet of snow mean blocked roads. I feel another contraction coming, and with a grimace I say, "What if I need to be taken to the hospital?"

"Don't worry too much. Khateen is an expert. You're in good hands."

Unsatisfied, I take a few shallow breaths and ask again, anxiously, "But will Segvan take me to the hospital if I need it?"

Shukriya steps away from the window, letting the shades fall against each other again and darkening the room. "Don't you see how excited he is? He's dying to see his son! He would carry you on his back if need be. Now, you need to take deep breaths and not fight the contractions."

The contractions intensify, their frequency and pain increasing, while my cries reverberate against the concrete walls and back into my ears. I try to relax my muscles in hopes of the process reversing itself and the baby somehow going backward in and disappearing forever. But Khateen announces she can see the head emerging.

The baby finally arrives in the late morning hours after much pain, sweat, and screaming. A sharp cry wakes my tired and sleepy body, reminding me yet again this is not a dream. This is reality, and rather a sad and terrible one. Exhaustion overcomes me, and I can barely follow the conversations around me.

Khateen brings me the baby, wrapped in a purple cloth, and says, "Congratulations, my dear. She has your eyes."

She! A girl! I hear Shukriya whisper something to Khateen as she leaves the room.

In the hallway, I hear Khateen yell at Segvan, "Where is my fee? Show me the money! We got you a beautiful girl."

I'm still catching my breath and don't know how much Segvan pays Khateen, if anything, but I hear him say, "God cut your life short, Khateen, for giving me such terrible news."

Moments later, Khateen returns to the room mumbling some curse words and says, "Men will never change."

With the first touch of my baby's face against my body, my soul is rejuvenated. Everything but this beautiful little face becomes trivial. Everything! Go on, my little baby. Take the milk and let me see those hazel eyes. I don't care what he says or does. You have my eyes. And together, we'll leave all pain and sorrow behind.

I will name you Helan, "to leave behind."

51

Azad

Mardin refugee camp, Turkey, October 1989–March 1991

We close the infirmary at five. Our Kurdish dikhtor asks me and the young Turkish trainee doctor if we want to join him for a soccer match, and we both nod.

Doctor Altan, the trainee, graduated from medical school less than a year ago. Born and raised in Ankara, he was initially unhappy to be shipped to Mardin for his first year of rural medicine training, but he soon settled into the place and found his work exciting.

He says his mother is Kurdish, but he only knows a few words of the language, certainly not enough to communicate, so he and I speak in English to each other. We both struggle at times, but I have a lot more ground to cover than he does. He's a good practice companion, and he convinced the camp administrators to keep me as an interpreter. I make three times as much money doing this job than I did as a laborer at the nearby market.

Dr. Altan helped one of my tentmates, a photographer prior to the Anfal Campaign, find and purchase a used video camera, which he has been using to capture life inside the camp. Altan also pushed the camp administrators to run a dedicated phone line to the office in case there's a medical emergency. Although we can't use it to make regular outgoing calls, some families here have received incoming calls from abroad. The last one was from a guy in Germany who insisted on staying on hold, neverminding the expensive international costs, for over half an hour as we searched for his parents.

When I head back to the tent after the soccer match, I find Jamil playing with his son. Little Wahid has grown! He's on his knees as Jamil gently throws a small ball at him.

A nearby tent became vacant a few weeks ago when an entire family reunited with their extended family in the Mushe camp. I and the rest of the single guys moved over there so Jamil could move his wife and son in with him. It took some convincing for Jamil to agree to that, but he took it as a sign that I had turned myself around even though it was only partially true. He has a family now. His wife and baby need him, and I can't allow my emotional wreckage to get in the way. At least the nightmares don't torment me as often as they used to.

～

BY THE SUMMER OF 1990, I expand the camp school to include classes for ladies, although some elderly men take issue with "the ways of city folk," as they put it. Finding a few young female teachers helps mollify them a bit. Now our school offers classes in the Kurdish language, Kurdish history, and the Quran. For those interested, I'm also offering English courses.

On the afternoon of August 2, 1990, while I'm hanging around the infirmary and exchanging some jokes with the dikhtor, Jamil rushes through the door. "Check the news," he says, panting.

He hands me my cassette player, which includes a radio, and says, "Iraq has invaded Kuwait."

The news creates an uproar in the camp. Those of us with family members back home still serving in the army understand the grave prospects of another war. And there's real fear about what more Saddam could do after he's finished with little Kuwait. The evening chatter is constant:

"He has the power and the army. He'll keep going until he swallows all the Arab gulf nations."

"It's the fault of those Arab idiots for giving him money and weapons to use against Iran. Now they're going to drink from that same cup of poison."

"He may turn around and attack Turkey, and guess who will be his first bite!"

"You're an idiot and never understood politics."

"Nothing is too much for the Ba'ath Party."

Later, as an international coalition swells against Iraq and an attack grows imminent, talk in our camp becomes even more animated.

"I hope that when the January deadline comes, Saddam

is still in Kuwait so the Western allies can crush that son of a bitch."

"As if he'll be harmed. Didn't I say you know nothing about politics?"

"I've been to more wars and shot more guns than your brain can count."

IT'S AN UNUSUALLY cold day in late November. I stand in front of my class of some fifty kids going over a basic English lesson. Many of the students are visibly shivering from the cold weather. The three electric heaters are barely helping, and kids are taking turns sitting near them to stay warm.

A young voice outside the tent calls my name. I step outside and see a boy standing there. "Why aren't you in school?"

"My father said it's urgent," he says defiantly. "Someone is here to meet you. Hurry!" His next words trigger a rush of adrenaline: "Our guest says he knows where your family is."

I hurriedly follow the boy to a large tent. Once inside, I struggle to catch my breath.

One of the men says in a welcoming tone, "Here comes our camp professor. Welcome, Mr. Azad."

I study the faces of the men inside the tent, and one of them is unfamiliar. He's wearing a thick navy-green military jacket, and I fix my narrow gaze on him.

He clears his throat and says, "My name is Tahir. Aren't you Wahid Barwari's son?"

I shake his hand and sit across from him. My fingertips

are numb and cold, my nose sniffling, and a fury of questions erupt from my mouth.

He walks me through every step of his encounter with my mother and the rest of our family members, including Mam Yasin. His ability to recall specific details and dates is astonishing. My chest nearly explodes when he tells me he handed them over to a smuggler named Segvan, who promised to take them to his small town near Urmia in Iran.

I turn to the boy and instruct him to go find Jamil for me. When Jamil joins us, we both ask Tahir so many questions so many times over dinner and tea that we keep him up way past his bedtime.

He looks exhausted. "I'm sorry it took me so long to look for you and to find you. I spent months locating my own family scattered in various villages near the border. But as soon as I heard about your whereabouts, I came here."

NEARLY TWO AND a half months pass slowly and heavily as Jamil and I anxiously clear one hurdle after another. First, two major snowstorms block access to the mountains. Then there were reports of military movement and potential unrest along the border, giving our potential guides and smugglers cold feet.

But we're finally ready to go. Our guide is a local Kurd from Mardin who is charging us arms and legs for his services. I sold my TV and cassette player and paid him all the money I had saved from working. Jamil added his own savings plus money he got from selling his wife's necklace. It will be too late by the time Siti finds out about it. We also borrow some money from Husain Ziway.

Everyone believes the guide is taking advantage of us beyond imagination, but I'm not willing to wait any longer, and although Jamil was reluctant initially, he agrees with me now that the longer we wait for a cheaper option in the spring, the more likely the area will explode before we go.

We're coming for you, Mother. I am finally coming for you, Juwan, my love.

52

Juwan

Hesenlu, Iran, February 1991

It's February 27, and my lovely baby Helan has just turned one. She doesn't spare any opportunity to stand up and walk. In the last few weeks, she's fallen backward and forward more times than I could count.

I'm standing against the stairs by the bathroom, watching her play with Shukriya's daughter Shahla, who is gently holding her hand as if declaring herself responsible for her safety. Shukriya is upstairs on the rooftop, hanging wet laundry.

"So he stayed with you last night?" I say as she walks down the stairs.

"Oh, honey, you can keep him any time you want. He smelled of alcohol and cigarettes, as usual."

"Why does he do this?" I ask as she passes by me.

She turns around to looks at me, the red plastic laundry basket in her hands, and raises her eyebrows, wondering what I meant.

"I mean, why is he evil-hearted toward women?" I whisper.

She giggles and says, "Don't worry, he can't hear you. He's deep asleep, hung over, and probably wouldn't wake up if you blew up dynamite next to his ear."

She sets the basket down and walks back toward me. "I'm convinced he hates women because of his childhood. Of course, no one knows his real family story, but my brother once said he heard that Segvan's mother poisoned her husband and ran off with another man, stranding the kid on the streets."

She's whispering too now even though she said I needn't bother.

Shahla bosses Helan around, instructing her to hold on to the wall so she doesn't fall over.

Shukriya picks up the basket and says, "Have you asked yourself why he was so disappointed that you didn't give him the boy he always wanted?"

I hear a knock on the front door. Helan and Shahla head toward it, but I pick up Helan and walk to the door myself. Helan kicks and attempts to break free. I hold her tightly and say, "No, my baby. You can't walk out. You will fall and get hurt."

I open the door, and what I see can't be real: Azad, Jamil, and another man I don't recognize are standing there.

I can't even breathe. Azad looks as shocked as I feel.

"Hi, Juwan," Jamil says. "Thank God you're safe."

So it's true. This is real?

I look from Jamil to Azad. He's leaning against the door, exhausted and in shock, as if seeing my face is enough to knock him out at the knees. His face is pale, his hair long and dirty. His jacket is muddy and dotted with small holes from fire sparkles.

He sees that I'm holding Helan. My daughter—Segvan's daughter—is trying to break away from me, so I set her down, and she crawls back inside.

"Juwan," Azad says, and reality breaks over me like a wave. It's his voice, but it's surprised, shocked, and strangely hesitant. My legs feel weak, and the images of the three men blur together as my head becomes lighter.

I hear Shukriya's faint voice behind me as if at a great distance, but her hands are on my shoulders, I'm falling back against her body, and everything turns to black.

I WAKE UP IN BED. Helan is crying somewhere in the room, and Segvan is leaning over me and saying my name.

"Hey, there you are. What happened to you?"

I'm still half asleep as Segvan's barrage of questions continues. What happened at the door? Who was out there? Are you sick? Did something happen that I need to know about? Why did you pass out? Is this the first time this happened to you?

Shukriya tries her best to deflect the questions. "I think she's low on water, or maybe her blood level is low. It happens after pregnancy."

I motion for them to bring Helan over to me, and she climbs onto my chest as I slowly regain my orientation.

Segvan's questioning continues, and Shukriya tries to keep up.

"There was no one outside," she says. "She followed her daughter to the door as a street seller was passing by, but she lost consciousness before she got a chance to look at his merchandise."

When Segvan finally leaves the room, Shukriya sits by the head of the bed and whispers in my ear. "Girl, that was Azad?"

I close my eyes for a few seconds while Helan pulls on my hair, desperately seeking my attention. "So it's real?" I say, opening my eyes, tears falling down to my ears.

Azad is back. He's back in my life, only to see me belonging to someone else. Does he know I'm married? Did he figure out that the little girl I held in my arms is my daughter? What will he think of me? Does he know his mother died?

So many questions run through my mind as Shukriya describes her brief encounter with him at the door as I passed out. She's raising her voice only enough for me to hear her without being overheard by the octopus around us.

"I was worried Segvan would wake up because my kids started to scream when you passed out. Poor Azad was already in shock when you fell into my arms. I told him to come back tomorrow at noon when my husband, our husband, won't be home. I closed the door and don't know what happened to them afterward."

I push my daughter off me and close my eyes again. I have a terrible headache. I'm sick to my stomach. I want to be dead, to lose my ability to think, remember, and feel. I vomit violently on the floor and continue to wretch for a few minutes. I catch a glimpse of Segvan standing at the door, looking at me and shaking his head, then disappearing. God, please take me!

53

Azad

Hesenlu, Iran, February 1991

I'm confused. Who was the girl Juwan was holding in her arms? Why did Juwan look so shocked and disappointed when she saw me at the door? Where are my mother and sisters? Where is her dad? Dammit! And who was the other woman? Why did she desperately try to get rid of us?

It's obvious to me, Jamil, and even our guide that something isn't right, and it's obvious that Juwan is married.

Now I'm smoking again and have already burned through a whole pack in this dirty hotel room somewhere outside Urmia.

"Azad," Jamil says, "you need to calm down. Don't jump

to conclusions. We'll find out what's going on when we go back there. Just rest."

I take a long puff from the last cigarette, looking through the fogged-up window overlooking the street. "Didn't you hear the lady? She said 'our husband.' And I want to know what happened to Mother, Shireen, and Dilveen. She didn't even want to talk to us!"

At the requested time, we present ourselves at the front door again. This time, Jamil asks me to step back so he can do the talking.

The other lady opens the door, anxiously looks around, and says, "Juwan is ill. She can't get up, and I think it's better if she doesn't come out. My husband could come home any time, and you guys could get in a lot of trouble if he sees you here, trust me."

I step forward and say, "Just tell us where my mother and sisters are."

A car drives past, and the lady jumps in fear. She follows the car with her narrow eyes, then sighs in relief when it turns away at the end of the street. "Your family is not here. We don't know where they are."

Jamil clears his throat and says, "What do you mean you don't know? Juwan lives here, so where are the rest? Where is her dad? We want to talk to him."

She offers me a piece of paper and says, "Juwan's father is dead. Here is where you may find your family or get some information. Now please leave. I don't want trouble."

At three in the afternoon we arrive at the address, which turns out to be some kind of clothing factory. A well-dressed older man greets us at the door, and we're relieved when he speaks Kurdish. He lets us inside when we tell him we just have a few questions. He leads us into a messy office, where two young men are already sitting.

When our guide asks him about Dilveen and Shireen and if they used to work here, the gentleman turns hateful and uninviting. He immediately gets up and motions for us to leave. "I thought you were here for a clothing inquiry. Please go, and don't bring me any more headaches."

I desperately plead with him. "Please, sir, just give us a second. I'm looking for my sisters, and I just need you to listen to us."

He's not having any of it, and moments later, we find ourselves standing outside, puzzled and angry.

The guide points at a small restaurant across the street. "Let's go eat and think of what to do next. I'm am starving."

Jamil and I follow him, a million questions running through our heads.

Somebody approaches us from behind, calling, "Hey, you guys, slow down."

I don't make much of it until a hand grabs my shoulder. I turn around and I'm certain he's one of the young men we just saw in the warehouse. The young man says he caught part of our conversation and wants to know exactly who we're looking for. I give him a quick description of Dilveen and Shireen and otherwise as few details as possible in case he has ill intentions.

"What's your name, and how do you know these girls?"

"They're my sisters, man. What do you know about them? I'm starting to lose my patience."

Realizing I may lose my cool anytime, our guide steps between us and tries to placate this young man who won't even tell us his name. We invite him into the restaurant with us to eat, but he declines, saying he has to get back to work.

"Look, I don't know where the girls are now, but I can try to find out. They used to work here. But I need to know who you are first. It's not a safe world anymore, you know?"

Despite my attempts to get him to talk, the man insists that he first has to check his sources and then he'll get back to us if he has any leads. He takes our names and our hotel information. His condition: don't come by the warehouse again. He promises he will come looking for us if he learns anything.

"We'll be in the hotel for two more days," the guide says.

The next morning, Jamil and our guide go outside to get us breakfast and cigarettes. I refuse to leave the room. The hotel is in an industrial area crowded with sketchy people. It smells of urine out front, and the building itself looks as if it might collapse at any moment. At night, mice of various sizes wander around in the room at ease.

I'm in the bathroom trimming my beard when I hear a knock on the door. The receptionist told us not to open the door if we're not expecting someone because beggars have been breaking in and robbing guests. But I am expecting someone, or at least hoping for someone, so I open the door.

It's the young man from yesterday. "Azad," he says panting, "I know where your sisters are." I invite him in, and he says, "I'm Ramo. Forgive me, but I couldn't tell you anything until I checked with your sisters to make sure you are who you claim to be. They're safe, and we can go see them now."

I reach for my pack of cigarettes and realize it's empty. I ask Ramo for one, but he says he doesn't smoke. "Where are they now? How's my mother?"

Ramo puts his right hand on my shoulder and says, "It's

a long story, my brother. I'm ready to take you to them whenever you are."

Jamil and the guide enter the room, announcing excitedly, "We have fresh bread, a plate of yogurt, and hot tea."

They freeze when they see Ramo. Before they can even set the food down, I say, "Let's go, guys. Ramo is here to take us to our family."

PER RAMO'S ADVICE, we pack with no plans to return to this dump of a place. On the way and via two buses, he gives us a brief version of events without getting into too much detail. He's especially evasive about our mother.

When we reach the village, Dilveen and Shireen are already outside, pacing around anxiously, and they run toward us once they see us. Had Ramo not told me that my sisters thought we had died, I would think they'd gone crazy with the way they inspect me and Jamil before embracing us.

"Where's *Dade*? Mother? Where is she?"

The more Jamil and I ask, the more Dilveen and Shireen avoid eye contact with us.

An old man approaches me from behind, places his hand on my shoulder, and says, "It's our destiny, my son. We all shall taste from that glass of death. To Allah we belong, and to him we shall return."

I struggle to keep my balance. Jamil shouts at Shireen and Dilveen, demanding an explanation.

Shireen buries her head in my chest and sobs. "Mother is gone. She's dead. She left us. Where have you been? Why did you both leave us?"

My body is breaking down from the accumulated exhaustion. My mind is crumbling too. My younger sister continues to pound on my chest, demanding an answer for why we abandoned them to a foreign country.

I'm startled by a sudden clap of thunder.

A lady steps out of the house and introduces herself as Ramo's mother. "Please, come inside before it rains."

There's a cold breeze in the air, and the wind starts to pick up as we accept our host's invitation.

"Go easy on yourselves and on your sisters," Ramo says as we step inside. "They've been through a lot, and they need you two to be strong."

54

Dilveen

Hesenlu, Iran, March 1991

I t rains all night, making it too muddy to walk across the village to the cemetery. Out of respect for our privacy and emotions, the host family calls bedtime early. The five of us—Shireen, Azad, Jamil, the guide, and I —sit near the fireplace as wood slowly burns and twists, making an already heated room even more charged.

Shireen and I recount in detail everything that transpired since we left BerAva. Whenever we mention Juwan and Segvan, Azad's facial expression stiffens, and his pacing turns more rapid. He sits next to the window for hours, waiting for the rain to stop so he can pay a visit to Mother.

Jamil, on the other hand, wants to know even the tiniest details about how Juwan ended up married to a smuggler and a stranger. He listens intently as Azad pretends a lack of interest but burns through a pack of cigarettes like the world will end tonight.

When we finish, Jamil shakes his head. "My God, I can't believe what I just heard. Allah has protected you so far, but it's sad what happened to Juwan, and mercy on Mam Yasin's soul. I can't imagine Juwan ever putting a stranger ahead of family and friendship."

Shireen adds a few more logs to the dwindling fire. "What I know is this: life's challenges reveal who people are so we can separate true friends from selfish clowns."

Azad turns toward her from the other side of the room, clearly offended, but maintains silence.

"You," I say without looking at her, "need to learn to shut up. You know less than a sheep's turd about life, and I'm tired of your mouth."

Sometime, long after midnight, Jamil says, "OK, dear family. We have an obligation to figure out what we can do for Juwan if she wants our help."

Shireen, surprisingly, says nothing.

Jamil continues. "Can we find a way to talk to Juwan to see if she wants to live with this man or not?"

Of course Shireen's silence can't last. "And what will you do if she wants to leave him? Are you going to kidnap her?"

I jump in and say, "I think the concern she and I both have is that this man is dangerous and well-connected. Just look at what he's been able to do to us so far!"

The rain is hitting the windows hard now. Azad gets up and lights yet another cigarette. My eyes follow him as he paces from one end of the room to the other. "We're leaving in two days," he says, "and we're not going to talk to her or get involved in her business. Start getting ready."

His tone is serious, and the idea of reaching out to Juwan now seems far-fetched.

With her back still to us while she's adjusting the logs in the fireplace, Shireen drops her biggest statement of the night: "I'm not going with you."

I can't say I am surprised, but I didn't expect her to come out and say it like this.

Azad abruptly stops pacing. "What did you say?"

Shireen stands up and faces Azad with daring eyes. "I'm not leaving this place. I've had enough of running around. You can beat me, drag me, or kill me, but I'm not going anywhere."

Our father never beat us or punished us physically when we were growing up. That was unusual in our village. Thankfully, Jamil and Azad took on that trait. But judging from the anger on Azad's face, I wonder if he's finally going to hit her.

He throws his cigarette into the fire. "Just what was missing from our family. Young girls defying those in charge." He repeatedly punches the wall.

Jamil shakes his head. "You're coming with us, whether you like it or not."

The defiant Shireen I know is not going to back down this easily, especially since I know what she has on her mind. The argument heats up until Azad finally screams at her with a barrage of cursing and shouting.

The guide is awake now, and so are the hosts. I have a strong feeling they've been up and listening all along. Come and join the party, everyone.

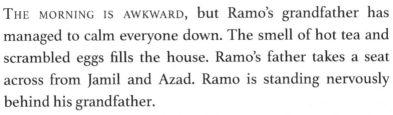

THE MORNING IS AWKWARD, but Ramo's grandfather has managed to calm everyone down. The smell of hot tea and scrambled eggs fills the house. Ramo's father takes a seat across from Jamil and Azad. Ramo is standing nervously behind his grandfather.

"You are our guests," his father says. "More than just guests. By now, you're like family to us. You've been through a lot, and the only way through is by sticking together. There's something we were planning to discuss later, but I'd better bring it up now."

All eyes are on him. But I know exactly what he's going to say. You've done it now, Shireen.

"Marriage is a blessing from God. And what more does a parent want for his son than a good bride from good upbringing? My son Ramo is someone any family would be blessed to have, and I'm not saying it just because he's my son."

Just get to the point.

Ramo nervously stands there as his mother watches from the kitchen.

"It is our honor to ask for the hand of your sister Shireen for my son Ramo according to the way of Allah and his messenger."

Shireen rushes into our room and closes the door. Sure, pretend you're shy. Go on. Act as if this is news to you. But then, who can blame a girl who has had to endure so much and yet finds a man and a family willing to embrace her and protect her as one of their own?

Jamil clears his throat. "We're humbled by your kindness and generosity, and it would be our honor to have kinship with a wonderful family like yours." Azad and I look at Jamil with puzzled eyes, but he continues. "As you know, we have a lot to sort out. Please give us some time to discuss this."

RAMO'S GRANDFATHER ACCOMPANIES ME, Jamil, and Azad to Mother's grave. After offering some comforting words, the gentle grandfather with the beautiful white beard leaves us alone and returns home.

Mother's grave is soaked from last night's rain. Both Azad and Jamil get on their knees in the mud next to her small headstone. Standing behind my brothers, I try my best not to cry, but it's impossible not to with both of them inconsolably sobbing.

Mom, I hope you hear our footsteps and our voices, and above all I hope you can finally rest knowing that your children are reunited and that your boys are alive.

I wipe my tears and pat my brothers on the back. "Let's head back. You both look exhausted."

On the way back from the graveyard, we pass fenced farms and old barns.

I slip and almost fall, but Jamil grabs my arm. "Careful, sister." He looks concerned. Even he, the most emotionally balanced among us, is buckling.

Azad is now a good ten feet ahead of us, walking alone with his head down.

"This place reminds me of BerAva and the good days," Jamil says.

I grab a long stick from the side of the pathway and use it to prevent myself from slipping again. "It's gone, Jamil. That beautiful life is gone."

He looks at me without speaking for a moment to emphasize what he's about to say. "Look, Dilveen, we've all been through a lot. More than we could ever imagine, but so have thousands of other people from our own blood and land. We're not giving up. We have to stay strong and stick together. Look at him." He points to Azad. "He's not handling this well. So for his sake, and for the sake of our youngest sibling who will be looking up to us, we have to stay strong."

"Speaking of that wicked little sibling of ours," I say, "we need to figure out what to do with her."

We catch up with Azad, and as we get closer to the house, he points to a stone fence. We head toward it and take a rest on the discontinued broken fence and discuss Shireen's marriage proposal.

Surprisingly, Azad is calmer than he was earlier, perhaps because he doesn't have the energy to fight another emotional battle. Jamil is skeptical of Shireen's ability to make a sound choice. While it's apparent to us that Shireen has already made up her mind about Ramo, I remind Jamil and Azad that they, as the men in charge of the family, get to make the final decision.

"Our family doesn't have girls who just run off and marry people on their own," I say, but I know my sister well.

"What exactly does she want here?" Jamil says. "Doesn't she want to live with her own family anymore?"

I run my stick in the mud, drawing random lines as I reflect on the thought that one day, perhaps very soon, my sister and I may be living in different countries. Am I enraged by her rebellion against me, us, the whole world? Yes. Do I fully blame her? I can't answer that. Am I jealous that she was courted by a total stranger at first sight? Call it jealousy or frustration or bitterness or whatever you want, but I'm not about to let my feelings get in the way of helping my sister decide what's best for her.

So what's best for her? Azad wants to go back to Turkey tomorrow. But then what? Can we fault Shireen for not wanting yet another journey into the unknown?

I lose track of time and my surroundings until I hear Azad's voice. "What do you think? Hey, Dilveen? Are you with us? Wake up!"

"Sorry, what did you say?"

"Jamil thinks we should say yes to avoid further problems, plus this family seems like good people."

"If you both feel that way, I'll support your decision."

"But what do *you* think? Don't let us stop you from voicing your opinion!"

"Look, guys. A lot happened after we left BerAva, and what I've seen makes me believe Shireen won't come back with us. I'm glad we're on the same page here, and I say we go back and give them our decision. We shouldn't lose the connection we have with her."

I look in the direction of the village, my eyes filling up with tears. I press the stick hard against the ground, and it breaks in half.

Jamil asks, "Why are you crying, sister?"

I hit my foot with the broken piece of the stick. "I think Shireen will end up being the wisest and luckiest of us all."

They both remain silent, knowing I'm not finished with

my thoughts yet. I wipe the tears away with the back of my sleeve and continue. "She'll get to stay close to Mother and be her neighbor."

Azad gets up and stretches his legs, followed by Jamil. The decision has been made.

Back at the house, Ramo's grandfather is outside and calling us to come in for breakfast. After we eat, Azad formally accepts the marriage proposal, and he and Jamil shake hands with Ramo, his father, and his grandfather. Ramo's parents promise to hold a well-deserved celebration of the marriage, but Shireen insists on the contrary. She says she could never enjoy a real wedding if our mother can't be there alive. The rest of us say nothing. We're leaving the next day anyway, but Ramo's father has a warning for us.

"Try to leave while the weather is good. And I caught some news on the radio about more unrest in Iraq. So you'd better go before things explode."

Great! More fighting!

ON THE MORNING of March 3, 1991, I wake up and find that my younger sister is not next to me in the room. Instead there's a small leather duffle bag with all my clothes and belongings in it.

I find Shireen in the kitchen preparing breakfast with her future mother-in-law. There are containers of food on the counter that will soon be filled with food for our journey. Ramo's mother pours hot tea in two thermoses that Ramo bought at the market yesterday.

Shireen starts crying as soon as our eyes meet. It's obvious that she slept very little last night.

An old brown-and-white SUV arrives at eight, and all of a sudden it's time to go. Shireen insists on accompanying Ramo and his father with us to the Turkish border, but Azad adamantly refuses. There's not enough space. Shireen and I embrace each other for what feels like eternity. "Please take care of yourself" is all I can manage to say.

I miss Mother already. Shireen promises me she'll make regular visits for me and never let the grave soil get dry.

With our wet cheeks against each other, I whisper in her ear, "Promise me you'll find a way to reconcile with Juwan and keep an eye on her. Open your heart, and let your heart open your eyes."

She nods, and Azad gently pulls my shoulder. "It's time to go, sister. We have a long way ahead of us."

Azad hands her a small piece of paper and says, "Here's the phone number at our Mardin camp. All you have to do is ask for my name."

WE RIDE in silence for a good hour or more before reaching a small abandoned village.

The driver says, "This is where we part ways. I'm not allowed to drive past here." We collect our belongings, and he points toward the mountain ahead of us. "You should be able to reach the top by dark, and I strongly recommend you don't stop there. The Turkish checkpoints on the other side will be able to see you in the daytime."

Our guide exchanges some information with the driver, who turns our direction and says, "You're fortunate to have such an expert for a guide. He'll deliver you to your destination in no time."

We follow our guide along a rocky trail up the mountain and disappear into the wilderness. Wolves are howling in the far distance.

I elbow Azad.

"Don't worry, sis," he says between panting breaths. "We're safe as long as we stick together. Go on, keep walking."

Preach on, brother. If only we had stuck together when we were forced to leave home. Things could have been a lot different now.

The cold wind hits my face, and while I'm sniffling and panting, Azad grabs my duffel bag and adds it to his load, allowing me to pick up my pace. When we reach the top of the mountain, I see scattered lights far away. Luckily, the weather is cooperative. There's no rain or snow in sight.

Our guide insists that we not stop until we're deep into Turkish territory and in a well-hidden area where we can rest and avoid being spotted. He keeps reassuring us that he has done this many times and knows what he is doing.

During the evening of the next day, while walking on the Turkish side of one of the border mountains with Iraq, we spot a fire from far away. The temperature has fallen drastically, and we're short on water. According to the guide, after we cross this mountain, we'll reach populated areas where we can find a ride.

Azad and Jamil are hesitant to approach the fire, but the guide reassures us that it's probably just a Kurdistan Worker's Party guerrilla unit that he can deal with, no problem.

When we're within shouting distance, the guide loudly announces that we're Kurds, unarmed and harmless, and that we need water and warmth. Relieved to not be ambushed or shot at, a man shouts back that we're welcome to join them.

Five men in total, only one of them armed, are sitting around a large fire. They stand up and greet us with smiles and create space for us near the fire. They speak the same dialect that we do and tell us that they're heading from the Mushe refugee camp to Duhok so they can join the Peshmerga forces that are slowly preparing for an uprising.

Jamil is thrilled. He spends the next hour asking them detailed questions about the state of things in Duhok while the men brief us about the lousy state of the military throughout Iraq.

"Saddam is done," one of them says.

Another coughs violently for a good minute or so, then says, "The Arabs in the south have risen, and now it's our turn."

Azad dozes off, but I sit there, my eyes closed, attentively listening.

"So what exactly is going to happen?" Jamil asks.

The man with the gun says, "All we know is that fighting has erupted between random Kurdish forces and the Iraqi army units scattered on the mountains near Erbil and Sulaymaniyah. We expect things to spill over into Duhok soon, so we're going to join the liberation forces that are being put together."

Jamil becomes antsy and insists that we get going. Azad agrees. We don't want to get caught in any crossfire.

WE REACH Mardin in late afternoon on March 5. Exhausted, cold, and hungry, we wait far away from the camp and decide, per Azad's recommendation, to wait it out until dark. Then we can sneak into the camp through a hole in the barbed wire fence.

The guide decides that his mission is complete, duty over, and says he's always available if his services are needed again. He leaves having scored a hefty payment.

Darkness falls. Lines of yellow lights glow above the tents. Somewhere a child is crying.

"That must be your wicked son," Azad says to Jamil.

They both smile, and I feel as if they somehow regret smiling as they get up. I follow them carefully, and we slowly walk toward the camp and march into another chapter of our lives in lost lands.

THE NEXT DAY, while still recovering from the trip, a commotion stirs throughout the camp.

My fears are later confirmed when Jamil returns to the tent and says he formed a group of two dozen or so men who are going to join the liberation forces in Duhok. He's determined. The decision is not subject to change.

His wife ambushes him with the news that she's pregnant again, but he ignores her and heads to a meeting.

I beg Azad to reconsider the decision to go to Duhok.

He chuckles and says, "Me? Do you think I'm crazy? I'm not made for politics. I don't even know how to shoot a gun. Leave me alone, I have enough ripping my head apart."

My poor brother. I know you're hurting deep inside, even if you refuse to admit it.

At night, every radio in the tents around us is tuned to a station, Arabic or Kurdish, covering the uprisings in Iraq. Men yell in celebration when the radio announces the fall of the town of Rania at the hands of local Kurdish rebels.

Jamil chuckles and with a wide smile says, "The days of the Ba'ath regime are limited now, and by the will of God, we will crush them."

The camp is ecstatic, but the mood is dim in our tent as Azad and I desperately try to change Jamil's mind. His wife sits there, quietly crying, while changing her son.

"Look here, Jamil," Azad says angrily, "don't let this nationalistic talk blind your mind. We're in a refugee camp, do you understand? A damn refugee camp!"

"So? Why should that stop us from pursuing dreams of freedom?"

"Look at your father-in-law and your brother-in-law. They're not going, and you can't tell me you're more patriotic than your father-in-law!"

"Everyone is free to make their own choices. I helped put this unit together months ago, anticipating and dreaming of such a moment. Nothing can change my mind, so save your energy."

"What about your wife and son?"

"What about them? They have my brother and sister here, don't they?"

The conversation was over before it started. I wonder how Shireen is feeling now, so far from us! My eyes tear up while Azad and Jamil continue their fight. I scream at them to stop and focus on what we can do to keep this family together instead of further division.

But Jamil is going, his decision can't be reversed, and we can't afford to have him leave on a bad note. So I pack him some food and an extra set of clothes while his wife puts her son to sleep.

He leaves on March 7 with twenty-seven men.

55

Juwan

Hesenlu, Iran, March 1991

All my life's sorrows have culminated during the past few days. I feel as if the ground has collapsed underneath me.

I've spent most of my time in my room as if I were chained to the bed. Shukriya's efforts to console me have all been in vain. When Segvan is home, I pretend to be asleep or in deep pain. Anything to keep him away. When he's out of the house, Shukriya rushes to my room with food, water, or tea, but life has no taste and no meaning.

Even when my daughter lays on the floor with dirty clothes soaked in urine or smelling of feces, I can't make myself change her or attend to her. She reminds me of him, and as mortifying as that is, at times I want to wake up and not see her in my life. I pinch myself for such thoughts toward an innocent life, but she carries his blood, and I just can't live with that.

I hate him. I hate the ground he walks on. I hate the air he breathes and exhales. I hate the day I met him, all the help he has given us, and I would rather have died at home under the bombs than become the prey of a predator in a foreign land.

On the morning of March 5, he makes another attempt to talk to me, but I refuse, which only makes him more frustrated. He heads out of the room and yells at Shukriya in the hallway. She screams back at him, and I immediately pull the covers over my head.

Sometime later, when Shukriya walks in with the breakfast plate, her left cheek is red, and I groan from pain and anger. She sets the tray next to me on the bed and stares at me. "So what now? What do you want to do?"

"I want to die and escape from this world."

"Don't say that, Juwan. God will punish you for such thoughts."

"Will God also punish the man who is the reason for our misery?"

"Everyone gets their punishment eventually," she says, moving closer to me. She pulls the covers off me and demands that I sit up and eat. "I'm sorry, Juwan. I'm sorry for being suspicious of you, for accusing you of things, and for everything bad I've ever said to you."

The last thing I want now is a rehash of our fights. I'm in no position to give or take sympathy.

"Tell me," she says, "what's on your mind? We need to find a solution. You can't keep living like this."

"Just leave me alone!"

"I won't. He'll know something is up, and we'll both be in trouble. Do you want me to find a way to contact Dilveen?"

"And tell her what? Please accept me back? After all my family has done *to* me and after what I've done *for* them?"

"You know they love you. This has been a nightmare for all of you, and I pray to God that everyone responsible gets the worst of punishments."

My chest squeezes as I envision Azad reuniting with his sisters and leaving me behind in this snake's hole. I feel disembodied imagining myself stuck in this life for even one more day, let alone months and years.

The front door opens, and moments later his yelling fills the house again. How much I hate hearing that sound, that voice, that barking, that growling.

He soon appears in the doorway and stares at the two of us. "I see a reunion of love taking place here," he says sarcastically. "Finally. All thanks to God." He enters the room and leans against the wall. With a cool yet angry and hateful tone, he says, "Are you going to tell me what's going on? You'd better not be hiding anything from me."

He stares at me, but I refuse eye contact with him. Helan and Shukriya's three girls barge into the room. Shukriya runs to the door and gently pushes the girls out and toward her room to play.

Looking straight to the large mirror ahead of me, I say to him, "Maybe you've been lying and hiding things from me."

He takes a few steps toward me, and with an unlit cigarette between his fingers, he waves his hand in my direction and says, "What do you mean by that? Don't play games with me. You understand?"

I collect my thoughts so I can formulate a response that will get his attention and rattle him at the same time. He's agitated by my silence, and he shoves the breakfast tray. Food clatters to the floor. Then he yells for Shukriya to get him a cup of hot tea.

She doesn't move, so he shouts louder until she heads toward the door. On her way out, she trips and falls to her knees. When she's on her feet again, Segvan slaps the back of her head and says, "You better not have poisoned her mind with your venom, you ugly witch."

My blood comes to a boil. "You lied to me about Azad. You lied to his mother and to his sisters, and you took advantage of us when we trusted you. Don't you have a drop of dignity?"

He clears his throat and gently says my name, trying hard to maintain a soft tone, and sits next to me in bed.

I head him off before he can say anything else. "Don't even try to lie your way out of it this time."

He takes a deep breath, exhales, and cracks his knuckles. "So you talked to the two bitches again and against my will."

I leap to my feet. "No, I actually *saw* Azad ... and Jamil. They are alive, and you are a monster, a monster, a monster."

Before I know it, he attacks me like a wild animal, his strong hands bracing my shoulders hard against the dresser. The large mirror shakes with the impact, then he pulls me to him with one hand and forces my face right up against his. His breath reeks of alcohol.

For the first time, I feel his violence and predatory wrath first-hand. I'm scared but refuse to show it. I finally understand how incredibly strong Shukriya is for standing up to him every time he assaults her.

I'm able to free myself from his grip momentarily and make a run to the door. Right as I open it, he grabs my shoulder and holds me in place.

Shukriya is at the door in front of me, a cup of tea in her hand. "Stop it!" she cries and sets the tea on the floor.

Segvan pulls me toward him again and shoves me against the wall. I try to scream, but he wraps his fingers around my neck. Our faces are nearly touching, his eyes bloodshot.

The kids are at the door now, and Nahla is crying.

His grip tightens around my throat. My breathing stops, and my head feels numb. My eyelids open wider, but the light becomes darker.

Shukriya desperately tries to pull him away from me, then disappears. The world turns to black, and it feels like an eternity passes before I'm finally released.

Before I even know what's happening, Shukriya screams: "Take this, you monster!"

"You bitch, what did you do?"

"What you deserve!"

I can't see. Everything is still dark. But I can hear. The children are screaming. Shukriya is screaming.

And Segvan is screaming. Shukriya and the children scream more, but Segvan's cries subside.

My vision slowly returns like a dark cloud sliding across the sky on a rainy day. Shukriya is standing a few feet from me, frightened and shocked, with a bloody knife in her hand.

Segvan is on the floor, face down, arms outstretched, a large pool of bright red blood growing around him.

I lean down to check on him, my hands trembling and freezing. He isn't breathing.

"I killed him," Shukriya says. "I stabbed the monster three times. I did what needed to be done a long time ago."

I take the knife from her hand as she stands there frozen. The kids are still screaming, their cries growing louder and more persistent. I shove Shukriya out of the room and close the door.

This can't be real. I have a dead body on the floor of my room, terrified children screaming outside, and the perpetrator in shock on the opposite side of the door.

Without further thought, I open the door again. Shukriya is still frozen there in the hallway, and I have to slap her face to get her attention.

"Here's what happened," I say. "He took a swing at you as usual and tried to choke you, and when I couldn't get him off you, I stabbed him. Now go outside and call the police or tell one of the neighbors!"

Shukriya is hyperventilating, seemingly collecting herself slowly and realizing the gravity of what has happened. Her lips tremble, and she struggles to mumble her objection. "No, I can't do that. You can't take the blame for it."

She falls to her knees, further rattling the children.

Yes, Shukriya, you're going to do it. This is finally coming to an end, and it was never going to end well. I'm tired. Exhausted. And I'm not going to take care of his kids while she is in prison. Let them take me instead.

KHATEEN ARRIVES FIRST, storming through the door and into the bedroom.

"*Khole b sar*," she says, "damn your life. What did you do?"

One of her daughters rushes in, and Khateen yells at her to go home and call the police. Then she pushes me and Shukriya into Shukriya's room and demands an explanation. "Did he beat you up again?" she asks, looking at Shukriya.

I say with a cold tone, "He tried to choke her and nearly killed her. I had to stop him." Shukriya opens her mouth, but I cut her off. "If I hadn't done it, he would have killed her and then me."

Everything that happens next is a blur. There's commotion as more neighbors stream into the house. A jumble of men's and women's voices. There's a faint sound of sirens. My head is swirling. I can't even stand. Then someone violently pulls me up from the bed and handcuffs my wrists.

56

Juwan

A jail in Iran, March 8, 1991

I 've thought of death plenty of times before, usually when I feared getting caught in the crossfire between the Peshmerga and the Iraqi military. I grew up worried about spending my youth alone if my father died at an early age like my mother did. And I thought of suicide when Segvan was the only thing in my life. But I never imagined sitting in a tiny jail cell surrounded by concrete walls in a foreign land, facing the consequences of murdering a man who's apparently important to the government.

I've been locked up for three days now with very little food and water. The room is about fifteen feet by ten, old, dirty, and reeking of urine. Four female inmates were already here when I was brought in. Two of them have not said a word. The third hasn't stopped mumbling, twitching, and making all sorts of strange sounds. The fourth asked me a few questions, all in Persian, but I try to keep a distance between us.

In the corner of the room is a small bathroom with no door. It has no running water, and I've never been so good at holding my bladder. A tiny window hangs far above us opposite the door. It lets in just enough light that we can recognize each other's presence.

I'm terrified each time the crazy inmate gets up and pulls on the bars. The rattling sounds send shivers down my spine. This time, a male guard approaches the cell and taps on the bars a few times with his stick, announcing the daily inspection and ordering us to make sure we're covered up and dignified. He inspects the room, including the bathroom area, and leaves. Moments later, another guard throws pieces of bread and cheese inside the cell. I hadn't touched any food until this morning, but I finally grab a small piece of bread and nibble on it while desperately waiting for my one cup of water for the whole day, which I gulp down all at once. Once food and water are served, that's it. There will be no more until the next day no matter how much you scream, beg, or ask kindly.

For the first two days, I was left in the cell without being interrogated or even visited. Then today, sometime in the morning or noon—it's hard to tell since the window gives out so little light—two guards call out my name. I jump to my feet. One of them yells something in Persian while I stand with my hands against the bars.

The other says something to him, then turns toward me

and in Kurdish says, "We'll open the door, and you'll follow us to the interrogation room, but any unexpected moves and you could be shot. Understood?"

I nod, lowering my head to further indicate my submission. The hallway is narrow and cold but well-lit. There are three rooms to the right, all with solid walls and no windows, and I hear men chit-chatting after passing the first two rooms. One guard walks in front of me while the other one, the Kurdish-speaker, walks behind me. I can feel that he's maintaining a close distance.

We turn left at the end of the hallway, and he whispers, "Do you have any idea how much trouble you're in? Who does that?"

My heart beats faster, a surge of anxiety overtaking my already shallow breathing. I can feel sweat running down my arms. I bite my lips to stay focused and to keep myself from passing out on the concrete floor.

We finally reach an office with a white door and a large glass window. Another guard motions for us to proceed, and I enter behind the first. Two more are inside sitting by a desk, their eyes fixed on me as we pass through their room and into a windowless room with a steel door.

They instruct me to sit on a small wooden chair across from a skinny officer wearing a neat long-sleeve shirt. He has a thick mustache that seems too much for his small stature. Separating us is a small wooden table, under which the officer has crossed his legs. His thin hair makes him appear older than he probably is. He studies my face while I sit as deeply in the chair as I can, doing my best to make myself disappear.

For the first time since I held the knife and claimed that

I had killed Segvan, I feel the heaviness of it, the weight, like a thundercloud is descending onto my head.

The officer aimlessly flips through the file in search of nothing in particular. I keep my gaze on my knees as long moments pass in silence. Suddenly, the door opens and the Kurdish guard from earlier greets the officer sitting across from me. The officer looks up at me and says something in Persian. Now I realize that he was waiting for the interpreter. Somehow his face looks familiar, but every stranger I meet in this place is similarly wicked and ugly.

The line of questioning starts with the interpreter shifting his focus between me and his superior.

"Do you admit to the killing of Mr. Segvan?"

"Yes, but—"

"You only answer to the specifics of what you are asked. Understood?"

"OK."

"Tell me what happened and why you killed him."

I keep my head down and my eyes on the handcuffs. "He was always violent with us, especially with his first wife, Shukriya. He was going to kill her by choking her."

The officer demands more details, his voice increasing in intensity now. I walk him through the altercation and Segvan's attack. I change nothing except swapping myself with Shukriya. His face turns red as I recount the details until he waves his hand for me to stop.

He abruptly gets up, says something to the guard, then storms out of the room with his files. I look up nervously toward the guard, begging for a look or gesture of reassurance, but none is offered. Instead, he says in a rather dry tone, "You killed one of his close friends," then instructs me to stand up and head to the door.

So that's it? No further interrogation? No one will listen to my full story?

"Keep walking, please," the Kurdish guard says as he leads me back into the hallway.

My steps grow heavy as I walk next to the guard, contemplating the mess I've gotten myself into. The shock is starting to wear off and being replaced with a waking nightmare with a cast of unseen monsters, all hungry to kill and destroy.

"I'm sorry, "I say as we turn the hallway toward the cell.

The guard says nothing.

"I have an infant daughter and I want to make sure she's OK."

When we reach the cell, another guard opens it. My opportunity to plead is dwindling.

"Please, help me arrange a visit with Shukriya, his first wife. She should have my daughter with her. I'm sorry about what happened. I didn't mean to do it. I'm sorry. I'm scared. What did I do!"

He removes the cuffs from my hands and closes the door. "The first wife will be here tomorrow for questioning. I'll see what I can do."

My thin blanket has disappeared, so I'm forced to sit on the bare concrete. I am too terrified to search for it because I'm convinced one of my cellmates will kill me if I do.

Nothing between these walls is normal, but I'm the biggest anomaly. How can I explain my unconditional love for Azad, whose personal goals always came before me or my total commitment to his family when they're so unappreciative—or at least that ungrateful whore Shireen? Above all, how can I take the fall for murder, especially for someone who always considered me a threat and antagonized me in every way possible? For that, I deserve to sit here as a worthless, misfit creature.

But the person I'm taking the fall for is taking care of my daughter. My baby Helan! I wonder what you're doing now, my angel. I'm so embarrassed that I haven't given you the love you deserve. It's not your fault, but his presence in my life as the only thing linking us together always made it difficult for me to bond with you. Now that he's gone—and good riddance to the deepest corners of hell—his absence has made room in my scarred heart that can only be filled with your love, the only love that could ever heal me.

THE NEXT MORNING, two guards drag out my crazy cellmate kicking and screaming. When she finally disappears down the hallway, one of my other cellmates yells, "Hey!"

She's pointing to my blanket, lying there coiled where the crazy one used to sit. I stare back at her, and she adjusts her head scarf, revealing a wide scar on the upper part of her cheek. I remain perfectly still. She reaches out to the blanket with her foot, and drags it across the floor, then kicks it in my direction. "What?" she says in Kurdish, her voice rough and thick. "You haven't seen humans?"

I slide the blanket under my legs and only now realize just how hard the bare concrete floor is.

I leap to my feet when I hear the crazy woman shouting again.

"Sit down," my cellmate says. "She's not coming back."

I wonder what she did to end up here. And the crazy one. And the others. One thing is for sure: I am not going to ask them.

~

THEY BROUGHT me to jail blindfolded in the back of a truck, so I have no idea where we are. It can't be more than half an hour away from the house, but in which direction? I want to ask my cellmates where we are, but what difference would that make?

The cell is more peaceful now that the crazy woman is gone, but the silence is growing more awkward. I feel like every whispered conversation is about me. I imagine myself as a high-profile killer the entire nation must be familiar with by now.

What have they done with your body, you bastard? Have you been buried yet? Wherever your body is, I hope your soul is burning in hell. Not fair if God allows an evil soul like yours into any merciful place.

Suddenly it hits me: I know where I saw my interrogator before. He has been to my house, to our house, to Segvan's house. He was there the night Segvan invited his friends and made me cook for them. I clench my fists and press my lips together, surrendering to the darkness awaiting me.

A jolt of fear hits me when I hear tapping on the metal bars.

"Juwan."

I look up and see Shukriya standing there. I pull on the bars, momentarily forgetting the door is locked.

The Kurdish guard appears and says, "Five minutes, no more. Make any noise, and I'll get in trouble. Which means you can both forget about visitation again. Understood?" He walks away without waiting for our answer.

Shukriya is crying, but she belts out a chain of questions. How are you? Are you OK? How are they treating you? Has anything happened to you? Have you been here the whole time?

I'm drowning in the heaviness of the moment, and every question she asks subtracts from my time to ask questions of my own. I want to ask: Is he really dead? Has he been buried yet? Has his body rotted yet? But I have to ask her first about Helan. There is no time to cry or relive the incident.

The inmates are talking to each other, and somewhere down the hallway two guards are laughing about something that's obviously very entertaining to them. Inside my head, a clock is ticking loudly. My five minutes have almost evaporated already.

"Helan is with me," Shukriya says, reassuring me. "She's fine and will be in good hands."

She'd better be, I think to myself. I wish I had an extra ten seconds to make that point clear, but before I say anything else, she lowers her voice, brings her face closer to the bars, and whispers, "We're in trouble. It's all over the news."

"I'm the one in trouble here, not you. Just find a way to get me out of here. They're not even talking to me."

Our hands are now touching, and she moves hers firmly against the bars as if to reassure me that we're on the same team. She gives me a quick rundown on Helan's well-being. She's eating well and enjoys playing with the kids. She's been crying at night and asking for mommy, but she doesn't mind sleeping next to the girls. Shukriya's brother dropped by for two days and left. Khateen has been staying at night.

"They're not allowing me to travel, but once the investigation is complete, I'm planning to stay with my brother for a while."

I press my fingers against the metal bars and lean my face closer to hers to emphasize my earlier point. "You've got to help me get out of here. Find a lawyer, talk to the police, do something, please. I can't stay here."

Shukriya rubs my hand gently. "I'm so sorry you got into this. I wish I hadn't let you take the blame. I want to tell them I'm the one who did it. Just—"

I put my palm against the bars across from her mouth, signaling for her to stop. "I'm terrified of what's going to happen. Please, just find a way to get me out. Talk to Zozan, let her ask her husband. Do something!"

The guard returns, his heavy voice announcing visitation is over.

"I'll do all I can," Shukriya says, "But you don't know these people." She whispers even lower and continues, "These are evil people. I'm really worried about us, about you."

Before she can say anything else, the guard yells at her to get moving.

As their footsteps grow softer, I hear Shukriya yell, "I promise you, Helan will be in good hands. I'll take care of her until Allah finds a solution for us."

I fold myself against the concrete wall, my face between my knees, and break down. For the first time since I arrived here, I let my emotions overtake me. Thunder slams through the walls of our cell, and rain hits the tiny window with accelerating force.

Where are you, Father? Why did you leave me behind? Even in your weakest moments, I know you wouldn't abandon me, but the mountains took you away.

57

Dilveen

Mardin Refugee Camp, Turkey, March 1991

I wake up gasping from a nightmare and sit bolt upright in bed. It's still dark outside. Berivan is asleep. Baby Wahid is startled by the noise of a few cats fighting outside. I gently rub his legs, and he falls back asleep.

I struggle to fall asleep once more, and not because of the cold. The nightmare hasn't loosened its grip on me yet even though I can't even remember it. Mother used to say never dwell on a bad dream you can't remember and never talk about it with anyone. Instead, ask God for protection from Satan and his army.

I repeat what she taught us to say. "*Astaghfirullah, A'othu-billah, ya Allah.*"

I'm worried about what we left behind when we crossed these borders. I turn over under the blanket, but I can't get Shireen's and Juwan's faces out of my mind. God, please let them be safe.

Finally I'm able to sleep again, but a loud noise wakes me up again. Women, children, and even men are crying. I rub my face to see if I'm in another dream, but Berivan jumps to her feet and grabs her son.

Someone is screaming, "Fire, fire, get water! The tents are burning!"

I'm on my feet at once, and both Berivan and I scramble to find our jackets. The commotion outside is growing more intense. Loud, painful cries are coming from multiple directions. I open the flap and stick my head out. Cold wind hits my eyes, and smoke fills my nostrils. Several men hustle past our tent carrying buckets of water through the narrow muddy pathway. The cries grow louder and more desperate.

Azad has been sleeping in the single men's tent, and when I close the flap and head back inside, I hear him yelling toward our tent. "Dilveen, are you OK? Are you all OK?"

Moments later, he barges inside, panting. He nervously looks around the tent then says, "Thank God you are all safe." Then he leaves.

I follow him out, asking for an explanation, and he shouts back, "There's a fire in the camp. Many tents are on fire. I have to go."

Suddenly, I see the top of a tent one row across from us engulfed in flames. I rush back inside and grab Berivan's arm, screaming, "Let's go, the fire is about to hit our row!"

We take shelter with Berivan's family in their tent, and an hour later, Azad appears and asks me if I still know how to treat wounds.

Of course I know how to treat wounds! As long as I have my scars, the caring of wounds will be a specialty of mine.

I follow Azad out. The wind has stopped, and the sky is clearing, but the cold chills me to my bones. I lift my dress a bit so it won't get dirty from the mud, but I let it go when Azad races too far ahead. I yell at him to slow down, but he turns to me, tears on his cheeks from the freezing temperature, and says, "A lot of people got burned. Some of them are in bad shape. We need to hurry to the infirmary." When I finally catch up with him, he coughs a few times and says, "Last night, some people burned wood next to their tents, and one caught on fire. The wind blew the flames from one tent after another. It took a miracle to put the fire out. Hurry, some people are in bad shape."

When we reach the end of the aisle of tents and turn toward the main gate, I see two men carrying a moaning old man by his legs and arms. When we get closer, I see that most of the skin on his upper right arm is gone and that a portion of his shirt sleeve was destroyed by the fire. The metal door to a concrete building opens, and the two men disappear inside with the old man.

"This the infirmary," Azad says. "Ready to see a war zone?"

He holds my hand and pulls me inside and through the crowd of people until we reach the main examination room where he introduces me to the dikhtor.

"This is my sister. She has experience caring for burn wounds."

Please don't ask me how I got my experience. Don't

remind me. Instead, the dikhtor points to a middle-age female victim whose family just brought her in. I turn, and Azad is gone. I hear him yelling at people in the hallway to make way for another victim.

I reach over to the burned lady. She's obviously in extreme pain, cringing and panting as she moves her right leg back and forth. Part of her dress has melted through her skin, and even the gentlest pressure summons loud cries. I turn to the dikhtor for help. Who am I to care for such tragic wounds?

He hands me a bottle of purified water and instructs me to pour it over a less serious wound on the back of a boy while he attends to the lady. In a single flourish, he rips off the clothing stuck to her leg, unleashing the loudest cry of pain I have ever heard in my life. She actually passes out before her family splashes water on her face.

The dikhtor asks me to call him Dikhtor. From the moment we entered, he has been barking orders with his deep voice. My count puts the number of burn victims at thirteen, including two teenagers, one child, and two elders. Four, including the lady I encountered when I first got here, are taken to the hospital by the ambulance while Dikhtor and I attend to the other nine with our limited supplies.

By noon, I'm exhausted and ready to leave when Azad shows up again. Not so fast! Three police cars arrive, too, and the officers demand to speak with some camp representatives about what started the fire.

"Who are you?" one of the officers asks me. "What are you doing here?"

"She's my assistant here," Dikhtor says. "She helped me care for the wounded, but she doesn't know anything about the fire, so she can go back to her tent."

Azad returns to the tent in the evening, looking and sounding exhausted but feeling satisfied. All the wounded have been cared for, and new tents replaced those that burned. Fortunately, the afternoon sun warmed the air and lifted the mood.

"So who is this guy Dikhtor?" I ask Azad while he finishes his dinner. "Is he a real doctor?"

Azad dips a piece of bread in the yogurt. "He's a trained doctor's assistant with lots of experience."

I refill his tea and offer a cup to Berivan, but she's busy feeding baby Wahid and wants to wait after he is fed.

Azad takes Wahid from Berivan and puts him on his lap. "His name is Dildar. He's best known for his services to the wounded Peshmerga in the mountains. A great guy."

Wahid bounces himself against Azad's chest, eager to get down and wander around the floor of the tent.

"Poor guy lost his wife on the border," Berivan says.

I grab baby Wahid from Azad and swing him up above my head and give him a long kiss on his cheek before I hold him tight to me while he fights to break free.

Azad asks Berivan, "So who is taking care of Dikhtor's children now?"

Berivan digs into the plate of mashed potatoes. "His married sister is. Plus he has extended family around him. His younger son is only five and doesn't understand what happened, but the older one is twelve and has been giving them a hard time. God help them."

THE NEXT WEEK proves to be hectic, with daily trips to the infirmary after breakfast until lunchtime to care for the burn victims. Camp administrators have regularly dropped off boxes of bandages, gauze, and other first aid supplies.

Dikhtor, as I have learned to address Dildar, is always there when I arrive, with prepared trays of necessary supplies ready to go. Most of the time, Azad hangs around the infirmary, sometimes attempting to strike up conversations in English with one of the armed camp officers.

When the workload lessens, Dikhtor asks me if I would be interested in working at the infirmary on a regular basis, mostly to help him with female patients. The camp no longer has a trainee Turkish doctor, and the load is proving to be too much for one person. I tell him I need permission from my brother, and he says he already has Azad's blessing. I would much rather be here than in the tent with overbearing Siti, so I accept the offer so long as I can direct traffic inside to avoid chaos.

THE CAMP IS OBSESSED with the news of an uprising in Duhok. Over dinner at Berivan's family's tent, the men listen attentively to the radio announcing a nearly complete liberation of Kurdistan from the Iraqi army.

"It's the blessing of Ramadan. Allah has finally hit Saddam with his punishing arm."

"It's a time of victory for Kurds. Who would have thought such a day would come during our lifetime?"

"Thanks to George Bush for leading the allied attacks on Saddam's army, weakening it down to a skeleton."

"Yes, *Wallah*, had Saddam not invaded Kuwait, he could have gotten away with anything."

"It's mind-boggling why Saddam invaded Kuwait! He was already king of the Arab world!"

"Man, the world's intelligence agencies no longer needed his services, so it was time to dispense with him."

"You and your conspiracy theories!"

The one voice I don't hear among all this chatter is my brother's. I wonder what he's thinking, but I don't actually need to ask. I know you're broken, my dear brother, but what can I do? I know you're hurting inside and burning to talk and let it out, but your pride won't let you speak.

On the third morning of Ramadan, I'm playing with Wahid inside the tent while his mother naps when a boy approaches our tent yelling Azad's name. With Wahid in my arms, I step outside. The boy is waiting there, panting. "My father sent me to get Azad, but I couldn't find him in his tent. My father says it's urgent."

"Who's your father?"

He wipes his nose and cheeks with his sleeve. "Dikhtor is my father. Dildar. Where can I find Azad? My father said he has an urgent phone call from Iran."

That last word lands like a bomb. I rush to the infirmary with the boy running behind me, still asking me where he can find Azad. At the door of the building, I turn to him and tell him to run to the far end of the camp by the fence behind the bathrooms.

I rush inside to where the phone is connected and find Dikhtor sitting by the desk, his back to the wall.

"What's happening?" I say nervously, leaning over the desk.

He sits up. "Someone named Shireen called claiming to be your and Azad's sister. She was asking for Azad. She said she was very short on time, and when I couldn't immediately locate Azad, she said she'll call back shortly."

My heart is racing, and the walls of the room seem to spin. "My God, my God," I repeat while pacing the room, barely able to stay on my feet.

Dikhtor offers me the chair with some words of reassurance. "I'm sorry, I don't know what she wanted. Is everything OK? I'm sure it's just a phone call to check on you all."

"No, Shireen wouldn't call if there wasn't a big problem. Oh God, please spare us tragic news."

The phone finally rings, and I jump to my feet, terrified and fully alert. It rings a second time, sending jolts of fear into me. I stare at Dikhtor, not sure if I'm allowed to answer. On the third ring, Dikhtor grabs the receiver and hands it to me.

When I bring it to my ear, Shireen is already yelling. "Hello, Azad, are you there?"

My breath stops when I hear the urgency in her voice. "Shireen, it's me, Dilveen. How are you, sister?"

She's sobbing into the receiver. It takes her a moment to collect herself. "Things are not good," she finally says. "I don't have much time. It cost me and Ramo a lot of trouble and money to make this phone call, and it may cut off any time so—"

"What happened, Shireen? Tell me."

"It's Juwan. She's in jail. They arrested her because she killed Segvan. She stabbed him!"

I can't move. I can't even breathe.

Ramo comes to the phone. "Dilveen, please let Azad know. It's bad. Juwan's life could be in danger, and I don't know what you want to do."

Azad suddenly appears, looking concerned. I hand him

the phone and withdraw to the opposite corner of the room. He shouts into the phone, then slams it down on the desk.

"The line cut off," he says. "The call ended. God damn it!" Then he punches the desk.

A Jandarma officer walks in and motions for us to leave. Dikhtor gently leads the two of us outside the building with Azad's gaze fixated on me, urgently demanding to be filled in.

"The news is not good, brother," I say, leaning against the wall of the infirmary"

"What happened? Tell me." His eyes are wide open, his face pale and full of concern.

"Juwan killed her hus—. She killed Segvan, and she is in jail now."

Dikhtor grabs Azad's shoulder, as if already declaring the gravity of the situation.

"What does that mean?" Azad asks with a hoarse voice, his mouth dry. "What do you mean in jail?"

Shireen's desperate words are still in my ear. Azad taps on my shoulder rather hard, pressing for further explanation.

"Shireen seemed worried. We are talking murder here, brother. Murder!"

Azad collapses to his knees while Dikhtor holds his left shoulder. I, on the other hand, push my back further against the wall of the infirmary, wishing it could open up and swallow me.

THE NEXT MORNING, we eat our *suhoor*, the early morning meal before our daily fast during Ramadan. Right after the morning prayer, Azad puts on his thick coat and announces it's time to leave.

The camp is mostly awake and preparing to fast even though it's still dark. Berivan's father, Husain Ziway, arrives minutes later, fully dressed and ready to join us. It took hours to convince Siti to allow her husband to leave. It took even more convincing to get Azad to allow me on the trip.

Berivan embraces me and whispers in my ear, "Inshallah, everything will go well. Please be careful and make sure Jamil returns with you."

I nod and assure her as best I can with tearful eyes. I step inside the tent and kiss baby Wahid on the forehead. I pull away before he wakes up, then head out. Husain Ziway leads the way out of the camp and through a vertical cut in the barbed wire fence toward the main road.

The plan is to walk until we catch some luck with a taxi or truck, then make our way to Silopi. There we can cross into Iraq near Duhok if the Turkish authorities cooperate, and if not, we'll cross illegally. There are many ways. And with a successful uprising in charge, our own Kurdish forces control the Iraqi side of the border. From there we can take a car all the way to the Iranian border without any trouble.

"Everybody stay focused," Husain Ziway says, "and help me wave down a ride."

58

Juwan

Iran, March 1991

My cell slowly empties as each inmate finally gets her turn in the interrogation room. All except one left without coming back. The last one returned with visible signs of torture on her face.

I've experienced every negative emotion and behavior possible in a prison cell: fear, anger, and hatred toward every human being I've met in Iran whether they did me wrong or not. I've screamed, withdrawn, mutilated my body with my fingernails and teeth, slept all day, and stayed up all night. Not a single person has come to visit me. Even the Kurdish-speaking guard ignores me.

I'm starting to wonder if God can even hear my prayers from behind these thick concrete walls.

The guards have taken me to the courthouse in Urmia, an intimidating building with a giant portrait of Iranian leader Ayatollah Khomeini out front. I'm in a large rectangular room with dark brown walls, a white floor, and dim yellow lights. A luxurious bench faces the entrance, where an old man sits in a black leather chair under another large portrait of Khomeini. From his attire, I assume he's a judge of some sort. He busily flips through some documents as the guards order me to sit in a metal chair at a small wooden desk facing the judge.

There are two women dressed in brown occupying two of the four seats to my right. Both follow me with their eyes as I get seated, the metallic rattling of my handcuffs the only sound in the room.

Two guards stand close behind me as if I'm somehow going to magically escape this suffocating room, run through hallways I'm totally unfamiliar with, then go out into the street and disappear in a country I hate, that I don't belong to, and that has no place for me.

Arriving now at the unoccupied table to my left are five men dressed in black suits, each holding a notebook. I'm struggling to control the shivers through my body as a young woman approaches me from behind and says in Kurdish, "I will be your interpreter." Before I can even look at her, she sits next to me and places her notebook on the desk.

All this for me?

The judge adjusts his thick glasses over the bridge of his wide nose, clears his throat, and announces something in Persian. All chatter in the room comes to a stop. He lowers his head toward the microphone, and with his eyes fixed on me, he yells something at me.

My interpreter instructs me to stand.

The judge yells something else, and the interpreter, now standing next to me, whispers, "You must look at the judge when he speaks to you."

I look straight in his direction, the large eyes of Khomeini looking down at me from above as if saying, "I'm watching you, wretched criminal."

The judge silently scans the documents in front of him, then says something in Persian.

"You have been charged with the crime of killing a man named Segvan," my interpreter says, "whom you claimed to be your husband. You confessed, is that true?"

I clear my throat and say, "I'm sorry for what happened, but I was defending myself."

Before translating, the interpreter asks me again, "So you admit to it? That's what the judge is asking."

I nod and look at my handcuffs. I attempt to speak, but the interpreter motions for me to be quiet while the judge brings a document closer to his eyes. He then waves the paper in his hand toward the back of the room. A familiar man answers and steps forward. He's the officer who interrogated me. He's dressed fully in black and approaches the bench.

For the next twenty-five minutes, the officer answers the judge's questions, occasionally producing photographs of the crime scene and showing them to the judge and the committee. More than once he points his finger at me in the most accusatory way possible. I can't understand his testimony, and my interpreter is just sitting there. Finally, the judge nods and motions for him to return to his seat.

Now I get to tell my side of the story. Relax! Take a deep breath. Be ready to recount the details exactly as they happened, keeping in mind that Shukriya is Juwan and Juwan is Shukriya.

But my turn doesn't come. Instead, the judge asks the committee something I don't understand. They immediately raise their hands, every one of them. No other reactions. No facial expressions, no words, nothing. They must be bored, I reassure myself.

When the committee members put their hands down, the judge turns to me, slowly adjusts himself in the seat, and makes a long, slow, careful statement that my interpreter translates even more slowly.

"On behalf of the Islamic Republic of Iran and the blessed revolution that brought justice and power to its people, the court hereby on this twentieth day of March 1991 finds you guilty of murder of an Iranian citizen by stabbing him to death, a crime you freely confessed to during a fair interrogation without duress. Furthermore, you have been determined to be an illegal citizen of another country who crossed our border by unknown and questionable means, in the process endangering the security of this great country and its valued citizens."

He sighs deeply, scans the room, looks back at me, and continues. "In light of the brutality of your crime, the illegal nature of your presence in our country, and the significant value this government placed in the victim, the court hereby declares your punishment to be death by hanging in a public square as an example for anyone else who might consider such a heinous crime. The punishment is scheduled for noon on March twenty-five. The decision is final with no chance of appeal. Court is adjourned."

BACK IN MY CELL, I spend hours upon hours yelling, screaming, cursing, punching the walls, pulling my hair, and shaking the bars of the cell door, but my shadow is my only companion, the echoes of my wounded voice the only answer. After exhausting myself, I stare at the wall for hours, trying to absorb the shock and understand how things could have turned this bad so fast. Just like that, you think you can sentence me to death and without a lawyer or even obtaining a proper testimony from me?

Some time passes. Perhaps a day or two or even three. I can't keep track anymore. But one day, suddenly, there's Shukriya, standing in front of my cell door. I'm lying on my side with my back to the wall. She says my name a few times, but I'm too exhausted to get up or even move. I slowly look up, and our eyes meet.

"Are you OK? Oh God!"

I close my eyes and answer. "I'm fine for someone counting the days to her death."

She says in a soft voice, "Your sentence was announced on the news. I can't believe it or accept it. I'm going to die. What happened during the trial? *When* did it take place?"

I slowly pull myself up, my eyes tired, my mouth dry, every muscle in my body stiff from lying on the bare floor for God only knows how many hours.

"Please talk to me," she begs. "Say something. I don't know what to do. God, what has happened to you because of me?"

I'm not going to waste my time with her dwelling over a lost cause, so I ask through my dry lips, "How is Helan? Please tell me she's well and safe!"

Excited to hear me speak, Shukriya responds, "Helan is fine. She is well cared for. I promise you that!"

Shukriya wipes a tear from the corner of her eye. "Look, Juwan, I'm going to the police. I'm going to tell them the truth, and I'm going to do it today."

Too weak to stand up, I slide across the floor and let my head rest against the bars. With our hands now touching, I gather enough strength to say, "You're going to keep your mouth shut!" I hit the bars with my weak shrunken hands.

She tries to grab my hands again, but I pull away from her. "You confess, and they'll just kill both of us. Our kids will end up in orphanages. Put your brain back in your head and keep quiet." Our eyes meet again, and I'm finally overcome with emotion. "They're going to kill me, Shukriya. I'm going to be hanged in a few days. Do you hear what I'm saying?"

I rest my head against the metal bars and sob.

Shukriya places her hand on my head and whispers, "Shireen visited me. She's devastated too. She told me to tell you that Azad and Dilveen might be on their way. You won't be left alone here."

I feel numb. Nothing can be done. It's all over for me.

The guard appears and announces the end of our visit. Finally I have enough energy to stand up.

"Please," I tell Shukriya. "Make sure I get to see my daughter before they kill me. Promise me that. Please promise me!"

59

Azad

Duhok, Iraq, March 1991

With the exception of a few small hurdles, our trip to Zakho goes more smoothly than anticipated. Money speaks the entire way. And here I am back in Zakho, two and a half years since we last left and hit the border and headed toward our unknown fate.

A lot has changed in the city, just as much has changed in us. Most importantly, Iraqi military personnel, police, and security forces are nowhere to be found. Instead, Kurdish uniforms are everywhere as are massive quantities of weapons carried by the simplest of citizens.

In the center of Zakho, Husain Ziway, Dilveen, and I find a Volkswagen taxi to take us to Duhok. The worn-down white-and-orange car looks like it could break down at any moment, but we get in anyway, Husain Ziway in the front and Dilveen and I in the back, hoping the taxi can actually reach Duhok.

We agreed earlier to tell no one our story until we reach Duhok. Yes, the place has been liberated from the Iraqi armed forces, and the population is euphoric, but surely there are still spies and other troublemakers who may have sold their souls to the enemy.

The driver doesn't waste much time with nosiness. With his oil-stained hand, he skillfully shifts gears, his thick neck and wrinkled face displaying years of accumulated hardship and neglected health.

Even though Duhok is barely sixty kilometers from Zakho, he can tell that's where we're from by our accents. "You folks from Duhok?"

Husain Ziway nods as we pass a burned tank on the side of the road. "How did the uprising start in Zakho? Was it similar to Duhok?"

I see what Husain Ziway did there. He's fishing for information about Duhok without doing so directly and without providing any of his own.

"Well, you see," the driver says with a sense of pride "I am from Darkar, and we lit the first spark in this region. That was on March 13 and 14. Truth be told, and I have to admit I was one of the doubters, but the Chatta forces, although originally intended by the Iraqi government to aid the military against the Kurdish liberation forces, were instrumental in facilitating the uprising, not just here but in many places."

He speeds along the open road between the massive flat, green fields extending to the horizons. "I cried from joy when I saw the locals bring down the statue of Saddam in front of the municipal building."

Dilveen fell asleep when we were still within the Zakho city limits, and now Husain Ziway is snoring heavily, too, so I decide to doze off as well.

We're all awake and alert when the city center appears in the distance. To the left and high above is the tall, yellow agricultural building next to my school. The driver points to another building ahead with bullet holes in it. I don't recall what it was used for, but there was obviously fighting here recently. Every other man on the streets appears to be carrying a weapon of some sort.

At the traffic light in the center of downtown next to the central police station, Husain Ziway rolls his window down and hollers at a teenage boy carrying an RPG-7 on his shoulder. "Son, what are you going to do with that? It's taller than you!"

The boy doesn't appear to be entertained. He positions the RPG-7 on his shoulder and against his neck, just as a seasoned fighter would when preparing to strike a target. His display of premature manhood draws giggles from Husain Ziway while Dilveen covers her face in disbelief.

The driver yells at the boy, "Where did you get it?"

"On the other side where the main military unit used to be," the boy says. "Their warehouse is empty by now, though. I could sell it to you?"

Husain Ziway waves the boy off, and for a second I worry that he'll use the RPG-7 against us for disrespecting him.

"Right there on the left is my uncle's shop," I tell the driver.

We park across from it, but it's closed. Memories flood

me as I get out and cross the street. It feels like only yesterday when Mam Khorsheed interrogated me about my school work and exams. If he saw any sign of slacking, he'd send me home and demand I give my work my full attention. "That's what you left your mother and sisters for," he often said. Yes, and it's also why I'm forever separated from my love.

I get back in the car and give the driver directions to my uncle's house. And thank goodness he's home. We have more to catch up on than he does since Jamil has already filled him in on every important detail.

Yet listening to Dilveen rehearse the events, relive the tragedy, and express her sorrow is just as hard for me the second time as it was the first time.

My uncle clears his throat, his large brown beads elegantly flowing between his fingers, and says with a broken voice, "Son, this is God's will. No one escapes fate. Each of us will taste what has been determined for us. Stay strong. Your father never gave up until his last breath."

"Right now, uncle, we need to get to Jamil as soon as possible," I say. "Now before tomorrow, tomorrow morning before tomorrow at noon. We must get to Iran, and Jamil is our key."

"Jamil is in Akre now. He's leading a battalion to secure some of the critical points outside Mosul. I know where to find him."

We hear shots outside followed by a few distant explosions, but Mam Khorsheed reassures us. "Don't worry, that's probably just kids playing with firearms. There's still some heavy fighting between Duhok and Mosul, but we're safe here. Rest assured."

"Where did all these weapons come from?" Husain Ziway says. "That's what I want to know!"

"From dozens of military warehouses in the city. The armed people you see outside are mostly the ones who fought during the uprising. As they finished taking over one army base, they took everything and moved on to the next."

WE REACH Akre just before noon. Mam Khorsheed tried to convince Dilveen to stay behind, but she wouldn't even think of it.

Some local Peshmerga men direct us to an elementary school turned into a temporary military outpost where we reunite with Jamil. His face is pale, his eyes tired, his hair dirty and unkempt. He looks like he hasn't changed his clothes since leaving the Mardin camp. He's proudly carrying a Kalashnikov over his right shoulder and a handgun on his belt. He's thrilled to see us, but he knows something must be wrong for us to show up like this unannounced. Maintaining his calm, he leads us into the principal's office, where a portrait of the late Kurdish leader Mala Mustafa Barzani has replaced the one of Saddam Hussein that used to hang on the walls of every official's office and every public building.

"So what are we going to do to save Juwan?" I ask, breaking the silence.

"We'll find a way to enter Iran, illegally of course. Then we'll gather more information and decide what to do, but this is not some rogue operation in a foreign country.

I want to leave now, but Jamil refuses for reasons that

are obvious to him but make zero sense to me. Every minute counts.

"It will get dark in a few hours," he says, "and any travel at night during times of unrest invites disaster."

"Jamil is the authority here," Mam Khorsheed declares, "because he has the power, the guns, and connections. We do what he says."

I shift in my seat, but Mam Khorsheed puts his hand on my knee and points toward Jamil and nods for me to listen.

"I know a guy," Jamil says, "a fighter who returned from Iran with a large number of men. He was here initially but then moved on to Shaqlawa. We'll pick him up tomorrow morning and head to the border. I'll have one of my men drive, but only Azad and I will go."

Dilveen leaps to her feet and says, "On my mother's grave, if you don't allow me to come, you will come back to find me dead. No. No. No!"

Jamil tries to talk her out of it, but she's relentless, so he finally concedes. "OK, you can come with us, but you will follow every single instruction and order I give you. Is that clear?"

"Understood," she says.

A LITTLE BEFORE SUNSET, Husain Ziway says he wants to see the old mosque of Akre. The rain has stopped, and Jamil says the mosque is within walking distance. We take a stroll down the road and climb the stairs through the busy alleys lined with small shops until we approach the large double doors leading into the mosque.

A shopkeeper nearby has his radio turned all the way

up. A Kurdish host screams, "Our revolution will succeed! It will flourish! Don't lose hope in our brave revolution." I sense desperation in his tone as he continues. "We will continue to push the enemy forces back. Bear with us, and keep your faith in the uprising."

I give Jamil a look, and he realizes I'm reading between the lines.

He shakes his head and in a soft voice says, "Things are not looking good, brother. The Arab uprising in the south is being crushed as we speak, and here we're facing fierce resistance from Saddam's forces, especially near the Mosul dam. Saddam is ruthless, and I'm worried he'll crush us now that the West seems to have turned its back on us."

I want to remind him that this is nothing new for us Kurds, but knowing how emotionally invested he is, I know he won't take it well.

We reach the mosque, and Husain Ziway points to a plaque above the door. "Look, it says this mosque was built in the year 1385 by orders from the second caliph, Omar Bin al Khattab."

While Husain Ziway remains absorbed by the details and history, we enter the building and take a flight of small stairs down to the main courtyard. It's full of people, dozens of Iraqi soldiers in their green military uniforms, some casually sitting in the courtyard, others laying down on the carpet by the door to the main prayer hall. I turn to Jamil with a look of astonishment, and he nods with a skeptical smile.

Jamil says to my shocked face, "Yes, they are Arab soldiers, and yes I share your feeling, but what can I do?"

I whisper to him as we both take our shoes off, "What do you mean what can you do? You have these savages sitting here like they're in a hotel? The same people who fought us and killed us? You saw the way they tortured us back in Nizarki!"

Jamil brings his face near mine and says, "If it were up to me, I would shoot every one of them, right here or out there or anywhere, I don't care."

Mam Khorsheed interjects. "It's not in our Kurdish manners to harm or disrespect guests or torture prisoners."

Guests? I want to scream so loud that everyone in this building can hear me. Instead I whisper to Jamil, "Why are you doing this?" As we walk inside the large prayer hall, I see even more of them laying comfortably against the walls and in the corners.

He whispers back, "We have orders not to hurt them. I wish they would just leave and go back to their homes, but they claim Saddam would kill them, and he probably would."

Minutes later, Jamil points toward the courtyard where several men descend the stairs carrying plates and pots of food along with bottles of juice.

"Want to hear something even crazier?" Jamil says. "See all that food? The locals brought it for our guests, our prisoners of war, the luxury guests. They break their fast on the best plates, courtesy of the generous townspeople."

Jamil shakes his head and leaves me standing there in shock and disbelief. I know that what Mam Khorsheed said is true. I can imagine my father saying the exact same thing, and they're right, but I don't even want to think about this anymore.

∽

THE FOLLOWING MORNING, March 23, just before dawn, we leave Akre in an old Land Cruiser with official Iraqi plates. The driver, a local who can't gush enough about Jamil's bravery and dedication, assures us that the car is fully loaded with fuel plus an additional tank in the back.

For the next four hours, I slide in and out of shallow sleep as we hurtle through the valley, the mountains alongside us like guards, fierce in their looks and determined in their silence. Somewhere along the way, we pick up our guide, Rozh, who skillfully directs the driver to where we can safely cross the Iranian border.

Once inside Iran, Jamil removes an ID from his inside jacket pocket and hands it to Dilveen. "Here, sister, this is my Peshmerga ID. Find a place inside your clothes to hide it. It's our best chance at getting back to Duhok from the border, but we can't get caught with it in Iran."

Rozh gives Jamil an address inside this border town where he'll return after dropping us off at Ramo's house. He'll wait a maximum of four days for us to return.

OUR REUNION with Shireen this time is of a different magnitude. She immediately passes out at our sight by the front door.

Moments later, after she has returned to her senses, she breaks down while hugging me tightly. "I'm sorry, brother. I'm so sorry. Why did this have to happen to you?"

I don't have the time or the energy for pleasantries and formalities, so I dive straight to the pressing matter for which we crossed borders. "Will someone please explain to me what happened and what's happening?"

A hush falls over the room as Shireen's new family stops talking, stops moving, and stares at me. I'm bracing for a hurricane of emotion the next time Shireen opens her mouth.

Instead, Ramo rests on his knees next to me and says with a soft voice, "I'm afraid we don't have good news, my brother. These ruthless people are going to execute Juwan the day after tomorrow."

Only Shireen will look at me, tears still in her eyes. "They're going to hang the girl of your dreams. They're going to break your heart and ours forever."

I don't even know how to react. Am I supposed to not cry or pretend I'm a paragon of Kurdish manhood? Am I supposed to withdraw to a corner or demand action? What action? Every answer to every question reinforces my despair. Yes, they've tried their best to get a lawyer, but the court has already made its decision. No, Juwan didn't get a fair trial. No, the jail can't be penetrated, so rescuing her is impossible. No, the Iranian government won't hesitate to hang a woman even in the holy month of Ramadhan if she is a Kurd. No, Shireen hasn't seen her because they require a government-issued ID to enter the jail and Shireen is still living here illegally even though she's now married to Ramo. Yes, No, Yes, No!

Then Shireen drops the biggest bomb of them all: "What kills me is that Juwan didn't even kill Segvan."

Did I just hear her correctly?

"The first wife did it," Shireen says, "but Juwan took the blame. And now it's too late."

I throw my chair against the wall and smash it to pieces.

60

Juwan

Iran, March 25, 1991

Daylight finally appears through the window above my head, starting the official countdown. The countdown for the dispatch of another miserable soul determined unworthy even for the worst of what life has to offer.

I can hear traffic outside and vendors passing by and hawking their products. It's just another day, rosy for some, doomed for others. I wonder if there just might be some beauty in this world that I have overlooked, some kindness I haven't unaccounted for. Maybe, just maybe, the death sentence is just a demonstration of power and they'll drop the charges and forget about me behind these sorry walls.

Who am I to them anyway? Why waste so much time and energy on legal procedures and media coverage to gin up public outrage? For what? My existence is meaningless to them in the first place. How can you kill something that barely even exists in your eyes? And who kills during the holy month of fasting?

I know it's all wishful thinking when I hear the familiar tap on the cell door. The heavyset guard with the shoulders made in hell stands there, holds his stick under his arm, and begins to slowly turn the lock, creating yet more drama and anticipation. I refuse to move until he tells me to. I won't take a single voluntary step on my own. This has all been a show of oppression from the first moment and will remain so.

He orders me to get up and, to my surprise, allows me to walk out of the cell without handcuffs. Another glimpse of hope! But is it real? I follow him down the hallway into the same room where they interrogated me.

The Kurdish guard appears later with a large piece of white clothing and hands it to me. "Here," he says in a cold voice. "Wear this over your clothes."

He heads out without giving me the chance to ask any questions. I unfold it and see that it's a baggy cotton dress. Every inch of it announces my fate. My sweaty hands start to shake, and I already feel as if my life is slipping out of my body, my lonely body that feels foreign to even myself now. I surrender to reality and slip into the clothing offered to me in my last few hours of life.

The door opens again, and the Kurdish guard is back, followed by a short and skinny old man dressed in formal clergy attire. The guard steps out of the way and stands in the corner as the man of God takes hesitant steps in my direction, stopping about two feet away. Avoiding eye contact with me, he clears his throat and starts to mumble some prayers. His voice is soft, too soft for the age revealed by his cleanshaven face. For someone in a position of religious authority, he sure appears faltering and shaky.

He then says to me in Kurdish, his eyes at his feet, "My daughter, I'm here to instruct you during your last hours and to guide you to ensure your submission to Allah, our lord and the possessor of our souls and lives."

Awkward silence. I can't think of a thing to say. The fear and feeling of disembodiment are beyond words.

"My child, I will say the words of the *Shahada*, and you will repeat after me."

"I know the *Shahada*. I am Muslim, in case you all have forgotten!" I regret this immediately. He may be my only source of hope for my last wish before I die.

I drop to my knees and beg. "Please help me see my daughter one last time before I die. I will do and say anything you ask of me. Please!"

But he continues to instruct me to say my last declaration of faith before death.

I plead with him again, louder and more persistently this time, until the guard intervenes. "He's not here to solve your sentencing or court problems. Listen to what he says so he can fulfill his responsibilities and leave."

Finally, the clergyman has heard and seen enough. He yells at me to stand up and be quiet. "Just repeat what I'm asking of you so I can clear my conscience and do the job the government has legally instructed me to do." His watery eyes twitch when they meet mine, as if he is begging me.

Tears fill my own eyes as I repeat the clergyman's words while resisting the urge to scream.

When we're finally finished, he turns to the guard. "Can you try to grant her wish to see her daughter?" The guard says nothing, so the old man looks at me again, his lips trembling. "May God be with you, my child" he says, then timidly walks out of the room.

As the guard walks out, I beg him one more time to help me see my daughter.

This time, he nods. "I'll see what I can do, but you have to promise me you won't cause a scene."

I give him my word, my promise, and swear on my father's grave and on my daughter's head, but he slips out of the room without seeming to hear me.

The wall clock reads fifteen after ten. I sit down at the table, exhausted and already lifeless. Surely the guard was lying to me. Less than two hours from my scheduled execution, I'd be a fool to believe they'd go through the trouble of bringing my daughter to me. I listen to the ticking of the clock, each movement heavier than a mountain as my final minutes run out.

But then: I hear her voice! It's her, my daughter. It's her voice, and she's crying. Anxiety overwhelms me, but no, I'm still alive. I prove it by pinching myself. I'm awake, and I'm not crazy. I heard Helan's voice. I pace the small room like a mad animal, worried I may have been hallucinating just a few seconds ago.

The door suddenly opens, and there she is, Helan in Shukriya's arms. I gasp and snatch her away from Shukriya as a guard looms by the door in case I make an unexpected move.

At first, my own daughter doesn't seem to recognize me, and she starts screaming. Maybe she was startled by my sudden movement or the way I snatched her from Shukriya.

Or maybe it's the clothes I'm wearing? Perhaps I really am already dead. I repeatedly kiss her, hysterically running around the room with her from one corner to another until she finally recognizes me and hides her head in my chest, her beautiful red bow loose in her hair.

I place Helan on the small desk and let her stand on her own. I wipe away her fearful tears and my own tears of sorrow, then gently play with her curly brown hair and sing one of her favorite lullabies. She giggles and jumps in my arms. I hold her tight, this time quietly and peacefully, allowing her beautiful, soft hair to soak up my tears as Shukriya slaps the concrete wall with the palms of her hands.

Shukriya finally settles down and gently places her hand on my arm. "We've been outside since first light, but they wouldn't let us in. It's a miracle they finally gave us permission. I'm so sorry, we tried everything we could think of. I wish it was me and not you. I'll never be able to sleep at night after this."

I wave my right index finger toward her mouth. "Stop all this nonsense. It's done and over with. I want to spend these quality moments with my daughter and in peace. Nothing else out there means anything to me."

She sniffles and wipes her tears. "Speaking of outside, I want you to know that Azad, Jamil, and Dilveen are there too. They came all the way from Turkey."

She gets my attention momentarily, but I say nothing.

"They're not allowed to visit you since they don't have government IDs, but Zozan is also outside. They only allow one visitor at a time. I'll leave for a few minutes to let her come and see you."

As Shukriya leaves, I wonder what the guards would do

if I decided to run with my daughter in my arms. Will they actually shoot me? Would they risk hurting a child to stop a fugitive? Will Azad hold my hand at the door and take me far, far away from here?

You had to come back for me twice now! Did you think I betrayed you the first time you found me? How sincerely were you trying to reunite with me? Why didn't *you* kill your rival, the monster who stole your love, your dreams, and *our* future?

Zozan enters the room and breaks down when our eyes meet. I don't let go of my daughter even when Zozan hugs me. She takes a few steps back, rubbing her hands against each other, not knowing what to say. What is one supposed to say in a situation like this? I'm sorry you will die soon? I wish you could live longer? We'll miss you?

"My husband used all his connections," she says in her ever-apologetic tone. "I pushed him way past his limit. He even had a mental breakdown, but they're not going to listen. They wouldn't even let us hire a lawyer." She brings her mouth to my ear and whispers, "Segvan was apparently a valuable informant. That's what my husband concluded, but don't tell anyone."

Don't tell anyone? Maybe I'll tell the dead once I join that party.

When Zozan runs out of words to say, she gives me another awkward hug and excuses herself. When Shukriya returns, her eyes red, the guard points to his watch, indicating it's time.

She embraces me one last time and says, "I'm sorry, I'm sorry, I'm sorry. I don't know what to say. Your cousin Shireen is also outside, and she's inconsolable. She begged me to ask you for forgiveness. She feels very sorry about all the things she said to you in the past. She won't stop crying."

The guard barges into the room, bluntly announcing visitation is over. He motions for Shukriya to take Helan away. And it is at that moment that my real execution is carried out. As Helan is forcefully snatched from my arms, the curtains start to fall.

Just before Shukriya leaves the room, I grab her shoulder, violently pull her to me, and say in the firmest tone I've ever been able to muster in my life, "You give my daughter to Dilveen. Tell her I'm entrusting her with Helan's life. Tell them I forgive them and ask for their forgiveness. Tell them that if they love me, they will show it all to my daughter. Please, will you do that?"

Speechless and with tearful eyes, Shukriya nods as the guard takes her away and locks the door in my face one more time. I close my eyes and flex every muscle in my body to block the sound of Helan's crying. I want my last memory to be her giggling while she pulls on my nose and scratches my face.

MY FATHER often told the story of a Kurdish political activist he met when they fled Iraq in the 1970s following a collapsed revolution. Even though the activist never picked up a gun in his life, the Iranian government hanged him high from a crane.

Although my father didn't personally witness the execution, every account of the story mentioned how the authorities left the body hanging there for days, with guards preventing onlookers from attending to the body.

So that's what I expect for myself. Along the ride from jail to where the truck stops, I imagine myself hanging there while people look upon me with curiosity and pity. I step off the back of the truck per the guard's instructions, and after a quick look around, I recognize the place. They've decided to execute me in Hesenlu, in Segvan's backyard. The pickup truck is parked on the edge of the soccer field barely two hundred feet from the bus stop I so often used.

I've looked at this field so many times on my trips to and from the bus station, so often finding boys playing soccer and solving their own conflicts over contested goals and penalties. I questioned their sanity during the hot hours of the summer and admired their perseverance during the coldest days of winter. Now the field will be the site of a much greater spectacle.

But there's no crane. What I see instead are masses of men, women, and children gathered in a tight line circling the field. There are men posted everywhere, on the street and in every corner of the field. Every one of them is heavily armed and masked up in dark helmets and blue sunglasses, making it impossible for anyone to identify them. This magnificent production just for me? How strange that the masses will celebrate the death of a miserable stranger who doesn't even exist here on paper!

An armed man waves his gun from side to side, silently ordering people to spread out and make room so the guards and I can pass. I can't understand what anyone is saying, but the murmuring and mumbling nauseates me. There's a large white pickup truck in the middle of the field with the flag of Iran painted on the driver's-side door. I momentarily slow down to focus, but the guards yell at me to keep walking. On the back of the truck is a tall structure of metal bars crossing each other in a rectangular pattern. From the top middle, a thick brown rope hangs down a few feet. As I step closer, the thickness of the rope seems to grow wider, and the distance between the end of the rope and the truck bed seems to grow higher.

The guard to my right motions for me to stop when we're about ten feet away. My throat tingles and my neck twitches as my eyes remain fixated on the noose. The lump in my throat thickens in defiance of the rope waving its own thickness from afar.

An overweight guard appears from the other side of the truck carrying two folded metal chairs and lazily throws them in the back. He then proceeds to turn the tailgate handle. He pulls the door, but it refuses to go down. He slaps it a few times, sending a jolt of fear through my body with each strike, and after the third blow it slams down with a crash of metal. He makes a hand signal, and another guard steps forward, big and tall with a prominent chin. He could easily pick up a person my size with one hand. He grabs a small wooden stepping stool from the back of the truck and places it on the ground under the tailgate. He then unfolds the two metal chairs, placing one under the rope and the other right across from it.

A hand touches my arm from behind, and I jump in fear. A woman dressed in all black with only her eyes showing instructs me to turn around. I'm shivering now and struggling to stop my teeth from chattering. I hear my name somewhere in the crowd, but I don't recognize any of the faces in the blazing sunshine. I can only imagine my daughter's face, her eyes following me everywhere.

The woman steps behind me while a male guard removes the cuffs from my wrists. I hear my name called again, but I can't even tell reality from imagination anymore.

The lady behind me barks an order at me in Persian, which of course I don't understand. After a moment, she sighs in frustration and grabs my arms from behind. Then she ties a rope around my wrists, every knot pushing my hands harder against my lower back. She then proceeds to push me toward the back of the truck, where the guard awaits and motions for me to step all the way back.

So this is it? The end of my miserable journey? Of a life spun from beautiful dreams and ugly reality? I heard so many stories of Peshmerga prisoners and army deserters caught by the Iraqi army and executed in public. The one that always stood out to me was the way Azad's father was shot in a public square. I always wondered why the victims didn't beg for their lives in their final moments. What did they have to lose? Little did I know that I would one day live the answer. Numb, emotionally deprived, cold, and shocked, I stand there staring into the distance at nothing in particular and listening to the noise and chatter, unable to recognize any familiar voices. Here I am, mere feet and moments from my own death, and I'm not crying, begging, or asking for mercy. Even the strong heartbeat I had when I walked onto the field earlier, which already seems like an eternity ago, has faded away.

I'm not ready to die. I don't think anyone can truly be ready, but there's nothing around me worth begging for.

Forgive me, my little baby Helan. Forgive my dark thoughts! But maybe I'm the one common factor in all the misery my family has endured on this journey. Maybe you'll have a better life without me. Forgive me, my daughter! I never thought I would love something that was forced into my womb against my will and against my wishes, but just as I was forced to have you, you were forced to come into this world as my daughter. And so our paths cross, but only for a few more moments. Then I fly away on this soft breeze of spring. I'm coming, Father and Mother. I'm tired, and I need to come back to you and relive my childhood! I have felt the weight of mountains on my back and strapped to my shoulders, repeatedly dragging me down. It's time for the load to come off—or should I say it's time for the load to lose its carrier. It's time! I'm tired! I am not giving up, but I am tired.

61

Dilveen

Iran, March 25, 1991

When Shukriya comes out of the jail building for the final time crying harder than ever, and once we're certain there's is no chance of going in to personally say goodbye to Juwan, we hurriedly head back toward Hesenlu. The streets are filled with police cars, and guards have been posted on corners. I ask Shireen to take Helan and head back to Shukriya's house. My heart has broken multiple times since the morning, and it's ripped out of my chest every time I look into my brother's eyes.

Zozan finds room for herself among the front line of

onlookers while I insist the rest of us stay back as far from any guards as possible.

Juwan, I see your heavy steps as the guards walk you toward the truck while spectators watch, some curious, some sad, and God knows how many happy and entertained. I watch your exhausted body, your distant mind, and your lost face as you process orders thrown at you from the guards and the evil lady who seems to take pleasure in tying your hands painfully behind your back. If I could have my way with her, I'd cut her hands off and stick her bloody fingers in her eyes. Scum of the earth.

I watch as your broken body stands on the field waiting to be loaded onto the back of the truck where the noose and hanging post have been prepped. I see you looking around when Zozan calls your name, and while I am scared to do the same, I nevertheless join her efforts in trying to get your attention by waving my hands from far away. But your blank looks and empty stares across the long line of spectators tell me you have already left us.

The breeze flows through my long hair, reminding me that I won't be able to brush your hair anymore like a sister and like a best friend. Now, after I left you behind not too long ago— against my will, of course—it's your turn.

And you, my dear brother! You stand here and watch the love of your life being led to her death. Brother, how much I begged you not to come, not to force yourself to endure the most gruesome chapter of our tragedy, not to let the beautiful image of Juwan be ruined by the image of her body lifelessly dangling in the open. But as always, you are stubborn and will only do what you want.

As for me, I have to bear yet the biggest share of the

weight by watching one life snuffed out physically and another destroyed emotionally.

I make one last plea to Azad to turn around or to walk with me to the street, but he shakes his head, his gaze fixed on Juwan while the guards adjust the noose a few times to make sure their mission is carried out perfectly. I have managed to slowly pull Azad away from the crowd and toward a small shop, holding his left hand while Jamil stands shoulder to shoulder with him on his right.

All hopes of a last-minute pardon have evaporated. There will be no heroic actions, not even in the middle of a blessed day of the month of fasting, the month of forgiveness and mercy. Instead, the guards fiercely instruct the onlookers to not dare move or speak as justice is carried out. To protect Juwan's dignity as a female prisoner, the woman in black ties a large fabric bag of some sort over Juwan's head and ties it above her waist.

I refuse to look. I won't allow them to force that image of defeat in my mind. Juwan, you will always be beautiful and lively to me. So I turn away and ask Azad to do the same, but he won't move an inch. When an officer starts reading a statement aloud, I close my tearful eyes and plant my feet on the ground, squeezing the urge to scream and yell. Moments later, the statement ends and silence looms over the field.

After a few heavy moments, an officer shouts in a loud tone, after which I hear the wooden chair being violently kicked away. The mass of onlookers gasps in unison, and I hear the sound of struggled breathing mixed with noisy chatter followed by warnings. I hold back a strong sob and the howling inside and feel Azad's body fall backward. He would have hit the ground had Jamil not caught him. He is pale and nearly out. His lips are shaking while Jamil gently pulls him a little farther away from the crowd and out of the sight of nearby officers and guards.

Azad opens his eyes and attempts to get to his feet but nearly faints again. A line of tears has formed on either side of his face down to his ears. Jamil is wiping away his own tears with the palm of one hand and holding up Azad with the other.

"Oh, brother," I say, "God help you. God help us all. What did they do to you? They have killed you and left you alive to live that death."

"Stop it with your nonsense talk," Jamil angrily says. "We have enough to deal with."

Ramo hurriedly joins us and says, "We need to get going. Any emotional display will reveal an association with the victim, and we'll all go down."

A few moments later, the chatter among the spectators grows louder, and the guards begin to disperse them with force, at times pointing guns at them. Zozan comes over, anxious as ever, mumbling insults under her breath as she turns around to look toward the truck one last time. My will to resist finally collapses. I give in and look in that direction with Zozan. Juwan's motionless body hangs by the neck from the pole, swinging with the gentlest push of the wind. Ramo pleads for us to get going when the guards get closer to us.

Azad refuses to go back to Shukriya's house, so Jamil stays with him near a local shop while Ramo, Zozan, and I walk back to get Shireen. At the door, Shireen stands in front of me with Helan in her arms and shoots a look of a million questions at me. When I shake my head in sadness, she breaks down and jumps in my arms with Helan still in her own arms.

When the emotional hurricane subsides, Ramo reminds us that we need to go. Shukriya recounts Juwan's last wishes regarding her daughter, that I should raise her as my own.

"I don't have any problem keeping her," Shireen says, "and will care for her as my own daughter."

I hold Helan tight to my chest and declare, "Absolutely not. No one will have her but me. She's all we have left of Juwan, and she wanted me to have her."

As Shukriya and I share one last embrace, I ask, "So what's next for you?"

"My brother is coming tonight to take me and my kids," she says. "I can't stay in this house anymore. Too much misery behind these walls."

She points toward the two bedrooms across from each other that witnessed two years of conflict, rivalry, hatred, misunderstanding, a common enemy, and ultimately tragedy. It's time to leave this house and everything behind except for this little angel that carries the blood and heart of my best friend and my brother's would-have been bride.

THE NEXT DAY, Ramo's grandfather and father disappear in the early hours of morning and return around noon in a pickup truck carrying a wooden casket.

Azad is lying down in the living room and staring at the ceiling. He leaps to his feet and runs to the door when Ramo's grandfather announces that he was finally able to get permission to receive Juwan's body.

He wipes sweat from his forehead and says, "It is all a

blessing from Allah that I was able to convince them that since she has no family, and a proper burial is obligatory in our religion, they should let me handle that responsibility."

He says he knows some people in the coroner's office who helped with the arrangements, but he's soon talking to himself as the rest of us rush to open the casket and see Juwan's silent body, her face pale and her lips dark. Her eyes are shut and circled with dark lines.

Shireen and I can't help but cry all over again, but Ramo's grandfather yells at us to stop. "For the sake of God and his mighty name, stop crying and yelling over a dead body. It's against our faith. We must bury her as soon as possible!"

For the next few hours, between the washing of her body, preparing her for burial, and the burial itself, Azad shifts from numbness and shock to a nervous breakdown when we finally say our last goodbyes to Juwan.

Grief takes a turn toward acceptance at night. After locking himself in our room for hours, Azad finally emerges and thanks Ramo's family for their kindness and support during this tough time. Then he turns to Jamil. "Brother, we must head out tomorrow. Our friend Rozh will be waiting for us, and we can't afford to miss him."

62

Dilveen

Iran, Turkey, and Iraq, March 27, 1991

Ramo's family is not rich by any means. In fact, they live basic lives at best. So I'm embarrassed when they go out of their way to make accommodations for us. Embarrassed to be a financial burden on them. Embarrassed not to have given them the benefit of the doubt at the beginning when Shireen said she wanted to stay and marry Ramo.

Ramo and his dad have rented a van and insist that the entire family will ride with us. The reason? We'll look more like a family if we're questioned at checkpoints. And I'll get to spend a few more hours with Shireen before we part ways again, almost certainly for a long time.

We meet Rozh in late afternoon after a few failed attempts to find his address, but the driver's deep connections prove helpful. Rozh insists on leaving immediately to take advantage of the impending nightfall. We should be able to cross the border with less trouble.

When it's time to take off, Shireen reluctantly hands me a cranky and sleepy Helan. I catch a glimpse of Rozh staring at her and shaking his head when he realizes this little girl will be coming with us. Although he heard about Juwan's story, it apparently hadn't occurred to him her daughter would become our responsibility.

I hug Ramo's grandmother and mother, then move to a final, tearful embrace with Shireen. In my peripheral vision, I see Azad and Rozh having a quiet conversation some ten feet or so away from us. When Azad returns, he clears his throat, hesitates for a few seconds, then says, "About this girl." He points at Helan with his head. "It's best if she doesn't come with us. I share Rozh's concern about our ability to travel safely with a toddler."

Azad doesn't look at me as he says this. I look to Rozh, and he turns away from me too.

I hold Helan even tighter to me and say, "I'm not leaving her. You and Rozh make whatever plans you must to get us across, but—"

"Sister, you can't force us to change plans if it threatens our safety. She can't come with us."

I step away from him. "I've been entrusted with this girl, and I will never let go of her. If she stays, I stay."

I'm in tears all over again. Shireen and Ramo's grandmother attempt to calm my emotions. In case there is still any doubt, I make my point with another loud emotional rant, this time directed at Rozh. Jamil gently grabs my shoulder and pulls me away. Azad shakes his head and mutters some insults under his breath, but I couldn't care less. The decision has been made. It's not up for discussion.

Azad won't talk to or even look at me. Every time Helan gets cranky, he shakes his head without turning to me or saying a word. Luckily for us, border patrols on the Iraqi side have all but disappeared since the uprising. In early evening, we walk parallel to the main road, bypassing the official border entries as we cross the frontier. Then we catch up with main road and walk alongside it.

"Someone will eventually pick us up," Rozh says. "Be patient."

Sure enough, a transport trailer truck starts slowing down once it passes Jamil, coming to a complete stop some ten or so feet from where Azad and Rozh flagged it down. The loud gurgling of the diesel engine wakes Helan, and she starts to kick and shift in my tired arms.

THE TRUCK DRIVER drops us off in a small town in the Erbil Governorate, but Rozh decides to stay on board to get closer to his destination.

We clean up and rest in a mosque by the main market, and Jamil accompanies me to a store to buy a set of new clothes for Helan, some milk, and some toys. Around noon, we find a taxi driver who agrees to take us to Akre, but for a hefty fare. It's the farthest he can go because things have taken a turn for the worse.

For the first hour of the trip, the driver seems to be on a mission to justify his outrageous fee, often addressing Jamil to his right instead of looking at the road. "Things are getting bad," he says.

"How so?" Jamil asks.

"There's a growing concern about the uprising failing. The Iraqi army is heavily mobilizing outside Erbil, Sulaymaniyah, and Duhok."

I overheard Jamil talking about this with Rozh on our way to Iran, but he looks more unsettled this time. When I'm finally too exhausted to handle Helan's hyperactivity, I hand her over to Jamil while he continues his discussion with the driver, who seems as concerned as Jamil if not more.

Paranoia is obvious in Akre. There's a sense of panic in the rapid movement of cars and people in the markets. And when we return to the Peshmerga center, only two of Jamil's men are present.

"Where is everyone?" Jamil says. "What's happening?"

"Things aren't good, sir. The uprising is collapsing by the hour. Quite honestly, it's only a matter of time."

"What do you mean collapsing? We shed too much blood and too many tears to let it all go!"

"I know, but this is the reality. You know as well as I do that we're no match for Saddam's merciless forces. Saddam was emboldened when Father Bush declared mission accomplished after liberating Kuwait and said that Iraq's internal matters were none of their business."

"He actually said that?"

"Yes, indeed. It was a slap in the face here and in the south after he had encouraged the Iraqis to rise up."

The young man hasn't told Jamil anything he didn't already know, but he presses on anyway. "Everyone is leaving, sir."

There's silence for a few moments, followed by the sound of a car approaching. The crunching of tires on gravel grows louder and closer before coming to a stop. I sit up, slide the window blinds aside, and look out. Three armed Peshmerga men step out of a pickup truck and are received by Jamil and his comrade. I recognize two of the men as part of the team that left the camp with Jamil at the onset of the uprising. They walk inside the building, and I try to listen to what they're saying, but all I hear is distant chatter.

Then I hear Azad join the conversation, which is becoming more intense by the minute. I quietly walk out of the room, leaving the door ajar in case Helan wakes up, and head to the main office. Jamil is now behind the desk once occupied by a principal while the rest of the men have taken seats on either side. All look broken.

Nobody acknowledges my presence. "What's going on?"

Silence ensues. Jamil runs his hand through his thick hair. Azad buries his face in his hands.

"I'm not stupid," I say, my voice rising in intensity. "Are you going to take me for an ignorant woman who knows nothing about what's happening?"

Jamil stands up. "No one is treating you like an idiot."

I step closer to him, our eyes locked. "Why don't you just say what's up? I've had enough of surprises, headaches, and heartbreaks."

Azad leans back on the couch and says in a cold tone, "The uprising is falling, Saddam's forces will take over in a matter of days, and as it has always been for the Kurds, everything will go down the drain again. I warned you, Jamil, and I don't understand why you thought a few hundred inexperienced men could stand up against an organized army."

"Watch your mouth there!" one of the men shouts. "It's not a few hundred men. It's an entire nation of people. And if the West hadn't abandoned us, Saddam would be ten feet underground by now. So why don't you just shut up!"

"Your dad would feel ashamed if he were here and heard what you're saying," the second man says.

Azad stands up and kicks the desk. "Don't you dare bring up my dad or try to shame me into thinking I'm any less patriotic than any of you. You just refuse to wake up from a dream because you know what the daylight will bring."

Helan is awake and crying now, so I run to the room to attend to her. When I return with her in my arms, Azad is gone and Jamil is whispering with his two companions from the camp.

This time he notices me. "Look, sister, these two gentlemen just returned from the frontlines near Mosul. They're no match for Iraq's heavy weaponry, so they returned, like so many others, to regroup and figure out what we should do."

"We didn't abandon our posts," one of the men says. "Nor did we give up. There's been a shift in strategy, and the leadership thinks a retreat might be inevitable."

This statement may have made this man feel better about himself, but it sure didn't help me. "So what are we doing here?" I ask Jamil. "Why are we not headed back to Duhok and straight to the border again?"

Jamil shakes his head in disappointment. "Just like that? We give up what we came here for?"

The third Peshmerga, whom I have never seen before, clears his throat. "You and your friends walked across the border to volunteer as fighters. That in itself is high bravery. But if you want my opinion, you'll take your family and whoever is left of your men here and head back to your families in Turkey before it starts to rain shit again."

Helan is tight against my chest, still cranky and unhappy about her interrupted nap. "Absolutely, Jamil. I wholeheartedly agree. You've done enough, and this uprising is in the hands and minds of people larger than you and me. Let them decide the course of things, and let's go before we get stuck again."

Jamil nervously paces the room, repeatedly shaking his head.

"And don't forget," I remind him, "Your wife is pregnant. Need I say more?"

Jamil turns red in the face.

THE DECISION TO leave is finally reached. While we still have the advantage of daylight, we hurriedly stuff our belongings in the back of the pickup truck. Our driver, the same man Jamil was talking to outside our window, played a big role in convincing Jamil that we should go.

The beautiful town of Akre rolls past us like a film on TV. The mountain stands tall overhead, proudly supporting rows of houses on its steep and rocky surface. Historic homes above and newer ones below stick to the mountainside like beautiful puzzle pieces. They may look random and unorganized from afar, but with a closer look, the architectural beauty is on full display.

But the usually vibrant streets of this forever welcoming town are lonely and empty. The sadness may be silent and invisible, but it's palpable.

Thinking about our truck ride after crossing the border from Iran into Iraq, I say, "I feel bad for the driver and his men who gave us a ride earlier. They moved their families back to Iraq, but now they'll have to return to Iran again."

"You actually believed them?" Jamil says.

Puzzled, I ask, "What do you mean? Weren't you listening to his story?"

Jamil giggles. "Sister, those were smugglers. They lied about their families. They're having a field day smuggling weapons and machines left behind by the army into Iran."

"They're making a fortune," our driver says.

Even more puzzled now, I ask, "Jamil, so why didn't you try to stop them?"

"We had bigger problems than smugglers. And should I have jeopardized our ride?"

Jamil plays with the radio, and I keep pushing. "So you knew those guys would be passing through?"

He looks at me through the rearview mirror. "Let it go, sister. Let me find some news about our godforsaken situation."

The young driver chuckles. I don't know if he's laughing at my stupidity or at the way Jamil reacted to my questions. Either way, I decide to let it go.

As we make our way out of this beautiful town, I remember my mother often talking about how much my father used to love the original Kurdish *khomali* rice from Akre, with its special texture and taste. Since it tends to be expensive, we cooked it only once or twice a year. I have to admit, I often couldn't tell the difference between that rice and the regular one, but Mother could smell it from the other side of the village. Shireen once mocked it as fraudulent, and Mother almost beat her up. Disrespect for Akre's rice was not allowed in our household, not when it was a favorite of my father's.

∾

WHEN WE REACH Mam Khorsheed's house in Duhok in the evening, we find him and Husain Ziway outside chatting with a few other men. I slept through most of the trip, taking advantage of Helan's long nap to catch up with some rest. I'm not sure what exactly Jamil and the driver noticed along the way, but as soon as we get out, Jamil walks up to Mam Khorsheed and asks about what's happening in the city, skipping the pleasantries and greetings. They both look concerned.

I take Helan with me inside, not wanting to hear any more bad news. When I reach the top of the entry stairs, a loud explosion detonates in the distance, and I nearly fall face-down with Helan in my arms.

Mam Khorsheed's wife meets me inside and says, "Welcome back, my dear, and don't worry. This has been going on for two nights now. Saddam's devils have been bombarding the outskirts of the city. Come on in."

Her words don't reassure me, but her calmness does, at least a little bit. She looks at Helan without saying anything. The look on my face tells her everything she needs to know about what happened. At least for now.

∾

THE SHELL STRIKES intensified last night, according to Mam Khorsheed. Half of the city has already left, hitting the mountains and the border in fear of an imminent military attack.

So the next morning, we're up before sunrise. There's no time to waste. We need to head out immediately.

A lot has changed in the week since we last passed through Duhok on our way to Iran. Once-busy streets are now empty. The few scattered passersby we do see are anxious. The market is deserted. Shops are closed. Few armed men are visible.

We pass through the city center and pick up the main highway toward Zakho. The roads are heavy with cars packed with people and supplies heading toward unknown destinations as far away from the city as possible. Just like that, we find ourselves staring at the end of a golden uprising for long-sought independence.

Mam Khorsheed insists on driving us to Zakho and as close to the border as possible so we can cross and reunite with family. He, on the other hand, plans to return to Duhok immediately, pack, and take his wife to join a few other families in the opposite direction, northeast, and head toward the border in that direction. We tried to convince them to come with us to Mardin, but they've heard horrific stories about the camps. Plus, my uncle would never survive far from Duhok for very long. If the army takes the city, he'll eventually find a way to return even if it means imprisonment or death. That's how much the city means to him, but there's little left for the rest of us.

Mam Khorsheed offers us a quick farewell somewhere outside Zakho. Before heading back, he pulls Azad aside for a discussion, which I'm sure is about what happened in Iran. Azad's face is distant and blank when he returns after giving Mam Khorsheed one final embrace. Somewhere in the far distance, another explosion further ramps up our sense of urgency. It's time for yet another goodbye. It's time for another trip across the border. It's time for another escape from our own homeland. We're all used to it by now.

GETTING BACK inside the camp proves to be more challenging than leaving it, especially now that we have a baby with us. We arrive after dark to find that the open part of the fence we escaped through has since been repaired with a new double-layer metal piece. Jamil, Azad, and one of the other men who accompanied us on the trip back pull on another corner of the fence, hoping to open it, but we soon hear Jandarma yelling and approaching us. I count five moving shadows. I hold Helan close to my chest, terrified as the angry soldiers point their guns at us and order us to walk toward the main gate.

Behind me, Azad whispers, "Don't worry, we'll be safe. This might turn out to be a more convenient way to enter the camp."

He turns out to be right to an extent. The soldiers allow us through the main gate, but they take the men to the administrative building and hold them overnight. The consequences of all of this? No more entry or exit to and from the camp.

We later learn that everyone who had left the camp with Jamil eventually managed to return except for a single young man who reunited with his immediate family in Duhok and had no more reason to return.

Azad withdraws over the next week, spending most of his time by the fence in solitude. I only get to see him briefly when he and Jamil come to our tent to eat. Having Jamil by his side doesn't help much. Jamil himself is having a hard time dealing with the collapse of the uprising. I, on the other hand, have freed myself from longing for the past and our lost lives. Instead, I search for new meaning as Helan learns to walk. Her radiant eyes are like rocks I can cling to after a shipwreck.

The entire camp is consumed with the collapse of the uprising. More than a million people have fled into Turkey and Iran. Everyone here has immediate or extended family from Duhok and can scarcely talk about anything else. Reports pour in about the miserable conditions in the mountains and the hundreds of thousands of civilians stranded at the border by the Turkish and Iranian governments.

The worst comes on April 16, the first day of Eid. A supposed day of celebration and happiness is nothing of the sort. Everyone is broken, so far from home for so long. Some of our loved ones are fighting snow, rain, hunger, and fear in the mountains. Worse, a brief news report on a local TV channel airs footage of humanitarian aid thrown from airplanes to the masses of refugees at the borders. Those who understand Turkish say the report touts the Turkish authorities' efforts to clear their airways so international help can arrive, but the news footage reveals horrendous conditions.

Many of us blame the Americans. I can't count how

many times men have mentioned George Bush's name in vain for not removing Saddam from power after liberating Kuwait—ironic since so many Kurds called him Haji Bush, or Father Bush, so recently.

63

Dilveen

Mardin Refugee Camp, Turkey, May–June 1991

S lowly, the camp administration loosens restrictions and allows people to leave on a limited basis to seek work and other sources of income. We learn about how our fellow Kurds in Mardin and other cities and towns throughout Turkey are shipping food and clothing to the million and a half refugees still trapped at the border. Foreign journalists and human rights activists have been pouring into the settlements to show the tragic conditions to the international community. A few have even paid unannounced visits to our camp, giving us hope that the camp administration may feel pressure to further improve our living conditions and let us out of this open-air prison.

In all fairness—and this is not a popular sentiment around camp—I suspect that the Turkish authorities are overwhelmed with our mass exodus during the past two years, but many in the camp are convinced that the Turks are discriminating against us because we are Kurds. If there's one thing I've learned throughout all this, it's that war is fertile ground for hatred, profiling, and misunderstanding. Can we fault a neighboring country for frowning over a mass exodus not of their making? Again, this is not a thought I would share out loud in the camp.

Azad used his connections with Dikhtor and a few of the camp guards to get permission to leave camp every day. I barely get to see him nowadays. He abandoned the school he established. Jamil bought him another cassette player, but he threw it in a box in a corner of the tent. According to Jamil, he's been hanging out with some questionable characters in Mardin's city center. The few times Jamil confronted Azad about his emotions or lack thereof, he said he feels responsible for what happened to Juwan. Of course, he would never confide this in me, and Jamil had to break his word with Azad to keep his feelings a secret.

Last night, I went to check on him, and when I got close, I heard him arguing with one of his tentmates. The man is known to play the tanbur and has a beautiful voice. As I stood there listening to their conversation, I heard Azad insist that the man now play a favorite song of the popular singer Erdawan Zakholi. When the man declined, Azad got up and threatened to punch him. If not for shame and dignity, I would have rushed into the tent, but I remained outside as the man finally gave in to Azad's demands and started playing the song.

I stood by the tent, arms crossed against my chest, eyes shut, and listened to the song, tears flowing down my face. Toward the end of the song, Azad started sobbing, and the singer immediately stopped singing and apologized for causing such an emotional upset.

Then Jamil yelled at Azad. "When is this going to stop? The man didn't want to upset you, but you kept pushing him. This is nonsense. It has got to stop!"

That was last night. This morning, I woke up very early to Helan's hungry cries. When a full bottle of milk finally puts her back to sleep, I lay in bed thinking about my brother. I try to put myself in his shoes as I recall everything that has happened and all the ifs and buts. What could we have done differently? Could we have extracted Juwan from Segvan's grip? Did Azad genuinely think that Juwan betrayed him or gave up on him? More important, did Shireen or I mistreat Juwan or fail to communicate how we felt?

Did Juwan die thinking she was neglected, unappreciated for the sacrifices she had made for us, especially for Mother? Did she feel rejected by Azad when the two finally met, however briefly, when he discovered she was married and had already conceived a child? I haven't had the chance until now to ask the questions that need to be answered. The problem now, of course, is that half the people involved in these questions are no longer with us.

THE CALMNESS of the morning is broken by men yelling outside, and I jump to my feet when I hear Azad's name.

While I'm looking for my shoes, someone runs between the tents calling out Dikhtor's name. Barefoot, I race toward Azad's tent where men are standing outside with concerned looks on their faces.

I scream Azad's name and frantically push my way through the crowd while a man yells for everyone to make way for the sister to go in. I fall to my knees when I see Azad laying on his back with Jamil next to him and calling out his name.

I lean forward to take a closer look. Azad's face is pale, his eyes are shut, and a line of white frothy discharge is running from his mouth down his left cheek. The world turns dark, and I try to scream, but I can't. I slap Azad to wake him, but his head rolls the other way without resistance.

He's dead. My brother is dead, finished. I still can't scream and can only manage to slap my knees.

I hear Dikhtor's assertive voice behind me asking everyone to get out of the tent. He then sits across from me and checks Azad's pulse.

Jamil says nervously, "I woke up and found him this way. He wouldn't respond."

Dikhtor motions for all of us to be silent while he puts his ear over Azad's mouth and checks his wrist. He pulls his head up and says, "He is alive, still alive. Make space for me."

Dikhtor instructs Jamil to move Azad and reposition his head over another pillow. He then yells toward the men outside the tent, "I need someone to run to the infirmary and call for an ambulance. Everyone stay clear of the tent."

I notice an empty white bottle of medicine under Azad's

left elbow. I pick it up, bring it closer to my face and yell, "He took medicine. He overdosed. Why, brother, why?"

Much to our surprise, the ambulance arrives half an hour after the call. Although Azad is still alive and breathing, they insist he be taken to the hospital immediately. After much insistence, Dikhtor is allowed to ride in the ambulance with him.

The next morning, I sit in the small clinic by the infirmary waiting for an update from Dikhtor. Although we now have a full-time phone operator hired from within the camp, I can't risk missing one of the most important phone calls of my life. So I keep myself busy organizing the medicine room, rearranging shelves, and doing any other chores to keep my mind occupied.

The phone rings before noon, and Dikhtor's hello gives me a sense of reassurance I haven't felt in a long time. "Azad is no longer in critical condition. Thankfully, the pills he took only temporarily affected his breathing and mentation, and the doctors think he'll recover fully."

I struggle to speak and hold the receiver tight against my ear.

"Dilveen? Are you there?"

"Sorry, I'm here." I wipe my tears, somehow thinking he'd be able to see me through the receiver. "Can I talk to him? Is he there?"

I hear a loud announcement in Turkish in the background, and Dikhtor waits until it's over. "No, I'm not with him now. I had to walk to the administrative station, and it took a lot of begging to get permission for this call. I just wanted to reassure you. I knew you would be worried." He clears his throat and continues. "They're saying Azad should be able to leave the hospital tomorrow if he continues to improve, so I'll stay here with him until then."

I'm so taken aback that I need a moment to put words together. "Thank you for all you have done for him, for us. You left your family behind to stay with him. I really appreciate that."

A loud and deep voice yells at him in the background, and he excuses himself in a hurry. Then the line goes dead, but I keep the receiver to my ear, hoping his voice would return. When a few silent moments pass, I stare at it in disappointment. Why did he not say goodbye? While I find myself judging Dikhtor for abruptly ending the call, wondering about all the possible reasons he may have done so, I am also impressed that he made the effort to call in the first place. Somewhere deep inside, a feeling is stirring, something new and foreign, faint and distant, and it makes my scars itch.

When Azad returns from the hospital, I expect him to disappear into his tent or to hunker down in his usual solitary spot by the fence. Instead, he shows up at our tent, cheerful, though still looking tired and pale, and demands a hot meal. I'm confused by his wide smile, but I'm not going to ask him about it. Instead, I jump up and hug him, kissing his head as if he's my little brother and not the oldest sibling. Jamil is standing behind him, having already received his share of puzzlement.

Berivan greets Azad, equally surprised at the change of attitude, but considering the alternative, we'll gladly prepare lunch for him, no questions asked.

I hear Dikhtor's voice outside, excusing himself while Jamil thanks him again for his help and support. Azad insists Dikhtor come in for lunch, but he's determined to see his kids.

"He could bring his family too," I say. "It's a blessing from God. We have a lot of food."

Azad turns to me, registering my words and nodding in agreement, then extends the invitation to Dikhtor.

"We will see," Dikhtor says and chuckles. "I'll try my best."

MOTHER USED to say life is a mystery. Just when you think you've figured it out, it shows you a new face to keep you on your toes."

Our lives have certainly twisted and turned over the past few years. From home to the fires of war, the darkness of imprisonment, the emptiness of hunger, and the hopelessness of death. And from all that to upgraded food in our camp and my brother changing from a walking corpse void of emotions to a seemingly content and stable man.

I watch him closely, fearing the darkness will return, but it doesn't—or at least it hasn't yet. Throughout this time, Dikhtor's visits have increased in frequency.

I'm behind the curtain separating me and Berivan from the men's side and pouring cups of tea. Dikhtor drinks his black with no water or sugar added. When I slightly slide the curtain and motion for Azad to get the tea tray, Dikhtor's eyes catch mine momentarily. Then he addresses a group of men arriving for an update.

"It appears the international outcry and media mobilization finally paid off," he says. I'm behind the curtain again but listening intently. "The humanitarian crisis has compelled the allied forces to order the Iraqi military out of the three main Kurdish cities in the north. They're calling it a no-fly zone."

The sound of metal teaspoons on glass fills the tent as the men stir the sugar in their tea. A cloud of smoke has settled above our heads, and I wonder if it isn't a humanitarian crisis to have two little children exposed to this much cigarette smoke.

"So Haji Bush finally kept his promise?" Husain Ziway says.

Azad fires back, "In all honesty, Bush and his allies have been good to us. If they weren't lurking from a distance, Saddam would have annihilated millions in the mountains without losing a minute of sleep."

More news arrives over the next few days about waves of refugees returning to their homes. Today, a team of foreign workers with cameras arrived at the camp accompanied by guards. According to Azad, they were studying the conditions of the camp and have already interviewed dozens of families. Opinions are unequally divided. The majority wants to be taken as refugees in the West, as far away from conflict as possible. Then there are people like Jamil who insist on returning home now that the allies have forced the Iraqi military out of the cities, handing power to the Kurdish leadership.

Jamil adamantly expresses that opinion to Azad over dinner. "We'll go back and rebuild from scratch. With freedom under the allies' umbrella, we can finally build the independent Kurdistan our forefathers always dreamed of and for which a lot of blood has been shed."

"Would you just enjoy your food and change the subject?" Berivan says, not wanting to ruin a family dinner with politics.

Jamil smiles and says, "Speaking of changing subjects, there's something we need to discuss."

Azad looks at me and smiles with Helan clinging to his back. He gently grabs her and pulls her to his lap. She playfully pushes her head into his chest, and I suddenly feel all eyes on me.

Berivan laughs and says, "Go on, Jamil, tell her."

With all three looking at me, Jamil clears his throat and says, nearly whispering, "Dilveen, Dikhtor has officially asked for your hand in marriage. The man is a great guy and—"

"What? No!" I drop my bread on my plate and push myself away from the table, my head down, embarrassed and anxious at the same time. These matters are usually channeled indirectly through women. I feel ambushed, but I don't want to feel surprised.

Azad says, "Why not, sister? Wallah, he would be a great husband."

I get up, show them my back, and say in an angry voice, "Do you so desperately want to get rid of me that you want me to marry a widower?"

Berivan gasps and asks Azad and Jamil to leave. Once they're gone, she berates me for what I said and the hurtful, unspoken meaning behind it.

I don't even understand what I'm saying or what I want. Realizing that discussing this further may make me look even worse or possibly close the door in my face, I tell Berivan to ask my brothers if I can talk to Dikhtor directly. Usually, a request like this could trigger a serious backlash.

How can a girl make such a bold demand? But both my parents are gone, and if the suitor isn't typical, why should my response be?

The next day, Berivan and I meet Dikhtor and his sister at the infirmary. He and I have sat across from each other numerous times in the treatment room, but it feels different today. Avoiding eye contact, I interlock my hands in embarrassment and anxiety.

Dikhtor breaks the silence. "Thank you for giving us a chance to talk. I'm told you have a few things to discuss?"

I can' help but leap straight to my question: "Why me?"

He chuckles. I don't even care if he's laughing at my question or simply feels good about where he thinks this is going. "I don't know, maybe because you are a great girl." He says this in a calm voice, then chuckles again. "Maybe you can ask my heart? I don't know!"

His answer, although romantic, doesn't land where I want, so I keep pressing. "Do you know I was burned during childhood?"

I nervously brush my hand against the opposite shoulder, slightly revealing the edge of the scar. I brace for his reaction, but he smiles.

"We all have scars," he says quietly and confidently, "some physical and some emotional."

My throat itches. "Some of us have both."

He nods, his smile replaced now with a serious look. "We must learn to paint happiness over our scars instead of hiding them."

His words land heavily this time. I doubt I will ever forget them.

Berivan calls out from the other room, "Are you both all

right? Please don't kill each other." Then she and Dikhtor's sister laugh.

"I understand you have two children," I say. "What about them?"

I don't know if he was expecting this question, but he responds right away. "My children are my world, and I will never give them up."

His eyes are red now. I realize I hit a nerve, but if I don't make myself clear, we could start off on the wrong foot or not have a start at all.

"No woman who asks you to do that is worthy of your commitment," I say. His face softens. "I ask because I'm entrusted with a little girl, and I'm not willing to give her up either."

"I know that," he says quickly, "and I respect you for it. I guess we're even now." He smiles.

But I'm anxious again, and vulnerable, too, but I push through my negative emotions and say, "Okay then."

He leans forward slightly. "We're okay?"

I smile and nod without looking.

He gets up from his seat and says, "I have one request to make. Considering that very soon they will be registering families for asylum through the United Nations, it would be great if we could formalize our marriage so I can write you down as my wife."

I nod to that as well. I can't tell if the ladies in the other room got tired of waiting for us or if Dikhtor sent them a signal, but they suddenly return to the room, his sister approaching him with a wide smile while I warn Berivan through my facial expression not to get excited just yet, but she's not about to listen to me.

IN THE EVENING and under the weak light above my head, I mull my decision to marry Dikhtor. It's tormenting me. I desperately want to step out of the dreary past into a brighter future even if it's still unknown, but a monstrous thing deep inside me still occasionally rears up, howling inside me and activating my scars, even in the middle of a smile or pleasant moment.

I shift and turn in my bed, my hair brushing against my face and neck. I haven't allowed anyone to brush it for me since the last time Juwan did. I sit up and pull my waist-length hair to the front. It's heavy, somehow pulling down on my mind as well as my head.

Helan is peacefully sleeping, the beautiful hazel eyes she got from her mother waiting for the light of the day so they can open and glow. I walk across the tent to a wooden box where we keep our sewing supplies and grab the large scissors. I run my fingers over the cold metal blades, thinking about how easily they can cut something and send each piece their own way. Then I gently tap Berivan's shoulder. Her motherly instincts are awakened inside her instantly. She's startled to see me standing over her and terrified when she sees the scissors.

"Bismillah, have you lost your mind?"

"No, I haven't," I say, chucking, however awkward it may be at this late hour.

"Then what's that in your hand?"

I smile and hand her the scissors. "Here, I want you to cut my hair."

"You *have* lost your mind! Do you know what time it is?"

"It's something I want done tonight before tomorrow. It will only take a minute."

I turn around and push all my hair to the back. She takes the scissors from my hand, still startled and puzzled, but she does what I've asked her to do, probably so she can go back to sleep.

"How short?" she asks, running her hand down the length of my hair.

"As much as you can cut without making me ugly"

She sighs deeply and pulls on my hair somewhere below the neck. I hear the blades meeting each other, back and forth. With each slow and calculated movement, some of the weight on my head and my mind eases.

When she's finished, I turn and say, "Thank you. My head feels so much lighter."

She shakes her head in disbelief and dives back under her blanket. "You've definitely lost it!"

I chuckle and say, "Some things are better not holding on to."

IT'S a hot and dry day in mid-June. A long line of people stretches from the restrooms all the way to the main gate, where a crew of United Nations workers have camped since early this morning. There are five in total, three male officers who speak Kurdish plus two foreign officials, a man and a woman, both blonde and older but active and healthy looking.

After two hours in line, we finally reach the front. It's been nearly two weeks since I agreed to marry Dikhtor, and while we haven't decided when to have a ceremony, we made our bond official in front of a clergyman and according to rules of God, just as my parents would have wanted. I'm carrying Helan in my arms and standing behind Azad and alongside Dikhtor and his family. His two boys have struck up a few conversations with me without much hesitation, so I'm comfortable with the prospects of Dikhtor probably having already told them who I am and who I will be to them.

Two men behind us have been arguing for a good half hour about whether or not the three Kurdish UN officers are spying for Turkish intelligence and planning to block anyone sympathetic to Kurdish nationalism from going abroad. Dikhtor is shaking his head at the conversation, but when our eyes meet, he gives me a smile wide enough to pull me out of any negative thoughts, even if temporarily.

It's finally our turn. The officer flips a page in his book and starts asking questions without looking up. "Full name, place of birth, married or single, how many immediate family members in total."

Azad answers the questions with details about himself and ends by saying, "There are two of us. Myself and my daughter."

He gently takes Helan from my arms as the officer finally looks up and says, "I see, and where is her mother?"

Totally taken by surprise, I try to get Azad's attention, but he takes another step away from me. I kick the back of his right foot to stop him, but I don't dare say something that might cast suspicion on us.

"Her mother died in the mountains," Azad says, sounding like he rehearsed those words a million times.

I pull on the back of Azad's shirt, but Dikhtor motions for me to stop. "We'll talk about this later," he whispers.

When the officer is finished writing down Helan's information and taking fingerprints, he looks up at Azad and says, "May God bless her soul. I pray for a bright future for you and your daughter."

Azad steps away with Helan in his arms, and when he's at least ten steps away, he turns and shoots a victory smile my way.

64

Azad

Mardin Refugee Camp, Turkey

I t's hot and dry, windy and dusty, but the heat doesn't bother me, and the dryness doesn't feel lifeless. The wind isn't punishing, the dust not blinding. Perhaps we, rather than the world, have transformed. It's as scary as it is interesting how capable humans are of adapting. The people in this camp have experienced more ups and downs than anyone can keep track of, yet the tired, sad, disappointed, and frightened will still find ways to keep going.

Reflecting back on my own life in the last three years, I see three different versions of myself, each estranged from the others. I'm not sure who I am anymore, but I'm definitely not the person I was yesterday or the day before, and this gives me comfort. I can't know who I'll be in the future either, but when I see a toddler crawling over my foot, I somehow feel like I belong to something larger than myself and my will. I feel something powerful through her that I can't even explain to myself. Whatever it is, I feel safe inside its circle. For the first time in my life, I'm content without knowing the answer. Let it be, Azad, I keep reminding myself.

THREE LARGE AND colorful buses have been parked outside the camp's gate for a few hours now with their engines running. The temperature has risen precipitously since they first arrived in the early morning. The camp was already awake and in full swing then, and emotions are now competing with the heat of the approaching noon.

Although they're a minority in this camp, the people who have decided to return to Duhok, to Kurdistan, have formed a line that feels longer than the miles between here and there. These are the people who have chosen to return home so they can feel at home. The rest of us have concluded that our homes are in our hearts, and we will settle where we feel safe. Considering the traumatic memories we so badly want to forget, moving far away may be our best way to carry our homes within our hearts in ways that won't pull us down.

Everyone has made peace with their decision to return home or wait to be taken abroad without feeling the need to judge others. Whatever our destinations, we will all carry mountains. Mountains of pain, sorrow, deprivation, and scars. Also mountains of hope, love, resilience, and determination. We will carry them wherever we go just as they carried us through both good and terrible days.

Jamil proudly holds little Wahid in his arms and stands close to his pregnant wife. His in-laws are a few steps ahead of them, slowly walking outside the camp and inching closer to the buses. Hundreds of other camp members have gathered around to watch their families, loved ones, and friends loaded into the vehicles in a manner dramatically different than the way they first walked into this camp.

Dikhtor and his immediate family are also standing next to us, his kids periodically looking Dilveen's way with curiosity. Before disappearing inside the bus, Jamil turns around one more time and waves in our direction with a large smile. Dilveen launches into an animated farewell that continues even after the three buses head down the narrow road out of the camp. This time, there are no tears. We have all agreed: no displays of sadness., I warned Dilveen.

She turns to me and asks, "When will it be our time to leave?"

"Hopefully soon," I say.

"Is it true they will take us to America?"

"That's what I'm hearing, sister."

"I told Dikhtor I won't go anywhere without my brother and Helan."

"Already bossing the guy around?" I say and smile.

She smiles back as we step into our tent behind Helan.

EPILOGUE

Azad

Nashville, Tennessee, May 2016

The Vanderbilt University campus feels like a maze you could get lost in forever if you don't know your way around. After looking for Dilveen for nearly half an hour, I finally meet her and her husband behind the medical center, the easiest landmark for them to find.

"Where's the rest of the family?" I say as I embrace her, still panting from walking.

Dikhtor, waiting his turn for a hug, says with a smile, "We left the youngest to watch over the supermarket. We're expecting a large shipment of fresh produce today. Everyone else is coming with their spouses."

Dilveen brings her face near mine and says with half a smile, "Am I not enough?"

I laugh and say, "You and your love are enough to fill the whole world, but I missed the kiddos."

We stroll down the concrete walkway through the large stretch of grass in the center of campus. Aged trees nearby stand as witnesses to history, the institution's legendary, colorful arboretum preserved after so many long years.

I check my watch, and it's already nine thirty. I pick up my pace while Dilveen and Dikhtor struggle to keep up with me.

The open pavilion is divided into three sections, each with a dozen or more rows of chairs. We pick our seats in the third row of the middle section, right across from the stage. Soft music is coming through the speakers mounted above our heads. Dilveen takes a seat to my right and flips through the "Vanderbilt Law School 2016 Commencement" booklet.

Dilveen turns to me in frustration and says, "There are hundreds of names here. Where do I find her?"

I'm already at page 11, the second one under the J.D. section, and there she is, the second name from the top: Barwari, Helan. A wave of pride washes over my heart while I leave the tip of my finger under Helan's name, forgetting that Dilveen and Dikhtor have their own booklets.

It was nearly twenty-five years ago that I stood at the United Nations table across from the immigration officer and pressed my finger under Helan's name, leaving blue fingerprints as a permanent declaration of kinship. Here I am again, a quarter-century later, pointing just under her name with my finger again, continuing the relationship that spans more time and space that I can comprehend. She will never fully understand the origin of our kinship, nor can she realize how far back her name takes me, through alleys lashed by merciless winds under dark clouds.

"Brother," Dilveen says. "Why don't you visit us more often? We miss you!"

Still trying to shake off my emotions and sense of pride, I say, "I know I should visit you more often, but work has been overwhelming. I've had to hire three more interpreters to catch up, but I know that's not an excuse."

"Oh, come on now," Dikhtor says with a grain of sarcasm. "You'd think he wasn't at our house eating *iprakh* less than ten days ago."

Dilveen gently slaps his left arm and says, "Don't you ever talk badly about my brother. I can never get tired of seeing him."

I catch a glimpse of Dilveen's arm with henna over her scar in a colorful design. "Helan and my daughters painted this. Don't you just love it?"

The music suddenly becomes louder. Dikhtor yells, "There they are," and points to the right of us.

Graduates slowly approach the pavilion, proudly carrying the golden letter V on either side of their black gowns. Dilveen stands up and waves while I struggle to spot Helan in the sea of black and gold. There she is, waving back, her stature tall enough for Dilveen to take photo after photo with her smartphone.

Everyone in the audience is on their feet now, waving and cheering, but I find myself dropping in my seat, overwhelmed. Before I can get up again, a voice comes through the speaker requesting everyone to take a seat as the commencement ceremony officially kicks off.

When Helan is finally up there with a wide smile on her

face, I am reminded of the person I once lived for and now live to remember. If only you knew, Helan, how much you resemble your mother—your eyes, your cheeks, your chin, and your gentle and reserved demeanor.

I stand and shout, "That's my daughter right there" and clap as hard as I can, Helan turning her head in embarrassment, the golden tassel shifting with her movement and declaring the magnitude of the moment. As Dilveen pulls me back into my seat, the professor on stage resumes her introduction while another member of the faculty walks up holding an award of some sort.

"The faculty of the Vanderbilt Law School would like to recognize Helan Barwari with the Community Legal Service Award for the most pro bono hours by a student in the class of 2016, with over 1,400 hours registered." A round of applause erupts, and the rest of Dilveen's family in the back shouts Helan's name in excitement.

When the dreadfully long post-ceremony photo session finally ends with a group picture under a large tree, I announce that I'm starving. "Whoever wants to stay behind and take pictures, be your own guest. Otherwise, be my guest for a royal brunch in celebration of our lawyer."

The mention of food is enough to get everyone's attention.

OUR SWEET, elderly waitress finally finishes taking our orders after we decide between breakfast and lunch. Dilveen is playing with her infant granddaughter, who appears well-fed and rested and willing to endure shaking and pinching with a smile. When the waitress disappears with our orders, my cell phone rings. I quickly pull it out of my pocket, anticipating a last-minute request for an urgent interpretation job. I answer without looking at the screen, and Jamil's voice comes through the speaker, loud as always. I head toward the exit, passing the waitress and reminding her to make sure my coffee is extra dark.

I push open the door with my foot and say, "Brother, my brother. How are you?"

Jamil is still yelling hello through the phone, and I have to scream over his yelling, "I can hear you, brother. You don't need to shout."

Then I realize I'm shouting too.

"Congratulations on Helan's graduation," he says. "I just wanted to call and offer my words. I was talking to Dilveen earlier, and she said they were on their way to the ceremony. How was it?"

I lower the volume on the speaker and say "It was great, thank you. We came to eat and celebrate. How have you been? How are the wife and kids? Any more babies on the way?"

He answers my chuckle with a couple of coughs, then says, "We're good. No more kids. Six is plenty. We are past that. Well, she's too old anyway. Unless I find another wife."

"Good luck with that! Her mother will come back from the dead and drag you out of this world before you say another woman's name."

He laughs.

This conversation could go on for a long time, but our food will arrive soon. "Jamil, let me go back inside and you can talk to the rest of the family. I don't know if they'll be able to hear you, though, because the restaurant is packed."

"No, brother. No need for that. Enjoy your time with

everyone, and I can talk to Helan another time. Just give her our warmest words."

I thank him and start heading back to the restaurant, but he shouts again, "Wait, don't go. There's someone else here who also wants to say hi."

After a moment, another voice comes on the line, a voice I haven't heard for more than a year. "It's me, Raqeeb. How are you, uncle?"

Even decades later, Raqeeb's voice sounds to my ears like that of the child we left behind with an Arab family while he begged us to not let go of him. I spent many years feeling like we had abandoned him, and when Jamil finally found him after so much searching, I had to ask for his forgiveness.

But the miserable boy we had to leave behind was healthy and hale when Jamil reunited with him. He never found his mother or sisters, but he emerged from his painful past with a wife and three adorable children.

The last time I heard his voice was over a year ago after ISIS had driven thousands of Yezidis from their homes, forcing them to seek refuge in Duhok. At the time, I connected him with a nongovernmental organization, and he set up a local office there. Since then, he has been the director of one of the largest refugee camps outside Duhok.

"Congratulations on Helan's graduation," he says. "Now she can help our organization with legal matters."

"Not so fast," I say and laugh as I head back inside. "She just graduated today. Give her a chance to learn the trade."

The noise grows louder, so Raqeeb hangs up after another round of greetings and regards.

Back at the table, everyone has already started eating. I

force my way through and take a seat between Dilveen and Helan and lay claim to my share of the bounty.

ACKNOWLEDGMENTS

Growing up, my family experienced a multitude of hardships, injustices, suffering, and political turmoil. Yet throughout this time, my parents maintained their hard work, dedication, and unconditional love for humanity, all humanity. They taught me and my siblings to love and respect others regardless of our differences of opinion. I am who I am because of my parents.

To my wonderful wife and my love, Areeman: thank you for being my biggest fan and fiercest critic and for your patience and big heart during the ups and downs of this project. To my lovely children, Jenna, Sahand, and Hamke: thank you for giving to me from your time. And I can't forget my three sisters, Zahra, Isra, and Noor, for being editorial hawks during this process. Special thanks to my childhood best friend and brother, Aryan Mazuri, who has been with me since this story was a little idea and when we were still teenagers.

While preparing to write this novel, I had the pleasure

of sitting down with some of the victims of the Anfal Campaign, whose life stories deserve a whole project. To all the victims who found ways to turn their tragedies into positive forces in life: You are my inspiration!

To everyone else who helped me, supported me, and encouraged me, I appreciate you.

ABOUT THIS BOOK

The idea for this novel goes back more than two decades. Throughout my childhood and adulthood, I learned more and more about the tragic Anfal Campaign carried out by the Iraqi army against the Kurdish minority during the 1980s. Everything about this campaign was wrong: the attempt to exterminate an entire population, the effort to suppress their voices, and the countless plans to strip them of their right to live a peaceful and dignified life.

To misuse the term "anfal" from the Quran, which means "spoils" or "profits," to describe genocide against another Muslim-majority population is yet more proof of how misguided and abusive the Iraqi regime was at that time. That campaign destroyed thousands of villages and hundreds of thousands of innocent lives. Many didn't live to tell their stories, while others have struggled, often in silence, with the trauma sustained during those times. The sad reality is that many of Iraq's citizens, including even some Kurds, didn't know the truth of what happened in the northern part of the country and in the mountains thanks to the totalitarian control of the Saddam regime. A balanced narrative of that tragedy is desperately needed to bring the different segments of Iraqi society together. We all need to feel each other's pain and understand each other's needs.

I have always wanted to write about that era through the eyes of regular people who lived it and felt it, without ideological biases. Just as it happened, with its sadness, mistakes, shortcomings, and misunderstandings but also the positives that one can use to build a better future for our next generations.

The characters in this novel are all fictional, as is the village of BerAva and small town of Hesenlu. If some details or names in this novel resemble the accounts of real victims, it is purely coincidental.

I struggled to get started writing this novel for many years, mostly due to my busy life as a medical student, a resident, a fellow in training, and finally as a physician establishing a practice. Yet during this entire time, the passion for writing followed me everywhere and sneaked up on me around every corner. When the COVID-19 pandemic started to take its mental toll on me and my colleagues as healthcare providers, I found solace in long, late-night hours of writing until I found myself on track at a rate faster than I ever imagined.

Finally, I would like to say that my role in writing this novel is neither as a victim nor as an advocate. Rather, I hope to have provided a clear lens through which readers can get glimpses of daily life and its struggles during that time. Hopefully, in understanding how things unfolded, an unbiased reader can connect the mind and heart and conclude that human life is sacred and above all other considerations.

Made in the USA
Coppell, TX
14 February 2022